NOTORIOUS

Hand in Hand Collection

MICHELLE REID and ABBY GREEN

POWER

May 2012

JANE PORTER CAITLIN CREWS

INFAMOUS

June 2012

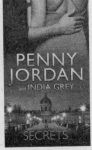

PENNY JORDAN and INDIA GREY

SECRETS

July 2012

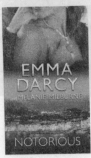

EMMA DARCY MELANIE MILBURNE

NOTORIOUS

August 2012

LYNNE GRAHAM MAISEY YATES

POSSESSION

September 2012

SHARON KENDRICK JENNIE LUCAS

PRICELESS

October 2012

EMMA DARCY
and MELANIE MILBURNE

NOTORIOUS

MILLS & BOON

Mills & Boon, an imprint of Harlequin (UK) Limited,
Eton House, 18-24 Paradise Road, Richmond, Surrey TW9 1SR

NOTORIOUS © Harlequin Enterprises II B.V./S.à.r.l. 2012

Ruthlessly Bedded by the Italian Billionaire © Emma Darcy 2008
Bound by the Marcolini Diamonds © Melanie Milburne 2009

ISBN: 978 0 263 90175 7

009-0812

Harlequin (UK) policy is to use papers that are natural, renewable and recyclable products and made from wood grown in sustainable forests. The logging and manufacturing processes conform to the legal environmental regulations of the country of origin.

Printed and bound in Spain
by Blackprint CPI, Barcelona

RUTHLESSLY BEDDED BY THE ITALIAN BILLIONAIRE

EMMA DARCY

Initially a French/English teacher, **Emma Darcy** changed careers to computer programming before the happy demands of marriage and motherhood. Very much a people person, and always interested in relationships, she finds the world of romance fiction a thrilling one and the challenge of creating her own cast of characters very addictive.

CHAPTER ONE

Sydney, Australia

'Miss Rossini…'

Another voice calling to her, using Bella's name.

Jenny struggled to understand. Her mind felt weirdly disconnected, taking in only snatches of what was said. She couldn't make sense of what she heard. It was as if she was locked inside a fog that almost cleared sometimes but then swallowed her up into a blank nothingness. Was this a nightmare that kept coming and receding? She needed to wake up, get a grip on what was real, but her eyelids were so heavy.

'Miss Rossini…'

There it was again. Where was Bella? Why did the voices use her friend's name as though it belonged to her? It was wrong. Her head ached with trying to figure it out. The fog swirled. So much easier to slide back into oblivion where there was no painful confusion. Yet she wanted answers, wanted the torment of this nightmare to end. Which meant focusing all the energy she could summon on opening her eyes.

'Oh, dear God! She woke up! She's awake!'

The screech hurt her ears. The sudden glare of light made her want to close her eyes, but she fought the impulse, frightened of losing the strength to open them again. Her blurred vision picked up a flurry of movement.

'I'll get the doctor!'

Doctor…white bed…white screens…tubes stuck in her arm. This had to be a hospital. Some kind of sling was on her other arm. She couldn't see her legs. The blanket on the bed was covering them. She tried to move them but couldn't manage it. Dead weight. Her mind filled with a galloping fear. Was she paralysed?

A nurse appeared at the foot of her bed, a pretty blond woman with anxious blue eyes. 'Hi! My name is Alison. I've paged Dr Farrell. He'll be here in a minute, Miss Rossini.'

Jenny tried to say that wasn't her name but her mouth wouldn't co-operate. Her lips, her throat were so dry they felt cracked.

'I'll get you a cup of ice,' Alison said, darting away.

When she returned she was accompanied by a man who introduced himself as Dr Farrell. Alison fed her a piece of ice which she rolled around her tongue, working moisture from it, grateful for the lubrication trickling down her throat.

'Glad to have you with us at last, Miss Rossini,' the doctor was saying, looking cheerful about it. He was a short stocky man, probably mid-thirties, dark hair given a buzz cut that seemed to defy the receding hairline, certainly no vanity about hiding it. His bright brown eyes twinkled approval of her wakeful state. 'You've been in a coma for the past two weeks.'

Why? What's wrong with me? Panic churned through her as she tried to telegraph the questions with her eyes.

'You were in a car accident,' he said, understanding her need to know. 'For some reason you were not wearing a seat belt and you were thrown clear of the wreck. However, you suffered a severe concussion, and the bruising of the brain undoubtedly contributed to the coma. You also had three broken ribs, a broken arm, deep lacerations on one leg and you have a cast on the other, fixing up a broken ankle. However, you are mending nicely and it's only a matter of time before you'll be on your feet again.'

Relief whooshed through her. She wasn't paralysed. However, her bruised brain wasn't working so well. It couldn't recollect any memory of a car accident. Besides, it didn't make sense that she hadn't been wearing a seat belt. She always did. It was an automatic action whenever she got into a car.

'I see you frowning, Miss Rossini. Are you up to speaking yet?' the doctor asked kindly.

I'm not Bella. Why didn't they know that?

She licked her lips and managed to croak, 'My name...'

'Good! You know your name.'

No!

She tried again. 'My friend...'

The doctor sighed, grimaced. His eyes softened with sympathy. 'I'm sorry to tell you that your friend passed away in the accident. Nothing could be done for her. The car burst into flames before help arrived. If you had not been thrown clear…'

Bella…dead? Burnt? The horror of it brought a gush of tears. The doctor took her hand and patted it, mouthing words of comfort, but Jenny didn't really hear anything but the tone. All she could think of was that being burned was a terrible way to die and Bella had been so kind to her, taking her in, giving her a place to live, even letting her borrow her name so she could work at the Venetian Forum since everyone employed there had to be Italian. Or of Italian heritage.

Was that how their identities had got mixed up?

The tears kept coming. The doctor left, appointing the nurse to sit at her bedside and talk to her. Jenny couldn't speak. She was too overwhelmed by the shock of her situation and the dreadful loss of her friend. Her only friend. And Bella had had no one, either. No family. Both of them orphans—a bond that had given them immediate empathy with each other.

Who would bury her? What would happen to her apartment and all her things…the home she'd made, waiting for her to come back…except she never would return to it.

Eventually the exhaustion of grief drew her into sleep.

Another nurse had replaced Alison when she woke up.

'Hello. My name is Jill,' she said encouragingly. 'Can I get you anything, Miss Rossini?'

Not Rossini. Kent. Jenny Kent. But there was no one to care about who or what she was now that Bella was gone.

Fear speared through the dark turmoil in her mind.

Where would she go when they finally released her from this hospital? Social Services would probably find some place for her, as they had throughout her childhood and early teenage years—places she'd hated—and if she was forced back into the welfare system because of her injuries, that sleazy abusive creep might hear of it.

Revulsion cramped her stomach. The officials hadn't believed her when she had reported their highly experienced social worker for *helping* down-and-out girls in return for sexual favours. He was too entrenched in the system not to be trusted, and the other girls had been too frightened of his vengeful power to back up her report. She'd been painted as a vindictive liar for not getting what she wanted from him, and no doubt he would revel in victimising her again if he became aware of her present circumstances.

Yet what other choice was viable? Simply to survive she would have to be dependent on welfare until she could stand on her own two feet again and make her way, selling her sketches on the street as she had before meeting Bella. Impossible to stay on at the Venetian Forum without the Rossini name.

The wild thought flashed into her mind—did she have to give it up?

Everyone thought Jenny Kent was dead.

There was no one to care if she was, no one to come forward to claim her. If officialdom believed she was Isabella Rossini…if she found out why they did…would it be too terrible of her to take over her friend's identity for a while…stay in the apartment…go on working at the Venetian Forum…build up some savings…give herself time to think, to plan out what to do when she felt up to coping on her own?

Wouldn't her friend have wanted that for her instead of all of it just…*ending*?

CHAPTER TWO

Rome, Italy
Six Months Later

DANTE Rossini unwound himself from Anya's voluptuous charms and reached for his cell-phone.

'Don't!' she snapped. 'You can pick up the message later.'

'It's my grandfather,' he said, ignoring the protest.

'Oh, fine! He calls and you jump!'

Her burst of petulance annoyed him. He sliced her a quelling look as he flipped open the cell-phone, knowing it could only be his grandfather because no one else had been given this private number—an immediate link between them. He'd bought the phone for this specific use when Nonno had been diagnosed with inoperable cancer, and yes, he was ready to jump whenever it rang. Three months at most, the doctors had forecast, and already a month had gone by. Time was running out for Marco Rossini.

'Dante here,' he said quickly, aware of a tight knot of urgency in his chest. 'What can I do for you, Nonno?'

Frustrated that her jeering words had had no effect on him, Anya flounced off the bed and strutted angrily towards the bathroom. Time was running out on Anya Michaelson, too, he decided. She always expected to be indulged, which he hadn't minded in the past, given her fantastic body and her talent for erotic games, but her self-centred core was beginning to irritate him.

He heard his grandfather wheezing, gathering breath enough to speak. 'It's a family matter, Dante.'

Family? Usually it was a business issue he wanted resolved. 'What's the problem?' he asked.

'I'll explain when you get here.'

'You want me to come now?'

'Yes. No time to waste.'

'I'll be there before lunch,' he promised.

'Good boy!'

Boy... Dante smiled ironically as he flicked the cellphone shut. He was thirty years old, already designated to take over the management of a global business, having met every challenge his grandfather had set for him from his teenage years onward. Only Marco Rossini had the balls to still call him a boy, and Dante excused it as a term of familial affection. He'd just turned six years old when his parents were killed in a speed-boat accident and he'd been his grandfather's *boy* ever since.

'What about me?' Anya demanded as he rose from the bed.

She'd propped herself provocatively against the

bathroom doorjamb, every lush naked curve jutting out at him, her long blond hair arranged in tousled disarray over her shoulders, her full-lipped mouth pouting. The desire she'd stirred earlier was gone. The only feeling she raised now was impatience.

'I'm sorry. I have to leave.'

'You promised to take me shopping today.'

'Shopping is unimportant.'

She was blocking the way into the bathroom. He took hold of her waist to move her aside. She flung her arms around his neck, pressing herself against him, her green eyes sparking anger. 'It is not unimportant to me, Dante. You promised...'

'Another time, Anya. I'm needed on Capri. Now, let go.'

His voice was cold. His eyes were cold. She let go, infuriated by his command but obeying it. He stepped past her and walked into the shower stall, not glancing back.

'I hate the way you switch off!' she screeched. 'I hate it!'

'Then find yourself another man, Anya,' he said carelessly and turned on the water, drowning out any extraneous noise. The last thing he wanted was to be subjected to a hissy fit, and he didn't really care if Anya found herself another man. Let someone else buy her clothes and jewellery for the pleasure of her body. There were always other beautiful women, eager to share his bed.

She was gone when he emerged from the bathroom and he didn't give her another thought. As he plunged into the business of getting ready to leave—calling the helicopter pilot to be on standby for a flight to Capri, dressing, grabbing some breakfast—his mind was sifting through the family positions, trying to work out who was causing his grandfather concern.

Uncle Roberto was currently in London, overseeing the refurbishing of the hotel, happily immersing himself in the kind of creativity he loved. He'd always managed his *gay* life with discretion and Marco tolerated his son's homosexuality, with the proviso that it wasn't paraded under his nose. Had something *unacceptable* happened?

Aunt Sophia had shed her third money-sucking husband a year ago, at the cost of several million dollars, causing Marco to gnash his teeth over his wayward daughter's total lack of judgement. She had married in turn an American evangelist, a Parisian playboy and an Argentinian polo player, all of whom apparently exuded enough sexual charisma to woo and win themselves a very wealthy wife. Had she started another unsuitable liaison?

Then there was his cousin, Lucia, Aunt Sophia's twenty-four-year-old daughter by the Parisian playboy, a sly little minx whom he'd never liked. Even as a child she'd had a habit of spying on people and tattling if she thought it would win her some advantage. But she was always sweetness itself to Marco. Dante couldn't imagine *her* giving their grandfather a problem. Lucia would avoid that like the plague, especially when there was a hefty inheritance in sight.

Marco himself had only married once. His wife had died before Dante was born, and Marco had satisfied himself with a string of mistresses over the years. They'd been treated well and paid off handsomely at the end of each 'arrangement.' None of them should be causing trouble.

Mulling over the possibilities was probably pointless, though Dante liked to be mentally prepared to carry out any directive his grandfather gave. Marco had drilled into him that knowledge was power. Anyone who was surprised at an important meeting had not done their homework and was instantly at a disadvantage. Dante was rarely surprised these days. Though he had been surprised by his grandfather's choice to spend his last months at the villa on Capri.

Why not the palazzo in Venice? The worldwide chain of Gondola Hotels, the Venetian Forums built in 'little Italy' sections of major cities...all were inspired by the place Marco called home. Of course, the air in Venice was not as sweet as on the island, the view not as clean, the sunshine not so accessible, not for a very sick man. Still, his grandfather had been born in Venice and Dante had expected him to want to die there.

He wondered again about that choice as the helicopter flew him towards Capri. His gaze swept around the high grey cliffs dotted with scrubby trees, the rocky outcrops spearing up from the sea, the predominantly white township sprawling around the top edge of the island, the water below a brilliant turquoise blue. There was nothing even faintly reminiscent of Venice.

The villa had always been a holiday place, mostly used by Aunt Sophia and Uncle Roberto. Dante had spent some of his school vacations there but his grandfather had only ever dropped in on them, not staying for long, certainly not ever demonstrating a fondness for the relaxed lifestyle it offered. He'd always seemed impatient to be gone about his business again.

The helicopter landed on the rear terrace of the villa grounds. It was almost noon and the sun was hot enough for Dante to be glad to reach the flag-stoned walkway, which was well shaded by pine trees and the profusion of bougainvillea spread over the columned pergola. He was not so glad to see Lucia at the other end of it, walking out to meet him.

She favoured her father in looks, more French than Italian, dark-brown hair cut in a very chic bob, her fine-boned face featuring a straight elegant nose, a full-lipped sensual mouth, bright brown eyes that were always keenly observant. She wore a coquettish, little-girl dress that shouted French designer class, geometrically patterned in brown and white and black, the miniskirt showing off her long slim legs.

'Nonno is in the front courtyard, waiting for you,' she said, turning to accompany him as he came level with her.

'Thank you. No need for you to escort me, Lucia.'

She stuck to his side. 'I want to know what's going on.'

'He called me, not you.'

She flashed him a resentful look. 'I'm just as much *family* as you, Dante.'

She'd eavesdropped on the call. He kept walking, saying nothing for her to get her teeth into. They entered the villa, moving towards the atrium, a central gathering place that connected the wings spreading out from it and led to the front courtyard.

Frustrated by his silence, Lucia offered information to tempt some speculation. 'A man came yesterday afternoon. He didn't give a name. He brought a briefcase with him and had a private meeting with Nonno. It left Nonno looking even more ill. I'm worried about him.'

'I'm sure you're doing your best to brighten him up, Lucia,' he said blandly.

'If I know what the problem is…'

'I have no idea.'

'Don't play dumb with me, Dante. You always have an idea.' The bite in her voice softened to a sweet wheedle. 'I just want to help. Whatever Nonno heard from that man yesterday has knocked the life out of him. It's awful seeing him so sunk into himself.'

Bad news, Dante thought, steeling himself to deal with the fallout as best he could. 'I'm sorry to hear it,' he said, 'but I can't tell you what I don't know, Lucia. You'll have to wait until Nonno chooses to reveal what's on his mind.'

'You'll tell me after you've talked with him?' she pressed.

He shrugged. 'Depends on whether it's confidential or not.'

'I'm the one here looking after him. I need to know.'

His grandfather had a private nurse and a whole body of servants looking after him. He shot his cousin a mocking look. 'You're here looking after your own interests, Lucia. Let's not pretend otherwise.'

'Oh, you…you…' Her mouth clamped down on whatever epithet she would have liked to fling at him.

It was clear to Dante she hated him for seeing through her artifices, always had, but open enmity was not her game.

'I love Nonno and he loves me,' she stated tightly. 'You might do well to remember that, Dante.'

An empty threat, but it probably gave her some satisfaction to leave him with it. They'd reached the atrium and she sheered off to the right, probably heading for the main entertainment room from where she could view what went on in the courtyard, though she wouldn't be able to hear what was said.

Dante continued on, only pausing when he stepped outside, taking in the scene before announcing his arrival. His grandfather was resting in a well-cushioned chaise lounge, his face shaded by an umbrella, the rest of his brutally wasted body soaking up the natural warmth of the sun.

He wore navy silk pyjamas, their looseness emphasising rather than hiding the loss of his once powerful physique. His eyes were closed. Sunken cheeks made his cheekbones too prominent, his proud Roman nose too big, but there was still an indomitable air about his jutting chin. His skin had tanned, probably from many mornings spent like this. It made his thick, wavy hair look shockingly whiter.

The nurse sat on a chair beside him, ready to attend to his every need. She was reading a book. A pitcher of fruit juice and a set of glasses stood on a table within easy reach. Tubs of flowers provided pleasing cascades of colour, and the brilliant blue vista of sea and sky generated a peaceful ambience. But Dante knew the sense of peace had to be a lie. Something was wrong and he had to fix it.

His footsteps on the terrace flagstones as he moved

forward alerted the nurse to his presence, and his grandfather's eyelids snapped open. The nurse rose to her feet.
His grandfather directed a dismissive wave at her and
gestured for Dante to take the chair she had vacated. He
didn't speak until she had gone and his grandson was
settled close to him. Greetings were unnecessary and any
inquiry about his health was unwelcome, so Dante waited
in silence to hear what he'd been summoned to hear.

'I have kept many things from you, Dante. Private
things, Personal things. Painful things.' A rueful grimace
expressed his grandfather's reluctance to confide them.
'Now is the time to tell you.'

'As you wish, Nonno,' Dante said quietly, not liking
the all too evident distress.

The usually bright dark eyes were clouded as his
grandfather bluntly stated, 'Your grandmother, the only
woman I ever really loved, my beautiful Isabella, died
in this villa.'

His voice faltered, choked with emotion. Dante
waited for him to recover, feeling oddly embarrassed by
so much feeling, never openly expressed before. The
only knowledge he'd had of his grandmother was the occasional reference in newspapers of Marco's one and
only wife having died of a drug overdose. It had
happened before he was born, and when he'd queried
the story, his grandfather had vehemently forbidden any
further mention of it.

Dante had privately assumed he had felt some guilt
over his wife's untimely and scandalous death, but given
she was the only woman he had ever really loved,
perhaps there had been a deep and abiding grief that he

couldn't bear to touch upon. It did answer why Marco had chosen to die here, too.

A deep sigh ended in another grimace. 'We had a third son.'

The missing Rossini 'wild child'—another sensational story occasionally popping up in newspapers, full of lurid speculation about the rebellious black sheep who'd obviously refused to knuckle under to what Marco wanted of him, dropping completely out of his father's world—speculation that was never answered by the Rossinis—a family skeleton kept so firmly in the cupboard, Dante's curiosity about the uncle he'd never known had always been frustrated. His jerk of surprise at the totally unexpected opening of this door evoked a sharply dismissive gesture from his grandfather, demanding forebearance.

'Just listen.' The command held no patience for questions. 'I banished Antonio from our lives. No one in the family was to even speak his name. Because of him, my Isabella died. He killed his mother, not deliberately, but he gave her the designer drug that led to her death. It was *his* fault and I couldn't forgive him.'

Dante's mind reeled with shock. It took him several moments to attach some current significance to the revelations of this traumatic family history. Had his exiled uncle resurfaced? Was this the problem?

'He was the youngest of our four children. Your father, Alessandro—' his grandfather sighed, shaking his head, still grieved by the loss of his eldest son '—he was my boy in every way. As you are, Dante.'

Yes, Dante thought. Even in looks, both he and his

father had inherited Marco's thick wavy hair, his deeply set dark-chocolate eyes, strong Roman nose, and the slight cleft centring their squarish chins.

'Roberto…he was softer,' his grandfather went on in a tone of rueful reminiscence. 'It was obvious from early on he would not be a competitor like Alessandro, but he does well enough with his artistic talent. And Sophia, our first girl…we spoilt her, gave her too much, indulged her every whim. I cannot really blame her for the behaviour I now have to pay for. Then came Antonio…'

His eyes closed, as though the memory of his youngest son was still cloaked in darkness. It took a visible effort to speak of him. 'He was a very bright child, mischievous, merry, given to creating amusing mayhem. He made us laugh. Isabella adored him. Of our four children, he looked most like her. He was…her joy.'

Dante heard the pain in every word and knew that Marco had shared his wife's joy in the boy.

'School was too easy for him. He wasn't challenged enough. He looked for other excitement, adventures, parties, physical thrills, experimenting with drugs. I didn't know about the drugs, but Isabella did. She kept it from me. When she died, Antonio confessed that she had been trying to make him stop and he had urged her to try the drug, to see for herself how marvellous it would make her feel and how completely harmless it was.'

His eyes opened and black derision flashed from them as he bitterly repeated, 'Harmless…'

'Tragic,' Dante murmured, imagining the horror of discovering how his wife's death had occurred, and the double grief his grandfather had suffered.

'Antonio should have died, not my Isabella. So I made him dead as far as my world was concerned.'

Dante nodded sympathetic understanding. None of this had touched his life and he still felt somewhat stunned that so much had been kept totally suppressed by the family. No doubt it was a measure of his grand-father's dominating and singularly ruthless power that not one word of the mother/son drug connection had leaked out, not privately nor publicly.

A mirthless little laugh gravelled from his grand-father's throat. His eyes seemed to mock himself as he said, 'I thought I might make peace with him. It's bad enough for any man to have one son die before him. Losing Alessandro was...but at least I had you, my son's son, filling that gap. Antonio was completely lost. And *is* completely lost. There can be no making peace with him.'

Dante frowned. 'Do you mean...?'

'I hired a firm of private investigators to find him, bring me news of the life he'd made for himself, infor-mation that would tell me if it was viable to set up a meeting between us. The owner of the firm called on me yesterday. Antonio and his wife died in a plane crash two years ago—a small private plane he was flying himself. Bad weather, pilot error...'

'I'm sorry, Nonno.'

'Too late for making peace,' he muttered. 'But he did leave a daughter, Dante. A daughter whom he named Isabella, after his mother, and I want you to fly to Australia and bring her here to me.' His eyes suddenly blazed with a concentration of life. 'I want *you* to do it, Dante, because

I know you'll do everything in your power to make her come with you. And there is so little time…'

'Of course I'll do it for you, Nonno. Do you know where she is?'

'Sydney.' His mouth twisted with irony. 'She even works in the Venetian Forum we built there. You will have no trouble finding her.' He leaned over, picked up a manila folder which was lying on the low table beside his chaise. 'All the information you need is in here.'

He held it out and Dante took it.

'Isabella Rossini…' The name rolled off his grandfather's tongue in a tone of deep longing. 'Bring Antonio's daughter home to me, Dante. My Isabella would have wished it. Bring our grand-daughter home.…'

CHAPTER THREE

SATURDAY was always the best day for Jenny at the Venetian Forum. It had a carnival atmosphere with weekend crowds flocking to the morning markets set up on either side of the canal, staying on for lunch at the many restaurants bordering the main square. In their stroll around the stalls, people invariably paused to watch her drawing her charcoal portraits, many tempted to get one done of themselves or their children. She made enough money on Saturday to live on the entire week.

It was even better when it was sunny like today. Although it was only the beginning of September—the start of spring—it almost felt like summer, no clouds in the brilliant blue sky, no chilly wind, just lovely mild warmth that everyone could bask in while they looked at the marvellous array of Venetian masks, original jewellery, hand-painted scarves, individually blown-glass works of art—so many beautiful things to buy. The photographer was busy, too, taking shots of people on the Bridge of Sighs, or on their gondola rides. He wasn't in competition with her. Hand-drawn portraits were different.

She finished one of a little boy, pocketed her fee from the pleased parents, then set herself up for the next subject in line, a giggly teenage girl who was pushed onto the posing chair by a couple of equally giggly girlfriends.

A really striking man stood to one side of them. Was he waiting his turn in the chair? Jenny hoped so. He had such a handsome face, framed by a luxuriant head of hair, many shades of brown—from caramel to dark chocolate—running through its gleaming thickness, and perfectly cut to show off its natural waves. It was a pity she couldn't capture the colours in a charcoal portrait, but his face alone presented a fascinating challenge; the sharply angled arch of his eyebrows, the deeply set eyes, the strong lines of his nose and jaw with the intriguing contrast of rather full, sensual lips and a soft dimple centred at the base of his chin.

She kept sneaking glances at him as she sketched the girl's portrait. He didn't move away, apparently content to linger and observe her working. A very masculine man, she thought, taller than most and with a physique that seemed to radiate power.

He was dressed in expensive clothes, a good quality white shirt with a thin fawn stripe and well-cut fawn slacks. The fawn leather loafers on his feet looked like Italian designer shoes. A brown suede jacket was casually slung over one shoulder. She guessed his age at about thirty, mature enough to have made his mark in some successful business, and carrying the confidence of being able to achieve anything he wanted.

Definitely a class act, Jenny decided, and wondered if he was idling away some time before a luncheon date, probably at the most expensive restaurant in the forum. It was almost noon. She half-expected some beautiful woman to appear and pluck him away. Which would be disappointing, but people like him weren't usually interested in posing for a street artist.

Gradually it sank in that he was studying her, not how she worked. It was weird, being made to feel an object of personal interest to this man. She caught his gaze roving around the chaotic volume of her dark curly hair, assessing the features of her face, which to her mind were totally unremarkable, skating down her loose black tunic and slacks to the shabby but comfortable black walking shoes she'd been wearing since breaking her ankle.

Hardly a bundle of style, she thought, wishing he'd stop making her self-conscious. She tried to block him out, concentrating on finishing the portrait of the teenager. Despite keeping her focus on her subject, her awareness of him did not go away. He remained a dominating presence on the periphery of her vision, moving purposefully to centre stage and taking the chair vacated by the teenager as the sale of the completed portrait was being transacted.

Jenny took a deep breath before resuming her own seat. Her nerves had gone all edgy, which was ridiculous. She'd wanted to draw this man, he was giving her the opportunity. Yet her hand was slightly tremulous as she picked up a fresh stick of charcoal, and the blank page on the easel suddenly seemed daunting. She had to steel herself to look directly at him. He smiled at her and her heart actually fluttered. The smile made him breathtakingly handsome.

'Do you work here every day?' he asked.

She shook her head. 'Wednesday to Sunday.'

'Not enough people here on Monday and Tuesday?'

'Those days are usually slow.'

He tilted his head, eyeing her curiously. 'Do you like this kind of chancy existence?'

She instantly bridled at this personal probe. It smacked of a much superior existence, which he had probably enjoyed all his life. 'Yes, I do. I don't have to answer to anyone,' she said pointedly.

'You prefer to be independent.'

She frowned at his persistence. 'Would you mind keeping still while I sketch?'

In short, shut up and stop disturbing me.

But he wasn't about to take direction from her. He probably didn't take direction from anyone.

'I don't want a still-life portrait,' he said, smiling the heart-fluttering smile again. 'Just capture what you can of me while we chat.'

Why did he want to chat?

He couldn't be attracted to her. It made no sense that a man like him would take an interest in a woman so obviously beneath his status. Jenny forced herself to draw the outline of his head. Getting his hair right might help her with the more challenging task of capturing his face.

'Have you always wanted to be an artist?' he asked.

'It's the one thing I'm good at,' she answered, feeling herself tense up at being subjected to more curiosity.

'Do you do landscapes as well as portraits?'

'Some.'

'Do they sell?'

'Some.'

'Where might I buy one?'

'At Circular Quay on Mondays and Tuesdays.' She flashed him an ironic look. 'I'm a street vendor and it's tourist stuff—the harbour, the bridge, the opera house. I doubt you'd be interested in buying.'

'Why do you say that?'

'I think a *name* artist would be more your style.'

He didn't rise to the note of derision in her voice, affably remarking, 'You might make a name for yourself one day.'

'And you want the pleasure of discovering me?' she mocked, not believing it for a moment and feeling more and more uneasy about why he was engaging in this banter with her.

'I'm here on a journey of discovery.'

The whimsical statement teased her into asking, 'Where are you from?'

'Italy.'

She studied his face; smooth olive skin, definitely a Roman nose, and that sensual mouth seemed to have Latin lover written all over it. His being Italian was not surprising. As she started sketching his features, she commented, 'If you wanted a taste of Venice, surely it would have been much easier to go there.'

'I know Venice very well. My mission is of a more personal nature.'

'You want to find yourself?' she tossed at him flippantly.

He laughed. It gave his striking face even more charismatic appeal. Jenny privately bet he was a devil with women and wished she could inject that appeal into his portrait, but the vibrant expression was gone before she could even begin to play with it on paper. The sparkle in his eyes gave way to a look of serious intent— a look that bored into her as though determined on penetrating any defensive layer she could put between them.

'I came for you, Isabella.'

His soft and certain use of her friend's name shocked her into staring at him. How could he know it? She signed her portraits *Bella*, not *Isabella*. Her mind reeled back over this whole strange encounter with him; the fact that he didn't fit her kind of clientele, his too-acute observation of her, his curiosity about her work, the personal questions. A sense of danger clanged along her nerves. Was she about to be unmasked as a fraud?

No!

He thought she was Bella. Which meant he hadn't known her friend. He must have got the name from one of the stall-holders who knew her as Isabella Rossini. Was he playing some supposedly seductive pick-up game with her? But why would he?

'I beg your pardon!' she said with as much indignation as she could muster, hating the idea of him digging for information about her, and thinking he could get some stupid advantage from it.

He gestured an apology. 'Forgive me for not being more direct in my approach. The estrangement in our family makes for a difficult meeting and I hoped to ease into it. My name is Dante Rossini. I'm one of your cousins and I'm here to invite you back to Italy for a reunion with all your other relatives.'

Jenny was totally stricken by this news. Bella had told her she had no family. There'd been no talk of any connections in Italy. But if there had been an estrangement, perhaps she'd never heard of them, believing herself truly orphaned by the plane crash which had killed her parents. On the other hand, was this man telling the truth? Even if he was, how would Bella have responded to it? No one from Italy had cared about her all these years. Why bother now?

Fear fed the burst of adrenaline that drove her to her feet. Fear chose the words that sprang off her tongue. 'Go away!'

That jerked him out of his air of relaxed confidence.

Jenny didn't wait for a response to her vehement command. She slammed down the stick of charcoal, ripped the half-done portrait off the easel, crumpled the sheet of paper up in her hands and threw it in the wastebin to punctuate an emphatic end to this encounter.

'I don't know what you want but I want no part of it. Just go away!' she repeated, her eyes stabbing him with fierce rejection as he rose from the chair, suddenly taking on the appearance of a formidable antagonist.

'That I cannot do,' he stated quietly.

'Oh, yes you can!' Her mind wildly seized on reinforcements. 'If you don't I'll go to the forum management, tell them you're harassing me.'

He shook his head. 'They won't act against me, Isabella.'

'Yes, they will. They're very tight with security.'

He frowned at her. 'I thought you knew the Rossini

family owns all the Venetian Forums. That you chose to buy one of our apartments here in Sydney because of the family connection.'

Her mind completely boggled. Had Bella known this? She had never mentioned it. And what did he mean...*all the Venetian Forums?* Was there a worldwide network of them? If so, the Rossini family had to be mega-wealthy and no one was going to take her side against this man. She was trapped on *his* territory.

'I've already spoken to the management here about you,' he went on. 'If you need them to identify me, assure yourself that I am who I say I am, I'm happy to accompany you to the admin office...'

'No! I'm not accompanying you anywhere!' she almost shouted at him in panic.

Her raised voice attracted the attention of passers-by, including Luigi, the photographer, who dropped his hustling for clients to stroll over and ask, 'Having trouble here, Bella?'

She couldn't rope him in to help her, not against the man who had the management in his pocket. Luigi depended on his job here. The two men were eyeing each other over—both macho Italian males—and the bristling tension told her neither one of them was about to back down.

'It's okay, Luigi. Just a family fight,' she said quickly. He would understand that. Her experience of working in the forum had taught her that all Italian families got noisy over a dispute and were best left to themselves to sort out the problem.

'Well, tone it down,' he advised. 'You'll be scaring customers away.'

'Sorry,' she muttered.

He shrugged and moved off, tossing an airy wave at Dante. 'Make him take you to lunch. He looks as though he can afford it. A bit of vino…'

'Excellent idea!' her nemesis agreed. 'I'll help you pack up, Isabella.'

He turned and collected the folding chair he'd been sitting on before Jenny could say a word. She felt totally undermined by his arrogant confidence, helpless to fight the situation, yet desperate to escape it. He wasn't *family* to her, and what had seemed a harmless deception—a temporary lifeline that would help her and not hurt anyone—was turning into a murky mess that she didn't know how to negotiate.

'Why turn up now? Why?' she demanded of him as he carried the chair over to where she stood beside the easel.

'Circumstances change.' He flashed that smile again. At close quarters it probably made every woman go weak at the knees and Jenny was no exception. Dante Rossini had megawatt sex appeal. 'Let me explain over lunch,' he added, his dark-chocolate eyes warm enough to melt resistance, his voice a persuasive purr.

Her spine tingled. Her heart pounded in her ears. Her mind screamed danger. No way could she give in to the charm of the man. If she didn't somehow extricate herself from this situation, it would lead to terrible trouble.

'You're too late,' she blurted out. It was the truth. Bella was dead. But she couldn't reveal that. 'I don't need you in my life. I don't want you,' she threw at him, wildly hoping he would accept that his mission was futile.

'Then why set yourself up in the Venetian Forum?' he shot at her, his eyes hardening with disbelief at her hysterical claims.

Bella had set her up. Confusion roared through Jenny. Had there been some artful plan behind her friend's kindness in inviting her to share the apartment, getting her employed here by using the Rossini name? Had Bella imagined it might catch the attention of the forum management enough to mention it to the Rossini family?

Was I bait?

Her first meeting with Bella…the offer that had seemed too good to be true…wanting to believe luck had smiled on her for once. Jenny shook her head. It was all irrelevant now. She shouldn't have stayed on, using Bella's name, getting herself in this awful tangle.

'Think what you like,' she snapped at the cousin who'd come too late. 'I'm out of here.'

She instantly busied herself, packing up the easel, her inner agitation making her hurry so much she fumbled and dropped the box of charcoal sticks. He swooped and picked it up, holding it out to her, making it impossible to completely ignore him. He was still holding her fold-up chair, as well.

'Thanks,' she muttered, snatching the box from him, stowing it in the carry-case.

'I'm not about to go away, Isabella,' he warned.

Her nerves quivered, sensing the relentless force of the man. With all that wealth and power behind him, he was undoubtedly used to people falling in with him. Being rebuffed and rejected would sting his ego, make him more persistent. It was imperative now to plan a disappearing act, get back to the apartment, pack only essentials, catch a bus, a train, a plane…anything that took *her* away. He wouldn't look for Jenny Kent. She was of no interest to him.

The carry-case was ready to go. She folded up the stool she used when sketching, tucked it under one arm, then steeled herself to face Dante Rossini and put an end to this danger-laden meeting. It took all her willpower to lift her gaze to his and hold it steady as she spoke to him, pouring a tone of flat finality into her voice.

'Don't waste any more of your time. Isabella Rossini has not occupied any place in your family all these years and that isn't about to change because you suddenly want it to.' She held out her hand. 'Just give me the chair and let me go.'

He shook his head, unable to come to grips with her stance, not about to accept it, either.

Jenny panicked at the thought of having to endure more argument from him. 'Keep it then,' she cried, her hand jerking in a wave of dismissal as she turned away and forced her trembling legs to march across the forum, heading for the elevator that would shut him out and take her up to the apartment he couldn't enter.

The chair didn't matter.

It would have to be left behind anyway.

The only way to disappear was to travel lightly, go fast and far, leaving no trace for anyone to pick up.

CHAPTER FOUR

DANTE had never failed to deliver what his grandfather asked of him. Failure in this instance was unthinkable. He had to get Isabella Rossini to Capri.

He followed her determined walk away from him, staying a few steps behind, not attempting to catch up with her. He needed time to process her reaction, make some sense of it before tackling her unreasonable negativity again. He had anticipated a pleased response. The fact that she'd chosen to live and work at the Sydney forum after losing her parents had suggested a wish for contact with the family. He now had to get his head into gear to deal with something entirely different.

Angry pride?

A fierce independence, grown out of being left to fend for herself for so long?

There'd been fear in her eyes just before she'd turned her back on him. Fear of what? Change? The unknown?

Beautiful eyes. Even without any artful makeup they were stand-out eyes, their amber colour quite fascinating, shaded by long, thick curly lashes. He liked her wide, generous mouth, too, another stand-out feature in her rather angular face. Her hair was an unruly mop, but take her to a good stylist, get it shaped right, hand her over to a beautician to polish up the raw material, put her in some designer clothes—her figure was thin enough under that shapeless black gear to wear them well—and Lucia would be as jealous as sin over her newly discovered cousin.

And spitting chips over another grand-daughter to inherit some of Marco's estate.

The money…

He could use that as a bargaining tool. Isabella's parents had left her enough to buy the apartment but little more than that. She wouldn't have to work another day in her life if she pleased Marco. She could live like Lucia, being pampered in the lap of luxury. No woman in the world would knock that back. He just had to lay it on thickly enough for Isabella to take the bait.

Confidence renewed, Dante quickened his pace. She was heading into the passageway where the elevator to the south bank of apartments was housed. He glanced up, smiling at the colourful concoction the architect had designed—pink, lemon, green, red, blue, orange, purple— reminiscent of the brightly painted houses on the islands of Murano and Burano, a short ferry ride from Venice. Isabella's apartment was the purple one on the third floor. She had pots of pink geraniums on her balcony, a nice homely touch.

I don't need you in my life.

Dante's chest tightened as he remembered those vehement words. Maybe she didn't, but she could give up two months of it for Marco. Especially when the reward would be substantial. He'd pay her himself—upfront—if she doubted there was a pot of gold at the end of this trip. He'd spent thousands on Anya Michaelson to keep her sweet while he wanted her. He didn't care how much it cost him to give his grandfather the solace of making some peace with the past before he died.

Her finger jabbed the elevator button—an action of haste and anxiety. In her fast flight across the square, she hadn't once glanced back to check on what he was doing. Nor did she acknowledge his presence when he stood beside her, waiting for the elevator doors to open. She stared rigidly ahead as though he didn't exist.

Dante was not accustomed to being ignored. As much as he told himself not to be piqued by her behaviour—it would change soon enough with the lure of wealth—it took a considerable effort not to reveal any vexation when he spoke.

'I'm sorry I've upset you, Isabella. That wasn't my intention,' he assured her quietly.

No reply. Her jaw tightened. Dante imagined her clenching her teeth, denying the possible spilling of any more words to him. The stubborn stance irked him further. She was throwing out a challenge he'd take great satisfaction in winning, if only to see that rude rigidity wilt.

'I'd appreciate it if you'd listen to a proposition which is very much to your advantage,' he said, wondering if the blank wall she was holding was actually a negotiation tactic. Resistance virtually guaranteed being offered more.

The elevator doors opened. Her head jerked towards him. Her eyes slashed him with a cut-throat look. 'I'm *not* interested!'

Having punched out those decisive words, she stepped into the small compartment and hit the button for her floor.

Dante stepped in after her.

She glared at him, clearly seething with frustration. 'I told you…'

'I'm carrying your chair up for you,' he said blandly. 'You are rather loaded down with the rest of your working gear.'

She rolled her eyes away. The doors closed and she pointedly watched for the floor numbers to flash up, once again set on ignoring him. He noted that every line of her body was tense, fighting the pressure of his presence. She might be ignoring him but she was acutely aware of him.

A pity she was his cousin. He'd like nothing better than to have her at his mercy on a bed, begging him to do whatever he wanted with her. Now *that* would be very satisfying—seeing her stiff body quivering, surrendering to his will! But a bit too incestuous, given the close blood link. His grandfather wouldn't approve of that tactic.

The sexual scenario raised the possibility that her love life might be a barrier. 'Is Luigi your boyfriend?'

The question startled her from her fixation on the upward journey of the elevator. 'No.' Worry carved a line between her brows. 'So don't pester him on my behalf. He's just a fellow worker. And don't go looking for other boyfriends, either, because there isn't one.'

'Good! No one to object to your coming to Italy with me.'

'Will you get it through your head I'm not going anywhere with you!' she cried in exasperation.

'Why not? There's nothing that can't be put on hold here. Why not satisfy a natural curiosity about the family you've never met?'

A frantic, cornered look in her eyes.

Was it a daunting prospect for her? Did she see herself being critically examined by a bunch of strangers?

'My grandfather...*your* grandfather...wants you with him, Isabella,' he pressed, then played his trump card. 'Marco is a very wealthy man. If you grant his wish, he will shower riches on you, give you access to more money than you've ever dreamed of. Financially your future—'

'I don't want his money!'

Horror on her face. Her whole body shuddered in recoil from the idea. Dante was so stunned by her reaction, he was totally at a loss to know what line of persuasion to try next. This woman was impossible. It was utter madness to be repulsed by the promise of financial security for the rest of her life.

The elevator came to a halt. She rushed out of it the moment the doors were open enough to make an exit, pelting along the corridor to her apartment as though the hounds of hell were snapping at her heels. Dante followed, grimly determined to get to the bottom of this crazy conundrum.

She shoved the key in the lock, was pushing against the door even before it opened. Dante knew she'd whirl inside and shut him out, given half a chance. He barged straight in after her before she could do it, not caring how outraged she'd be by the action. He'd run out of patience with trying to reason with her. If he had to tie her up and gag her, he would force her to listen to him long enough to be convinced that a trip to Capri was the best course for her to take.

'This is home invasion!' she yelled at him, her chest heaving in agitation. Nice breasts, Dante couldn't help noting.

'No reasonable person would think so. You didn't object to my carrying up the chair for you,' he calmly reminded her. 'Perfectly natural for me to step into your apartment with it.'

She dropped the carry-case containing her easel. The stool which had been tucked under her arm clattered to the floor. She reached out, grabbed the folded chair from him, and pointedly let it fall on top of the carry-case. Clenched hands planted themselves aggressively on her hips. Her eyes blazed rejection of any excuse he could give for entering her apartment without permission.

'Now get out!' she hurled at him.

'Not until I get satisfaction.'

He pushed the door shut and stood against it, blocking any move she might make to open it again. Dante wondered if she was going to fly at him and try to punch him out. Her eyes were wildly measuring his physique. Maybe she sensed that she'd stirred a dangerous male savagery in him, a savagery that would take pleasure in forcefully restraining any physical attack she made. His own hands were itching to demonstrate some mastery over her. She stepped back from the simmering flashpoint, lifted her chin to a defiant angle and spat out her next line of action.

'If you don't go right now, I'll call the police.'

'Go ahead. Call them,' he challenged without a flicker of care, confident of justifying his presence here.

She visibly dithered over the decision.

'While we're waiting for them to come, you can do me the courtesy of listening to why your grandfather wants you to visit him.'

She flinched at the mention of Marco, as though the idea of a grandfather wanting her was painful. Dante wished he knew what was going on in her head. He hated dealing blindly. But listening to him was a lot less bother for her than answering to the police, so he expected to win this round.

'Promise me you'll leave when you finish talking,' she demanded, hating him for forcing the choice.

He held up his hand. 'Word of honour.' He wasn't about to finish talking until she agreed to come with him.

She heaved a sigh, then with a much put-upon air, moved into the sitting room and settled herself in a bucket chair, hands folded in her lap, looking at him stony-faced. She reminded Dante of a rebellious student having to endure an unfair lecture from a headmaster before she could escape.

He propped himself on the well-padded armrest of a sofa, commanding the space between her and the door. 'What did your father tell you about the family rift?' he asked, wondering if his uncle Antonio had painted Marco in some false light to favour himself.

She shook her head. 'You talk. I'll listen.'

He talked, repeating his grandfather's story of what had led up to Antonio's banishment, filling in some facts about the rest of the family, the death of his own parents, Marco's grief at having lost two sons, the cancer that decreed he had only three months left to live—one month already gone—his search for Antonio which had led to Isabella, his wish to see her, get to know her.

He played on gaining her sympathy and was gratified when he saw tears well into her eyes. Sure that he could now clinch her co-operation, he finished with, 'He's dying, Isabella. The time is so short. If you can find it in your heart to give…'

'I can't!' she cried, covering her face with her hands as she sobbed, 'I'm sorry…sorry…'

'I'll organise everything, make it easy for you,' Dante pressed.

'No…no…you don't understand,' she choked out.

'No, I don't. Please tell me.'

She dragged her hands down her tear-streaked face, gulped in air, and raised a wet, bleak gaze to his. 'It's too late,' she cried in a grief-stricken voice. 'Bella died in a car accident six months ago. I thought she had no one. I didn't think it would matter if I took her identity for a while. I'm sorry…sorry that your grandfather thinks she's alive. Oh God!' she shook her head in wretched regret. 'I didn't mean to hurt anyone.'

Dante was totally floored. He'd been sent on an impossible mission. Another death. He closed his eyes, shutting out the imposter, thinking of his grandfather who'd been fooled into believing he had another

Isabella who might look like his beloved wife. Everything within him railed against delivering such a devastating disappointment.

Anger stirred. Why hadn't the private investigators picked up the identity swap? How had this woman deceived everyone? No problem now in understanding her responses to him. She'd been scared out of her mind about getting tripped up. He opened his eyes to glare furious hostility at her.

'Explain to me how you managed to take Isabella's place without anyone questioning it,' he commanded, pushing himself upright and walking over to where she sat, standing over her, using deliberate intimidation to draw what he wanted out of her.

She didn't try to fight him this time. Her connection to his cousin poured from her in a stream of pleading for his understanding…how she'd come to share Isabella's apartment and use her name to get employment at the forum, the car accident, her friend burnt beyond recognition, her own identification cards destroyed in the fire, the mistake made by the authorities because of a handbag she'd been holding when she'd been thrown clear…

'I remembered afterwards that was why I'd taken off my seat belt. Bella was driving and she asked me to get a bag of sweets out of her handbag which she'd thrown onto the back seat. I couldn't reach with my seat belt on, so I unclipped it and leaned through the gap between the front seats, hooked my hand around the shoulder strap and dragged it onto my lap.'

'Her handbag must have contained her driver's licence,' Dante tersely pointed out. 'The identification photo…'

'It wasn't a good one of her. We both had long curly hair, hers darker, but that could have been from bad lighting when the camera shot was taken, and she was smiling so you couldn't tell her mouth wasn't as wide as mine. Her eyes were squinted up so their different shape wasn't so obvious, and I guess my face was bruised and puffy from the accident, making it look rounder. Even so, there was enough doubt about who I was for the police to call in the employment manager from the forum to identify me and because of my working under Bella's name...'

'Very convenient for you.'

She flushed at his acid sarcasm. 'I was in a coma for two weeks after the accident. The identification was made while I was still unconscious. I didn't know about it until after I woke up, and then all the medical staff was calling me Miss Rossini...and I let them. I let them because I had nowhere else to go and I needed recovery time from my other injuries, and I didn't think Bella would mind...'

'How could she?' Dante savagely mocked. 'She was dead.'

'Yes,' she agreed miserably. 'I'm sorry. I didn't know about you. Bella told me she was an orphan like me. No family. I didn't think it mattered when the police came again after I woke from the coma and I identified the driver as my flatmate, Jenny Kent...a nobody who wasn't connected to anyone. And that was the end of it.'

'Not the end. You took over Isabella's life because she had more than you,' he accused mercilessly. Money *was* a prime motivation. It always was. She'd just proved him right again.

'I only meant to do it for a while. Until I could…'

'Well, you fooled everyone effectively. You can go on fooling them for another two months.'

He would not fail his grandfather on what was virtually a death-bed request. It didn't matter who this woman was. She could make up for the deception she had played by being a good and loving grand-daughter to Marco until he died.

She shook her head, pained bewilderment in her eyes. 'I was going to leave here tonight, become Jenny Kent again. I'm sorry I…'

Ruthless purpose surged in Dante, cutting her plan of escape dead. 'I will not allow you to destroy the hope that made my grandfather send me on this mission. You will come to Italy with me. You will stay with him in the villa on Capri until he no longer needs you. He will know you as Isabella…'

'No! No!' She leapt to her feet in panic, hands wildly gesturing protest. 'You can't! *I* can't!'

He gripped her flailing arms. His eyes burned through the glaze of horror in hers with unshakeable determination. 'I can and you will. If you don't do as I say, I'll call the police and have you arrested for identity-theft and fraud, and I promise you your term of imprisonment will be a lot longer than two months!'

Shock, fear, despair chased across her face.

'So what do you want to be, Jenny Kent?' he mocked. 'A common criminal rotting in jail or a pampered grand-daughter living in luxury?'

CHAPTER FIVE

Rome
One Week Later

JENNY stood in the bedroom assigned to her in Dante's palatial apartment and stared at her reflection in the mirror, barely recognising herself. She had been transformed into someone else—the Isabella Dante wanted to present to his grandfather. It was incredible what money could do; incredible, fascinating and frightening. It had the power to make anything possible.

She now had a passport in Isabella's name, an entire wardrobe of fabulous designer clothes—some acquired in Sydney while they waited for the passport, the rest bought during a stopover in Paris—a face that had been made over by a beautician, her once thickly tangled mass of hair cleverly cut into a tousled cascade of wild sexy curls, newly applied perfect fingernails, polished in a natural tone, plus a whole range of fantastic accessories to complement her new look—belts, bags, shoes, jewellery.

She'd flown halfway around the world in a private jet,

been waited upon hand and foot, eaten food she'd never been able to afford, stayed in penthouse suites at the Gondola Hotels, and any minute now Dante would come and collect her for the helicopter flight to Capri. A different life, she thought. A totally different life which still didn't feel quite real to her.

This image in the mirror was Dante's puppet, moving and acting to his will. Even how it was dressed…

'Wear the Sass and Bide outfit,' he'd instructed. 'This first lunch at the villa will be informal, and the design is something fresh and individual. Lucia would not have seen it anywhere. She's not into Australian fashionistas.'

Lucia…Bella's other cousin.

Every time Dante mentioned her it was with a cynical twist. He didn't like her. Jenny had the strong impression he wanted his Isabella creation to outshine Marco's real grand-daughter. Which felt terribly wrong to her, but maybe there was some good reason behind his antipathy towards his cousin. It was not her role to make judgements on the Rossini family. She had to follow Dante's edicts or… A convulsive shudder ran through her at the thought of imprisonment in a women's jail.

She couldn't face it. The rigid discipline of the orphanage still haunted her in nightmares. Being subjected to that kind of uncaring authority again—the unrelenting system of punishment for any infringement of the rules, fighting to survive with some sense of self intact—anything was better than suffering through another soul-destroying environment.

Somehow for the next two months she had to think herself into Bella's skin, be as true as she could to what her friend had told her about her life. If her presence helped Marco Rossini to die peacefully, maybe the deception wasn't such a bad thing. Whatever happened, this was Dante's choice, Dante's family, so he had to deal with the outcome. Though she was irrevocably tied to it.

No way out, she thought, hating the sense of being trapped, frightened of failing, frightened even more of never regaining her freedom. Two months…two months of a life she knew too little about. Would this incredible makeover Dante had orchestrated really help to blind the Rossini family to seeing she was not one of them?

The Sass and Bide outfit was startling, fascinating in its creative use of fabrics. The patchwork on the blue denim vest was quite wild with bits of lace, decorative buttons, braiding and embroidering. The short-sleeved white T-shirt underneath ended in jagged handkerchief points, just lapping over the matching blue denim hipster jeans which also had embroidery running down the legs, and buttons detailing the short side splits at her ankles.

She wore embroidered rope sandals on her feet, decorated with tiny lacy shells, and a matching rope handbag was slung over her shoulder. But that was where the trendy casual image ended. Dante apparently scorned costume jewellery. Sapphires went with blue denim; sapphire and diamond drop earrings and a gold chain watch with a sapphire face and diamonds marking the hours. In short, she was wearing a fortune, and the woman in the mirror could have stepped out of a magazine featuring incredibly wealthy celebrities.

'Ready?'

Her heart jerked. He even had a string on that, Jenny thought as she swung around to face the all-powerful puppeteer. She'd left the bedroom door open for his manservant to collect her luggage which was all packed and ready to go. The man moved in behind Dante to do precisely that while his master—her master—strolled towards her, his gaze taking in her appearance from head to toe, making every nerve in her body twang with the need to be approved.

She took a deep breath, stiffened her spine and answered, 'As ready as I'll ever be.'

He smiled, apparently satisfied with how she looked, his dark eyes glittering with a sexy appreciation of the woman he'd fashioned to suit what he wanted. 'You look beautiful, Isabella,' he purred at her, and her whole body seemed to vibrate with self-awareness.

She'd never bothered much about her appearance. Clean and tidy was all she'd cared about, buying most of her clothes in charity shops, shying away from spending money on non-essentials because she might need it for living. Being dressed like this, being looked at as Dante was looking at her, evoked feelings she'd never felt before and she wasn't comfortable with them.

'I guess fine feathers make fine birds,' she muttered mockingly, thinking he always looked superb. He probably never glanced at a price-tag to see how much anything cost. He hadn't while shopping with her. No doubt the blue jeans and white sports shirt he wore carried designer labels. They certainly showed off his top-of-the-line physique—mega-male, oozing classy sex appeal.

'Don't duck your head,' he instructed, lifting a hand
to her chin, tilting it up, forcing her gaze to meet his.
'Hold it high. You're proud to be Isabella Rossini.
You've led an independent life and you won't kowtow
to anyone. You're here because your grandfather invited
you and that gives you every right to be treated as a
respected member of the family, not Cinderella.
Understand?'

It was difficult to find breath enough to speak when
he was this suffocatingly close. 'Yes,' she choked out.

His thumb stroked her cheek. The hard ruthless
gleam in his eyes softened to a wry appeal. 'I may not
be allowed to stay at your side. If Nonno wants you to
himself…be kind to him, Isabella. Put him at ease with
you. I want him to be happy that you've come.'

Panic undermined the seductively soothing intent of
his caress. Being left alone with Marco Rossini was a
terrifying prospect. If Dante wasn't there to pull the
strings…if she made a mistake…if she unwittingly
revealed a different person to the one she had to portray…

Dante was frowning at her.

'I'll do my best,' she promised in a rush.

'There's nothing to fear,' he assured her, still
frowning, his dark eyes stabbing his own indomitable
confidence into hers. 'I've paved the way for this
meeting. Nonno will not be testing you about your
identity. He's an old man, facing a painful death,
wanting the pleasure of making your acquaintance. All
you have to do is respond to him as warmly as you can.'

He made it sound easy. Maybe it was, though the deception still weighed on her mind. She scooped in a

deep breath, trying to calm her jangling nerves, and
lifted her chin away from his touch, needing to feel
some independence. He had taken over her life to such
an extent, it was difficult to be confident of standing
alone, without his all-pervasive support.

'I'll do my best,' she repeated, and meant it, not
wanting to be a source of distress to a dying man.

'It's in your best interests to do so,' he reminded her.

'Yours, too,' she said with a flash of resentment at the
ruthless power he had wielded.

He smiled, amused by her counter-thrust at him.
'Yes. We're in this together, aren't we? You could say
it forms an intimate bond.'

The hand he had dropped from her chin took possession of one of hers, fingers interlacing, gripping hard, en-
forcing a physical bond that burned like a branding iron,
linking her inexorably to him. Jenny's heart fluttered
wildly as the heat from his hand spread through her entire
body, igniting a mad desire for an intimate relationship
with Dante Rossini that was not based on deception.

'Time to go,' he said.

And Jenny went with him, once more a slave to his
command, tugged along by his hand while her mind,
which he couldn't completely dominate, was in a
helpless whirl over the shocking realisation of finding
herself actually *wanting* him to want her as a woman.

This situation was playing some weird sexual havoc
on her. She'd been almost constantly in his company for
a week, compelled into his world, and she supposed it
was natural enough to have her normal, sensible self
seduced by how beautiful and powerful and masterful

he was—the kind of man that featured in foolish, romantic dreams, turning a Cinderella into a princess.

But this prince was not being driven by any desire for her.

She *knew* that.

He was determined on making his plan work, nothing more, nothing less.

It had to be these extraordinary circumstances causing her to be affected like this. They were thrown together by a conspiracy that probably bred a sense of closeness—a very temporary sense, she sternly reminded herself. When Dante no longer had any need for her co-operation, he'd cast her off as quickly and as ruthlessly as he'd picked her up.

To allow any attachment to him to develop was sheer stupidity. She had to keep remembering that Jenny Kent was not and would never be a person of serious interest to Dante Rossini. All he wanted of her was a brief impersonation of his cousin. If she played that role well enough, she'd be free to go at the end of it. That was what she had to aim for. Feeling swamped by this man's magnetic attraction could only create a problem for her and she had problems enough.

So don't go there.

Ever.

Dante was sharply aware of steel sliding into Jenny Kent's backbone as he walked her down to the car that would take them to the heliport. She held her head high, straightened her shoulders and adopted an aloof air, ignoring the fact that he was still holding her hand. He briefly wondered if the idea of having some blackmail power over him was inspiring the change. Or was she simply taking courage from his assurances?

For the most part, she'd given him passive obedience since he'd forced her to take on the role of Isabella. The only rebellion she'd staged was her refusal to talk about her own life, flatly telling him he didn't need to know. He wanted her to be Isabella and that was his only claim on her.

Oddly enough, it wasn't easy to shrug off his curiosity about Jenny Kent, probably because most of the women he met were only too eager to tell him about themselves, courting his interest, wanting him to know them. Of course, none of them had been an unwilling captive in his company, but he was willing to bet that a week of being pampered with luxury, beautified, outfitted with 'fine feathers' would normally thaw any resistance they might have to giving him whatever he wanted.

Not his manufactured cousin.

She didn't even speak unless spoken to. She soaked up what he told her about the Rossini family and offered nothing about herself. He wished there'd been time to have Jenny Kent investigated. He was taking a risk in trusting her to fulfil the role he'd insisted upon, trusting her fear of the alternative. His gut instinct told him she would deliver, which was all he should care about, yet it was definitely tantalising that she held herself so rigidly apart from any personal connection to him.

It gave him a perverse kind of pleasure to take possession of her hand. The urge to break her passivity kept niggling at him. But she didn't fight the contact, didn't respond to it in any way, just waited until he released it when she was stepping into the car, then sat with both her hands linked on her lap—a pointed picture of self-containment.

She did not so much as glance his way on the drive to the heliport, staring out the side window, apparently immersed in the sights and sounds of the streets they travelled. Dante felt himself challenged by her silence, by her stubborn determination to ignore him.

'What do you think of Rome?' he asked.

'It doesn't matter what I think,' she said dismissively, still not turning her head towards him.

'Nonno will ask. You might as well practice a reply.'

'Then I'd sound rehearsed. Better that I don't.'

'I've been rehearsing you all week. Why stop now?'

'Because time's up. I'm about to go on stage and stuffing any more into my head at this point will only make me more anxious about my performance.'

It was a fair argument so he let his frustration with her slide. Whoever Jenny Kent was, she was far from stupid. Not only did she have street smarts, but also quite an impressive natural intelligence, making his task of coaching her into meeting any expectation of Isabella a relatively easy one. Her life experience was obviously a far cry from his, yet he was confident she could now fit in to the family without feeling too much like a fish out of water.

In fact, she wouldn't just fit in, she'd shine. He'd been right about how she could look. Nonno was going to be proud to own her as his grand-daughter. She *was* beautiful. Quite enticingly beautiful. But he

couldn't afford to think of her like that. Nonno might
see it in his eyes. Just one slip—revealing that she
stirred a devilish desire in him—and the deception
might unravel.

They arrived at the heliport. As Dante escorted his
newly found cousin across the tarmac he watched his
pilot's reaction to her. Pierro was standing by the opened
door of the helicopter, waiting to greet them and help
them to their seats. He'd seen Dante with many beautiful women in tow. 'Isabella' lit up his eyes with a look
that said 'Wow! Knockout!' in no uncertain terms.

Pierro couldn't do enough for her, fussing over
getting her comfortably settled in the helicopter. It won
him a smile and sweetly appreciative words, neither of
which had come Dante's way all week. It was absurd to
feel a twinge of jealousy, but damn it! He'd done a hell
of a lot for her and she was barely civil to him.

You've done it *to* her, not *for* her, he reminded himself,
but he was still piqued that with him she wrapped herself
in a cool dignity he couldn't penetrate. But he would. It
was only a matter of time, and he'd make sure he had
plenty of that with her while she was on Capri.

They landed at the villa just before noon.

Lucia, of course, was hot to meet her Australian
cousin and size her up, actually coming down to the
helipad instead of waiting in the shade of the colonnaded walkway. Dante felt the rush of adrenaline that
always fired him up for critical meetings.

Game on! he thought, and hoped 'Isabella' was up
to it.

* * *

'Your cousin, Lucia,' Dante murmured as he took Jenny's arm, holding her steady for the high step down from the helicopter.

Jenny had already mentally identified her. Due to the shopping experience with Dante in Paris, she instantly recognised French chic. Lucia Rossini personified it: short black hair artfully cut in an asymmetrical bob; a gorgeous scarlet-and-white dress that skimmed her slim, petite figure; elegant white sandals with intricate straps around her ankles. She also carried herself with the same arrogant confidence that Jenny now associated with great wealth.

Without Dante's intervention in dolling her up, she would have felt like dirt beneath the other woman's feet. The style he'd chosen for her was very different, but it had more than enough unique class to make Lucia look quite miffed as she eyed her newly arrived cousin. It made her wary as Dante moved her forward for introductions.

'Lucia, how sweet of you to welcome Isabella so eagerly!' he drawled, his lightly mocking tone putting Jenny even more on guard.

'Well, naturally I'm curious about a cousin I've never known, Dante,' she tossed back at him, a flash of venom in her dark eyes.

Certainly no love lost between these two, Jenny thought.

'*You've* had her to yourself for a whole week. Now it's my turn,' Lucia said, re-arranging her expression into a smile which didn't quite reach her eyes. 'Welcome to Capri, Isabella. I aim to make you feel at home here very quickly.'

She stepped forward, put her hands on Jenny's shoulders and air-kissed both cheeks. Jenny instinctively reared back, not used to people invading her personal space and not liking the over-familiarity, particularly since she felt no warmth coming from this cousin.

'Thank you,' she muttered. 'Very kind.'

'Isabella is Australian, Lucia,' Dante dryly reminded her. 'She's not accustomed to the Italian style of greeting. A hand-shake is more their style.'

'Oh! How stand-offish!' Lucia shrugged. 'I thought Australians were known for their open friendliness.'

Jenny flushed at the implied criticism. 'I'm sorry. I guess I'm feeling a bit strange at the moment. All this is very new to me.'

'Well, you'll have to learn to be Italian, too, if you want to fit into this family.'

The sheer arrogance of that statement stung Jenny's deep resentment at being forced into this situation. 'Maybe I won't want to fit in.' The words were out in a flash and she didn't regret them. In fact, it gave her a fine satisfaction to see Lucia's eyebrows shoot up in *unplanned* astonishment, as though being in the Rossini family was the most desirable thing in the world. It wasn't, as far as Jenny was concerned. 'I didn't ask to come here,' she added for good measure.

Lucia turned an arch look to Dante, her eyes glinting with malicious glee. 'This must be a first for you,' she drawled, 'running into resistance from a woman, not having her falling on her knees to please you. Nonno should have sent me to collect Isabella. I would have done a better job of it.'

'I doubt your brand of sly sniping would have achieved anything,' he replied sardonically. 'But then you wouldn't have wanted to, would you, Lucia? Isabella is too much a wild card for your liking, coming in at the death, so to speak.'

'Oh!' She feigned hurt shock. 'That's such a mean thing to say! Don't take any notice of him, Isabella.' A cajoling smile was directed at her. 'That's just a payback for being teased about his famous charm. I'm delighted that you're here for Nonno.' She waved an open invitation. 'Now do let's go up to the villa. It's so hot out here.'

Jenny glanced back at the helicopter, wishing she had never set foot in this place.

'Pierro will bring in our luggage,' Dante quickly assured her, taking her hand again, pressing it hard to remind her there was no escape, not until he allowed it, and that would be no time soon.

She hated him in that moment, hated having no choice, hated being thrust into such foreign territory, hostile territory if Lucia's attitude was anything to go by.

Capri was supposed to be a romantic place, a paradise for lovers. As they moved from the open heat to the shade of a colonnaded walkway, Jenny couldn't help thinking there was at least one serpent in this Eden.

How many more would she have to meet?

She was imprisoned on this island as surely as she would have been in a women's jail, having to work out how to deal with the other inmates and survive. The luxury of it was supposed to sweeten her term here, but wasn't there a saying—wealth is the root of all evil?

She yearned for her own simple life.

And hated Dante for forcing her into his.

CHAPTER SIX

THE colonnaded walkway was beautiful, shaded by pine trees and masses of brilliant bougainvillea. Jenny could imagine a Roman emperor with a string of courtiers strolling along it, sandals slapping on the flagstones. She wondered if Marco Rossini presided over his family like an emperor, parcelling out power to those who pleased him. Like Dante.

'I've had the blue suite in the guest wing made ready for you,' Lucia cooed at her. 'I'm sure you'll enjoy staying there. It has a lovely view of…'

'I don't think so,' Dante cut in with an air of haughty command. 'Isabella will feel much more comfortable in the suite adjoining mine. Makes it easier for her to come to me if she has a problem. I did promise her my protection on this journey.'

It was the first Jenny had heard of his promised protection, but she didn't contradict him, thinking she might need it if Lucia was planning to sink her snaky fangs into her. Putting her in the guest wing, away from the puppeteer's support, was probably a ploy to make her more accessible to hostile action, as well as making her feel like an outsider, which she was, but she wasn't supposed to be.

'But Isabella is safely here,' Lucia argued. 'What possible problem could she have now?'

'Do as I say, Lucia.' No moving him on that point.

'It can't be done,' she said with a much put-upon sigh and a smug look at Dante. 'Anya Michaelson is already in the suite adjoining yours. Which is where *you* wanted her on previous visits.'

Dante's grip on Jenny's hand tightened, revealing a rise in tension. She glanced at his face. Displeasure was written all over it. 'Anya came here uninvited?' he bit out in cold anger.

If Anya was his current girlfriend, she'd just made a bad move, Jenny thought. Dante Rossini liked to order things his way, and not even the lure of sexual pleasure right next door changed that aspect of his character.

'No, no. I invited her,' Lucia replied, still smug about her initiative. 'I flew over to Rome to do some shopping and ran into her on the Spanish Steps. She was most upset about your leaving so abruptly, without a word to her, so I explained about Nonno sending you off to fetch Isabella, and then I thought you'd like some relaxation with Anya after such an arduous trip....'

'In short, you interfered with what was none of your business.'

His tone would have made most people shrivel, but Lucia obviously thrived on his anger, positively enjoying herself.

'You should be more caring of your women,

Dante,' she trilled back at him. 'I was simply saving you from a nasty scene with Anya when you finally caught up with her again. I'm sure she'll now be ever so sweet to you, all primed to smooth away your travel fatigue.'

Jenny felt a strong distaste for this conversation. She looked at the pots of flowers spaced between the columns, pretending total disinterest in Dante's sex life, trying to keep herself emotionally separated from affairs that had nothing to do with her. Absolutely nothing.

Of course he would have a woman. What man like Dante Rossini wouldn't? And no doubt Anya was beautiful and very beddable. Despite his annoyance at Lucia's interference, Jenny expected him to choose the ready pleasures of a lover, especially since the arrangement was already in place. The potted flowers were lovely; geraniums, petunias, impatiens…

'Bad judgement, Lucia,' he said contemptuously. 'Family takes priority at a time like this. You can deal with moving Anya out while I'm introducing Isabella to Nonno.'

A huge tide of relief swept through Jenny. His connection with her remained firm. *She* was more important to him than anything else. No, the *deception* was, she quickly corrected herself. He wasn't about to abandon her during this testing time, not when his grandfather's peace of mind was at stake. That came first. She kept her gaze trained on the flowers, but she heard real shock in Lucia's response.

'Don't be so unreasonable!' she snapped. 'It's not going to hurt Isabella…'

'This is not open to argument, Lucia. You chose to invite Anya. She's your responsibility. Do whatever you like with her, but Isabella is to occupy the suite next to mine. Make no mistake about that,' he said with steely authority.

'Anya won't like it!'

'Anya should have waited for me to contact her. *If* I wanted to.'

'How can you be so cruel! She loves you.'

'Since when have you become an authority on love?' he mocked.

'The two of you have been an item all this year.'

'Don't play games with me, Lucia. You'll lose. Every time.'

His tone had moved to studied boredom. Jenny had no doubt that for him the issue was closed. She could feel Lucia seething with frustration, but had no sympathy for her. To her mind, people who set out to make mischief should be caught in their own net and made to pay.

'One day your insufferable ego will be your undoing, Dante,' Lucia warned venomously.

A little shiver of apprehension ran down Jenny's spine. It was probably Dante's ego that refused to accept failure, forcing her into this false identity. If Lucia somehow uncovered the deception…

'Don't hold your breath waiting for that day, Lucia,' he drawled, emitting a confidence that eased Jenny's spurt of fear, though didn't completely eliminate it. Two months was a long time to be under the gun from *this* 'cousin.'

'Anyway, I can't deal with Anya now. Nonno is waiting for us on the terrace.'

'He's not waiting for you,' Dante coldly corrected her.

'I won't be shut out of Nonno's first meeting with Isabella. He expects us to be all together.'

'I'll tell him you've already met Isabella. I doubt you'll be missed. Nonno will want to focus all his attention on the grand-daughter he doesn't know yet.'

'It's a point of hospitality, Dante,' she grated out angrily.

'If you insist on accompanying us, I'll let him know just how inhospitable you've been, putting *your* guest ahead of the very special family member Nonno wants to feel welcomed here.'

'There's nothing wrong with the Blue Suite! Isabella, I promise you it's beautiful.'

Jenny didn't want to be dragged into the argument, but the direct appeal to her couldn't be ignored. The colonnaded walkway had led into a fantastic atrium where they had come to a halt while the conflict was settled. It had a central water feature—a pool covered with gorgeous water-lilies—and she reluctantly lifted her gaze from these to look at Lucia.

Her younger 'cousin's' dark eyes burned with the demand that she fall in with her plan, woman to woman against the man who divided them. For a moment Jenny was almost tempted, just to rattle Dante's overbearing power, but the situation was too tricky for her to negotiate alone.

'I'm sorry you're being put to so much trouble on my account, Lucia,' she said as calmly as she could, trying to maintain a composure that hid a growing mountain of nervous tension. 'It *is* difficult, being a stranger to all this.' She gestured to the exotic surroundings. 'Dante has shepherded me around all week. Having him close by will make it easier for me.'

The hand holding hers squeezed approval, making her feel too connected to him again, too aware of him in a way that would not lead to anything good for her. He was her captor, her jailor, and while he probably meant to give her a sense of safety, he kept shaking her up with an attraction she knew was treacherous. Having him in the suite next to hers was not going to make life here easier for her, yet being separated from him was too scary to contemplate.

'A fine start, Lucia,' Dante mocked. 'You've had Isabella apologising twice to you in the past ten minutes, making her feel uncomfortable.'

'I didn't mean to,' she flared at him, furious at being out-manoeuvred.

'Then you can demonstrate a kinder nature by making instant amends.' He waved her towards one of the wide hallways which ran off from the atrium. 'I'll make your excuses to Nonno.'

Her jaw clenched. Every atom of her being exuded hatred of defeat, the knowledge that she was forced to accept it. *This time around.* Dante had her cornered with no way out. He was very good at that, Jenny thought with black irony.

Lucia managed to stretch her mouth into a smile aimed at her. 'I truly had no intention of making you feel uncomfortable, Isabella. Please forgive my thoughtlessness.'

'I don't mean to be difficult, either,' she replied with an answering smile. 'I guess I haven't yet recovered from the shock of being presented with a family I knew nothing about. I can understand it's a shock to you, as well.'

Lucia seized the excuse. 'Yes. Hard to know what to do for the best. I'll go and fix everything up for you and join you on the terrace as soon as I can.' With a last challenging glare at Dante, she turned on her heel and walked briskly to the hallway he'd indicated.

'Well done,' Dante murmured, his warm breath wafting over Jenny's ear, making her flinch away from the tingling sensation.

Her head jerked up, her eyes rejecting any form of intimacy with him as they met and held his. 'Bella might very well have walked away after one day of this rotten family rivalry,' she said in a fierce whisper. 'Why don't I do that, Dante? Remove any danger of being caught out. You got me here, which is all your grandfather asked you to do. Be satisfied with…'

'No!' He cut her off, ruthless determination stamping on her rebellion. 'I've paid for the performance. You give it.'

'One day is enough,' she argued on a wave of panic.

'It won't be for Nonno.' He released her hand and took hold of her upper arms, forcing her to face him. His dark eyes blazed with relentless purpose. 'While ever he lives, you stay here, giving him whatever he wants of you.'

She instinctively fought against the overwhelming pressure of his demands, frantically searching for some way out. 'What if he doesn't like me?'

'He will.'

'Why should he? He doesn't know me.'

'Neither do I but I like you, Isabella.' The tension on his strong face broke into a slow, sensual smile. 'I'm beginning to like you very much.'

Her heart skittered in wild alarm as she felt her resistance melting. Her mind screamed that he had a woman and she must not allow his famous 'charm' to get to her. 'I haven't given you any reason to,' she snapped.

He laughed, effectively zooming up his attraction quotient which was already far too discomforting for Jenny. Her head whirled with the need to block it out, stay indifferent to him.

'All this time we've spent together, not once have you whined or wailed or wept about your fate.'

'There was no point in kicking and screaming over what I can't change.'

'Exactly. Which is a surprisingly intelligent response from a woman.'

'Then you can't know many intelligent women.'

'Or you're not practised in using feminine wiles to win what you want.'

He was right. She'd never learnt to use feminine wiles, never been in the kind of environment where they might have been of use. In any event, if she read his character correctly, they would have been futile weapons in this situation.

'Would they have worked on you?' she asked, showing her scepticism.

'No. But that wouldn't have stopped most women from using them.'

'Waste of time and energy,' she muttered.

'True. And I appreciate your pragmatic attitude. Needs must to get the job done. You've actually given me many reasons to like you, Isabella. Not least of which was the deft way you handled Lucia.'

'As you said, you've paid for the performance. I was simply following your lead.'

'With a nice little embellishment of your own at the end.' He smiled again as he lifted a hand to touch her cheek in an admiring salute. 'I'm sure you'll handle the meeting with Nonno just as well.'

Her skin burned under the light caress. Her eyes burned with resentment over the cavalier way he touched her as he liked, always reinforcing the inescapable link between them. An increasingly dangerous link in Jenny's mind.

'Let's get on with it,' she said tersely.

'It will go better if you relax.'

'I'll relax more quickly if you get your hands off me.'

He raised his eyebrows at the too-revealing comment and Jenny cursed herself for letting it slip. He lifted his hands out in a gesture of meaning no offence, and she felt herself flushing as she rushed into answering the heart-pumping speculation in his eyes.

'You might own me in one sense, Dante Rossini, but there are some liberties you have no right to take.'

He nodded but the speculation didn't go away and she inwardly squirmed under it, knowing she had just shown a vulnerability that completely undermined any pose of indifference.

'Another first,' he murmured in dry amusement. 'No woman has ever objected to my touch before.'

'I'm your cousin,' she fiercely reminded him. 'And don't you forget it.'

'Cousins can and do show physical affection.'

'I can do without Lucia's brand of affection. And yours.'

He cocked his head musingly. 'Nonno will like your feisty sense of independence. I think you're ready to meet him now.'

'Do I have a choice?'

'No.'

'I didn't think so.' She waved a careless hand, doing her utmost to appear relaxed. 'Lead on. I'm as ready as I'll ever be.'

Out of the corner of her eye she could see him smiling as he ushered her over to a set of double glass doors which opened to a terrace overlooking the sea they had flown over only a short while ago. The old saying—'caught between the devil and the deep blue sea'—slid into her mind. It was precisely how she felt.

Focus on what Bella would be feeling, she swiftly told herself. Here she was, meeting her grandfather for the first time, a man who'd wanted nothing to do with her family until now. Any sense of affection was impossible. Curiosity, yes. Perhaps resentment, too, at being called in so late in the day, too late for her own father who'd died in exile, never knowing any forgiveness for his grave teenage sin.

She mentally blocked out Dante, training her gaze on the old man being helped up from a sun-lounge by a woman caregiver. He still had a full head of thick wavy hair, shockingly snow-white, framing a face that seemed all bones, the flesh obviously wasted by the cancer that was eating him from the inside. His skin was tanned from lying in the sun, possibly in an attempt to look healthier than he was. He wore a loose white tunic over baggy white trousers. Neither hid the frailty of a body which had probably once been as big and strong as Dante's.

He was a dying man, maybe in considerable pain, warranting some sympathy despite the other circumstances that had brought her here. It was clearly an effort for him to stand straight and tall, determined on meeting her with dignity. Pride doesn't die, Jenny thought, and Bella might well be prickly with pride, too, the outcast who hadn't asked to be rejoined to this Rossini family and had no reason to bow to this patriarch.

Hold your head high, Dante had instructed.

She did.

And met Marco Rossini's penetrating dark gaze with determined steadiness.

I am Bella. You are my grandfather and you don't know me. This is not just a test for me. It's a test for you, too.

CHAPTER SEVEN

THEY stood, face-to-face, studying each other in a silence that stretched Jenny's nerves so far she could feel them twanging with tension. Marco Rossini was taking in every feature of her face as though trying to match them against some picture in his mind, and fear squeezed her heart as she read disappointment in them. Inevitable, she knew, because she had no Rossini genes, though maybe his disappointment was good for her. He mightn't want to keep her here, since she didn't look like the son he had banished.

His mouth finally broke into a wry little smile. 'Thank you for coming,' he said, his voice furred with emotion.

'I'm sorry it was too late for…for my father.' She hated speaking the deception that had to be carried through, but the sentiment was right if she'd been Bella.

'So am I, my dear. So am I,' he repeated sadly.

And her heart went out to him. It *was* sad, sadder than he knew with his grand-daughter gone, too. Tears welled into her eyes, remembering Bella's dreadful death, and Marco Rossini reached out and took one of her hands in both of his, patting it comfortingly.

'Your loss is even more grievous with both parents gone,' he said in gentle sympathy. 'I hope I can make up in some way for not being there for you.'

The tears overflowed, spilling down her cheeks. It was awful, pretending to be someone she wasn't. This should be happening to Bella, getting a grandfather who would care for her. She shook her head, bit her lip, swallowed hard, desperate to regain some control. 'I'm sorry,' she choked out. 'I didn't mean to…'

'It's okay, Isabella,' Dante soothed, quickly stepping over to a small table beside the sun-lounge, pulling some tissues out of a box and thrusting them into her hand. 'I'm sure Nonno understands this meeting isn't easy for you.'

'Come and sit down, my dear,' the old man invited, drawing her over to a bigger table shaded by a large umbrella. 'Pour her a drink, Dante.'

The table was round, the chairs well-cushioned. Marco dismissed his caregiver as Dante poured the three of them drinks from a jug of fruit-juice, adding ice from a more expensive version of an esky. The men sat on either side of her and Jenny did her best to regain some composure, mopping her cheeks, hoping the eye-makeup she'd been taught to apply wasn't completely messed up, taking several deep breaths to ease the tightness in her chest.

'Where is Lucia?' Marco asked his grandson, diverting attention from her while she recovered from her distress.

'Re-arranging accommodation for Isabella. She had designated the furthermost suite in the guest wing for her, which I didn't consider appropriate.'

'Ah! So typical!' the old man remarked ruefully. 'I should have directed the choice.'

'Lucia is used to being your only grand-daughter, Nonno.' He nodded towards Jenny, a silent warning that his cousin could be spiteful towards her.

'I'll take that into account. But for the most part, you'll have to be my watchdog, my boy.' It was a reluctant admission of weakness.

'I will,' Dante assured him.

'Put all business on hold. I want you here now. It won't be for long.'

'I've already done that, Nonno. I want to spend this time with you.'

The old man heaved a weary sigh. 'I don't have much energy these days. Thank you for bringing Isabella to me, Dante. She should not have been left alone.'

'I'll see that she is never without family support again.'

Jenny couldn't let that pass. 'I'm all right. I don't need anything from you,' she declared, shooting a frown at both Dante and Marco. 'I didn't come to get your family support. I can look after myself.'

The old man eyed her quizzically. 'Why did you come, Isabella?'

'Because...' *He forced me to,* but she couldn't say that. 'Because I wanted to know where my father had come from. Dante told me why you banished him, but you know, it must have been terrible for him, too, knowing he caused his mother's death. I think now he punished himself, taking on the hardships of living and working in the Outback. It's a very isolated life. But he was a good man, a good husband, a good father. You could have been proud of what he made of himself.'

She barely knew where the words came from—

stories Bella had told about her growing-up years on the cattle station in far west Queensland, her own instinctive spin on the tragedy that had led to Antonio Rossini's exile, a need to resolve the bad feelings that Dante wanted resolved because that would free her in the end.

Her earnest outburst seemed to drive Marco back inside himself. He closed his eyes. His face sagged. His skin took on a greyish tinge.

Dante leaned forward, anxiously touching his arm. 'Nonno, Isabella didn't mean to be accusing.'

The heavy lids slowly lifted. 'My boy, I've been saying the very same things to myself, ever since I read the investigator's report.' He turned deeply regretful eyes to Jenny. 'What was done was done in anger and grief. I loved my wife very much. And I believe what you tell me. Antonio loved his mother very much. He gave you her name.'

Dante hadn't mentioned that to her. It made more poignant sense of Marco's disappointment. 'You wanted to see her in me.'

'Yes. Antonio looked very like her. I thought...' He made an apologetic grimace.

'It's Isabella on my birth certificate but I've always been called Bella,' Jenny said defensively, shying from being linked to the woman whom Marco had loved and lost. It made her feel even more of a fraud.

'Bella...' he repeated softly. 'A fitting name. You're a beautiful young woman. Your mother must have been beautiful, too.'

Jenny flushed at the compliment, knowing it wasn't really deserved since her 'beauty' had been engineered by Dante. 'I thought so,' she answered stiffly, judging it to be the safest reply.

'Do you have photographs of your parents you can show me?'

Jenny shook her head, answering with Bella's own words explaining why she had none of the usual me-mentoes of her family. 'The old homestead on the station burnt down when I was eighteen and in my last year at boarding school. My parents were away at the cattle sales. Nothing was saved.'

'Another loss for you,' Marco murmured sympatheti-cally.

'And you.' Her eyes flashed understanding of his desire to see a pictorial record of the son who had lived out his life on the other side of the world.

'Yes. But I chose to bring my loss upon myself. You didn't.'

It was fair comment and she nodded her appreciation of it. She was beginning to like Marco Rossini. He didn't come over as a cruel tyrant, ruthlessly wielding his wealth and power to punish or reward, more a man in the winter of his life, regretting mistakes he could not re-write.

She picked up the drink Dante had poured for her and sipped the fruit-juice, grateful for the cool moisture sliding down her throat. It tasted of pineapple and oranges. She needed the refreshment for the next round of questions.

A glance at Dante showed him watching her with an air of curious respect, as though she'd met more than his expectation in her performance so far. Which was a huge relief, since she'd been winging it with a mish-mash of her own feelings and what she'd imagined Bella's would be.

'Since you chose to live at the Venetian Forum, I thought Antonio must have told you some of his family history,' Marco put to her. 'Yet you said you knew nothing of us.'

'He never spoke of you,' she answered, though she had no idea of whether that was true or not. The question of why Bella had bought an apartment at the Venetian Forum had been tormenting her ever since Dante had brought it up. She had to produce a logical reason for it.

'We had an Italian name. I asked my father where it had come from. He told me it was an old Venetian name. His family had lived there but when he'd lost them he'd emigrated to Australia, and Venice was a place in the past for him. He said I should only think about being an Australian.' She lifted her chin proudly. 'Which is what I am.'

The old man nodded. 'It's a fine country. I spent some time in Sydney, purchasing suitable property for our hotel and the forum. It's a beautiful city.'

'Yes. I love it,' Jenny said strongly, wanting him to know she had no desire to leave her life for anything he could offer. Bella might have made that change but Jenny Kent couldn't.

'A big change for you from life in The Outback,' he remarked, possibly thinking if she could adapt to that, she could adapt to moving to another country.

'I had no heart for trying to run the cattle station after my parents died. There was a large mortgage on it because of the drought and…'

'Too difficult for you in every respect,' Marco murmured sympathetically.

'Yes.' She sighed over the immediate difficulty of trying to relive Bella's life. 'After everything was settled up, I wasn't sure what I wanted to do, so I went on what you might call a journey of discovery, travelling around until I found a place that appealed to me. When I came to Sydney, I found the Venetian Forum and...'

'And you remembered your father was originally from Venice,' Marco supplied helpfully.

'It felt right. Like a sense of belonging. I loved the artiness of it, the colours of the apartments, the markets around the canal. I've always loved drawing and I thought about signing up for an art course but I had to wait until the beginning of the new year to do that. I made a good friend who was also into art and asked her to share my apartment so I wasn't alone. She didn't have any family, either. We were like sisters.'

Jenny desperately hoped that covered everything. 'But then I lost her, too,' she finished off, her voice losing traction under the dampening weight of sorrow that Bella's death always evoked in her.

She closed her eyes and ducked her head, fighting another rush of tears. Bella should be here, not her. Jenny Kent had no one to care if she was dead or not. And Bella had been so kind to her, so generous in her sharing, so good to be with. She had deserved more from life, and maybe she had secretly yearned for this reunion with the Rossini family.

Jenny wept for her in her mind.... *I can't do this for you. I'm not you.* Yet to survive she had to take Bella's place for Marco Rossini. Dante would not let her go until the performance was no longer needed for his grandfather.

'You have us now, Bella,' the old man assured her quietly.

She shook her head and lifted a bleak gaze to the man she had to satisfy. 'You don't feel real to me, Mr Rossini. None of this feels real. I'm apart from it.' That was the truth.

'Give it time, my dear. I know about the accident that killed your friend. You've suffered one tragedy after another and it's taken a good part of this year for you to recover from your own injuries, delaying the career plan you'd decided upon. Let this visit to Capri be a healing time for you, in many respects. We'll get to know each other…'

Panic churned through her again at the thought of keeping up this deception every day for months. She couldn't do it, couldn't… 'But you're going to die, too,' she blurted out, wildly hoping he would understand she couldn't bear it. 'Dante wouldn't take no for an answer, so I came to see you, but…'

There was an instant hiss of indrawn breath from Dante, a tense leaning forward.

Jenny was too scared to look at him, too scared to utter another word. Her eyes frantically pleaded with his grandfather to let her off the hook.

The old man raised a commanding hand to his grandson. 'There's no need to be protective of me, Dante. Why should Bella risk growing fond of a man she knows is dying?'

'You're her grandfather,' he answered vehemently.

Jenny trembled at the sound of his displeasure.

'Who has never played any part in her life, never done anything for her,' Marco replied reasonably. With an air of sympathetic understanding, he turned to Jenny, addressing her kindly. 'My dear, I have no doubt Dante did everything in his power to steam-roll you into this visit. I'm sure he would have played upon your natural urge to see where your father came from.'

She flushed, ashamed of the lie.

'Antonio was my son for eighteen years,' he went on in a tone of sad yearning. 'He was a boy of great promise. One thing I can do is fill in those years for you, if you'll allow me.'

Her heart sank. Bella would have wanted that. Any daughter who'd loved her father would. She could feel Dante fiercely willing her to agree, hanging the threat of prison over her head if she didn't. There was no way out.

'I have very little time left, Bella,' Marco added softly. 'Will you help me to spend it well, correcting a wrong that weighs heavily on my heart? Think of me, if you will, as a treasure chest of memories you can open now, but will be forever closed once I'm gone.'

It was too persuasive an appeal to deny. 'All right. I'll try it,' she conceded, surrendering to the inevitable once again. 'I'm sorry. I shouldn't have thrown your…your failing health in your face. It just seems that…'

'Death keeps cutting through your life?'

She nodded, feeling too uncomfortable to say anything more.

'It's different with me, Bella. My journey is simply drawing to a close. Only this business with you remains undone.' He smiled encouragement at her. 'Let's finish it together.'

She managed a wobbly smile back. 'I hope it will be good for you, Mr Rossini.'

'Good for you, too, my dear.'

Not in a million years, Jenny thought darkly.

She threw a defiant look at Dante, not really caring about his reaction to her performance since Marco was satisfied with the end result. Besides, she was too drained of feeling by this traumatic meeting to worry about him at this point.

'It will be all right, Isabella. I promise you,' he said quickly, determined on soothing her fears.

He'd stand between her and any trouble. Jenny had no doubt about that. But he couldn't promise it would be all right for her. It never could be. The deception was tearing her apart. The bitter irony was she had thought surviving a term in a women's prison would be harder.

Bad choice.

Bad, bad choice.

Jenny Kent was more in danger of losing herself here than anywhere else.

CHAPTER EIGHT

'You like living dangerously?'

The angry threat in Dante's voice was like a hammer beating on Jenny's head, which was already aching from the stress of the meeting on the terrace. Lucia had joined them there. Lucia had shown her to this suite so her new cousin could freshen up before lunch. Dante, of course, had tagged along to ensure everything was 'all right,' and once they had entered the appointed room, he'd very purposefully ushered Lucia out, closing the door firmly behind her, intent on securing a private tête-à-tête with the puppet who'd done her own little dance with his grandfather.

Jenny gritted her teeth and turned to face him, determined on standing the ground she had just established with Marco Rossini—an independent person who'd make her own choices. Trapped here she might be, but she wasn't going to bend to Dante's will anymore. She met his blazing gaze with stubborn defiance.

'I adapted to circumstances. Isn't that what you wanted of me?'

'You saw a chance to extract yourself from the situation and you took it,' he fired at her.

'I'm not what he wanted,' she retorted fiercely. 'I couldn't be, could I? You should have foreseen that, Dante. You disappointed him.'

'No. I have never disappointed my grandfather,' he declared with vehement conviction. 'One of his wishes didn't come true. You don't look like Antonio. That was unavoidable, but you can and will supply everything else he needs from you.'

'I said I'd try.'

He crossed the room to where she stood at the foot of the bed, towering over her with intimidating power. 'You were *trying* to twist your way out of this. Don't *try* it again or I'll make you pay for it.' His eyes bored into hers. 'Believe me, I'll make you pay for it.'

She believed him.

He was as much tied to this deception as she was, and failure was unacceptable.

Dante Rossini didn't fail.

The force of the man in such close proximity made her quake inside. It was like being blasted by an electric energy that jangled her nerves, kicked her heart into a faster beat, tore at her muscles, leaving them quivering. She stared back at him, refusing to let him see any weakness in her, silently fighting her lonely fight to survive him as well as everything else.

'Nothing more to say?' he mocked.

She swallowed convulsively, trying to get some control over her throat muscles. Her mouth was as dry as the Sahara Desert, making it impossible to speak, so she simply shook her head. He didn't want to hear anything she might say, anyway.

The threatening tension on his face slowly relaxed. The laser-like heat in his eyes simmered down. His mouth actually quirked into an ironic little smile.

'On the whole, you did quite well out there. Not the warm response I told you to give, but the emotional tears were good. Nonno was moved by them. He liked your independent stance, too.'

The approval, coming straight on the heels of his attack, turned Jenny's mind to mush.

'Just don't hold that line too hard,' he went on. 'You've made your point. You're not about to suck up to a grandfather who hasn't been a grandfather to you. That's okay. It's an attitude he respects, but soften it with kindness. And courtesy.'

She nodded.

He huffed an exasperated sigh. His eyes snapped with annoyance. 'We're back to the silent treatment, are we?'

It goaded her into a challenging glare and re-activated her vocal chords. 'Less grief for me if I remain a submissive doll who doesn't buck your authority.'

'Huh!' he scoffed. 'Submissive is the last word I'd apply to you! I'm not fool enough to believe something meek and mild resides in the fortress you've built around yourself. You can fly the white flag as much as you like but I know…'

He stepped closer, raising her tension level to screaming point. His hand gripped her chin, fingers pressing into the curve of her cheek, and his eyes were glittering with heat again, not angry heat, not threatening heat, more a very male sexual heat wanting supremacy over a woman. He was touching her, touching her aggressively, and she was paralysed with panic.

'I know rebellion is seething behind it,' he said with arrogant certainty. 'And maybe the best way to quell it is to storm your defences and seduce you into wanting to stick with me.'

His fingers slid into her hair. His other arm scooped her body hard against his. She had no time to react with any physical or vocal protest. His mouth covered hers, and the shock of his kiss, of being enveloped by the heat and strength of his powerful body, completely robbed her of any resistance. He invaded her mind, possessed it with a host of sensations.

She'd never been kissed like this before, never been held by a man like him, never experienced such an explosion of excitement. His mouth ravished hers, his tongue sweeping over her palate, making it tingle with intense pleasure, driving her own tongue into a duelling response. He had read her character rightly. Submission was not in her nature. Every primitive instinct she had was suddenly triggered, dictating a need to fight back, to do to him what he was doing to her.

The self-discipline that had ruled her life for so long broke into an angry passion. He held her body by force. She flung her arms around his head, hands burrowing fiercely into his thick hair, holding him just as forcefully. Her lower body ground against his. Her breasts thrashed his chest. No control. Every action was driven by a wild urge to assert herself, not surrender to his dominance, make him feel what he was making her feel.

The arm around her back tightened, his hand pressing down, grasping the fleshy curve of her bottom, lifting her into intimate contact with the erection she had aroused. Part of her mind registered danger. The rest of it revelled in her power to seduce him out of his formidable control.

He'd taken her out of the life she knew. She wanted him to pay for that, screw up his puppet plan, storm him with crashing waves of feeling, drag the devil into the deep blue sea he'd plunged her into. Awash with incoherent emotion, she was barely aware of him moving, carrying her with him. His mouth was locked on hers, kissing with ravaging intensity. Only when he'd tumbled her backwards onto the bed, did it break away.

Her eyes snapped open. He was kneeling over her, breathing hard, a dark confusion on his face. Words flew off her tongue in a silky taunt. 'Not what you wanted, Dante?'

His eyes blazed with the desire to crush her spirit, grind it so far down she'd be enslaved to his will. *Never,* she silently shot at him, exhilarated by the contest between them.

A knock on the door startled them out of the intense connection with each other. Dante cursed under his breath, backed off the bed, hauled her to her feet. 'This will keep,' he muttered savagely, releasing her to head for the door, putting respectable distance between them.

Jenny's legs were too tremulous to walk anywhere. She sucked in air to get a blast of oxygen through her scattered brain and sat back down on the bed, needing recovery time and wanting to hide any crumpling of the duvet where she had lain on it. Her heart was pumping with horror at what she had almost done with Dante Rossini, horror at her own mad elation over it.

They were supposed to be cousins. She bit down on a bubble of hysterical laughter. If this deception fell apart it would be his fault. He'd started it. He'd forced it. And be damned if she'd take the blame for it!

Another knock on the door.

He opened it. 'Anya?' he said in a tone so cold, it automatically denied there'd been any boiling heat in this room.

Anya...the woman he usually housed in this suite for his sexual convenience...here to smooth away his travel fatigue.

The hysterical laughter bubbled up again and Jenny clamped down on it, pride insisting on an appearance of absolute decorum. She sat up straight, hands in her lap, her mind seething with curiosity over how Dante was going to handle *this* deception, dealing with his current girlfriend after he'd just been conducting a sexual assault on *his cousin.* Was he incredibly adept at switching himself on and off?

She was curious, too, about the type of woman who usually attracted him. No doubt someone as fabulous as him in the looks department, she thought cynically, determined not to feel in any way jealous. This was not her world and she wasn't about to forget that reality.

'Excuse me, Dante,' Anya pleaded in a honeyed voice. 'Some of my toiletries were left in the bathroom. I've come to collect them.'

She didn't give him the chance to deny her entry, sliding into the room as she spoke, obviously keen to get a look at the cousin for whom she had been evicted from this suite. Anya Michaelson was a honey all over. Men probably flocked to her like bees. She had a glorious mass of silky blonde hair. Her figure was sensational, voluptuous curves barely encased in a bright yellow mini-dress. Perfect long legs gleamed as though they'd just been rubbed with scented oil. And the face she turned to Jenny was strikingly beautiful: flawless skin, stunning blue eyes, a full-lipped mouth with a very sexy pout.

'Sorry to break in on you like this,' she directed at Jenny, the blue eyes gobbling up every detail of her appearance, sharply assessing the attraction of the woman Dante was supposedly protecting. 'I'll only be a minute.'

She was already crossing the room, heading for a door which had to lead to an ensuite bathroom.

'Say hello to Isabella, Anya.'

The whip-like command from Dante stopped her in her tracks. 'Oh!' she exclaimed apologetically. 'I didn't mean to be rude.' A row of perfect white teeth was flashed at Jenny. 'Hello, Isabella. Don't you love Capri?'

'Not particularly,' Jenny answered, bridling at the condescending tone.

'Well, you've just arrived. I'm sure it will grow on you. Excuse me while I remove my things, won't you? I expect we'll be meeting properly over lunch.' She threw an appeasing smile at Dante. 'Pardon me, *caro*. A careless oversight by one of the servants, not being thorough in checking what might have been missed.'

'Make sure you collect everything, Anya. I don't want you returning,' he said balefully.

She kissed her fingertips and tossed it at him, sashayed into the bathroom, leaving the door open behind her, not so much for an easy exit, Jenny thought, but to eavesdrop on any conversation in the bedroom.

No satisfaction for Anya on that score.

Jenny didn't even look at Dante, let alone speak to him. She rose from the bed and, finding her legs much steadier now, strolled over to the glass doors on the other side of the room to him. Outside was another colonnaded walkway, shading the area between this wing of the villa and the stone wall running along the cliff edge, beyond it the sea. She pretended to take in the view, her mind ferociously engaged on far more internal territory.

The sexuality Dante had aroused in her was still tingling through her body, making it feel vibrantly alive. Part of her wanted to pursue this experience with him, but what self-respect was there in that? The blonde bombshell in the bathroom represented his world—the beautiful people with money to burn. No doubt he'd poured out his famous charm to acquire her.

No charm for Jenny Kent. He was knowingly using his mega-strong physical attraction to get what he wanted from her. He'd probably been doing that with women all his life, given the male assets he'd been born with. Did she really want to fall victim to a cynical sexual play?

No.

It would be totally stupid of her.

Getting more deeply involved with Dante Rossini

would only muddy what was already dangerous waters. She had to keep a clear head, not get distracted from what she had to do to earn her freedom.

'Got them,' Anya trilled, as though it had been a triumphant feat of discovery.

It struck a false note in the loaded silence.

Jenny turned to acknowledge her presence but didn't get a glance from the other woman. Anya's gaze was concentrated on Dante, who had remained by the opened bedroom door, pointedly waiting for her to depart.

'Then there's nothing to stop you from speeding on your way,' he drawled, dark eyes glittering impatience.

She flounced over to him, pausing to tilt up her beautiful face, pout her sexy mouth and say, 'I did apologise for the intrusion.'

'Curiosity killed the cat, Anya.' It was a cold indictment of her behaviour.

'I just wanted...'

'You've got what you came for. Go!'

His stony face did not invite argument. She left. He closed the door. Jenny steeled herself to rebuff any continuance of the scene Anya had interrupted. Dante turned to face her, his dark gaze skating over her stiff stance, his mouth curling into a twist of irony at the defensive wall so firmly back in place.

'Why don't you follow her?' Jenny flung at him. 'I don't need you to help me settle in here, and since you're obviously feeling some frustration, I'm sure your girlfriend would welcome the chance to ease it for you.'

'Ah, but I wouldn't welcome her efforts.'

Her heart skipped at the change of tone from icy

distaste to seductive sensuality. It raced into a gallop as he started strolling towards her, his eyes mocking her attempt to reject what had happened between them.

'I don't welcome yours,' she stated vehemently. 'Your Casanova mentality doesn't appeal to me one bit.'

Her jeering contempt did not hold him back. He shrugged it off and kept on coming. 'Casanova romps are not my style. I'd decided to end my relationship with Anya before I flew to Australia for you.'

'She can't know that or she wouldn't be here.'

'Anya only listens to what she wants. Apparently my suggestion that she move on to another man made her think she'd better work harder to keep me, and she seized the opportunity Lucia held out to her.'

'Then let her work hard.' Anything to keep herself safe from what he could do to her!

He shook his head. 'I don't want her anymore.'

His eyes told her very graphically that she was now the object of desire. Jenny was hopelessly torn between her own secret desire for him to want her and the certain knowledge he intended to use sex to keep her in line with him. He wanted abject surrender from her, not a relationship that carried caring with it. He had no reason to care for her, never would.

'Don't look at me like that!' she cried. 'I've just seen the type of woman who attracts you and I'm not it. If you think you can fool me, think again!'

Dante did pause to think again. The fierce antagonism flowing from her would only deepen if he physically forced the issue. Persuasion was now the tactic to use to get her back to where he wanted her. And he did *want* her. The desire still surging through him was stronger than any he'd felt in a long time. Anya's sexual expertise was a tame thing compared to the powerhouse of passion he'd found in this woman.

He had to move Anya out of this villa, off Capri, get rid of that bone of contention before attempting another seduction, which would have to be carefully planned, given the level of resistance Anya's intrusion had forged.

'And get this straight,' the little spitfire hurled at him. 'I'll be Isabella for your grandfather whenever he wants my company, but I don't like Lucia and Anya and I'm not going to mix with them when he's not there.'

'Anya will be gone before lunch.'

'Fine! Then you can lunch with your real cousin by yourself. Tell her I have a headache. Tell her I'm still suffering jetlag. Tell her anything you like to excuse me from having to put up with more stress, because I'm going to rest in this room all afternoon. *By myself.* Or I won't answer to how I conduct myself with your grandfather over dinner tonight,' she finished with threatening defiance.

'Good idea!' he approved, which instantly took the wind out of her battle sails. 'I'll have one of the maids bring you a tray of refreshments. Would you like headache pills, as well?'

She lifted a hand to push at her forehead. 'Yes, I would. Thank you,' she muttered, visibly sagging with relief at his response.

'Lucia can be a trial, but it will be impossible to

completely avoid her,' he warned. 'I'll do my best to keep you apart. Okay?'

She nodded, looking too drained of energy to argue anymore.

'I'll leave you to rest.'

The deception had to be maintained at all costs, Dante reminded himself as he let himself out of the suite. It was probably reckless of him to pursue a sexual connection with his 'cousin.' In all honesty, he couldn't pass off this move as a means of winning her willing co-operation. He wanted to experience all of her.

The way she challenged him stirred his highly competitive instincts, driving a need to strip her of her armour, take her so totally she would concede everything to him. But he had to be careful, too, not incur any suspicion of the connection he intended to have with her. Control was paramount in this situation. He'd almost lost it, back there.

He smiled.

It didn't matter if he lost it behind closed doors.

CHAPTER NINE

HAD she made Dante think again?

Jenny stared at the closed door, not knowing if he'd decided that any further attempt at sexual domination was not a good idea, or if this was merely a reprieve. Her head *was* aching. She felt totally exhausted, her nerves frayed by an overload of tension. Whatever Dante intended, she was grateful he'd left her alone for a while, grateful not to have to be constantly thinking about what she had to say and do to remain safe in this place.

She dragged her gaze from the door and slowly swept it around the bedroom which was supposed to be her own private sanctuary. The fabrics used were mostly peaches and cream with touches of pale lime green. The furniture was white. Two armchairs and a coffee table holding a platter of fresh fruit were placed for the enjoyment of the view outside. A writing desk was graced by a beautiful arrangement of pastel carnations. A large plasma television set provided easy viewing from the bed which was king-size.

The room was so large, the big bed did not swamp

the space, but it did swamp Jenny's mind with dark thoughts. It was so clearly a bed for two people, a bed for sex, a bed where Anya had lain with Dante, playing erotic games, using her lush femininity to keep him. What wiles would she try to make him reconsider his decision to end their relationship? Obviously she didn't want to let him go.

Would Dante reconsider, using a resumed affair with Anya to defray any suspicion of sexual interest in *his cousin*? He was certainly capable of doing anything to achieve what he wanted, Jenny reminded herself, hating her own vulnerability to the power of the man. Somehow she had to remain emotionally cold with him, not let him see he could get to her, though how she was going to manage that after losing her head with such mad passion she didn't know.

Sighing over the wretched mistake, she dragged her feet over to the door that led to the ensuite bathroom. Except it didn't directly. It opened to a short corridor which bisected the bathroom on one side and a dressing-room on the other, and at the end of it was another door. Shock squeezed her heart as she remembered this suite adjoined Dante's. He had private access to it. No one would see him if he chose to come to her at night.

She rushed over to try the door-knob. It didn't turn. Locked. But was there a key? Could he unlock it on his side? She fought down a wave of panic. There was nothing she could do about this now. When the maid came with the tray of refreshments, she could ask her about it, insist she be assured of absolute privacy.

Her head was throbbing. She needed to wash off her

makeup and lie down. Her legs were shaky. She shoved herself back to the bathroom doorway. All her toiletries were neatly set out on a marble vanity bench. A glance back to the dressing room showed the rest of her luggage unpacked as well, clothes hanging up or stowed on shelves. Even her shoes had been stacked in pairs on a rack.

This was how the rich lived, she thought derisively, having everything done for them, having their wishes carried out, acquiring whatever they wanted, *including a grand-daughter.* How was she going to fill in these two months with the Rossini family, having nothing to do apart from chatting with Marco whenever he was well enough to want her company? Hiding in this suite day after day would be too unnatural. She couldn't see Dante allowing it. But at least he had left her to herself this afternoon.

She slept most of it away. When she woke it was almost five o'clock. Mercifully her headache was gone. A note had been slipped under her bedroom door. She picked it up with some trepidation, not knowing what to expect, but it was only a helpful list of instructions:

Call kitchen on telephone intercom for service when wanted.
Dinner is at eight.
Be ready by seven.
Wear Lisa Ho dress.

No signature but it had to be from Dante, doing his puppet-master thing again.

Having missed the two-o'clock lunch, and with dinner still three hours away, Jenny decided she needed some refuelling before her next performance. The platter of fruit did not appeal as much as a cup of coffee—a whole pot of coffee—so she called the kitchen and requested it, along with a serving of bruschetta. Her empty stomach was growling for something more substantial than grapes and peaches. It took a lot of energy and a sharp mind to keep on her toes with the Rossini family, and having to fight the perilous attraction to Dante took even more.

She tried not to fret over what might happen next with him. Nevertheless, it was impossible to suppress some anxiety as the meeting time approached. She had eaten, showered, dressed, made up her face in appropriate tones to complement the green and gold hues in the filmy, frilly, ultra-feminine Lisa Ho creation, put on the gold jewellery, fluffed up her hair, was satisfied that she was presentable, then had nothing to do in the last twenty minutes, except pace around the room and worry about things she couldn't control.

Getting some fresh air seemed like a better activity. She opened the glass doors, crossed the colonnaded walkway and leaned against the stone wall, breathing in the salty scent of the sea and watching the shifting colour of sky and water as the sun set. The seeking of some peace of mind was short-lived. She'd barely started to relax when Dante's voice snapped her back to full-on tension.

'I hope you're not thinking of jumping.'

The sardonic drawl seemed to crawl down her spine. Her heart leapt into a jitter-bug. She gritted her teeth and fiercely told herself not to get rattled, to adopt a cool aloofness that denied she was in any way affected by his presence.

'I'm not yet defeated by life,' she replied, turning to see him stepping out of *her* bedroom, which was an instant reminder of the set-up he'd orchestrated. 'Did you just use the connecting door between our suites?'

He shrugged as though it was totally inconsequential. 'I knocked first. When there was no response, I thought I'd better check on you.'

It sounded reasonable but Jenny glared her dislike of the too intimate situation. She'd decided not to fuss about having a key, realising he either had one or could acquire one, and making a fuss to anyone else might raise eyebrows over questions of trust where there should be none, not between *cousins*.

'Don't assume you can invade my privacy any time you like, Dante,' she said tersely.

His mouth twitched into a smile as he crossed the walkway to the stone wall, his gaze flicking down and up, assessing her overall appearance. 'I see you're in fine form again. Headache gone?'

'Yes, thank you.'

She whipped her gaze back to the view when he joined her at the wall, standing too close for comfort. He was wearing a white suit and an open-necked black shirt—a striking combination that oozed sex appeal on him. She was so acutely conscious of his nearness she could barely breathe, and her mind's eye was so occupied with his image the sunset was a blur. It was an act of will to keep her voice working in a fairly natural tone.

'Who will be at dinner tonight?' she asked, more fixated on Anya's presence than anyone else's, torn between wanting her gone and needing to have Dante's sexual drive diverted away from herself.

'Just Nonno and his three grandchildren. He's been resting all afternoon, as well, looking forward to this evening. I trust we'll have a pleasant dinner together.'

A touch of steel was added to his voice on those last words—a warning to behave as he wanted her to behave with Marco. Remembering his other warning, she couldn't stop herself from mockingly asking, 'Has Anya paid for not pleasing you?'

'Oh, I think Anya profited quite well from our relationship,' he said cynically. 'Which is why she wanted to extend it past its use-by date. I told her in no uncertain terms that I'm not interested in an extension, and she flew back to Rome this afternoon. With *all* her toiletries.'

Gone...

Jenny didn't know if she was disappointed or relieved. One source of possibly hostile attention had been eliminated, making the situation less complicated on the social level. On the other hand, Anya's departure meant she couldn't be used as a line of defence against any disturbing move Dante made on her.

She shot him a hard look. 'Have you always ordered your world how you want it?'

He grimaced. 'If I could do that, my mother and father would still be alive, and Nonno wouldn't be dying of cancer.'

'Family,' she murmured, thinking it was the one thing he couldn't choose.

'My parents died when I was six,' he went on. 'Nonno took me under his wing. He was always there for me. He's given me so much, I had to give him you, Isabella. I couldn't tell him you were dead, not when he's dying.'

Was it an appeal for understanding? Another play for her co-operation? Ruthless blackmail, sexual connection, a pull on her emotional strings…anything and everything was grist for his mill.

Yet maybe it wasn't ego driving him. Maybe he was half-crazed by grief at the imminent loss of the grandfather who had nurtured and supported him since he was a little boy.

She shouldn't have taken over Bella's identity. None of this would have happened if she hadn't made that decision—taken when her mind had been torn by grief for her friend and desperation on her own account. Impossible to imagine then she was setting up a collision course with Dante Rossini and would end up here, paying for that decision. And maybe it was right that she should pay for it. Marco's investigators had been deceived into reporting Isabella was alive. Her fault.

She heaved a regretful sigh. 'I'm sorry I caused this mess. I *will* do my best to give your grandfather what he needs from Bella, Dante. You don't need to…to force more from me.'

A rush of hot embarrassment burned her cheeks. She hadn't fought his kisses. It shamed her that her response to them had not been negative. Dante wasn't likely to forget that explosive passion. Her mind squirmed over it, wondering if she could explain it away, say it had erupted from anger, nothing at all to do with an attraction that was still tearing at her, despite common sense dictating how dangerously stupid it was.

She stared out to sea, painfully aware he had swung towards her and was studying her profile. Did he believe her? Would he trust her to continue behaving as Bella might have done? Her skin kept burning under the intensity of his probing gaze. He made her so tense she could hardly think.

'Who were your parents?'

The soft curious tone washed through her jangling mind like cool water. The relief from hot pressure was so great, she forgot about denying him information about herself. It seemed harmless to tell him the truth, easier than prolonging a silence that fed her fears.

'I don't know. No one does. I was an abandoned baby, only a few hours old when I was found. Public appeals were made for the mother to come forward, but she never did.'

'Probably a student,' he mused. 'For whatever reason, she must have had to hide her pregnancy, hide the fact she'd had a baby.'

Surprised by this sympathetic reading from him, she shot him a quizzical look. 'Why do you say that? Why not someone who simply didn't want to be loaded with me, who didn't want to bother with the fuss of handing me over to officials for adoption?'

'Someone who didn't care would have had an abortion.' He shook his head. 'I think your mother was very young and had a lot to lose by admitting to the mistake of getting pregnant, but you were her flesh and blood and she couldn't bring herself to deny you life.'

She frowned at his persistence in drawing this picture of her unknown mother, whom Jenny had privately condemned for dumping her baby daughter in a limbo of not belonging anywhere. 'I don't know why you're going on about her like this. It makes no difference to what happened to me. No parents. No family. The nurses at the hospital named me Jenny and I was found in Kent Street. There you have it. Jenny Kent.'

His question was answered.

But he didn't let it drop.

The speculative interest in his eyes didn't even waver.

'I believe genetic inheritance contributes far more to one's character than environment. I think your mother was a student because you're remarkably intelligent. I think she felt trapped and scared, and just as you denied your own identity to survive, she denied being a mother to survive.'

'I'd never give up a child of mine,' she cried emphatically, resenting the parallel he was drawing.

'No, I don't think you would,' he said in measured judgement. 'That's where environment comes in. I doubt your mother had the experience of being an abandoned child herself. But in traumatic situations, people do make decisions they later regret.'

Like me, coming out of the coma, faced with too many problems to cope with.

Maybe she should think more kindly of her mother.

What was the old saying? 'Don't judge people until you've walked a mile in their shoes?'

It suddenly struck her how strange this conversation with Dante was. What was the purpose behind it? Why would he care how she thought about her mother? It had nothing to do with his high-powered life, nothing to do with…

'Like my grandfather turning his back on his youngest son,' he added quietly. 'Then it becomes too late to turn back the clock.'

Ah! He was setting up a more sympathetic bond between her and Marco, tapping into her own background to establish an emotional link, pulling strings again. Had he decided the sexual angle might be too volatile to be safely handled? Was she off that hook?

She turned and looked him straight in the eye. 'I said I'd do my best, Dante. I meant it.'

His long, hard, assessing stare was difficult to hold, making Jenny feel stretched on a rack with him tightening the screws, testing every nerve in her body. Nevertheless, she was determined on making him believe her and it was not her gaze that dropped first.

It was his.

Slowly sliding down to her mouth, stopping there.

And she knew he wasn't thinking about the words it had just delivered. He was remembering how she had responded to his kisses, wanting to test the memory, relive it.

Her breath caught in her throat. Her heart hammered her chest. Her stomach contracted. Tremors ran down her thighs. One hand gripped the edge of the stone wall, fingers spread wide for supporting traction. The other curled into a fist. Her mind screamed not to show weakness, to fight him off if he touched her.

He didn't move. His gaze lifted to hers again, dark eyes simmering with a sensuality that sent a convulsive little shiver down her spine. Fear or excitement she didn't know, couldn't let herself think about it. He was so damnably sexy and his eyes were promising pleasure she'd never get with anyone else.

'You look so beautiful tonight, Nonno will be proud to own you as his grand-daughter,' he said huskily. 'He'll put aside the fact there is nothing of Antonio in you. That's half the battle won. The rest should be easy as long as you're committed to it.'

Her breath released itself in a shaky sigh. 'I am,' she assured him, feeling she had just been given another reprieve.

He smiled, the warm satisfaction in his eyes making her skin tingle. It was impossible to stop her body reacting to this man.

He gestured an invitation to move. 'Shall we stroll along the walkway to the terrace? We can go from there through the atrium to the entertainment wing of the villa.'

Game on again, Jenny thought as she set out with him, trying to direct her mind away from its acute awareness of the physical chemistry that seemed to buzz between them. 'What reception am I likely to get from Lucia this time?' she asked.

'All sweetness and light under Nonno's eye,' he answered dryly.

'How did she take Anya's departure?'

'Oh, she put on a fine act of having misunderstood the situation, believing she was doing me a good turn in inviting Anya here. Lucia is an expert at cutting her losses when she no longer sees any advantage for herself in holding a stand.'

'You sound very cynical about her.'

He shrugged. 'It's just the way she is. Aunt Sophia has veered between indulging her and neglecting her. Lucia worked out how to manipulate her mother and everyone else around her at a very young age. It annoys the hell out of her that I see straight through her games.'

'Being a master game player yourself.'

His eyes glittered acknowledgement of that truth. 'It's how one stays on top.'

Ruthless control, Jenny thought.

And couldn't help wondering what it would be like to feel all that power in bed with him.

CHAPTER TEN

THEY dined in a room overlooking a fabulous swimming pool. Underwater lights gave the water a blue brilliance and sparkled through a glorious fountain at the far end. Statues of Roman gods stood in the surrounding grounds amongst trellises of grapevines and urns of flowers. The outlook was so stunning, Jenny's gaze was drawn to it every time there was a lull in the conversation. It provided relief from the tension of having to be Bella with every word she spoke.

She wasn't so much under the gun from Marco Rossini tonight. He seemed content to sit back, watch and listen while Lucia directed a barrage of questions at her new cousin, most of which were easy to handle.

'Do you have a boyfriend waiting for you back home?' was thrown at her after the main course had been cleared away.

'No. What about you? Do you have one?'

A careless shrug. 'No one special. I can pick up anyone I want whenever I want.'

The arrogance of great wealth, Jenny thought. Dante

probably had the same attitude. Discarding Anya had not worried him one bit. No emotional involvement. She'd do well to remember that.

'What do you do with your time when you're on your own?' Lucia carried on.

'I draw. Or paint.'

'What do you draw?'

'Portraits mostly.' It gave her a perverse kind of pleasure to shock Lucia with the truth. 'I've been what you'd call a street artist. People who come to the Venetian Forum in Sydney pay me to do a portrait of them on the spot.'

'*Dio!* That's not much better than a beggar!'

'I like it. There are so many interesting faces. Like Dante's.' She smiled at him, revelling in rebelling against caution for once. 'I wanted to sketch it before he asked me to.'

'Dante asked a cheap street artist to do a portrait of him?' Lucia sounded scandalised by such a lowly activity.

His dark eyes stabbed a warning at Jenny that she was playing with fire before turning a bland look to Lucia. 'It was my first meeting with Bella. I wanted to get to know her at least a little before identifying myself and telling her why I had come.'

'I'd like to see the portrait,' Marco said, drawing everyone's attention to him. His eyes sparkled with interest, dark pinpoints of vitality in a face that looked almost grey with fatigue or pain. 'Did you bring it home with you, Dante?'

'No,' he said ruefully.

'I didn't finish it,' Jenny explained. 'When he told me who he was…'

'She packed up her things and stormed away from me, wanting nothing to do with any of us,' he finished dryly.

'Why ever not?' Lucia cried in disbelief.

'Because we were of no significance in her life…and should have been,' Marco answered heavily. He turned to Jenny in appeal. 'Perhaps you would do a portrait of Dante for me while you're here.'

She shrugged an apology. 'I didn't bring any art materials with me.'

'No matter. I will supply them.' He turned to his grandson. 'You'll see to it, won't you, Dante? Everything Bella needs for her drawing and painting, now that she is staying with us.'

'First thing tomorrow, Nonno,' he promised.

'Just a sketchpad and some sticks of charcoal will do,' Jenny put in anxiously, not wanting to accept any more from them.

Marco waved a dismissive hand at her protest. 'What artist would not want to capture the colour of Capri? You do me the favour of giving me your company. Let me give you the pleasure of doing what you like doing while you're here. Get everything, Dante,' he repeated, not to be denied on this point.

It *would* fill in the hours…days…weeks…months…

Jenny grabbed the idea with gratitude, realising it would provide her with an escape from both Dante's company and Lucia's. She could be herself in her own world for as long as she was occupied with art.

She smiled at the old man. 'Thank you. I would enjoy trying my hand at doing some landscapes.'

He smiled back. 'And I will enjoy seeing you happy at work.'

'Have you sold any of your paintings?' Lucia asked with a lofty air, clearly peeved by her grandfather's indulgence towards the new grand-daughter and wanting to downgrade the talent being indulged.

'Yes. But not for very much,' Jenny answered, quite happy to downplay herself since it was the truth.

A condescending little smile played across Lucia's mouth. 'I know one of the top gallery owners in Rome. If I asked him, he'd be happy to give you an opinion of your work.'

Jenny shook her head. 'Thank you, but I'm not up to that standard.'

'Oh!' It was almost a sneer.

'Bella is planning to get some formal training next year,' Marco said, a slight reproof in his voice. 'It's time you thought of putting some structure in *your* life, Lucia, furthering your education so you can pursue a more rewarding occupation than attending parties.'

'They are fund-raisers for charities,' she quickly justified.

'Charities are better served by work,' came the terse reply.

Lucia gestured a pretty appeal. 'What would you have me do, Nonno? Just tell me…'

'Find some drive within yourself that gives you satisfaction,' he answered wearily. 'I can't tell you what it is.'

'But I'm absolutely satisfied with my life,' she blithely argued.

'Then you are cheaply satisfied, my dear, and you'll end up like your mother, being exploited by others.'

'No one will ever exploit me,' she retorted in gritty anger. 'I've seen what happens with my mother and I've learnt from it.'

'Sophia has nothing to fall back on, nothing to fill the emptiness when it comes,' he said sadly. 'You should find something for yourself, something that can always give you a sense of personal achievement, Lucia. That's what I'm telling you. This will never be a problem for Dante. I doubt it will ever be a problem for Bella. But you risk losing yourself in meaningless pursuits unless you find a more solid direction for your life.'

The long speech drained him. He sucked in breath and gestured to Dante. 'Take me to my suite. Must rest.'

Lucia leapt to her feet. 'I can help you, Nonno.'

He waved her down. 'Dante.'

There was no arguing with that firm edict.

His caregiver had brought him to dinner in a wheel-chair, evidence that he hadn't felt well enough to walk. Not well enough to eat much, either. He'd been served only small portions of the pasta entrée and the main veal dish, most of which had been pushed around his plate. As Dante wheeled him away from the table, it really shot home to Jenny that time was running out for Marco Rossini. He was dying, perhaps faster than the doctors had predicted.

Be kind to him...

She took Dante's request to heart at that moment, silently vowing to give his grandfather whatever pleasure she could. Tomorrow she would try her best to capture the essence of Dante in a portrait.

No sooner had the two men left the room than a maid came in, carrying the sweets course—small balls of different flavoured sorbets, easy for Marco to eat, Jenny thought, except he wasn't here anymore. The maid hesitated at the absence of half the dinner party.

'Serve us and take the rest back,' Lucia commanded snippishly, still put out at having her help rejected.

Jenny waited until the maid had departed, then attempted to reduce Lucia's smouldering annoyance. 'Dante told me he'd been with his grandfather since he was six. It's only natural…'

'Oh, shut up!' The dark eyes blazed absolute fury. 'You might have won over Dante and Nonno with your smarmy, agree-with-everything act, but I know what you're after.'

'I'm not *after* anything,' Jenny stated emphatically, feeling her own temperature starting to rise.

'A clever card to play,' Lucia jeered. 'It worked on my mother every time—lovers who didn't go after her for the money, except they took her big-time once she fell for it. It's quite marvellous how you didn't want anything to do with us, yet here you are, feeding Nonno a guilt-trip about you so he'll bend over backwards to give you everything he can.'

Jenny took a deep breath, telling herself to stay calm. 'I'm sorry you've learnt to be so cynical about people, Lucia,' she said reasonably, 'but you're wrong about me. I…'

'I don't have any art materials with me,' she mimicked mockingly. 'It was a deadset certainty that Nonno would supply you with the best range of stuff that can be bought. Not a bad start, Bella.'

The acid sarcasm bit. 'I won't keep it. It's just for here. I'll leave it all behind when I go home.'

Lucia's eyes lit with malevolent triumph. 'So the art thing is an act, too. No wonder you didn't want an expert opinion on your work.'

'No, it's not an act,' Jenny retorted heatedly. 'I have my own stuff at home. I don't need to take anything from your grandfather. And I won't!'

'Only the inheritance that would have gone to your papa. Don't tell me that's not on your mind.'

'It's not. But even if it were, why should it matter to you? What will you lose by it? Aren't there enough Rossini billions to go around for you? How much do you need, Lucia?'

'It's not the damned money!' She slammed her hands down on the table and stood up, leaning forward to spit vicious words at Jenny. 'You arrive here, thick as thieves with Dante, and Nonno immediately takes to you, even throws you in my face as an example of how I should lead my life. As if he's ever cared about my life!'

'He's just shown you he cares,' Jenny pointed out quietly, realising Lucia was fuming with jealousy.

'He's never done anything for me!' That was fired straight back at her. Her hands sliced the air in exasperated fury. 'It's always been Dante, Dante, Dante. His precious grandson got all his attention while I was dragged around the world by my mother, different minders, different schools, whatever suited her convenience.'

Her hands slammed down on the table again, eyes burning with hatred. 'Do you know how many times I wished I was an orphan so Nonno would take me in and give me what he gave Dante? And now he's found another orphaned grandchild to shower his attention on.'

Jenny shook her head. 'He's dying, Lucia. I won't have much time with him.'

'It should be *my* time. I wish he hadn't found you. I wish you were dead like your parents.'

'Lucia!'

Dante's voice thundered across the room as the blood drained from Jenny's face. Bella *was* dead...*was* dead... had been dead these past six months. She had no right to be here, taking up time that a real grand-daughter should have.

'Don't think you can order me to leave, Dante!' his cousin yelled, the harsh decibels in her voice hurting Jenny's ears. 'This villa isn't yours yet! I have as much right as you to say and do whatever I like.'

'If abusing people is your style, do it to an empty room. I won't have Bella subjected to your spite.' He strode over to Jenny, hauled her up from her chair, tucking her protectively to his side, a strong arm around her shoulders.

'Right! Run off together!' Lucia jeered. 'I've always been alone anyway. Nothing new there.'

'Try thinking of others instead of how everything affects *you,* and you might have a different result. Wishing Bella dead because it would suit you better is beyond contempt.'

The lash of his voice brought scarlet flags to Lucia's cheeks. 'I wish you were dead, too,' she said venomously.

'You always have. But you know what, Lucia? I've never once complained to Nonno about the malicious traps you've set for me. But try it on with Bella and I *will* tell him what a nasty piece of work you are. He doesn't have much tolerance for wrong-doing. He banished his own son so completely, we didn't even know of his existence until a week ago.'

The power of that threat hung in the silence that followed it—a silence loaded with violent emotion, barely held in check. Dante swept Jenny out of the room, her legs feeling as wooden as a marionette's, her mind pummelled by a dreadful sense of wrong-doing. She should never have agreed to this deception. There were too many repercussions to it. Dante had tunnel vision if he thought it was as simple as granting a deathbed wish. Nothing about it was simple.

'Don't fold on me now,' Dante muttered fiercely, sensing the turbulence weakening her earlier commitment to staying on here, almost carrying her down the long corridor to their bedroom suites, enveloping her with his own strength of purpose so she couldn't break away.

Once inside her room he locked the door against any possible intrusion, but he didn't release his hold on her. Before Jenny could say a word, she found herself locked in his embrace, her head gently pressed onto his broad shoulder, his hand stroking through her hair with soothing intent, his mouth warmly brushing her ear, his breath wafting over it as he spoke, his voice a deep rumble that rolled through her, making her feel even more shaky.

'There's no turning back. Whatever Lucia said to you, it makes no difference.'

She should be fighting the dominating power he was exerting, yet she couldn't summon the strength to do it.

There was comfort in being held so tightly, being stroked, feeling his caring about the stress she'd been put through. Tears spilled into her eyes. Tears of weakness. She didn't want to stand alone. Her whole body craved this seductive togetherness with him. Though part of her torn mind insisted that his caring was centred on protecting his own interests, wanting her to keep doing what he wanted.

She swallowed hard, blinked back the tears and forced herself to say, 'Yes, it does. It does make it different. I'm taking time away from her. Time that shouldn't be mine. And since I was the one who created this situation, I should take the blame for it. I'll tell your grandfather and Lucia I deceived you about being Bella. That won't bring you down in their eyes, Dante.'

It didn't matter what happened to her. Not meaning to do any harm did not excuse the wrong she'd done. She was filled with guilty shame and didn't want to live with it any longer.

His fingers entwined themselves in her hair, gently tugging her head up from his shoulder. She wanted to keep her eyes closed but the need to let him see she'd spoken the truth forced her to open them, to meet his dark questing gaze without any wavering.

He stared at her. For long, nerve-wracking moments, his eyes burned into hers as though they were scorching a path to her innermost soul. She was suddenly acutely conscious of the tension in his body, the pressure of his thighs against hers, the arm around her waist holding her firmly pinned to him, her breasts crushed against the hard hot wall of his chest.

Her heart started hammering.

The expression in his eyes changed to a glitter of satisfaction as though he sensed the loss of focus in her concentration on the deception issue and liked the physical awareness of him much better. 'I don't want to let you go, and you don't want me to, either,' he said with arrogant certainty.

He kissed her.

And she let him do it, knowing it was foolish, yet overwhelmingly tempted to feel whatever he could make her feel, before she returned to her own life. She'd never known a man like him, never would again. Only extraordinary circumstances had brought about this connection and it had to end, but she could take one night with him away with her.

Recklessly abandoning any sense of caution, she kissed him back, wanting to incite the explosion of passion that had blown her mind earlier today. He tasted her surrender, revelled in it, his mouth plundering hers for more and more of her giving, as though he couldn't get enough of it, and the wild intoxication of his need drove her own for more of him.

Excitement pumped through her body. His was moving sensuously against hers, making her aware of the excitement pulsing through him, making her crave the power of his sexuality. She wanted to be taken by him. He stirred something terribly primitive in her, a rampant desire to possess the essence of the man, to hold him in *her* power, if only for a little time.

Her arms were still by her sides. Her hands dragged up and down his hard muscular thighs, blindly transmitting the need that was clawing through her. A convulsive little thrill ran down her spine as his fingers burrowed through her hair to the zipper at the back of the designer dress and drew it down, baring her skin to his touch.

His mouth broke from hers, muttering something in Italian. His face wore a look of urgent intensity, his eyes blazing a command for her to remain exactly where she was while his hands worked quickly at stripping her of the fine feathers he'd clothed her in.

Yes, Jenny thought fiercely, wanting to be shed of the designer image, which was all part and parcel of the deception, wanting to feel free of everything, just be the woman she was, naked with nothing, and still being desired by Dante Rossini. His hands and mouth assured her this was true…long, shivery caresses down her back, over her buttocks, hot intimate caresses, kisses drawing her breasts into throbbing peaks, kisses on her stomach, her thighs. She was awash with exciting sensation.

Then he was surging up to his full towering height again, tearing off his own clothes, and she silently exulted in his wild haste, her eyes feasting on the magnificent maleness being revealed: satin-smooth olive skin, stretched tightly over perfect muscles, his whole physique in pleasing and heart-pummelling proportion. She could barely wait to run her hands over him, to feel his nakedness against hers. He was a beautiful man— his face, his body, the aggressive energy emanating from him, flooding her with an intense sense of being the weaker sex.

Which probably should have frightened her, but it didn't. It made her feel very female, meltingly soft, her whole being yearning for his hard strength to envelop her, fill her, take her to places she had never been, places she'd read about but never experienced in the few un-satisfying sexual encounters she'd had in the past. This man was different. She knew it in her bones, knew it from the uncontrollable responses he drew from her, knew it from the most basic of basic instincts.

He picked her up and carried her to the bed like a caveman claiming his woman. Her arms were around his neck, hands wantonly kneading the taut muscles in his back, her breasts crushed to the heaving wall of his chest, glorying in the silky heat of his naked skin. He knelt between her legs as he lowered her onto the bed, hovering over her like some dark beast of prey intent on devour-ing her, and she laughed at her own wild imagination, laughed with a mad joy in his ravenous desire for her.

He choked off her laugh with a long, driving kiss that turned her joy to a feverish passion. She wound her legs around his hips, her feet stroking his legs, pushing at them, goading him to act. The kiss was not enough. It promised. It incited. It tantalised. But it didn't deliver what she wanted, needed, her whole body screaming to feel him deep inside her, deeper than the kiss, much deeper.

She arched in sheer ecstasy when he finally entered her, plunging hard and fast to the place that had been waiting to welcome him, the place that pulsed with intense pleasure at his filling of the void, so brilliantly intense she could hardly bear it. He retreated from it, then came again, and again, and again, building an exquisite tension that splintered into sweet chaos, bringing wave after wave of euphoria crashing through her entire body.

And still he came, stroking through the waves, riding the crests, sucked into the honeyed heart of her, until he, too, spiralled beyond all control, spilling himself in great spasms, a stream of life eddying and swirling, hot, urgent, gloriously fulfilling her wish to possess some of him…if only for a little while.

She held him to her, filling all her senses with him, smelling the musky scent of after-sex, listening to his ragged breathing, feeling the thumping beat of his heart, seeing the glisten of sweat on his skin, loving the intimacy of it all. He rolled onto his back, carrying her with him, his arms holding her just as tightly, tucking her head under his chin, making her feel like his cherished possession.

It was as though they were cocooned together in a silent world of their own, content to be as one in it. She knew it had to end soon, knew they had to be parted, but not yet…

Please…not yet.

Let this night be long.

One night…before tomorrow.

CHAPTER ELEVEN

DANTE stretched his legs over hers, squeezed the lush roundness of her bottom, entwined the tangled curls of her hair around his fingers, holding her tightly in his grasp. No way was he about to let her slip away from him. She was something else…this woman.

Apart from stirring the animal in him, she had one hell of a strong pull on his mind. He was used to women in the Anya mould—women who counted the score, knowing how to work the wealthy social scene, giving enough to get what they wanted. Despite Jenny Kent's different background, he'd still assumed she'd fall in with his plan. It was in her best interests to do so. Yet she was bucking his judgement at every turn.

She cared about deceiving his grandfather.

She cared about deceiving Lucia.

She cared about taking what wasn't rightly hers to take, though she had taken over Bella's identity. As a short-term survival measure, she'd told him. Reasonable enough in the circumstances when she'd believed it wouldn't hurt anyone.

And now she didn't want to hurt him—the man who'd forced her into this situation—prepared to shoulder the whole fraudulent conspiracy herself rather than take him down with her.

Amazing that she cared so much for others.

But she didn't realise her confession would not serve any good whatsoever. Lucia would go on being a spoilt brat, making as much capital as she could out of *the mistake*, crowing over Nonno's disappointment instead of trying to assuage it by being the kind of granddaughter that gave him what he wanted given to him. Impossible anyway. Only Bella could do that—Jenny being Bella.

The status quo had to be maintained.

Besides, he wanted more of this woman.

Much more.

Right now she lay passively in his embrace. *Physically* passive. Passion spent. He wondered what had driven such wild passion in her. This hadn't been an act of seduction, though he'd meant it to be whatever was needed to keep her on track. From the moment he kissed her…it had to have been a wilful decision or an irresistible impulse on her part to embrace the strong chemistry between them, give it free expression. There'd been no inhibitions to overcome.

Maybe for her it was a release from all the tension he'd put her through this past week—a physical venting of all the feelings she'd kept bottled up behind her wall of silence. And, of course, he was the focus of those feelings, having forced her into this high-pressure situation.

No matter. The sex had been unbelievably fantastic.

Which was all to the good. Except…he suspected that sex, however fantastic it was, would not hold her against her will. It could be that she'd let herself have it—taking it from him—because tomorrow she would be gone.

Dante gritted his teeth in determination.

One way or another, he had to make her stay.

He'd try pushing the sex first.

He unclenched his jaw, forced himself to relax, then slowly and languorously rolled her onto her back, propped himself on his side, and gently stroked her hair back from her face, smiling into the eyes that fluttered open, looking at him with an expression of anxious wariness.

'Tell me why you laughed,' he invited, using a tone of indulgent curiosity.

It surprised her into a reminiscent smile. 'It's so mad…you and me.'

'But right at that moment you didn't care.'

'No. I didn't.'

'Neither did I.'

Her smile turned wry. 'A one-off thing for both of us.'

'I don't want it to be.' His gaze dropped to her mouth as he ran feather-light fingers over her lips. 'I haven't had nearly enough of you.'

She breathed in hard, knocked his hand away and spoke with fierce pride. 'I might be a nobody with nothing to my name, but don't think you can keep me as your secret little whore, Dante. I had sex with you because I wanted to but I'm not staying around for more of it.'

He raised a mocking eyebrow. 'Not good enough for you?'

She flushed. 'That's not the point.'

'It is to me. I can't recall ever having had it so good.' He glided his hand down her throat to her breasts, caressing them as though there were exquisite to his touch. Which they were. Even more so because of her reluctance to concede to him. 'Can you say differently?' he purred, confident of her response.

Confusion swirled in her eyes. 'That's not the point,' she repeated with an edge of desperation. 'I don't belong in your world. You know I don't.'

'My world is what I make it. I've already made you part of it.'

'As your cousin. A cousin you shouldn't be touching.'

'We both know that isn't true so we're not doing anything wrong. Why not enjoy what we can have together?' He reached down to the hot moist cleft between her legs, gently stroking a reminder of how intimately they had connected. 'It's about mutual pleasure, which is so far removed from your being degraded by the two of us being lovers that it's absurd for you to think like that. Secrecy will have to be maintained but I would never view you as selling yourself to me. It's not in your nature. You'd be milking this situation for all you could get if that was your mindset.'

'The situation is wrong, Dante,' she argued, her breathing quickening at the excitement his fingers were slowly re-igniting.

'No,' he quickly assured her. 'You're providing my grandfather with a distraction from his pain, giving him an outlet for memories he wants to open up before he dies. Only your presence can soothe the feelings of guilt he has over banishing his son.'

'But I'm not Bella.'

It was a cry of anguish.

Dante leaned over and tenderly grazed his lips over hers, wanting to soothe the turmoil in her mind. 'Whatever kind of person Bella was, you do her credit by being the person you are in her place. You're doing good.'

She grabbed his face, lifting it to make him look into eyes that were still pained. 'It hurts Lucia. I'm taking your grandfather's attention away from her and she has the right to it.'

Anger boiled up in him and with it a surge of aggression. He ceased the intimate caressing, lifting his hand to her chin, holding it firmly as he inserted his leg between hers and half-covered her body, instinctively using physical dominance to add pressure to his claim on her mind.

'Lucia...' he snarled contemptuously, his eyes blazing a conviction that couldn't be refuted. 'What was she doing this past week when she could have had all Nonno's attention? Off shopping in Rome and fixing a visit from Anya. Does that speak of a need to be with her grandfather to you?'

No answer. She stared up at him but the lack of sharp focus in her eyes told him his argument was registering in her mind. All he had to do was nail it home to her.

'Lucia could have spent that time reaching out to Nonno if that's what she really wanted. But no. She likes the power of playing her games with people and you were her target tonight, putting you down, stirring you up, making you feel like an unwanted interloper. And she was doing that to Bella, remember. Bella, your friend. Your friend who was like a sister to you. She had no right to do that. No right at all. How would Bella have felt if she'd been here?'

She frowned, not liking the reality of what her friend might have faced.

'It was cruel,' he hammered in. 'And if you let Lucia win, you'll hurt my grandfather, not her. She'd be preening over your departure, having scored a hit against me for having brought you here, never mind how Nonno would feel about it. And he's the one who counts. The only one. This is *his* time—the little time he has left—and he chooses to have you with him. You…'

He kissed her, trying to tease a response, but it wasn't there.

'You with your caring,' he murmured, and slid his tongue between her lips, wanting her to open up to him. Which she did, but passively, her mind still too full of other things.

'You with your giving,' he pressed, kissing her more deeply, using all his erotic expertise to get her focus back on what *they* could share together while she was Bella.

Her grip on his face eased, fingers sliding into his hair. Elation buzzed through him as her tongue slowly tangled with his. He'd won, and the win fired his desire for what she could give *him*. He wanted to feel the fire in her, wanted to build it to white-hot passion again, so he concentrated on keeping control this time, revelling in pleasuring her, feeding her sensuality with a slow journey of kisses and caresses all over her body, exulting as she squirmed in heat, when she clawed his back, wildly wanting the ultimate completion of his flesh plunged into hers.

Her need heightened his, the first deep thrust inside her feeling like a sunburst of incredible satisfaction. Control instantly evaporated. She made him feel like a great eagle, soaring and swooping, riding currents of air that zinged with sensation. It was brilliant, flying towards the highest of highs and she was taking him there, bucking and squeezing, drawing him on until he was utterly driven by her journey to the peak of ecstasy, reaching it with her, exploding like a nova that radiated out from the molten inner core of her to every cell in his body.

His mind was gone.

His strength was gone.

He floated in a weird kind of vacuum where she was the only anchor. Eventually his senses returned and he realised his body-weight must be crushing her, yet her arms were wound around him as though she didn't want him to move, or couldn't bear to break the closeness. He didn't want to break it, either, but he raised himself enough to kiss her forehead, her closed eyelids, her nose, her lips, and whisper, 'Say you'll stay.'

He breathed in her breath as she answered, 'Yes.'

He'd won.

She'd surrendered to his will.

And through him ran a sense of triumph that was sweeter than any he'd known.

CHAPTER TWELVE

JENNY sat at the newly acquired easel which had been set up close to Marco's sun-lounge on the terrace so he could watch her attempt to capture his grandson in charcoal. His caregiver, Theresa Farmilo, a middle-aged private nurse with a kindly manner, sat on the other side of him, ready to attend to his needs. A large umbrella shaded all three of them from the late-morning sun.

Dante was seated at the table, a few metres away, shaded by another umbrella. She'd asked him to chat with his grandfather, rather than hold a still pose. Silence and being the focus of all attention would have made her more nervous about doing the portrait. Besides, the vitality of his face when he talked was more interesting to work on than a simple sketch of flesh and bone and hair. More challenging, too.

He was an extremely challenging man. She no longer had any clear idea of what was right or wrong. He'd swamped her with intense sexual pleasure last night, argued her out of her concern for Lucia, re-asserted the need to indulge his grandfather with Bella's presence, and she had been unable to find the will to deny him anything.

Just do what he wants, kept running through her mind. It was too hard to fight him. Besides, this was his family and his judgement of it had to be better than hers. Though what Lucia had revealed about her life still touched a chord of sympathy—no settled home, a stream of minders, the lack of any deep personal interest being shone on her. In a weird kind of way, it echoed Jenny's own life. Wealth didn't really make up for the sense of inner loneliness. It only meant basic survival was never an issue.

Maybe she could speak to Marco about Lucia when they had some private time together, without Dante listening and butting in. If she could do some good there she would feel better about staying. Though Lucia might resent her interference, however well meant it was. Jenny had not seen her this morning, had no idea if she was ashamed of last night's cruel outburst or didn't care what hurt she had inflicted. No doubt their next meeting would reveal more of her nature. Best to wait and see.

More troubling than the question of Lucia was the new intimacy with Dante. She hadn't planned to have a prolonged secret affair with him. Her intention had been to end everything this morning. Now he clearly expected them to continue being cousins during the day and lovers at night—another deception that didn't sit easily in her mind. Yet her body was saying *yes* to it, regardless of how stupid and reckless it was to get so deeply involved with him.

Here she was, studying his mouth to draw it right,

and all she could think of was how it had kissed her...everywhere. Just looking at him stirred a host of exciting memories. He'd said he wanted more of her and she couldn't deny wanting more of him. If he came to her room tonight, she knew she wouldn't be able to refuse him.

This was time out of time, she told herself. A brief madness that would end when Marco died. Then she would return to her real life, and her connection to Dante Rossini would seem like a dream. She hoped she would be able to remember it with a smile—an experience that would never have come her way in the ordinary course of events. In the meantime she had to keep filling the grand-daughter role, make sure she didn't get anything too wrong.

The pleasant peace on the terrace was interrupted just as Jenny was putting the last touches to the portrait.

'Good morning, all!' Lucia trilled, arriving via the cliff walkway, obviously having enjoyed a recent swim in the pool. She wore a red bikini, the bottom half covered by a matching sarong, and a large, floppy, red straw sunhat drooped fashionably over her face. 'How's the portrait going, Nonno?' she asked, smiling at him indulgently as she sashayed over and dropped a kiss on his forehead.

'Look for yourself,' he invited, smiling at Jenny. 'I think you'll have to credit Bella with more talent than you had imagined, Lucia.'

'Really?'

The incredulous tone in her voice instantly made Jenny bridle. It was difficult to care about a person who was bent on being critical. She felt herself tensing as Lucia moved around to stand behind her and examine the likeness to Dante. She tensed even more when Lucia started laughing.

'You're going to love this, Dante. It's the most romantic version of you anyone could turn out.'

'Romantic?' he queried, looking at Jenny in a bemused fashion.

'I guess that's what street artists do, try to please the person they're drawing,' Lucia rattled on mockingly. 'Never mind about their true character, which, of course, they don't have a clue about. Though I must say, Bella, you should have picked up some of Dante's by now. You've been with him long enough.'

A horrible flush of self-consciousness flooded up Jenny's neck as she stared at the portrait, realising she had poured her feelings into it, making his eyes more gentle and loving than they really were, giving his mouth the kind of sensuality that reeked of sexual promise.

'Where's his master-of-the-situation arrogance?' Lucia demanded. 'The cutting-edge cynicism? All those innate qualities that make him such a force to be reckoned with?'

'I obviously don't know him so well,' Jenny muttered, shooting an anxious look at Marco. 'I'm sorry if you're disappointed.'

'Not at all, my dear. I'm glad Dante has shown you the softer side of himself.' He held out his hand. 'If you've finished, let me see it more closely.'

Jenny stood to pass over the portrait, achingly aware that Dante had stood, too, and was coming over to view it with his grandfather. Would he be amused to see himself *romanticised* by her? Or would his sharp mind pick up the fantasy of a dream lover that her subconscious self must have been weaving as she drew? Her insides writhed with the humiliation of revealing what should have been kept hidden.

He looked.

He said nothing.

His gaze remained lowered, fixed on the portrait. There was no telling expression on his face.

'I like it,' Marco said in a gruff, wistful tone. 'I like it very much.'

'Then Bella should do one of me, too,' Lucia said petulantly, annoyed by her grandfather's warm approval of Jenny's work.

'She might not see you as you would like to be seen, Lucia,' Dante tossed at her dryly.

'If she can do such a romantic version of you, she can do the same for me. Then Nonno can have the best of both of us to look at,' she argued, flouncing over to the chair Dante had vacated at the table, seating herself in an exaggerated pose, waving a command at Jenny. 'I'm all yours, Bella. Let's see what you can make of me.'

'Where are your manners, Lucia?' Marco asked sharply.

She flashed a saccharine smile at Jenny. 'Pretty please. As a gift to Nonno.'

'I'll do my best,' Jenny hastily agreed, grateful for the distraction from Dante and his reaction to the portrait she'd done. Besides, if she 'romanticised' Lucia, he would think that was her style, nothing personal to him.

She sat herself at the easel again, picked up a stick of charcoal and began drawing, emptying her mind of the spite and jealousy that soured Lucia's character, trying to see her as a lost child who was still occupying a frighteningly empty world, wanting the love she had missed.

Dante stretched out on another sun-lounge, remaining quiet as Lucia babbled on to her grandfather, telling him of the call she'd taken from her mother this morning. Apparently Sophia was waiting for her brother, Roberto, to join her in Paris before both flew down to Capri for the weekend to visit their father and meet Bella. Jenny hoped her pseudo aunt and uncle were not going to put her through any hostile hoops while they were here.

She listened to Lucia's rambling on about her family, knowing that meeting the rest of the Rossinis was inevitable. It was only natural they would want to spend time with Marco before he died. Bella might not be a welcome addition to the scene at this late juncture, but they would have to accept her presence.

It would be interesting to see how they responded to Dante, being the person designated to take over from Marco. Did they resent him as Lucia did, or were they content for him to carry the responsibility of the family fortunes?

Not that it was any of her business. She had to remain apart from all family politics. This wasn't her life. It was simply time out of time.

'I'm done,' she told Lucia, silently vowing not to let this 'cousin' upset her again. Since the portrait had been requested for Marco, she took it off the easel and handed it to him. 'Your gift,' she said with a smile.

'Thank you,' he murmured, staring at her work as his two real grandchildren moved to satisfy their curiosity about it.

Again Dante said nothing.

Lucia rushed into a string of protests. 'This isn't what you did for Dante. The eyes are too dark and intense. They should be bright and happy. You've made me look edgy instead of romantic. I don't like it.'

Jenny shrugged off the criticism. 'I'm sorry it doesn't meet your expectations. I'll try again another day if you want me to.'

'I wanted Nonno to have it today.'

'No, Lucia,' Marco said firmly, shooting her a quelling look. 'I'm satisfied with this one and Bella has indulged us enough. It's ungracious of you to demand more.'

'But, Nonno…'

'Enough!' he repeated sharply. 'I want you and Dante to leave me with Bella now. I'm tired and I'd like a few minutes alone with her before Theresa wheels me off to bed.'

'Then I'll go back to the pool. You can join me there later, Bella,' Lucia tossed at her with a show of cousinly grace as she left them.

Dante moved to pack up the easel. 'I'll take this back to your suite, Bella,' he said, his eyes stabbing a command for her to join him there when his grandfather was finished with her.

'Theresa, go and look at the sea,' Marco instructed, waving towards the cliff wall, obviously wanting his caregiver out of earshot, as well.

Tension streaked along Jenny's nerves as she waited

for the private tête-à-tête Marco was intent upon. This would be another test she had to pass, completely on her own this time. Fatigue was drawn on the old man's face but it hadn't dulled the sharp intelligence in the eyes he turned to her.

'You are a very talented artist, Bella. No question about that,' he said with authority.

'Thank you.' She smiled at the compliment, hiding her angst over what questions he *did* have in his mind.

'Sensitive to your subjects,' was his next comment.

The probe in his eyes made Jenny squirm inside. She was too frightened to say anything in case she revealed even more than she had done already with her unwitting interpretation of Dante.

Marco still held both portraits in his hands and he spread them apart, studying them again before quietly stating. 'These speak to me. I don't know if you meant them to...' Again the sharp probe, striking at her heart, making it flutter with fear. '...and perhaps they tell me more about you than they do about Dante and Lucia.'

'No, no...' She shook her head, her mind frantically searching for a defence of what she'd drawn. 'You asked me for a portrait of Dante, and what I do know about him, with absolute certainty, is that he loves you very much. I tried to show it.'

He nodded, but she wasn't sure he completely accepted her explanation.

'Love...yes,' he murmured. 'Thank you, my dear. It's good to be reminded.'

Relief coursed through her. He wasn't going to attach

it to anything personal in her. His gaze moved to the other portrait.

'You've captured something quite different in Lucia.'

'I didn't mean to suggest she doesn't love you,' Jenny said quickly, hoping she hadn't hurt the old man.

He shook his head, a wry twist on his mouth. 'I doubt Lucia is capable of loving anyone. She thinks of herself too much.'

'Is that her fault?' The words were out before Jenny could think better of the criticism they implied. She immediately tried to mitigate them. 'From what Lucia told me last night, she's had a difficult life, having to change schools and go wherever her mother wanted to go. She never had the kind of relationship Dante had with you. I think she's a very unhappy person.'

'Yes.' He heaved a deep sigh. 'It is unfortunate. If my Isabella had still been alive to guide Sophia into being a better mother…more consistent in her caring for Lucia…' He grimaced. 'And Sophia's husbands have been worthless as fathers. Bad choices.'

His eyes sought her understanding. 'I have done all I could for Lucia, offered her every opportunity to make her life count for something other than the wealth attached to her name. She chooses to be a dilettante, and while she sticks to that course, she will not attain any inner happiness. I can't make her change. And be warned, my dear, she will tear your sympathetic heart to shreds, seeing it as a weakness to be exploited.'

'Why? I thought she felt lost. Like no one ever cared enough about her,' Jenny pleaded. 'I'm sorry if that's presumptuous, but—'

'No. Lucia is very clever at painting the pictures she wants to present. Which is whatever will suit her purpose at the time. Care was certainly lavished on her when she was a little girl, but even then it was in her nature to destroy rather than build something good. She is not a lost child, Bella, more an *enfante terrible* who enjoys wreaking havoc.'

'Because she wants more notice taken of her?' Jenny suggested, still reaching for more understanding of what sounded like psychotic behaviour.

'To make herself the centre of attention, yes. But not to care about the effect of her actions on anyone else. She has long had a habit of engineering situations that give her a destructive control. I have come to believe this behaviour stems from a personality disorder, perhaps a genetic inheritance from her father who had no conscience at all. I don't know. I only see how it is. But Lucia is family and I will never again turn my back on family. When I'm gone it will be Dante's responsibility to look after her, see to her needs as best he can.'

Jenny frowned over what she saw as an extremely strained relationship between the two cousins. 'Surely her mother should do that.'

'Oh, I'm sure Lucia will milk the guilt trip she loads on Sophia for all she can, but Dante will hold the reins on how much is given. He knows where to draw the line, and draw it he will with authority that cannot be bucked.'

As he had already done twice since she had been here. But would he be as tolerant as his grandfather when he was left in charge of the family? 'You trust him with a great deal,' she said musingly.

'He has earned my trust a thousand times over. Not once has he ever let me down.'

Nor would he at the end of Marco's life, Jenny thought, feeling more sympathetic towards the deception Dante had enforced. His grandfather had sent him on an impossible mission and she had been the answer to it.

'I think it must be very rare…what you and Dante share,' she said in wry appreciation.

'Yes. As rare as finding the love of a good woman. I have been fortunate with my wife and my grandson. And I'm glad he found you, my dear, and brought you home with him.'

Embarrassed by the linkage to people who were truly dear to Marco, Jenny muttered, 'I had to come. But please don't feel you have to do something for me. Just being here is enough.'

'I hope it will be.'

His smile was so benevolent, Jenny wished she was his grand-daughter. It would be so nice to belong to him.

'Thank you for the portraits, my dear. And don't let Lucia spoil your stay here. Dante will keep you company when I can't. Trust him to deal with any situation that arises. Will you do that?'

She nodded, acutely aware there was too much family history she didn't know.

He waved a dismissal. 'Time for me to retire. Will you tell Theresa I'm ready to go?'

'Of course. I hope you have a good rest.'

Having taken her leave of Marco, she strolled along the cliff walkway which would take her to her suite, looking out at the deep blue sea and thinking

over all he had told her. Patterns of behaviour did
reveal the person. Lucia only wanted Marco's attention when he was giving it to others. 'Bella' wasn't
taking up what could have been her time with him.
Lucia only wanted it to take it away from Bella. Or
Dante. Not to use it for anything that might be good
and meaningful.

Don't let her spoil your stay here.

I won't, Jenny resolved.

Which left only Dante weighing on her mind—
Dante, whom she now saw waiting for her outside her
suite—Dante, propped casually against the stone wall,
watching her with a dark intensity that sent little quivers
through her entire body.

Her feet faltered to a halt.

She burned with embarrassment, remembering the
'romantic' portrait. Love had nothing to do with what
he'd done with her last night. He wanted to keep her
here for his grandfather, by any means—a ruthless
manipulator. Her head told her that, but her heart...
her heart was drowning in a deep blue sea, beating
against conflicting waves of emotion that could not be
held at bay.

CHAPTER THIRTEEN

DANTE saw her leisurely stroll along the walkway come to an abrupt halt when she caught sight of him waiting for her. The pensive look on her face instantly changed—a self-conscious flush bursting onto her cheeks, a tense defensiveness in the sharp tilt of her chin, wariness in the eyes that met his—and he knew without a doubt that she had exposed her heart in the portrait of him. In both portraits, but the one of Lucia did not concern him so personally.

His conscience had been pricking him from the moment he took in what she had drawn. It wasn't the man he'd been to her. If she'd portrayed what she wanted him to be, he'd taken too many liberties with the person she was, been blindly selfish in going after what he wanted, not giving any thought to how his actions would affect her, except in so far as they achieved his purpose.

His sense of righteousness over using her had received one hell of a hard knock. He'd known she was vulnerable, and he'd exploited her vulnerability, telling himself the end justified the means. He'd overlooked the fact that she had been an abandoned child whose need to be loved and cherished had never been answered. It had only been sex to him last night, but if she had fantasised love, she could end up deeply hurt by her connection to him.

This wasn't a woman he could kiss off with some lavish gift when the mutual pleasure wore thin. He knew she would be insulted, mortally offended, believing he truly had used her as his 'secret little whore.' Jenny Kent was essentially a good person, not wanting to do harm to anyone. It was in her every word, every action. He'd known it last night. She was a giver, not a user.

He shouldn't keep taking from her.

Yet he couldn't bring himself to tell his grandfather the truth—that Bella was dead and he'd brought Jenny Kent in her place to ease the guilt and pain over his lost son. Nonno wanted her here. He liked her. It was helping him get through this bad time.

Apart from which, Dante wanted Jenny Kent to stay for himself. Desire for her was burning through his body right now, urging him to dismiss his concern over how deeply she was responding to him. He wasn't *forcing* her to have sex with him. It was her choice. She had made that clear to him last night. *Her choice...*

Yet his instincts were telling him this was not the time to push for the physical satisfaction of having her again. It had been a pressure morning for her and she probably needed space to herself—a rest from the inner conflict of having to be Bella. On the other hand, if he gave her room to think too much, her mind might be torn over the deception again. What had his grandfather said to her after he had dismissed Lucia and himself?

Her shoulders straightened and she pushed her feet forward again. Dante sensed a proud refusal to be intimidated by anything he thought or said. Jenny Kent made her own way, regardless of the forces she had to contend with—a survivor, no matter what. He had to admire her spirit. In fact, there was nothing he didn't admire about her. She was a beautiful woman, inside and out.

'I didn't break your trust,' she assured him, once she was standing at the stone wall, close to his position but not in touching distance. Her lovely amber eyes looked directly into his to drive the point home. 'Your grandfather still thinks I'm Bella.'

Which was why she was here.

Dante got the message.

Having sex with him was a side issue, not the main event, and whatever it meant to her was not to be discussed. It would happen—if it did again—behind closed doors and that was where Jenny Kent would leave it when her life moved on beyond this time on Capri. Dante told himself he should be feeling relief at her attitude. It freed him from any guilt over treating her too cavalierly. Yet for some unfathomable reason, he didn't like her return to rigid self-containment. He wanted her. He wanted *all* of her.

Maybe it was the lure of forbidden territory.

The challenge she continually posed.

Whatever...now was not the time to pursue it.

'What did he want to talk to you about?' he asked.

'Lucia mostly. He wanted me to understand her per-

sonality so I wouldn't get too upset by anythi...
did or said.'

To Dante's mind, that underlined his grandfather's
need to keep Bella here. 'Nonno well knows her
penchant for creating scenes when she's not getting her
own way,' he commented, nodding to himself. 'Lucia
has been quite a malicious little manipulator all her life.'

'You're not too backward at manipulation yourself,
Dante,' she shot at him, a weighing look in her eyes as
though she was measuring his integrity.

'My actions are never motivated by malice,' he stated
unequivocally.

'But you are ruthless when it comes to executing
your vision of the greater good. And cynical in your
judgement of people. Lucia was right in pointing that
out to me.'

'Lucia's aim is to divide and conquer. She doesn't
want us to be close. The more she can drive a wedge
between us the better she'll like it.'

'I'm not stupid, Dante. I know that staying close to
you is my best chance of holding all this together. I need
your support and protection and I trust you to give me
both. But I'm well aware of when our togetherness will
come to an end, so please don't think I'll fool myself
into getting *romantic* about you. Your grandfather
wanted a portrait of you. I gave him a loving one.'

She spoke coolly, but her eyes hotly denied any other
interpretation of what she'd drawn. Pride, he thought,
and an array of conflicting emotions coursing through
the pragmatism she had persistently demonstrated since
he'd forced her into this situation. The problem was that

the mind could see a logical reality and accept it, but how the heart reacted to it was not so easily governed.

'Thank you for using your artistry to give me such a kind treatment,' he said quietly, feeling an odd spurt of tenderness for this woman who cared so much. 'It was very generous of you. Nonno was touched by it.'

She sucked in a deep breath and managed a shaky smile. 'He did like it. I should have done the same for Lucia instead of annoying her by portraying her differently.'

'It was, I thought, a sympathetic portrait of her,' he posed, wondering if she would shield herself against Lucia's poisonous darts or suffer from them.

She shrugged as the smile turned into a rueful grimace. 'Don't worry. Anything Lucia says to me will be water off a duck's back from now on. She's your business, not mine.'

'A cross I have to bear,' he said dryly. 'And speaking of Lucia, do you want to brave a swim in the pool while she's there?'

Out in the open where she could please herself—swim, laze in the sun or shade, chat or flip through the magazines Lucia always had handy—a place to relax, Dante thought, and regather herself, without any push for more intimacy from him. He could almost see the same train of thought going through her mind before a smile of relief spread across her face.

'Yes. A swim would be good.'

He nodded agreement. 'I'll meet you at the pool.'

Which took away any fear he might invade her room while she was getting changed.

The smile brightened. 'Okay! See you there!'

She left him with an eager bounce in her step—the bounce of freedom from expectations she wasn't up to facing right now. He had kept her on a tight rein, intent on covering every problem that could arise from the situation. The most critical time had already been successfully negotiated. She was doing really well in the role of Bella, better than he had ever anticipated. It was time to loosen up, give more consideration to Jenny Kent's needs.

Dante wondered if he should keep away tonight.

Did she want him to?

That was the more pertinent question.

Jenny actually enjoyed the time they spent in and out of the pool. Lucia was with them which ensured Dante acted in a cousinly manner, affably fetching them drinks when requested, making occasional droll comments on the conversation about fashion in different countries, which Lucia kept rolling as she leafed through magazines.

Jenny had very little experience of designer-wear— only what Dante had acquired for Bella—but her general ignorance didn't matter. Lucia enjoyed being the expert, showing off all her inside knowledge of the subject, gossiping about top models with whom she was personally acquainted. It obviously made her feel superior to her Australian cousin and that was fine. Nothing really nasty was said. Dante's presence was undoubtedly an inhibiting factor on that front.

Certainly neither cousin was the least bit inhibited about exposing their bodies. The bottom half of Lucia's red bikini was virtually a G-string and so was Dante's swimming costume which was not much more than a black pouch, forming a tantalising magnet for Jenny's eyes. She continually had to make a conscious effort not to keep looking *there*. As it was, the rest of his magnificent physique was more than enough to flood her mind with memories of last night's intimacy.

It made her doubly conscious of her own body. She wore a more modest bikini in a pretty apple green, a Zimmerman design featuring feminine little frills on the side of the bra and across her hipline, bought by Dante but chosen by her. She felt comfortable in it, except when *his* gaze roved over her. Several times she was driven back into the pool to reduce the heat of wanting this man too much.

She knew it wasn't sensible.

But the sexuality he'd stirred in her had a life of its own, pulsing a constant rebellion against any common sense.

When would she ever meet a man like him again—a man who could make her feel like this?

Most probably never.

As long as she kept in her head, there would be no happy-ever-after with him, why not take whatever he gave of himself? She wanted it, more than anything she had ever wanted. If he came to her tonight...but that was hours away and she had to keep cool in front of Lucia. Cool to him, too, because she didn't want him to know how besotted she was becoming with him.

The three of them had a leisurely lunch beside the pool. Jenny concentrated hard on enjoying the food—delicious Atlantic salmon served with a scrumptious side salad containing wedges of sweet orange and roasted pecan nuts. Fresh fruit was served afterwards; little balls of different melons and pineapple sprinkled with mint. They drank a lovely refreshing white Italian wine which was so pleasant to the palate, she drank too much of it, ending up feeling so drowsy, she was glad when Dante announced it was time for a siesta.

He accompanied her back to her suite, maintaining a relaxed manner as they walked along. Jenny was careful not to reveal any sexual tension, asking questions about Italy and showing interest in his answers. He left her at her door, casually moving on to his own suite, and she wondered if he had decided not to get too entangled with her.

Had the portrait suggested to him a risk of emotional attachment that might cause problems for him further down the line, problems he didn't want to deal with?

It was no use worrying about it, Jenny told herself. She'd done her best to tell him she knew the score where their relationship was concerned. What Dante chose to do about it was beyond her control. *He* was the controller, of every sphere in his life. It was so imbued in his character, Jenny couldn't imagine him any other way.

She took a long, cool shower to reduce her body heat, decided not to wash her hair until after siesta, and had just wrapped herself in a towel when she heard a knock on the door that linked their suites. For a few moments she dithered over answering it. Should she pretend to be already asleep? Had he heard her shower running? What did he want?

Her heart was suddenly pounding in her chest, thundering in her ears. She was acutely conscious of her nakedness under the towel—less naked than in her bikini, yet more instantly available if sex was on his mind. Her body felt like a mass of zinging nerve ends, urging her to go to the door, open it, find out where she was with him.

She did.

He, too, wore only a towel. It was tucked around his waist. She stared at his bare, beautifully muscled chest, the satin-smooth olive skin stretched tightly over it, her hands itching to touch, to feel him as she had felt him last night. It took an act of will to lift her gaze to his and project an innocent inquiry.

The dark eyes blazed raw desire at her. 'Do you want to be alone?' he asked.

A simple question but they both knew it wasn't simple.

It carried an undertow of danger which could sweep them away from any safe ground.

She knew he would force himself to clamp down on his rampant sexual need to have her again if she said yes. The determined restraint he was holding screamed of almost unbearable tension, and something deeply primitive in her revelled in the fact that he had been driven to this door, probably against his better judgement.

The decision was hers to make.

Her mind had already made it.

'No,' she said.

And didn't care where it led for her...further down the track. Regardless of what pain it might bring, she would take the pleasure now.

CHAPTER FOURTEEN

Six weeks passed.... For Jenny, the days blurred into each other, the pattern of them only broken by visits from Uncle Roberto and Aunt Sophia each weekend, both of whom accepted her as Bella without question. Their curiosity about her was easily satisfied and they weren't the least bit concerned about having a late addition to the family getting attention from their father.

Regret was expressed over Antonio's unfortunate death. They would have liked to meet him again. 'He was a terrible scallywag in his youth,' Sophia remarked, which Roberto had hastily discounted with, 'No, no, he was a darling boy,' smiling kindly at his new niece. As far as they were concerned, if it pleased Papa to have her here, it was good that she had come.

Perhaps it also took some emotional pressure off them. They were uncomfortable in the face of Marco's physical decline. Sophia's rather brittle personality was prone to gushing tears over her father. Roberto would set out to amuse—too anxiously—then fall into a glum silence. Jenny felt Marco suffered their visits, trying to soothe their distress when they were with him.

They looked to Dante to take care of everything. There was certainly no resentment of his designated position as the future head of the family. It was obvious they had no wish to carry the load, and Jenny noted that Dante treated them gently, like fretful children whom he knew were incapable of coping with any heavy responsibility.

He was The Man.

In every respect, Jenny thought, having long lost her resentment over his dominating strength of mind and purpose. Not many people had the force of will to do what had to be done, and he didn't use his power without any sense of caring. She'd seen the caring in action, felt it for herself, and understood why his grandfather had placed so much confidence in him.

Only with Dante was Marco completely relaxed. Lucia he more or less indulgently tolerated because she never showed any sign of being unhappy about his dying. As for herself, Marco indulged himself with her, reliving memories that encompassed his whole life, not just the part that was centred on his lost son.

Conversations with him were not the strain she had expected them to be, particularly whenever he insisted that Dante or Lucia leave them alone together. He didn't question her about Antonio's life in Australia which she would have found difficult, and she enjoyed listening to his memories: his boyhood and family background, meeting his Isabella and the life they'd had together, how he'd built up his huge business empire, the hotels, the forums, the pride he took in them, the pride he took in Dante, who would carry what he'd built into the future, not waste it.

'A good boy…'

She didn't know how many times she heard that phrase, always imbued with love and approval. She grew genuinely fond of the old man and felt sorry for the life that was slipping away—a remarkable life, fully lived in so many ways. Sometimes he patted her hand, saying she was, 'A good girl,' making her wish she *was* his grand-daughter.

Though, she was glad there was no blood relationship when she was alone with Dante. They spent siestas and the nights together, pleasuring each other, and it wasn't only hot, urgent sex. She loved the physical intimacy of simply being held close to him, going to sleep in his arms, the mental intimacy of being locked into a secret world of their own.

Quite often they talked late into the night, she relating things his grandfather had told her, he elaborating on them, connecting them to the life he'd shared with Marco. She told him things about her own life she'd never confided to anyone, even about the nasty clash with the sleazy welfare officer. Somehow it didn't matter that he knew. This was time out of time, and once it was over, nothing she said to him would come back to hurt her. The one thing she wasn't open about was how much her heart had filled with loving him.

Occasionally she worried that Lucia was suspicious about how close they were—unguarded moments when a look or a comment revealed an intimacy that shouldn't be there, not between cousins. She grew more and more conscious of Lucia watching, making snide little remarks about how amazingly occupied Dante was with her company, how considerate he was to her needs— taking her off to various parts of the island for her to paint pretty landscapes, staying with her while she did them— and how incredibly well they clicked when they talked.

'Anyone would think you were lovers,' she tossed off one morning while they were lazing on lounges by the pool, her keen bright eyes sharply observing their response.

It was impossible for Jenny to stop a tide of heat from racing into her cheeks.

'You're embarrassing Bella again, Lucia,' Dante rolled out with an air of impatience over her pretend playfulness. 'I promised Nonno I'd look after her as best I could and I'm grateful that Bella is making it easy for me. Which is something you rarely do.'

'No fun in that, dear cousin,' she flipped back at him.

He glowered a warning. 'Don't inflict your brand of fun on Bella.'

'Big Brother is watching,' she intoned in a robotic voice, her eyes merrily mocking him.

'Nonno asked me to,' he said, as though he was simply fulfilling a duty of care.

Lucia smiled sweetly. 'Well, Little Sister is also watching, Dante, and one day…one day you'll slip up and I'll get the better of you.'

He shrugged. 'A rather petty aim in life.'

'But, oh, so satisfying,' she drawled, relaxing back on her lounge with a smug air.

Dante brushed off the incident as just another gambit

from Lucia to make mischief, wanting to discomfort Jenny into being less responsive to him. Still, it made her more wary of how she acted in front of Lucia and only truly relaxed in his company when they were alone together.

Marco grew too weak to leave his bedroom suite. Visits to him were necessarily brief. He was in bad pain and his doctor organised a morphine drip, monitored by shifts of nurses to ensure he had twenty-four-hour care. Warned that the end was near, Dante immediately notified Sophia and Roberto to come to Capri and be on hand for their father's last days.

My last days, too, Jenny thought, but she couldn't wish for Marco to suffer any longer than he had to. Nor did she speak of *the end* to Dante, knowing he drew comfort from having her to come to at night. The imminent loss of his beloved grandfather weighed heavily on his heart. Being with her was helping him through a bad time, and Jenny refused to spoil one precious moment with him by bringing up what could wait until there was no longer any need for her to be Bella.

The role did not worry her anymore. Dante had been right. It didn't hurt anyone, and Marco had liked having her here—someone with whom he could recount his life, dwelling on what had been good for him. She had served him well and had no regrets over anything she'd done.

The morning of Sophia's and Roberto's expected arrival came. Dante left her bed to return to his own suite and get ready for the day—one that was sure to be harrowing for him, Jenny thought, having to handle his aunt's and uncle's emotions, as well as his own. She watched him walk towards the door that linked their suites, hoping she could take some of the burden off his broad shoulders, make herself available to be sympathetic company.

She had thrown off the bedclothes and was heading for her own bathroom to get ready for the day when he opened the connecting door. He stepped inside his suite, and Lucia's voice rang out in gleeful triumph.

'Got you!'

Jenny froze in her tracks, shock ripping through her.

Lucia was in Dante's bedroom.

He was naked, coming from her suite.

His voice cracked out in anger. 'What the hell are you doing here?'

Then he slammed the door shut behind him, protecting her, but Jenny knew, knew as sickeningly as the nausea that rolled through her, that Lucia would revel in telling Marco that Dante was sleeping with his cousin. Never mind if the shock of it killed him. Lucia would not deny herself the pleasure and satisfaction of taking Dante down in his grandfather's eyes before he died.

Dante glared at Lucia, his mind scrambling to grapple with the situation, knowing she would make capital out of it. Was there a price he could pay—anything she'd take to keep quiet about it and let Nonno die in peace?

She rolled off the top of his pristine bed—the bed he obviously hadn't slept in—and bounced to her feet, her face alight with malicious delight. 'I paid Nonno an early-morning visit and he asked me to fetch you, Dante. I knocked on your door but you didn't answer so I came in to wake you up.'

He'd forgotten to lock his door. Stupid oversight! And he should have stayed in his room, given that Nonno might want him at his side. No excuse that he had wanted to be with Jenny.

'Better get dressed,' Lucia mockingly advised him, heading for the door she'd left ajar. 'I don't think Nonno will appreciate the *naked* evidence that you've seduced his precious Australian grand-daughter into sleeping with her first cousin.'

'Wait!' he commanded, needing to stop her, to reason with her.

She scuttled the rest of the way to the door, hanging onto it for a moment to throw back at him, 'Oh, I can't wait to tell Nonno what you've been up to.'

'Lucia, don't!' he shouted at her, galvanised into action, wanting to grab her, shake some sense into her.

She laughed as she leapt into the corridor and shut the door in his face. By the time he wrenched it open again, she was running, putting distance between them too fast for Dante to catch her before she reached their grandfather's suite. Even if he did, he knew she would make a scene, and with him stark naked…

No. He had to get dressed, present himself to Nonno as fast as he could with a measure of calm dignity, minimise the damage. His mind jagged to Jenny. She must have heard Lucia. She'd be in shock, worried sick about this outcome from their intimacy. But he didn't have time to go to her. Nonno had to come first.

Clothes on, hair combed, mind tumbling through replies to Lucia's accusations, heart pumping hard as he strode towards a showdown he'd been unable to avoid.

The door to his grandfather's suite was open. He could hear Lucia reeling off a string of outrage, pretending to be appalled at his moral transgression.

'Having sex with his first cousin…it's disgusting, Nonno. Incestuous.' She loved rolling out that word. 'Dante has no morals at all. He has the arrogance to believe he can get away with anything. You have to—'

'No!' Dante thundered as he stepped into the room, jolting Lucia into turning to him.

'You can't order me around, you dirty beast!' she jeered.

'You've said your piece. Now get out.'

'I will not.' She folded her arms in defiant righteousness. 'I'm not going to let you lie your way out of this.'

'I have no intention of lying.' He shot an anxious look at his grandfather, who, surprisingly, did not appear to be upset or agitated, his wasted body lying completely still, his dark sunken eyes regarding Dante with the same trust he'd always shown. No shock in them at all.

Did he think Lucia had been lying?

'Leave me with Dante, Lucia,' he commanded in a wheezy whisper.

She instantly wheeled to him in protest. 'But, Nonno…'

'You heard him. Go!' Dante cut in fiercely, advancing on her, prepared to throw her out bodily if she refused to move.

'Go…' their grandfather weakly echoed.

Lucia huffed her displeasure at this second dismissal. She hated missing the fun, but had to accept that she couldn't push her presence any further. 'I've told you the absolute truth, Nonno. It's only right that you know what he's really like,' was her parting shot as she flounced to the door.

Dante shut it behind her, knowing she would eavesdrop if she could. He wouldn't give her *that* satisfaction. It was impossible to pretend that she had been lying, impossible to betray the trust in his grandfather's eyes, though he had been betraying it these past two months, presenting Jenny as Bella, maintaining the fiction. He couldn't do it anymore, not now at the end.

He sucked in a deep breath, walked over to the chair at his grandfather's bedside, drew it close, sat down, reached out and took his hand, pressing it gently, his eyes begging for understanding as he said, 'I'm sorry, Nonno.'

The almost skeletal hand squeezed back. There was no criticism in his eyes, no judgement, only trust. 'No need…for apology.'

'There's a lot I must tell you.'

'No…only one thing.' He struggled for more breath.

Dante waited, his mind racing in search of the one thing his grandfather wanted to know—the one thing that was more important to him than all of Lucia's vitriolic accusations.

He wasn't expecting the question that came. He hadn't ever asked it of himself. Nor had Jenny. It completely bypassed the deception they had played and bored straight into his heart. A simple question, loaded with the implicit demand for a truthful answer.

'Do you love her?'

CHAPTER FIFTEEN

JENNY stopped her fretful pacing at the sound of the connecting door being opened. Was it Dante or Lucia? Driven by the frightened need to hide her own nakedness and look presentable, she'd thrown on some clothes, pushed her feet into sandals, brushed her hair into reasonable order, and tried to apply some makeup, though her hands had been shaking too much to attempt more than basic stuff. She had no idea how many minutes had passed since Lucia had confronted Dante in his bedroom, but her heart was still racing so hard, her hand instinctively lifted to cover its wild beat as she whirled to face whoever came into her room.

Dante!

She sagged with relief.

Though the relief was short-lived.

His grim face told her he'd been unable to stop Lucia from doing her worst, running to his grandfather with the news that they were lovers. Her heart sank. The deception they'd played successfully right up to this eleventh hour had surely come unstuck. Dante could not carry the horrible stigma of sleeping with his first cousin.

'You've been alone, Jenny?' he asked, sharp concern in his eyes as he crossed the room to where she stood.

'Yes.'

'I'm sorry. I'm grievously at fault for not locking my door, allowing Lucia the chance to—'

'Tell me what's happened,' she cut in, only too aware that what was done was done and couldn't be undone.

He drew her into his embrace, held her tightly for a few moments, then eased back, his eyes begging her to understand and support whatever he'd put into place.

'Lucia got to Nonno before I could. She told him I'd been sleeping with you. He ordered Lucia out. He didn't want to listen to any explanations from me. He was concerned about you. He asked me to bring you to him now, Jenny. Can you handle this?'

No escape.

There never had been from the moment Dante had walked into her life.

She was tied to him for as long as he wanted her.

'I'll do my best,' she said.

Worry lines drew his brows together. 'If you'll just give him the answers he wants, Jenny, give him whatever he needs from you…'

'I understand,' she said, trembling inside at the prospect of facing Marco and having to set his mind at rest.

'Thank you. Let's go then. I told the nurse to lock his door and keep Lucia out. He's waiting for us.'

He dropped his embrace and hugged her shoulders as they began to move, assuring her they were together in this, right to the end. He wouldn't abandon her in Marco's room, though what either of them could do there was very much up in the air.

She half-expected to find Lucia lurking along the corridor, revelling in her triumph over Dante, wanting to gauge how much trouble she had caused, but it was empty of any other presence apart from theirs. Tension tore at her nerves as they waited for the nurse to let them in to be with Marco. She fiercely wished there had never been any deception, yet without it, there would not have been this time with Dante. This final hurdle had to be crossed…somehow.

The door opened. Dante ushered her to the chair at Marco's bedside. He stood just behind her, one hand resting on her shoulder in a show of togetherness. His grandfather lay still, his eyes closed, his face so gaunt and grey, her heart instantly went out to the old man who clearly had little time left in this world. He'd always been kind to her and she desperately wanted to treat him with kindness in these last hours of his life.

'I'm here, Marco,' she said softly.

A little smile curved his lips. 'Good girl!' he murmured, then slowly lifted his eyelids, turned his head on the pillow and looked directly into her eyes. 'Now tell me, my dear…who are you?'

For one paralysing moment, she thought he had lost the power to recognise people. Then she realised there was no dulling of intelligence in the knowing dark eyes that sought the truth from her, and shock pummelled her again.

Marco knew she wasn't Bella.

She had no idea when he had come to this conclusion. Maybe he had suspected it from quite early on, given that he had accepted the sketchiest details of Antonio's life in Australia without probing for more. Maybe the fact that she and Dante were lovers had clinched it for him. The grandson he knew so well would not have slept with his first cousin.

A huge sense of relief swept through her as the burden of deception was lifted. She would not be breaking Dante's trust to speak the truth now. He'd asked her to give his grandfather whatever he wanted.

'My name is Jenny Kent,' she said openly and honestly.

They were the words she should have spoken in the hospital when she'd woken up from the coma. Dante's fingers dug into her shoulder with bruising strength. Was he appalled at her confession? It was too late to take it back. Besides, it was right to give up the truth. Marco's eyes told her it was right.

'I was Bella's friend,' she went on. 'Neither of us had family and we became like sisters. I shared her apartment and she lent me her Italian name so I could work in the Venetian Forum. I'm sorry, Marco, but she was the one who died in the car accident, and the authorities mistakenly identified her as me.'

The whole story poured out, from convincing herself that taking on Bella's identity for a while would not harm anyone to Dante's insistence that she come to Capri in Bella's place. '...because he loves you, Marco, and he couldn't bear to tell you Antonio's daughter was dead, too. I hoped I knew enough about Bella's life to...to satisfy you...but I can tell you now—' she leant forward earnestly '—your grand-daughter was a wonderful person, generous and kind, endlessly curious about everything, more fun than I am and I wish she had been alive for you.'

He lifted his hand to wave aside her concern, dragging in breath to speak. 'You…you are more important, Jenny.'

'Me? But I'm no one,' she protested painfully.

'Listen to me…'

The rasping urgency in his voice silenced her. It hurt to watch him summoning the strength to speak, the effort it took to deliver what he wanted to say. All she could do was respect his request for her to listen and hope that Dante wasn't hating her too much for spilling out his part in the deception. Maybe she should have taken all responsibility for it herself, as she had once planned to, but then he would still be guilty of sleeping with a woman he believed to be his first cousin. Better that he hear the truth.

Her heart ached with the knowledge she had just ended her time with him. Jenny Kent had no part to play here. When the helicopter arrived with Roberto and Sophia, it could take her away, out of the Rossini family where she had never belonged, out of Dante's life where she wouldn't belong, either.

Marco wheezed in another deep breath and said, 'I saw your feelings for Dante…in the portrait.'

No, no, no, her mind screamed. She'd tried so hard to hide them. For his grandfather to point them up in front of Dante now…

'I put it together then,' he went on. 'No family likeness…your reticence about Antonio…so many careful reservations…Dante, too watchful…'

So soon, Jenny thought, anguished over being seen as a fraud almost from the very beginning.

'Why didn't you say, Nonno?' Dante asked, his voice gruff with the emotions coursing through him.

Marco's gaze lifted to his grandson. He struggled to reply. 'I wanted her to stay…to observe the connection between you…to see if you would come to feel for her…what I felt for my Isabella. To have a good woman at your side, Dante…sympathetic, strong, caring, sharing. I wished that for you, my boy…more than I wished for a grand-daughter I'd never known.'

Tears welled into Jenny's eyes. This was a dying man's dream, wanting to believe his beloved grandson would be happily settled with a good woman in the future. It wasn't going to happen. Not with her. As much as she would love to be at Dante's side for the rest of her life, she knew his involvement with her was only a *pro temps* thing, bound up in sexual pleasure and secrecy, but she remained silent, unable to bring herself to tell Marco that. It was up to Dante to speak the truth this time.

But he said nothing and Marco reached out to her. 'Give me your hand, Jenny.'

She did, desperately blinking the tears away so she could meet his gaze without blurred vision.

'I want you to know…you've been very good for me.'

The tears welled again. She couldn't stop them.

Marco pressed her hand gently. 'You do love Dante, don't you?'

Such a direct question…Dante's voice in her head, telling her to give the answers his grandfather wanted, his hand squeezing her shoulder again. 'Yes,' she choked out. It was the truth anyway.

Marco's breath whistled out on a long sigh. He sucked in again. 'Don't waste time, Dante. Marry her soon.'

Marry?

'I will, Nonno,' came the strong promise.

The blank shock in Jenny's mind receded at the quick realisation that Dante was giving the answer Marco wanted to hear.

'In the safe…in my study…give her Isabella's ring.'

'It will honour our commitment to each other. Thank you.' Dante's voice was more furred this time.

'You have my blessing. Both of you.'

He patted Jenny's hand.

She couldn't speak over the huge lump of emotion in her throat.

'You'll always be with us, Nonno,' Dante said.

'Good boy.' A last benevolent smile, then, 'Go now. I must rest…for Sophia and Roberto.'

Dante stepped forward, leaned over and kissed both his grandfather's sunken cheeks. 'Rest easy,' he murmured. 'And thank you for all you have given me.'

The dark eyes he turned to Jenny as he straightened up were shiny wet, pleading eloquently for one last effort from her. She swallowed hard to clear her throat, stood up and kissed Marco as Dante had, pouring her own genuine fondness for the old man into what were probably her last words to him.

'Thank you for letting me be Bella. It made me wish you were my grandfather. And thank you for giving me time with Dante. I will always love you for that, Marco.'

No matter what, she thought.

Dante's arm around her waist scooped her away from his grandfather's bedside, swept her quickly to the door the nurse opened and closed behind them. Once outside in the corridor, he swung her into his embrace, tucking her head into the curve of his neck and shoulder, his chest heaving against hers, his cheek rubbing over her hair as he fought to bring his churning emotions under control.

Jenny held him tightly around the waist, hugging this final closeness to him, wanting him to take comfort from it. At least he now knew her confession had not been a mistake. Marco had wanted it. And what had ensued from it was not her fault. She had carried through what Dante had asked of her, and he would not be holding her like this if he didn't feel a mountain of grateful relief.

'*Dio!*' Lucia's shrill voice rang out again. 'You two are absolutely disgusting! Right outside Nonno's door!'

Dante lifted his head. 'Oh, shut up, Lucia!' he barked at her. 'Jenny is not Bella. She was only pretending to be for Nonno's sake, for my sake. He knows that.'

'Not Bella?'

Jenny turned her head and saw Lucia in a frozen pose of utter incredulity.

'Not Bella,' Dante repeated emphatically. 'Jenny Kent, the woman I'm going to marry. And Nonno has just given us his blessing, so you might as well go away and sulk over your failure to *get me.*'

'Marry!'

Jenny empathised with Lucia's shock. What was Dante thinking to make such a public announcement? He couldn't really mean to marry her, could he?

'You're looking at my future wife, so be careful how you treat her, Lucia.'

The warning was loaded with threat. Dante's emotions were still running high. He dropped his embrace, hugged her shoulders again, and walked her straight towards his meddling cousin. Jenny's own emotions were in chaos. Her mind was clogged, incapable of making sense of anything. Her feet went with him, letting him be the puppet-master again.

'That's the helicopter arriving now,' he threw at Lucia as the distinctive sound came from overhead. 'Go and meet your mother and Uncle Roberto. Jenny and I have other business to attend to for Nonno.'

Lucia's face contorted with rage. 'You…' She threw her hands up in the air in furious exasperation. 'You get away with everything!' Then she spun on her heel and marched off ahead of them, her back rigidly rejecting any congratulations on an engagement she could never have envisaged.

Neither had Jenny. Was Dante now determined on carrying out his grandfather's wishes—his deathbed wishes? He was certainly set on it while Marco was still alive. Maybe afterwards, as well. They reached Marco's study before she could sort through her feelings about what was happening. Dante released her and moved to a painting on the wall, swinging it aside to reveal a safe.

'Stop!' The word croaked from her throat, driven out by a desperate need to understand the situation.

He looked back at her, resolute purpose carved on his face, the dark eyes burning up the distance between them, shooting a debilitating bolt of heat through her, weakening her own resolve. She loved him. She wanted to be with him for the rest of her life. But was this real or just another deception?

'You can't marry me just because your grandfather wants you to, Dante,' she cried.

His chin jerked up as though she had hit him. Aggression flared. It pumped through every stride he took back across the room. Her heart kicked into a gallop as she felt the overwhelming power of the man directed straight at her.

She didn't move.

Couldn't move.

He cupped her face, strong hands holding her captive, his eyes blazing into hers. '*I* want to,' he declared with vehement passion. 'And *you* are not going to run out on me, Jenny Kent.'

It almost killed her to say it but she had to. She would not go along with another deception, not one that involved her whole life. 'It's over, Dante. Your need for me has no basis anymore. Your grandfather…'

'This has nothing to do with my grandfather.'

'Of course it has! You said what he wanted to hear. You asked *me* to say what he wanted to hear.'

'Did you lie, Jenny?' he shot at her point-blank, his eyes drilling hers with such penetrating force, all her insides felt pummelled.

Her mind flew into a chaotic whirl. If she admitted the truth, would he wield it like a weapon, beating her into submission to his will?

His fingers pressed at her temples, demanding entry to her thoughts, feeling the wildly leaping pulse under his touch. 'You said you loved me,' he bored in. 'I don't believe that was a lie. All this time with you…I've felt your love in so many ways, you can't deny it. I won't let you deny it!'

But he hadn't said he loved her. Not once had he said it or even implied it. 'I won't be a puppet wife for you!' she cried in desperate protest. 'I want the man I marry to love me, Dante.'

'You think I don't?' His brows jagged together. His eyes fiercely challenged any disbelief on her part. 'I love everything about you. Mind, heart, body and soul…everything! I love you. I need you in my life. I won't let you go.'

Mind, heart, body and soul… A fountain of joy exploded inside her.

'Now say you love me,' he insisted with riveting intensity. 'I know you do. Say it!'

The words spilled out at his command. 'Yes. Yes, I do.' Yet was love enough? Doubt screeched through her mind. 'But, Dante, I wasn't born to your world. You know I'm not a suitable wife for you.'

'I don't care about your background,' he declared in ruthless dismissal of it. 'I've been with you day and night long enough to know the person you are inside, Jenny. It's the person I want to spend my life with.'

Still she couldn't quite bring herself to accept it. 'You shouldn't judge on what we've shared here. It's not your normal life, Dante. Nor mine,' she pleaded, frightened that their relationship wouldn't stand up under other pressures.

'I told you before. My world is what I make it. What *we* will make it together, Jenny. Trust me. It will be good.'

He spoke with such forceful conviction, her fear wavered. She wanted to trust him, yet if he ever came to see her as a mistake, regretting a decision made in an emotionally fraught moment...

'How can you be so certain it will stay good?' she pleaded, desperately worried that she might fail to meet his expectations of a wife.

There wasn't the slightest glimmer of doubt in his eyes. His whole formidable energy force was focused on making her believe. 'Jenny, at the centre of our marriage will be the love we have for each other. Our life will revolve around that, I promise you.'

He believed what he said. *He* would make it happen. What Dante Rossini set out to do, he did.

Jenny's defensive resistance started to melt. Hope surged into her battered mind. She was a survivor. She could adapt to circumstances. Hadn't she done so umpteen times? So long as Dante loved her, she could make their marriage work, too, do whatever had to be done.

'Are you sure, Dante?' she asked, needing to hear his indomitable confidence once again.

'Yes, my love. Very sure.'

His eyes said, 'Enough talk.'

He dropped his hold on her face, his arms sliding around her, bringing her into the warmth and strength of his love, linking them together, bonding them in the union that their marriage would make firm forever.

He kissed her, and Jenny gave up her heart to him.

With the deepest passion she had ever felt.

With all the love she'd tried to keep bottled up.

With trust in the future they would build together.

And afterwards, she accepted the ring that had been the symbol of Marco Rossini's love for his Isabella. She gazed down at it, understanding how very special a gift it was, representing the faith Marco had that their marriage would be as happy as his had been.

'Do you know what a ruby means?' Dante asked.

She shook her head. It was a magnificent ruby, surrounded by diamonds, probably worth a fortune, and she was silently vowing it would never leave her finger, never be mislaid or lost or stolen from her.

'A priceless love,' Dante said softly. 'I know that's what I have with you, Jenny, and I'll always cherish it.'

She looked up, saw in his eyes the promise of everything she had ever dreamed of in her long years of lonely survival, and knew she was truly blessed. This wonderful, amazing, beautiful man would be there for her, filling the rest of her life with love.

CHAPTER SIXTEEN

Four Months Later

JENNY woke up in the Rossini palazzo in Venice and a happy excitement instantly welled up in her. This was her wedding day. She rolled out of bed to draw the curtains on the long windows. The sun was shining. Venice was shining. She smiled and lifted her hand for the beautiful ruby and diamond ring to shine in the light. Another ring would join it today—Dante's ring—but this one would always be very special.

'Isabella,' she murmured, knowing it was the memory of his beloved wife that had been foremost in Marco's mind when he had sent Dante on his mission to bring Antonio's daughter to him, and it was the memory of their love that had kept Marco silent when he could have rightly denounced her as a fraud and sent her packing—the same kind of love he wanted Dante to know and have.

If it had not been for the two Isabellas, grand-daughter and grand-mother, she would never have met

Dante. Her life would have moved along a very different path, instead of which, here she was, about to marry the most wonderful man in the world. And it was not only a marriage blessed by his grandfather, but happily embraced by the rest of the Rossini family.

Even by Lucia. More or less. Poking her nose into all the wedding arrangements, advising Jenny at every turn, meddling so much Dante had confronted her over such zealous interest, suspecting some hidden agenda designed to spoil the big day.

'I actually quite like your chosen bride, Dante,' she had loftily declared. 'There's not a bitchy bone in her body. And given the power she obviously has over your life, I have hopes she might show up a few flaws in you that I'll enjoy making use of. But first and foremost, I would find it quite intolerable if the Rossini name was not attached to the most spectacular high-society wedding of the year. It's a matter of family pride. And the only way to downplay your bride being a Cinderella is to highlight your status as a billion-dollar prince, never mind your feet of clay.'

'Maybe you'd like to advise me on what shoes to wear,' he'd answered dryly, deciding Lucia's motives were reasonably free of malicious intent.

Jenny hadn't thought there was any at all. Lucia enjoyed showing off her expertise in creating a social event, enjoyed 'Cinderella's' total ignorance of where to go and what to do. Jenny Kent, who had nothing else to her name, *was* much more to her liking than Bella the cousin, who would have rivalled her own position in the family.

Sophia, also, had closely involved herself with the

wedding plans, insisting she take on the role of mother of the bride, since Jenny had no family of her own. She didn't have her daughter's drive for organisation, but fluttered around, being supportive. An ineffective mother, Jenny thought, observing how Lucia imposed her own will on Sophia, who invariably wilted over any decision-making but was always well meaning.

As were Roberto and his partner, Jonathon. They had been having a lovely time refurbishing the palazzo's grand reception room for the wedding party that would follow the marriage ceremony in the cathedral. Apparently Marco had not wanted to be openly faced with his son's gay life, but Dante had no reservations about it, and Roberto was delighted that the family ban had been lifted on Jonathon being with him—his joy in this freedom overflowing into a warm benevolence towards Jenny, seeking her approval of the décor changes they had been making, wanting to please.

All in all it seemed to Jenny that the family had grasped her and Dante's wedding as an affirmation of life moving on after the sadness of losing Marco. Even on the day he died the revelation of her real identity and the news of her engagement to Dante had been a distraction from their grief, and there had also been some solace in knowing that Marco had given his blessing to the marriage and had gone to his final rest in a happy, peaceful state of mind.

He'd seen Isabella's ring on her finger and smiled... his last smile. She and Dante had been with him at the end, Dante holding his hand. She could imagine him smiling in spirit today as Dante took her hand in marriage, and she silently promised him her love for his grandson would be as unwavering as Isabella's had been for him.

The blood-red heart of the ruby glowed at her.

A priceless love.

Dante stood in the grand foyer of the palazzo, waiting for his bride to come down the staircase, which was festooned with white ribbons and roses. Roberto and Jonathon were fussing around, assuring themselves that all the floral arrangements in the foyer were as stunning as they should be for when the guests would arrive.

They had already passed approval on the flotilla of black-and-gold gondolas outside, saying that they looked magnificent and the gondoliers splendid in their matching uniforms. The musicians in the lead gondola had also pleased them, perfectly attired in formal black dinner suits and white ties. They had reported that the tenor was in fine voice, entertaining the crowd of spectators lining the canal with love songs while they waited to see the bride and groom.

None of this really mattered to Dante, except in so far as he wanted Jenny to be happy with everything on their wedding day. He loved seeing her glow with pleasure, her lovely amber eyes lit with joy and love for him. She was so different to all the other women he'd known, so very special. Uniquely special.

He was glad his grandfather had seen that she was the right wife for him, pushing him into realising it before he'd thought of it himself. Though he would have come to it. All along, he had wanted to keep Jenny with him, sharing with her what he could not imagine sharing with anyone else. Not once had he looked ahead to her walking out of his life. She was there for him. Always would be now.

We'll have what you had with your Isabella, Nonno, he thought, a little stab of sadness in his heart that his grandfather couldn't be here to see them wed. But they had his blessing and he'd died content with the outcome of the mission to Australia, not getting to know a grand-daughter but a grand-daughter-in-law who had won his approval in every sense…Jenny, who had done so much good.

Even with Lucia, who seemed to have given up mischief-making these past few months in favour of being Jenny's chief advisor on how to fit in with what was expected of a Rossini in any public arena. He gave her an appreciative smile as she came prancing down the staircase, Sophia in tow, both of them looking fabulous in frilly, fuchsia pink designer gowns and wearing happy grins on their faces.

'We're coming down to get the full effect of the bride making her first appearance,' Lucia announced. 'You only have to cool your heels for another minute or two, Dante.'

'Thank you, production manager,' he said, grinning back at her.

She preened. 'I happen to be good at it.'

'Yes,' he agreed. 'I think you would make a brilliant special events organiser in our hotels, if you ever have a mind to take on such a position.'

One eyebrow arched in surprise. 'You'd let me do that?'

'If you really want it, yes. I can't imagine you not making a great success of it.'

Lucia hated failure as much as he did, and if she did seize this opportunity, it might give her a sense of power that would be constructive instead of destructive.

'I'll think about it,' she said, looking immensely pleased. 'We need to get this wedding right first.' She cast a critical eye over him. 'I have to concede you are star material, Dante, but you are about to be outshone by the bride.'

'As it should be,' he replied.

She laughed and turned to stand beside him, Sophia next to her, Roberto and Jonathon arranging themselves on his other side, all faces uplifted as they watched for Jenny to appear.

His bride…

Love and pride swelled his heart as she came floating down the stairs, a vision of such ethereal beauty in her glorious gown and veil, the need to touch her, to assure himself she was real powered through him. He had to force himself to remain still, let her enjoy this moment in the spotlight—his Jenny, who had struggled to survive with so little in her life. He wanted to give her everything.

As she reached the last stair, he did step forward, holding out his hand to take hers.

'Will I do?' she asked, her lovely eyes twinkling with happy confidence, but if she needed some vocal assurance from him, Dante was not about to fail her.

'Beautifully,' he declared, his voice a husky throb of emotion.

She gave him her hand.

And so much more, Dante thought.

A love that filled his life with a deeper pleasure than he had ever known.

A love that cared about everything he did.

A love that had no price on it.

True love.

And he was absolutely committed to giving it right back to her.

* * * * *

BOUND BY THE MARCOLINI DIAMONDS

MELANIE MILBURNE

Melanie Milburne says: one of the greatest joys of being a writer is the process of falling in love with the characters and then watching as they fall in love with each other. I am an absolutely hopeless romantic. I fell in love with my husband on our second date and we even had a secret engagement, so you see it must have been destined for me to be a Mills & Boon author! The other great joy of being a romance writer is hearing from readers. You can hear all about the other things I do when I'm not writing and even drop me a line at: www.melaniemilburne.com.au.

Dear Reader,

Well before I started writing I was a devoted reader of romance. Whilst juggling family and career and further study I used to treat myself to armfuls of Mills & Boon novels and indulge in a reading fest that would last for days. One of my favourite authors was Emma Darcy. I loved her passionately intense stories and full-of-life characters.

In the year 2000 I came second in the Emma Darcy Award in Australia. I had only been writing about a year so it was an incredible thrill. But what was even more exciting was when Emma met with me privately at the RWA conference in Sydney to talk about my entry. During those few minutes she expressed a belief in my talent that has inspired me, encouraged me and sustained me through my journey as a writer ever since.

To have my name joined with hers all these years later in a two-in-one book is truly a pinch-me moment!

I hope you enjoy our stories and many more to come.

Warmest wishes,

Melanie Milburne

I have often seen books dedicated to editors or agents in the past, and thought—No, I don't need to do that. This is business. But I am afraid I cannot write another book without publicly thanking my current editor, Jenny Hutton, who has been the most amazing support to me both professionally and personally. This one is for you, Jenny, and I hope we get to do many more together. XX

CHAPTER ONE

IT SEEMED like only weeks ago that Sabrina had attended her best friend's wedding, now she was attending her funeral. Any funeral was sad, but a double one had to be the worst, she thought as Laura and her husband Ric's coffins were solemnly carried out of the church by the dark-suited pallbearers.

Sabrina caught the eye of the tallest of the men bearing Ric's coffin, but quickly shifted her gaze, her heart starting and stopping like an old engine. Those coal-black eyes had communicated much more to her than was fitting for a funeral. Even with her head well down, she could still feel the scorch of his gaze on her, the sensitive skin on the back of her neck feeling as if a thousand nerves were dancing with excitement in anticipation of the stroke of his hand, or the burning brush of his sensual lips.

Sabrina cuddled Molly close to her chest and joined the rest of the mourners outside the church, taking some comfort in the fact that at only four months old the little baby would not remember the tragic accident that had taken both her parents from her. Unlike Sabrina, Molly would not remember the sickly sweet smell of the lilies and the sight of the grief-stricken faces, nor would she remember the burial, nor watch in crushing despair as her mother was lowered into the ground, knowing that she was now all alone in the world.

The procession moved to the cemetery, and after a brief but poignant service there the mourners moved on to Laura's stepmother's house for refreshments.

Ingrid Knowles was in her element as the grieving hostess. She brandished a rarely empty glass of wine as she chatted her way through the crowd of mourners, her make-up still intact, every strand of her perfectly coiffed bottle-blonde hair lacquered firmly in place.

Sabrina kept a low profile, hovering in the background to keep Molly from being disturbed by the at-times rowdy chatter. Most of Laura and Ric's close friends had left soon after the service—apart from Mario Marcolini. From the moment he had entered the house he had stood with his back leaning indolently against the wall near the bay window, with a brooding expression on his arrestingly handsome face, not speaking, not drinking…just watching.

Sabrina tried not to look at him, but every now and again her eyes would drift back to him seemingly of their own volition, and, each time they did, she encountered his dark, cynical gaze centred on hers.

She quickly looked away again, her heart skipping a beat and her skin breaking out in a moist wave of heat as she remembered what had happened the last time they had been alone together.

She was almost glad when Molly started to become restless so she could escape to another room to see to the little baby's needs.

When Sabrina came back out a few minutes later, Mario was no longer leaning against the wall. She let out a breath of relief, assuming he had left, when all of a sudden she felt every hair on the back of her neck rise to attention when she felt a hard male body brush against her from behind.

'I did not expect to see you again so soon,' Mario said in his deeply accented, mellifluous voice.

Sabrina took a shaky step forward and slowly turned around, cradling Molly protectively against her breasts. 'No, I…I guess not.' She lowered her eyes from the startling intensity of his dark brown ones, her brain scrambling for something else to say to fill the gaping silence. What was it about this man that made her feel like a nervous schoolgirl instead of a mature woman of twenty-five? He was so sophisticated, so urbane, such a man of the world, and she was so—she hated to say it but it was true—gauche.

'Um, it was very good of you to come all the way back to Australia when you'd only just left,' she mumbled.

'Not at all,' he said in a tone that had a rough, sandpaper sort of quality to it. 'It was the least I could do.'

There was another loaded silence.

Sabrina moistened the parchment of her lips, trying not to look at him, trying not to think of how close he was standing to her, and how foolishly she had reacted to that closeness just a matter of weeks ago. Would she *ever* be able to erase that totally embarrassing—no, mortifying— few minutes from her mind?

'Laura's stepmother seems to be enjoying herself,' Mario commented.

Sabrina met his sardonic, midnight gaze. 'Yes. I'm kind of glad now Laura's father isn't around to see it,' she said. 'Laura would be so embarrassed if…' She bit her lip, unable to speak, fresh tears springing to her eyes as she bowed her head.

She felt a warm and very large hand touch her briefly on the shoulder, the tingling sensation it set off under her skin feeling as if a million bubbles of an effervescent liquid had been injected into her blood.

She brought her gaze back to his once more, a rueful grimace contorting her face. 'I'm sorry,' she said. 'I'm trying to be strong for Molly's sake, but sometimes I just…'

'Do not apologise,' he said in that same deep, gravel-rough tone. He paused for a moment and, lowering his gaze to the sleeping baby in her arms, asked, 'Do you think Molly is aware of what is happening?'

Sabrina looked down at the tiny baby and released a sigh. 'She's only four months old, so it's hard to say. She is feeding and sleeping well, but that's probably because she is used to me looking after her occasionally.'

Another silence tightened the air, tighter, tighter and tighter, until Sabrina could feel the tension building in her throat. She felt like a hand was round her neck, the pressure slowly building and building.

'Is there somewhere we can speak together in private?' Mario asked.

Sabrina felt that same invisible hand suddenly reach inside her and clutch at her insides and squeeze. She had sworn after the last time that she would never allow herself to be alone again with Mario Marcolini. It was too danger-ous. The man was a notorious playboy; even in a state of grief he was unable to shake off his air of rakish charm. She felt the warm waves of male interest washing over her even now, those sleep-with-me dark eyes of his sending a shiver of reaction racing up and down her spine every time they came into contact with hers.

Her eyes flicked briefly to his mouth, her stomach

knotting all over again at the thought of how she had been tempted to taste its promise of passion in the past. Her lips had never felt quite the same since, nor had the rest of her body, which had been jammed up against him so tightly she had felt every hard, male ridge of him…

Sabrina gave herself a mental shake. This was hardly the time or place to be thinking of her one and only lapse into stupidity. She squared her shoulders and nodded towards a room off the main living area. 'There's a small study through there,' she said. 'It's where I put Molly's pram and changing bag earlier.'

She led the way, conscious of his gaze on her with every not-quite-steady step she took. No doubt he was comparing her to all the glamorous women he cavorted with back home in Europe, she thought with a kernel of bitterness lodging in her throat. His latest mistress was a catwalk model, tall and reed-slim, with platinum-blonde hair and breasts that would have made sleeping on her stomach uncomfortable if not impossible. But then he had probably moved on to someone else by now. He was known for changing his girlfriends like some people changed their shirts.

It was a lifestyle Sabrina could not relate to at all. The three things she longed for most in life were love, stability and commitment, and she knew she would be nothing but a gullible fool if she thought for even a moment that someone like Mario Marcolini could give them to her. He might be as handsome as sin and as tempting as the devil, but he was way out of her league, and always would be. Her gauche attempt to get him to notice her at Molly's christening had more than confirmed that.

She opened the study door and, moving across to where the pram was, gently tucked Molly under the pink-bunny rug before turning to face Mario. Yet again she had to fight the urge not to stare at him. He was so impossibly good-looking it was heart-stopping even to glance at him. At six-feet-four, he towered over her five-feet-seven, and with that ink-black, glossy hair and those equally dark, glinting eyes he made her feel mousy and grey in comparison.

He closed the study door with a click that immediately dulled the sound of the chatter and clatter of the wake going on without them. It was like a volume switch suddenly being turned down; it made the silence of the study all the more intimidating, the closer confines of the room making her all too aware of the fact that he only had to take a stride or two to reach out and touch her.

His eyes met hers, holding them as if he had some sort of secret, magnetic power over her; she couldn't look away if she tried. 'We have a problem to solve and it needs to be solved quickly,' he said.

Sabrina paused for a moment to moisten her lips with the tip of her tongue. She had been preparing herself for this, but even so, now that it came to the crunch, she felt devastated. She knew what he was going to do. He was going to take Molly back to Italy with him and there would be nothing she could do to stop him. She would never see her little god-daughter again if the very rich, very powerful and very ruthless Mario Marcolini had anything to do with it.

'You have been informed that we have been appointed joint guardians of Molly, correct?' he said, still watching her with that brooding, hawk-like gaze.

Sabrina nodded, her throat moving up and down over a knot of despair. She had been informed a couple of days ago of the terms of the guardianship Laura and Ric had nominated in their wills. She had also been told it was going to be challenged by Laura's stepmother, who believed she and her new husband could offer Molly the more stable and secure future.

The lawyer had been up front about Sabrina's chances of keeping Molly in her care, and it didn't look good. The court would decide on the basis of the best interests of the child: for instance who had the most to offer in terms of security, of the child's welfare and future provision. Sabrina was not only single, but currently out of work, while Ingrid Knowles and her husband, Stanley, although on the wrong side of fifty, were more than well off and had made no secret of their wish for a child.

'Y-yes,' she said, running her tongue across her chalk-dry lips again. 'I am well aware of Laura and Ric's wishes, but the legal advice I have been given is I stand very little chance of fulfilling them due to, er, my current circumstances.'

He gave her an inscrutable look. 'Your current circumstances being that you are single, unemployed and lately labelled a home-wrecker, correct?'

As much as it galled Sabrina to agree with him, what choice did she have otherwise? The press had made her out to be a bed-hopping babysitter with her eyes on the main chance. She had wanted to defend herself, but knew she could not do so without upsetting the Roebourne children by exposing their father for the perfidious and lecherous creep he was.

'Pretty much,' she said with a grim set to her mouth. 'Laura would be heartbroken to think her stepmother will get custody of Molly. She hated Ingrid with a passion. She told me so only a few days before...' she gulped back her emotion '...before the accident.'

Mario began to slowly pace the room back and forth,

like a caged lion meticulously planning an escape. Sabrina stood with her arms crossed over her chest like a shield. She kept her breathing as shallow and steady as she could, but even so she felt her nostrils flare as the exotic spices of his aftershave insinuated their way into her system, making her feel intoxicated, as if she had breathed in a powerful, aromatic drug.

'I will not allow that woman and her husband to have full custody of Ric's child,' Mario said, turning to face her, his dark eyes diamond-hard with determination. 'I will do everything, and I mean *everything*, in my power to prevent it.'

Sabrina felt her heart sink at his adamant statement. This was it. This was the part where he would state his intention of taking Molly back with him to Italy. Her stomach churned with anguish; how could she let this happen? Surely there was something she could do? She had grown up without her mother, without someone who loved her and understood her. How could she let the very same thing happen to little Molly?

'I have a temporary solution,' Mario said.

'Y-you have?' Sabrina's voice was barely audible.

'We are Molly's godparents, and legally appointed guardians. These are both responsibilities I intend to take very seriously.'

'I understand that but, as you say, we are both responsible for her, and I too take those responsibilities equally seriously,' she said, wishing she had sounded more determined and less intimidated. Wishing she *felt* less intimidated.

His eyes held hers for a tense moment. 'Then we shall have to share those responsibilities in the best way we can.'

'What are you suggesting?' Sabrina asked, conscious of a frown tugging at her forehead. 'I live in Australia, you live in Italy. It's not as if we can share custody of an infant, or at least not in what the courts will acknowledge is an acceptable way with Molly's best interests at heart. She can't be shifted back and forth between countries. She's just a baby, for God's sake. I'm not sure what it's like in your country, but here the courts are big on what is best for the child.'

His jaw was set in an intractable line, his black-brown gaze still drilling into hers. 'Ric was my best friend,' he said. 'I will not stand by and let his daughter be brought up by a couple who in my opinion are not worthy of the custody of an animal, let alone a small infant.'

'All the same, I think it's going to be almost impossible to present a case against Ingrid and Stanley over Molly's custody,' she said, tearing her gaze away from his mouth with an effort. 'I don't know what else I can do. I have looked at this from every angle, and I can't help thinking the odds are against Laura's and Ric's wishes ever being granted.'

There was another silence, weighted with something Sabrina couldn't quite identify. She felt the tension in the air, the humidity of the atmosphere, the pressure of the unknown, the calm before the tumultuous, uncontrollable storm that was stealthily approaching.

'I think we should get married as soon as possible.'

The words fell into the silence like boulders into a calm pond. The rings went outwards, rolling towards her, each one threatening to swamp her. Waves of panic washed over her; she swallowed great, drowning mouthfuls of it before she could speak.

'W-what did you say?' she choked.

He gave her a level look. 'It is the only way we can secure Molly's future,' he said. 'We are her godparents; if we marry, it will convince the court we are the most suitable candidates for her guardianship.'

Sabrina felt her brain start to whirl like an out of control adventure-park ride. Surely she was hearing things; had he *really* just suggested they marry each other? They were practically strangers. They had only met twice, and each time had circled each other like wary opponents. How could she agree to such a preposterous plan?

'Think about it, Sabrina,' he said. 'I am a rich man who can provide everything Molly will ever need. You are an experienced hand at looking after infants and small children. We are also young enough to be good substitute-parents. It is a perfect solution.'

Sabrina finally located her voice, but it came out sounding like a rusty hinge. 'You're asking me to—to *marry* you?'

Mario's eyes flickered in irritation at her tone. 'It will not be a real marriage, if that is what is making you baulk at the prospect,' he said. 'We can each live our own lives— but of course you would have to live with me in Italy, at least until Molly is of an age when she does not need you so much. After that, we can reassess the situation and take appropriate action.'

Her grey eyes blinked at him, her soft mouth falling open, her cheeks developing a faint blush. 'Live with you…in Italy?' she said on a gulp.

Mario felt his annoyance rising at her. He was the one putting himself out on a limb here; he had sworn marriage was something he would never submit to. He loved his freedom; he relished every minute of being his own man, living the life he wanted to live without the ties of a permanent relationship. But, after receiving the news about his best friend's death, he'd realised he would have to step up to the plate, and quickly.

Ric had once risked his own life to save Mario's during a skiing trip in the Swiss Alps when they were nineteen. Mario knew he would not be alive and well today if it hadn't been for Ric's courage and persistence at digging him out of that avalanche with his bare hands. The bond of friendship that had always existed between them, had become so strong after that day Mario had felt sure even way back then that only death would be able to sever it.

Ric had trusted him to see to Molly's interests and he would honour that trust, even if it meant temporarily tying himself to a woman with a more than tarnished reputation. Sabrina Halliday was all demure girl-next-door on the outside, but Mario had tasted a tiny morsel of what was simmering on the inside of that slim but all-woman figure. No doubt that was why she was playing the hard-to-get game with him now. He knew how gold-diggers worked, and as far as he was concerned she was a text-book case. She might have genuine affection for Molly, but that didn't mean she wasn't aware of how much she could gain out of this situation.

'I am prepared to pay you for every year we remain married,' he said. 'I am even prepared to negotiate with the amount.'

The frown she gave him seemed too quick to be anything but genuine, but he was well used to the guiles of women with dollar signs in their eyes.

'You think I want to be *paid* to be your wife?' she asked.

He pinned her grey gaze with his. 'You can have what you want, Sabrina, name your figure. I want Molly under my care and I will pay anything to achieve it.'

This time her face went pale and her small, white teeth began to gnaw at her bottom lip. 'I think you've got the wrong idea about me—'

'Let's not dawdle any longer over this, Sabrina,' he cut her off impatiently. 'I realise moving to another country is a big step to take—but, with what has been happening here recently, do you not think it is an ideal time to escape from all the innuendo and speculation that has surrounded you?'

Sabrina felt her face crawl with colour. Just like everyone else in Sydney, he thought she was guilty. She could see it in his eyes, the way they ran over her as if he could see right through her clothes. The press hadn't done her any favours, certainly, but surely he of all people knew how the media worked? He had been subjected to it all of his life, so how unfair was it for him to so readily assume she was as she had been portrayed?

But *marry* him?

Her stomach dropped at the thought of being in the same country as him, let alone the same room. He was everything she was not. Hadn't she proved that by her clumsy attempt to kiss him that day? How could she possibly agree to marry him and subject herself to daily temptation? And, even more worrying, would she be able to withstand any attempt on his part to consummate the union if he took it upon himself to do so? He was temptation personified. She could feel the sexual energy of him here and now. Every time his eyes connected with hers it was like being exposed to powerful radiation, making her body hum inside and out.

'You have not found a new position as a live-in nanny, and it is my guess you will not be able to for quite some time,' he continued. 'After all, what self-respecting wife would want to employ a well-known seductress to take care of her children?'

Sabrina ground her teeth. 'I am no such thing. I was used as a scapegoat and no one would believe me.'

His expression was brimful with cynicism. 'It is of no concern to me what you did or who you did it with,' he said. 'I need a wife in a hurry, and as far I can see you are the most suitable candidate.'

She curled her top lip at him. 'I find it surprising you would want a wife with such a track record as mine. Aren't you concerned I will be a bad influence on Molly?'

'I have seen you with Molly, and I do not have any doubts over your love and care for her,' he said. 'Besides, she is used to you handling her, and I do not want her routine disrupted any more than it has been already. I do not know the first thing about babies, and quite frankly nor do any of the women I normally associate with. Plus, it was the wish of Laura and Ric that we should care for Molly.'

Sabrina felt a tiny hook-like tug somewhere in the middle of her chest at the thought of all the women he would continue to see if she married him. 'A marriage of convenience' was the term, a mutual agreement that bene-fited both parties, this time for the sake of a small, tragi-cally orphaned child. Mario would continue his playboy lifestyle while she would act the role of the long-suffer-ing wife. Oh, she would be well and truly compensated, of that she was sure. Money was no object when it came to the Marcolini bloodline. Upon his father's death a few months ago, Mario had taken over the Marcolini invest-ment business even though he was not the eldest son. His older brother Antonio was a high-profile plastic surgeon who travelled the world lecturing on his ground-breaking techniques for facial reconstruction surgery.

Between the two of them the money they had inherited and earned was beyond anything Sabrina could imagine. When she had lost her mother at the age of ten, the foster family who had taken her in had by no means been on the breadline, but they'd been frugal and conservative with their spending and their lifestyle. Necessities were saved for and purchased, but never luxuries. Sabrina had not even been to a proper restaurant until the age of sixteen, when she had saved up enough money from her various babysitting jobs to go out to celebrate a friend's birthday.

Mario Marcolini on the other hand had probably been fed by five-star chefs all his silver-spooned life. The suit he was wearing looked as if it was a designer label; the silver watch on his tanned wrist probably cost more than her car. Everything about him spoke of wealth and privilege, which was no doubt where he had obtained his air of arrogance. His cleanly shaven jaw had a hint of stubbornness to it, and although she knew from experience how sinfully sensual his mouth could be she suspected it too could be equally intransigent if anyone stood in the way of what he wanted.

The sound of a tiny cry came from the pram, and Sabrina blinked herself out of her stasis to soothe Molly, who was due for a feed and change. 'Hey there, little one,' she cooed as she picked up the little pink bundle. 'What is all the fuss about, hmm? Are you hungry?'

'May I hold her?'

Sabrina turned with the baby in her arms, surprised at how deep and scratchy Mario's voice had sounded. 'Of course,' she said, stepping towards him.

He took the baby carefully from her arms, one of his

hands brushing against her breast as he did so. Sabrina tried to disguise her reaction, but she could feel the heat pooling in her cheeks all the same.

She watched as he cradled Molly against his broad chest, his large hands and long, strong forearms making the infant look so small in comparison. A corner of his mouth began to lift in a wistful smile as he looked down at the little girl, one of his long fingers stroking her tiny cheek. *'Ciao, piccolo; sono il vostro nuovo papa,'* he said.

Sabrina found it amazing how one small infant could effect such a change in a man's demeanour. Gone was the cynical glint in his dark gaze; in its place was a tender warmth that made her wish he would look at her like that. She pulled back from her traitorous thoughts, shocked at how she was reacting to him. Perhaps it was his out-of-the-blue proposal that had weakened her normally rigid resolve. Like him, she would do anything to protect Molly, but what he was suggesting made her feel as if she was wading out of her depth into very murky, dangerous water.

Being formally tied to him would mean much more than sharing a house and the care of a child. In spite of his assurance, the marriage would not be a real one. She couldn't help but think living with him over any period of time would blur the boundaries, for her if not for him. From the first moment she had met him at Laura and Ric's wedding eighteen months ago, she had felt a zapping sensation when his deep brown eyes had meshed with hers. It had made every nerve beneath her skin tingle with awareness; her stomach had felt hollow and her legs watery. He had flirted with her outrageously, and yet somehow she had managed to play it cool even though inside she had been simmering with reaction, a reaction she had not been able to control when she had met him again just a few weeks ago. She was not normally the sort of woman to have her head turned with suave good looks. She had always been so guarded around men, which made the fiasco with the Roebournes all the more ridiculously ironic.

There was a sound at the door, and Ingrid Knowles came sweeping in. 'Where is my grandchild?' she asked, her words slurring slightly. 'I want to show her off to some of my friends who have just arrived.'

Sabrina felt her back come up like the fur of a cornered cat. 'Molly needs changing and feeding first,' she said. 'And she is not your grandchild—she is no relation to you whatsoever.'

Ingrid's mouth pulled tight as she gave Sabrina an up-and-down look that had talons attached. 'You think you're going to keep her, don't you? Well, you are not. I have already spoken to my lawyer. You don't stand a chance—not after what you did to poor Imogen Roebourne, seducing her husband behind her back.'

Sabrina felt one of Mario's arms go round her waist, while the other cradled the baby against his broad chest. 'You have been misinformed, Mrs Knowles,' he said with cool authority. 'Sabrina was totally innocent in the Roebourne affair. The press made it out to be something it was not.'

Ingrid gave a grating laugh. 'And you believe her?'

'Yes, I do, actually,' he responded smoothly. 'I would not be marrying her otherwise.'

Ingrid's penciled eyebrows shot upwards. 'You're marrying *her*?' she choked in stunned surprise.

His arm subtly tightened around Sabrina's waist. 'We will be married as soon as it can be arranged and take Molly with us back to Italy.'

Ingrid turned her attention to Sabrina. 'Is this true?' she asked, with a gaze as narrow as a starling's. 'Are you really marrying this man?'

Sabrina felt the seconds ticking by as she hesitated before she answered. The band of Mario's arm was warm about her; she could feel every one of his splayed fingers on her hip, the warmth spreading to her inner thighs like a trail of slow-burning fire. By opening her mouth and agreeing to his plan she knew she was not just stepping onto hot coals but throwing herself into the flames.

Her eyes flicked to where Molly was nestled against Mario's chest, her sweet little doll-like face turned in Sabrina's direction. Her little Cupid's bow mouth smiled as she looked at her, and for Sabrina that clinched it. How could she possibly say no now?

'Um...I...yes,' she said. 'That's right. We're, er, getting married.'

Ingrid gave her another scathing look. 'Then you are an even bigger gold-digger than I thought. You hardly know the man. You've met him—what?—twice? How can you possibly think of marrying him unless it's for money? That's what this is about, isn't it? You've always fancied being the wife of a rich man, and who is richer than a Marcolini?'

Sabrina felt her face suffuse with colour. 'This is not about money.'

'That is correct,' Mario interjected. 'It is about what is best for Molly. It's what her parents wanted for her.'

Ingrid threw Mario a malevolent glare. 'You don't stand a chance. Stanley will engage a top lawyer who will make mincemeat of you.'

Mario's eyes glinted with steely implacability. 'Before

he does that, perhaps you had better tell him I know all about what he has been doing with the Whinstone account.'

There was a throbbing pause.

Sabrina could see how Laura's stepmother was clenching and unclenching her teeth, her green eyes darting about nervously. She almost felt sorry for the woman. For all Ingrid's beverage-fuelled bravado, what chance did she stand with Mario Marcolini as an opponent?

'You're not going to win this,' Ingrid said through thin lips, although her defiant stance had visibly sagged.

Mario's hand tightened possessively on Sabrina's hip as he gave the older woman an imperious smile. 'I believe I just did,' he said. 'Sabrina has agreed to be my wife, and that as far as I am concerned is the end of it.'

No, Sabrina thought with a funny, moth-like fluttering sensation in her stomach as Ingrid stalked out. *It is just the beginning.*

CHAPTER TWO

'YOU DO not need to look so worried, Sabrina,' Mario said as he gently handed Molly over. 'I don't think we will hear from Mrs Knowles again once we are officially married.'

Sabrina busied herself with seeing to the baby's needs rather than meet his eyes. Oh, dear God, what had she committed herself to? There was no way she could wriggle out of this without compromising Molly. Mario had hinted at something untoward in Stanley Knowles's business dealings. And, knowing what Laura had felt about her step-mother and what Sabrina had seen for herself, how could she step aside now to let such people be the guardians of her little god-daughter?

The tiny baby girl cooed at her as if to confirm it, her tiny arms reaching towards Sabrina's face, the little starfish hands touching her on the cheeks, a gurgling chuckle of delight coming out of her rosebud mouth.

'I will arrange for a special license,' Mario said, watching as she leaned forward to press a soft kiss to the middle of each of Molly's tiny palms.

Sabrina continued to dress Molly with hands that were not quite steady. 'How soon do you expect it will be before we…?' She faltered over the word. 'Er, marry?'

'As soon as it can be arranged,' he answered. 'No longer than a week, maybe even less.'

Sabrina felt her stomach lurch sideways. *A week?* She picked up the baby and laid her against her right shoulder as she faced him again. 'That seems…rather rushed.'

'Do you have a current passport?' he asked.

'Yes, but—'

'Good,' he said. 'I will need that and your birth certificate to make all the arrangements.'

'Mario, I—'

'It is imperative we get going on this, Sabrina,' he said with an indomitable look. 'Besides, I want to get back home to where my business commitments await me.'

No doubt your mistress awaits you too, Sabrina thought resentfully as she took out Molly's bottle, which was encased in the Thermos container, and settled down to feed the restless baby. Once Molly was sucking contentedly, Sabrina looked up at Mario who was standing a short distance away, watching her like a predator with its targeted prey.

'You said it wasn't to be a real marriage,' she said, feeling her cheeks bloom with colour, and her whole body shiver in reaction as she thought of what a real marriage to him would involve if he put his mind to it. 'You also intimated it was temporary. What sort of time limit are you thinking of?'

'Molly is a tiny infant,' he said. 'She needs a full-time mother at least until she is of nursery-school age.'

Sabrina felt suspicion crawl up her spine, making her sit more upright in her chair. 'So what happens then?' she asked.

'I will engage the services of a nanny and then you can have your freedom.'

Sabrina frowned at his arrogance. 'So I am to be expelled from Molly's life just like that?' she asked.

'Not necessarily from Molly's life,' he said. 'But from mine. We can have a quiet dissolution of the marriage and then both get on with our lives.'

'So let me get this straight,' she said with a guarded look. 'You get full guardianship of Molly in Italy while I get sent back to Australia, is that what you're suggesting?'

He gave an indifferent lift of one broad shoulder. 'That will be entirely up to you, of course,' he said. 'As my ex-wife you will have full residency in my country, but whether you choose to live in Rome or Sydney will ultimately be your decision.'

'Do you really think I would just walk away from Molly as if she meant nothing to me?' she asked, still frowning furiously. 'And what about what Molly wants? She will have come to look upon me as her mother. She's practically doing it now. What you are suggesting is not just outrageous, it's cruel to both Molly and to me.'

He lifted his dark brows at her vehemence. 'Come now, Sabrina,' he said coolly. 'You have looked after young children before, becoming involved with every aspect of their lives, only to leave when the family no longer requires your services.'

'That's not the same thing at all,' Sabrina argued.

'Are you saying you did not have any affection for the children you were employed to look after?' he asked.

Sabrina could feel her hatred of him simmering in her veins. It was pulsing through the intricate, narrow network in her body, threatening to burst out at any moment. She knew what he was doing; he was going to sideline her right from the start. She would be more than useful to him during the next two or three years while Molly was a baby and toddler, but after that she would be dismissed, just like any other servant in his employ.

'Of course I develop great affection for the children in my care, but Molly is my godchild, the daughter of my best friend. It's an entirely different relationship, especially given the circumstances now.'

'Your marriage to me will not be permanent,' he said. 'As long as you understand that, there will not be a problem if you wish to continue to see Molly once our marriage is brought to an end.'

Sabrina stood and lifted the baby against her chest to wind her, gently patting the tiny back, her eyes still tussling with his. 'You think you've got this all worked out, haven't you? I know what you are doing, Mario. You want a cheap babysitter while you continue to live your playboy lifestyle.'

He gave her a smile, his eyes reflecting its mockery. 'Cheap, Sabrina?' he said. 'Is that how you would describe yourself? Certainly the press called you such, and a whole lot more, if I recall.'

She gave him a flinty glare. 'I am not going to be dismissed from Molly's life at your say-so. I want to remain a part of her life no matter what happens between us.'

'Nothing is going to happen between us, Sabrina,' he said. 'Or have you got other ideas, hmm? A little affair with me to pass the time, just like you did with Mr Roebourne, *sì*?'

This time her look was withering. 'I have met some creeps in my time, and up until now Howard Roebourne was at the top of that list. But you, Mario Marcolini, have just bumped him off.'

His smile was still mocking as he came up close and stroked a long finger down the baby's cheek. Sabrina sucked in a breath; he was so close she could see the sand-papery stubble on his jaw, and the unfathomable black holes of his pupils in the deep, dark chocolate of his eyes. The air around her face carried a trace of his scent, a mixture of aftershave and male pheromones, making her heart give a funny, out-of-time beat.

She quickly lowered her eyes and encountered the flat plane of his chest and stomach; she could almost imagine the six pack of ridged muscle lying beneath his designer shirt. She daren't look any lower; she had spent too many nights as it was thinking about how he was made. The hardened length of him in full arousal as he had taken control of her amateur kiss at Molly's christening had made the blood race frantically in her veins both then and since.

She felt his finger beneath her chin as he lifted her face upwards. 'Is that how you did it?' he asked with a curl of his lip and a hard glint in his eyes. 'Is that how you lured a respectable married man away from his wife, by looking at him with those smoky, grey come-to-bed eyes of yours?'

Sabrina would have pulled away from his touch but she didn't want to disturb Molly, who had drifted off to sleep against her shoulder. 'I did not seduce him, or anyone,' she said, glaring back at him.

His finger moved from beneath her chin and came to her mouth, tracing a pathway over the fullness of her bottom lip, barely touching, making every sensitive nerve begin to leap and dance beneath the skin. 'Ah, but that is not quite true, is it, Sabrina?' he said in a low spine-loosening murmur. 'It is not hard to see why so many men would find it hard to resist a taste of its sweetness. I have not forgot-ten how tempting it was to taste it myself when you so very kindly offered it to me.'

Sabrina stood very still, barely able to breathe in case she betrayed herself. She wanted to taste his finger, to draw it into her mouth, to suck on it, to see if his pupils would flare with desire the way she suspected hers were currently flaring. Her gaze flicked to his mouth, the sensual contours of it pulling on the secret strings of desire deep and low in her belly. It was like torture to stand so close and not touch him. She had blamed the champagne the day of the christening, but she was stone-cold sober now, and still she wanted his mouth to set hers alight. What was wrong with her? Was she somehow turning into the raunchy Jezebel the press had made her out to be?

His hand dropped from her face. 'I need to get going,' he said, glancing at his watch. 'I will come by your apartment this evening with some papers for you to sign.'

Sabrina could feel the walls of her prison starting to close in on her. When Mario Marcolini wanted something done, he was like a freight train going at full speed. This was the time to say, *no, I won't be a part of this*. Why then wasn't she saying it? The words were on the tip of her tongue, hovering there, but somehow she couldn't utter them out loud. Saying no to Mario would be saying no to Molly; she was sure of it.

He had already demonstrated how ruthless he could be in his dealings with Laura's stepmother earlier. What was to stop him doing the same to her? If she refused to marry him he was quite likely to use her sullied reputation against her. He would apply for full custody of Molly, and with his wealth and status there wouldn't be a judge in the country who wouldn't give it to him. With his pedigree and fortune he had so much to offer a little orphaned child. And Sabrina knew full well if he didn't marry her to secure his claim he would simply marry someone else, and then she would never see Molly again. She was lucky he had offered her a compromise, although why he had done so was anyone's guess. Stripped down, it was nothing more than blackmail, and yet she had no choice but to agree to the terms. What else could she do? Other women before her had made sacrifices for those they loved. She would do the same.

Sabrina bit her lip as she gently tucked Molly back into the pram. If Mario thought she would be shunted aside some time in the future, he had better rethink his plans. She wasn't going to desert little Molly, no matter what the cost to her personally.

Mario escorted Sabrina out past the other mourners, one or two of them stopping to look in on the sleeping baby, murmuring their condolences; others, like Ingrid and Stanley Knowles, carried on with their drinking and chatting as if they were at a garden party.

Once Molly was safely strapped into the baby carrier in her car, Sabrina turned to look at Mario. 'Do you have my address?' she asked.

'I looked it up in the phone book,' he said. 'I will be round about eight or so.'

Sabrina's gaze flicked back to the house, her brow pleating with worry. 'What if Ingrid comes round before then?' she asked, swinging her gaze back to Mario. 'She's come round each day since Social Services released Molly into my care. The last time she was quite abusive. It was embarrassing for me, not to mention for the neighbours, most of whom are elderly. I was sure someone was going to call the police. I considered doing it myself, except I didn't want the press to get wind of it.'

He drummed his fingers on the roof of her rusty car for

a moment. 'Then it will be best if you and Molly are not there if she should take it upon herself to drop round.'

Sabrina felt another frown pull at her brow. 'But where will we be?'

'You will be at my hotel with me,' he said.

'I-is that such a good idea?' she said, her frown deepening, her heart stuttering in panic. 'I mean…will there be room for us?'

The look in his eyes was inscrutable, but there was a hint of amusement lurking around his mouth. 'Molly can sleep in her pram, and you can sleep in my bed.'

Sabrina's eyes widened, her heart giving that annoying little extra beat again. 'Are you by any chance going to be there too?' she asked with an attempt at an arch look.

'In my bed, do you mean?'

She nodded, hastily disguising a nervous swallow.

'Only if I am invited,' he said with a sexy slant of his mouth.

Sabrina pulled her own mouth into a prim line. 'That is not going to happen.'

'No, of course not,' he said as his smile turned to a sneer. 'You have a taste for the forbidden, do you not? The married man is more your style.'

'I can assure you that all of your married friends will be quite safe from me,' she said with a lift of her chin.

He took her chin between his finger and thumb, his eyes boring into hers. 'I perhaps should remind you at this point of the behaviour I expect from you during the period of our marriage,' he said.

Sabrina considered pulling out of his hold, but, though it was firm enough to make her think twice, it was somehow gentle enough for her not to even want to try. She felt the slow but steady burn of his touch, the heat of him going to her core where a cauldron of need was still on the boil from the last time he had come this close. She ran the tip of her tongue over her lips, her stomach giving a little kick of awareness when he brushed the pad of his thumb over where her tongue had just been. It was like negative meeting positive, fire meeting fuel, flame meeting tinder. She felt her whole body respond; her breasts peaked, her inner thighs trembled and her heart didn't just pick up its pace, it all-out sprinted. 'I—I'm not sure what you expect me to do,' she said, trying to steady her out-of-control breathing. 'It's not as if we are, er, in love or anything—and for that matter I am not prepared to pretend we are.'

His eyes continued to hold hers. 'I am glad you mentioned that particular four-letter word,' he said. 'You are more than welcome in my bed, but do not get any ideas about making this arrangement more permanent. I know how a woman's mind works, so any vows of love from you will be disregarded henceforth.'

Sabrina was taken aback by his words. She bristled at his arrogant assumption that she would fall in love with him so readily or, even more insulting, pretend to do so for personal gain. It just went to show the sort of women he sought to warm his bed. He wanted shallow and short term, not deep, caring and committed. 'I could never love someone like you,' she threw back. 'You are the very opposite of what I want in a partner.'

He smiled that mocking smile again. 'Is that so?'

She pulled her shoulders back, her eyes flashing their dislike of him. 'You are selfish, for one thing,' she said. 'And ruthless, and…and…' She hunted for some other words to describe him, but it totally confounded her that all she could think of was how good he was with Molly. For a playboy he certainly was astonishingly at ease around a tiny baby. He handled Molly with care and confidence. He had been the same at the christening, kissing her tiny nose and each of her miniscule fingertips one by one, his normally cynical and hard, black-brown eyes all but melting.

'But I am rich,' he said, still smiling. 'That surely makes up for what else I lack, *si*?'

'You do not have enough money to tempt me,' Sabrina said with a toss of her head.

'We will see,' he said, and opened the passenger door.

She frowned at him again. 'What are you doing?'

'I am holding the door open for you.'

She rolled her eyes. 'Yes, I can see that, but why? I can't drive it from this side, in case you haven't noticed.'

'I will drive,' he said. 'You can tell me where to go.'

'That will be the easy part,' she said with a pert look. 'Go to hell.'

His dark eyes glinted with amusement. 'Not unless I get to take you with me,' he said. 'I have a feeling we could really ramp up the heat down there with just a kiss or two, let alone the full works.'

Sabrina pressed her lips into a flat line of disdain. 'You don't get to sample the goods, Mario, they're not on offer.' *Not any more*, she mentally tacked on, not entirely sure if it was a promise or a prayer for help in resisting temptation.

'I know what you are doing, Sabrina,' he said. 'You have been doing it from the first moment we met. You like to slowly reel a man in, do you not? That is your modus operandi, no? Little by little you up the ante until he finally capitulates.'

She took a step backwards. 'I am doing no such thing.'

He leaned closer, capturing her chin again, his eyes locking on hers. 'I will take your slim little body any time you like,' he said in a low, spine-tingling drawl. 'Any time, any place, any position. You just have to say the word. Just like the last time.'

Sabrina felt her insides erupt into flames, the hot spurts of need anointing her intimately as she thought of what he would be like as a lover. Inexperienced as she was, she knew enough about him to know he would be everything a woman could want in a sexual partner: demanding, exciting, daring and dangerously attractive. The one kiss they had shared had shown her that and more. It had sent shooting sparks from one end of her body to the other, licking her senses into a frenzy of want. She could feel the pulse of her blood now, hectic and overly excited at his nearness. Her eyes went to his mouth, his fuller lower lip drawing her gaze like an industrial-sized magnet. All she had to do was step up on her tiptoes and their mouths would touch and burn…

The sound of other guests spilling out of the house was the only thing that saved Sabrina from making a total fool of herself all over again. She pulled out of Mario's hold and slipped into the passenger seat, her legs still trembling long after he had stridden around and got in behind the wheel of her four-cylinder car.

Once he was sitting beside her, she suddenly realised how very small her car was. It was like a child's toy; although he pushed back the driver's seat to its maximum distance from the wheel to accommodate his length, every time he worked the gears she was aware of his suited arm within touching distance of her thigh.

'I thought you would have hired some swanky Italian

sportscar while you are here,' she said once they were on their way. 'Isn't that what rich men like you do?'

'I saw no need to waste money on one when I was only going to be here for such a short time,' he answered evenly.

Sabrina chewed over that for a moment. 'What if I hadn't agreed to your plan?' she asked, not trusting herself to look at him.

'Then I would have found some way of convincing you,' he said, equally smoothly.

This time she did look at him. 'With blackmail, like you did with Ingrid and Stanley Knowles?'

He met her eyes for a brief moment, before turning back to the traffic. 'I see no reason not to use a bit of pressure when it is warranted,' he said.

Sabrina huddled in her seat, wondering how far he would have gone to make her change her mind if she had said no—not that she'd really had a chance to say no. Ingrid had come in and the words had tumbled out of Sabrina's mouth, words that now tied her to a man she knew so little about.

It was a disturbing thought. All she knew was Mario Marcolini was ruthless in business and equally so in his private life. Women came and went from his life like clouds in the sky, none of them lasting long enough to make an impression on him. She wondered if he had been hurt by a past lover, or if he was just one of those men, all too common these days, who shied away from commitment. All she knew about his background was what Laura had told her in snatches, and, because Sabrina hadn't wanted to sound too curious, she hadn't asked the questions she had longed to know the answers to. Questions she had no right to even be thinking, let alone asking.

'Where to from here?' Mario asked when he came to a crossroads.

'Turn right at the next lights,' she said. 'My flat is in the fourth building on the left, but really I don't think it's such a good idea for me to move into your hotel with—'

She stopped when she saw a news van parked outside her building, the cameras already being set up. 'Oh no…'

'Put your head down and ignore them,' Mario said as he parked the car in the tenants' parking area behind the tired-looking inner-city building. 'I will deal with them while you go in and pack what you need. I can always send someone over later to get the rest.'

Mario fielded the press with a few short statements about his intentions, even embellishing the facts a little for his own amusement. He watched as the news team drove away a few minutes later, and then with a sigh of satisfaction turned and entered the building.

Sabrina's flat was neat and tidy inside, but he could see why she had always sought employment in the upper echelons of society. Like the many gold-diggers he had met or had dealings with in the past, she was obviously looking for a way out of her current situation. A rich man, even if he was married, could set her up as his mistress. Things had backfired on her with Howard Roebourne, but no doubt there would be other rich men once he put an end to their temporary marriage, Mario thought sceptically.

'How long have you lived here?' Mario asked as she came out with a battered suitcase into the tiny lounge area.

'A couple of years,' she said. 'I'd like something bigger and in a nicer suburb, but there's really not much point when most of the families I have worked for have required me to live with them for extended periods.'

'It must at times be difficult to have a private life when you are living with other people,' he said, taking the bag out of her hand and placing it near the door. 'No wonder you have been tempted to work and play under the same roof.'

Her grey eyes flashed as they hit his. 'You think I'm a slut, don't you? And yet the papers are full of your sexual exploits. Your double standards make me sick.'

'I have not resorted to sleeping with married women,' he said. 'I have plenty of single and unattached ones to work my way through first.'

She swung away from him, snatching up her handbag and hoisting it over her shoulder. 'I suppose you have a revolving door on your bedroom?' she said, flashing him another glare.

Mario grinned at the thought. 'Not yet, but it sounds like a great idea,' he said.

Her glare intensified. 'I think you are disgusting,' she spat. 'You have no morals. You probably don't even spare the women you bed with another thought once you have done with them. It's such a shallow and selfish way to live.'

'It is no more shallow and selfish than touching what does not belong to you,' he pointed out.

'You know nothing about me,' she said with a mulish jut of her chin as tears welled up in her eyes. 'You think you do, but you don't.'

He pushed himself away from the door frame where he had been leaning. 'I know what Howard Roebourne told me about you.'

Sabrina felt her face drain of colour as her heart began to pound sickeningly. 'H-how do you know him?' she asked.

'The business world is not as big as you might think,' he answered. 'Roebourne and I move in the same financial circles. I happened to run into him at a corporate function when I was here the last time.'

'W-what did he say?' she asked, even though she wasn't sure she really wanted to know. After that last horrible scene with her previous employer, she could not think of a single thing he could say that would paint her in an attractive light.

'Nothing I had not already worked out for myself,' he said with an enigmatic smile.

Sabrina silently ground her teeth. So *that* was why he had allowed her to kiss him on the day of Molly's christening, to see if what he had heard about her was true. Her shameless grasp at him hadn't done her any favours, she realised now when it was far too late to do anything to change things. If he had only suspected she was a wanton woman before, her behaviour at the christening would have been more than enough confirmation that his suspicions were accurate. She had acted so out of character that day. She had blamed the three glasses of champagne she had consumed, but she had only drunk them out of sheer nervousness in his presence.

It had started the day of the wedding when he had captured her gaze and held it. Something had passed between them that day, something visceral. And then at the christening it had been activated all over again by Mario's debonair charm, his lethally attractive smile, and the sensual glide of his hand on her bare arm as he had taken the baby from her. She had felt it as soon as his eyes had locked with hers, drawing her to him, holding her, making her burn for him as if he had turned on a switch inside her body. Try as she might, she hadn't been able to locate it since and turn it off. She had felt that same tingle of awareness even when his name had been mentioned, let alone standing in his presence as she was doing now.

'Are you ready to leave?' he asked as he picked up Molly in the baby carrier in one hand and her old suitcase in the other.

'Yes,' she said, avoiding his eyes.

Once Molly was back in the car and the suitcase stowed, Mario got back behind the wheel. 'I suppose I should warn you that the press will go wild about our forthcoming marriage,' he said. 'I know you are not keen on the idea, but I think the best approach is to let everyone believe this is a genuine love-match. That is what I told them back there at your flat. They seemed to be delighted by it.'

Sabrina stared at him in wide-eyed alarm. 'You told them I was *in love* with you?'

He grinned at her wickedly. 'Of course I did. I have my reputation to maintain, don't forget. I can't have people thinking you married me for my money. It's demeaning.'

'But I am only marrying you because of Molly, and it was your choice to pay me,' she pointed out wryly.

He gave a shrug of indifference. 'Yes, but no one else needs to know that. Have you decided how much you want?'

Sabrina swallowed tightly as she turned to look out of the passenger window. There was no amount of money on this earth that would ever bring her best friend back, but if she could put any of the money Mario gave her into an investment account for Molly it would be something. When Sabrina's mother had died, she had been left with nothing. The stigma of being penniless and at the mercy of others' charity had never left her, even after all these years. Of course Molly, being under Mario's protection, would want for nothing, but Sabrina wanted to demonstrate her commitment to her godchild by herself providing her with a nest egg when she came of age. She was determined not to touch a penny of it for herself.

'I can almost hear the ching-ching of the cash register in your brain,' Mario said. 'You are doing the sums, calculating how much you will need to set yourself up for life.'

She sent him a spiteful glance. 'I want half a million for every year we are married.'

'In Australian dollars or euros?' he asked without flinching.

Sabrina tried to recall the current exchange-rate. 'Um… in euros,' she said, wishing she had asked for more just to annoy him.

'If you give me your details, I will make sure the first instalment is in there once we are married.'

Sabrina toyed with the strap of her handbag for a moment. 'You said earlier you expected me to take your name,' she said, pausing to glance at him again. 'Is that really necessary in this day and age?'

'Sabrina Marcolini,' he drawled. 'Now that has rather a nice ring to it, does it not?'

She pursed her lips. 'I prefer Halliday. It was my mother's maiden name.'

'You don't have a father?'

'Not that I know of,' she said, fiddling with her handbag strap again. 'My mother never mentioned him. I think he might have been married or something. She seemed reluctant to give me any details. I found a photo once, but when I asked who it was she scrunched it up and I never saw it again.'

There was a momentary silence.

'You said it *was* your mother's name,' he said. 'Does that mean she has since married again?'

'No, it means she is dead,' Sabrina said, stripping her voice of the aching emotion she still felt. 'She died when I was ten. The train she was travelling to work on was derailed. She was the last to be pulled out of the wreckage.'

'I am very sorry,' he said. 'Neither Ric nor Laura ever mentioned it to me.'

'Laura understood how hard it was to grow up without a mother,' she said. 'She lost hers when she was a little older than I was, but when her father married Ingrid only weeks later she was totally devastated. She felt she had lost both of her parents right then and there. Her father died just before she met Ric...but I suppose you know all this?'

He shifted the gears, a frown stitching his brow. 'I did not really know Laura all that well,' he said. 'I only met her for the first time at the wedding, where, if you remember, I also met you. Ric and I went to elementary school together. We remained in close contact even when his family emigrated to Australia when he was fourteen.'

'Did you ever visit him?'

'Yes, I have been to Australia seven times now, and Ric came back to Italy on holidays occasionally,' he said. 'My brother was here in Sydney just a couple of months ago.'

'Yes, I read about it in the paper,' Sabrina said. 'I saw the name and assumed it was your brother. He was here for a lecturing tour, wasn't he?'

'Yes, but also to sort things out with his estranged wife.'

Sabrina felt her brows lift up in intrigue. 'Oh?'

He changed the gears again. 'They were living apart for five years but they are back together now,' he said. 'They renewed their vows only a few weeks ago. They are expecting a child in a few months.'

'Are you pleased about their reconciliation?' she asked, watching his expression for a moment.

'I am very happy for them both,' he answered after a pause. 'I might not be a family man, but I recognise when a couple belong together. There was a time however when I thought Antonio would have been better off moving on without Claire, but I am prepared to admit I was wrong.'

'I don't think it is wise to take sides in a marital dispute,' Sabrina said, thinking of all the times Laura had let off steam about Ric's hot-headed stubbornness, only to be madly in love with him the next moment.

As the silence stretched Sabrina couldn't help feeling Mario's brother's situation explained a lot about his cynical attitude towards relationships. He had seen his brother go through a lengthy estrangement. There was no way he was going to give any woman in his life the same opportunity to put his life on hold. His relationships were on his terms and his terms only. Love didn't come into it, nor did permanency, even when there was a child involved.

Mario needed her now to act as a substitute mother to Molly, but she was on borrowed time, and if she had any hope of coming out of this with her heart intact she had better keep reminding herself of it.

This is not for ever.

This is not for real.

She took a mental gulp and added: *this is dangerous.*

CHAPTER THREE

THE hotel Mario was staying in was exactly where Sabrina had expected someone of his ilk to stay: top-end luxury, panoramic harbour views, several five-star restaurants, as well as a piano bar and an in-house gym, and a health spa which was second to none in terms of decadent indulgence. His penthouse suite was superbly decorated with the latest in high-street trends, the modern open-plan design making it feel more like a mansion than a hotel apartment.

The views from every window were breathtaking, even for someone who had lived in Sydney all of her life, Sabrina conceded. The harbour was dotted with colourful yachts and the bustle of passenger ferries criss-crossing the sparkling waters to take commuters and tourists wherever they needed to go.

Molly was still sleeping in her carrier, which gave Sabrina time to unpack a few things into the spacious wardrobe Mario had told her she was to use during their short stay.

However, she resolutely turned her back on the massive king-size bed made up in a thousand threads of Egyptian cotton, with numerous feather pillows, and a doona that looked as if it was filled with air. But even so she couldn't help thinking of Mario lying there, possibly naked; yes, she decided, he would *definitely* be a naked sleeper, his long, tanned limbs splayed out in any number of erotic poses.

She gave herself a stern mental shake and concentrated on the job at hand. She had a tiny baby to settle into yet another routine, and in a few days a long-haul flight to another country, a country where she knew only the basics of communication, in spite of Laura's giggling tutorage over the last few months.

It struck Sabrina again, then, how surreal the last few days had been. Laura, the one friend who had understood her passion for connection and belonging, was gone, never to return. She kept thinking someone was going to shake her awake and tell her it was all a mistake, that the bodies taken from the wreckage of Ric's car were not those of him and Laura but someone else, strangers, no one she knew—no one she loved so dearly and would miss for the rest of her life.

Just like the day her mother had died, Sabrina was alone again… Well, not quite alone. She had Molly, dear, precious little Molly, who was thankfully oblivious to what had passed in the last few days. There would be a day when she would need to be told the truth about her real parents. Sabrina could only hope she would be around to tell Molly what a wonderful and loving mother Laura had been, how much she had loved her baby and had wanted the best for her, leaving her in the care of the two people she had trusted most in the world: her husband's best friend and hers.

How ironic that those two people hated each other, even though they both loved the child, Sabrina thought as she folded another pink baby-suit and laid it on the shelf.

The baby gave a grizzling sound, and Sabrina went over to her, scooping her out of the carrier and cuddling her close, breathing in that sweet infant smell, her hand cupping the black down of that tiny, silky head. 'Shh, my precious,' she said softly. 'I know this is all new to you. It's all new to me too. We'll have to take one day at a time until I can think of a way out of this.'

Mario heard Sabrina's voice just as he came to the door of the bedroom. So she was thinking of an escape route, was she? Not while he had anything to do about it, he determined. She would likely face a kidnap charge if she left without consulting him as co-guardian.

Ric's wife had had nothing but good to say about her friend, but that didn't mean Sabrina hadn't personally woven the wool she had pulled over Laura's eyes. Mario had to admit Sabrina had an innocent look about her that was beguiling to say the least. Ric had obviously fallen for it too; he had told Mario at the wedding how delightful Sabrina was, how charming, how unworldly, shy and self-effacing, even dropping broad hints about what a suitable partner she would make for him. Mario had laughed off the suggestion; he had met plenty of supposedly shy women in the past and in his experience they were the ones who turned out to be the most devious and coolly calculating. It was the quiet ones you had to watch.

And he had been right about Sabrina. His interesting little conversation with Howard Roebourne the evening before Molly's christening had confirmed what a go-getter Sabrina was behind that sweet girl-next-door exterior. The woman who had thrown herself into his arms for those few stolen moments had been hot and hungry, her mouth like an open fire, her tongue a flame that had scorched his, branding him with an imprint he had not been able to erase. He could still taste the sweet temptation of her cushioned lips, the way they had moulded so perfectly to his. Their passionate clinch had been interrupted before he'd been able to take things any further, but he was in no doubt he could have had her then and there. In fact, he was in little doubt he could have her any time he wanted to if he put his mind to it. He saw the way she looked at him with those smoky-grey eyes of hers, the sensual need in them unmistakable.

Mario entered the bedroom and Sabrina turned to face him, the baby cuddled close to her chest. 'Have you everything you need?' he asked.

'Yes,' she said, lowering her eyes to concentrate on tucking in the label of Molly's baby-suit at her tiny neck. 'Everything's…lovely.'

'I have to pick up some legal documents but I should be back within an hour,' he said. 'Make yourself at home. If you want anything for yourself or Molly, call room-service and charge it to me.'

Sabrina hadn't realised she had been holding her breath until he left, the door of the penthouse closing firmly on his exit. The air in the room seemed to lose its tightness once he had gone; her chest felt less restricted, and her heart rate not so hectic.

Molly seemed restless and, although Sabrina had fed her, she decided a warm bath might help the little baby to relax. She carried her through to the *en suite* where twin bowl-like basins were set on top of a highly polished marble bench. She half-filled one basin with warm water and squirted in some baby-bath liquid. Once she had Molly undressed and splashing delightedly in the basin, the little girl's giggles replaced her grizzles. It was times like these that made Sabrina wonder if she would ever have a baby of her own some day. Being tied to Mario for the next three or four years was hardly going to improve her chances of finding a partner.

He on the other hand would no doubt continue his numerous affairs, leaving her to hold the baby, so to speak. The way he had orchestrated things meant he was always going to be in control. But then that was the sort of man he was; he was nobody's lackey, he was as alpha as they came. It still surprised her how much he wanted Molly, however. It just didn't fit with her knowledge of him as the playboy the press made him out to be. Bouncing a blonde bombshell on his knee rather than a baby was more his thing, but then perhaps he was not interested in fathering his own offspring and was content to have the responsibility for a small child's upbringing instead. There was no doubt he cared for Molly, but then how many people could resist a cute, gummy smile and big china-blue eyes?

Once Molly was dried and dressed and, after a cuddle, back in her pram and sleeping peacefully, Sabrina sat on one of the plush leather sofas and flicked through the hotel entertainment and facilities guide, trying not to think too much about the night ahead.

The door opened and Mario came in with a briefcase in one hand. He placed it on the coffee table in front of her, clicking it open and retrieving a sheaf of papers.

'You had better read through these before the lawyer joins us,' he said. 'He's meeting us here in a few minutes. He is still downstairs. He had to take a call from another client.'

Sabrina took the thick pile of paperwork and began reading. It was wordy, as legal documents generally were, but she plodded her way through it, realising that in signing it she was relinquishing the right to any of Mario's assets acquired prior to their marriage. Pre-nuptial agreements didn't sit well with her on principle. She'd always reasoned that if a couple was truly committed to making their marriage work there would be no need for a back-up plan. But then, this marriage was hardly what anyone could call a romantic union. It was little more than a business transaction, and for that reason she decided there was no point in making a fuss about signing on the dotted line. She didn't want Mario's money; all she wanted was for Molly to have a secure and loving home.

The lawyer arrived and after brief introductions he went through the document with Sabrina and indicated where she was to sign.

'That's it,' the lawyer said once the last space had received Sabrina's signature. 'I will speak to the accountant about having an allowance deposited into your bank account, as per Mario's instructions.'

Sabrina felt a tide of colour slowly ebb into her cheeks. She wondered just how much the lawyer had been told about the circumstances between Mario and herself. She was being paid to be a wife to him on paper only, and substitute mother to Molly, and yet as far as she could tell there was nothing in the lawyer's expression that suggested he thought their relationship was anything other than normal. But then perhaps Mario had lied to him as he had done to the press earlier—for the sake of his own reputation, certainly not hers.

Once the lawyer had left, Mario began to tug at his tie. 'I thought I might do a few laps of the pool,' he said. 'You can join me, if you like.'

Sabrina gave him a testy look. 'We have the custody of a baby, remember? You can continue to have your freedom, but I for one am taking my responsibilities seriously where Molly is concerned.'

His eyes collided with hers. 'Are you suggesting I am not taking my responsibilities seriously?'

She folded her arms across her body. 'Let's be right upfront about this, Mario. You hardly have to do a thing where Molly is concerned. That's why you've got me, isn't it? Your life can continue without interruption while I am left to look after the baby.'

His tie hung loosely around his neck as he came up close. 'Forgive me if I am wrong, but I thought your chosen career was to care for babies and small children?' he said. 'Or are you being particularly bitchy because you do not like the fact that I have prevented you from getting your hands on my fortune when our marriage is eventually terminated?'

She glared up at him, desperately wanting to step backwards, but forcing herself to stand her ground. 'Everything is always about money to you, isn't it? You think I want anything from *you*? I hate you. I can't believe Laura agreed to nominate you in her will as Molly's guardian. In fact, I can't even believe Ric suggested it, since he knew you longer than Laura ever did. He of all people should have known how unfit for the task you are. I have never met a more unsuitable father figure in my life.'

His dark eyes hardened to smouldering black coals of contempt. 'You are a fine one to talk, Sabrina Halliday. You have the morals of an alley cat in heat, opening your legs for the highest bidder.'

Her eyes flashed with pure venom, her whole body quaking with rage. 'At the risk of repeating myself—you are disgusting.'

He stepped closer, so close she had to flatten her spine against the wall. 'How about if I *were* to make a bid for you, hmm?' he asked in a slow, sexy drawl. 'One that your greedy little hands will not be able to resist?'

Sabrina felt the valves of her heart tighten as his warm breath skated over her face. Her breathing became even more ragged; her legs felt like dampened paper, barely able to keep her upright. 'No amount of money would tempt me to sleep with you,' she said, flashing him a feisty glare.

'Oh, I do not want you to be asleep when we come together,' he said with a sinfully sexy smile. 'Far from it. I want you writhing and convulsing and panting beneath me. That is what you want too, is it not, Sabrina? That is what you have wanted from the first moment we met.'

Sabrina had never felt such an explosion of heat erupt in her face or in her body before. His words, his incendiary, carnal words, had set off fires all through her, each one singeing her like a burning ember pressed to her skin. Images of their bodies locked together in passion flooded her brain, shockingly erotic images that were disturbing, not because she didn't want them to happen but—God help her—because she did.

Denial was her only defence, and as hastily assembled defences went hers was about as unstable as any could be. 'You are mistaken,' she said in a voice that was not quite as steady and controlled as she had hoped. 'I have no interest whatsoever in becoming another notch on your belt.'

He picked up a few strands of her hair, coiling them like a silky rope around two of his fingers, his eyes still burning down into hers. 'It is early days, *la mio piccolo* seductress,' he said. 'We are not yet married; perhaps when you have my ring on your finger and your body in my bed you will change your mind.'

'Don't hold your breath,' she said, still glaring at him, her heart beating like a hyperactive jackhammer.

He gave her hair a gentle tug, pulling her inexorably closer to the hard ridge of his body. Sabrina felt her breath skid to a halt in her chest, her body set alight by the arrantly male and primal probe of his.

The atmosphere tightened; the air around them was brooding, dangerous, and suddenly full of irresistible temptation.

Sabrina felt each 'thud, thud, thud' of her heart like a swinging anvil against her chest, her insides quivering at the brooding intensity of his dark gaze as it held hers. She moistened her lips—discreetly, she had thought—but his gaze flicked downwards, the thick screen of his dark lashes giving him a heavy-lidded, sexy look that sent every thought in her head scattering like startled sparrows.

'I could have you right now, Sabrina, and you damn well know it,' he said in a low, deep tone, his warm, hint-of-mint breath caressing her lips.

Sabrina's gaze was mesmerised by his mouth. Those firm lips were tilted in a smile that promised mind-zapping passion, and her lips tingled in response, aching for the pressure of his. All she had to do was stand up on tiptoe to close the gap between their bodies, like she had that first time. His fire would melt her ice with one brush of that commandeering mouth of his on hers.

Just in time she felt the undertow of commonsense tugging at her, pulling her back from temptation. Oh, she wanted him all right, but that would be feeding right into his cynical opinion of her as a good-time girl after a fast buck and an even faster tumble in his bed.

With the sort of strength she had no idea she possessed,

she pulled out of his hold. 'I don't think so,' she said, mentally berating herself for not sounding as determined as she had planned. The trouble was she didn't know if it was possible to resist him. She was fighting herself more than him, and wondered if he knew it. Desires and needs she had never felt before shuddered through her almost constantly in his presence. Her body felt hijacked, hijacked by a need to be possessed by his hot, hard heat. The heat she could still feel on her skin even though she had put some distance between their bodies.

He waited a beat before asking, 'If it is not more money that you want, what exactly is it?'

Sabrina turned away. 'I realise you are used to having whatever you want, but I am not for sale.'

'Every woman is for sale,' he countered cynically.

'Not this woman,' she said, turning to face him again, her chin up.

The smile playing about his mouth was sardonic. 'We will see.'

'I mean it, Mario,' she insisted.

He rocked back on his heels, his eyes still holding hers. 'Do you ever think about that kiss?' he asked.

She schooled her features into indifference, although her mouth was tingling at the mere mention of that mind-blowing moment when she had tasted his mouth. 'What kiss?'

His smile deepened the grooves either side of his mouth, making him look even more devastatingly attractive. 'You know what kiss.'

'Oh, that.' She waved her hand dismissively. 'I forgot all about it. I was drunk. I can barely remember what I did that day.'

His dark eyes glinted. 'Liar. You remember every last

detail, don't you? And you were not drunk—a little tipsy, perhaps, but definitely not drunk.'

She pulled back her shoulders. 'I was not in control of my behaviour that day, and for that I am deeply ashamed,' she said. 'I promise you, it won't happen again.'

'You had better be able to control your behaviour in future, Sabrina, for during the time you are in my bed I expect it to be an exclusive arrangement.'

Sabrina gave him a glowering look. 'Are you usually so confident in the face of rejection?'

His glinting gaze teased hers. 'Always.'

'Then this time you are heading for disappointment,' she said, wondering if she was tempting fate by sounding so confident when she was anything but. He was so potently attractive; every pore of his strong, male body promised an explosive passion. One kiss had shown her how weak her defences were. Hating him clearly wasn't a big enough barrier, for she knew if he took it upon himself to capture her mouth right now she would be lost within seconds.

'If you would like to stretch your legs, I can mind Molly for an hour if you tell me what I need to do if she wakes up,' he offered after a moment.

Sabrina met his dark eyes. She wished she knew what was going on behind that enigmatic expression of his. Was he sizing her up, calculating how long it would be before she capitulated to his advances? Did he know how seriously tempted she was? How could he tell what sort of turmoil her body was going through? Was she giving off some secret signal or something?

'It's all right,' she said, shifting her eyes just out of reach of his. 'Her routine is a little out of sorts just now.

She might not wake at all, or she might wake as soon as she hears the door opening and closing.'

He pulled his loose tie away from his neck, coiling it as he stood before her. 'When we get to Italy I can engage a part-time nanny for the times you feel you need a break,' he said. 'There will be the occasional function we will be expected to attend as husband and wife, so we will need the services of a nanny in any case.'

Husband and wife.

Oh, how casually he said those words, Sabrina thought with a savage twist of her insides. They meant nothing to him; they were just words. They did not signify for him the relationship as it was meant to be, the relationship she had longed for all her life—one of closeness, security and friendship. Her mother had been denied it and now Sabrina was suffering the same fate. Life was cruel.

'I would also like Molly to learn my language,' he added. 'It is important she hears you speak it as well as me.'

'But I am not qualified to teach her,' Sabrina said, frowning at him in agitation. 'I can only speak a few words of Italian. I can barely say please and thank you. I'm afraid I don't have much of a talent for languages.'

'I will organise some tuition for you,' he said. 'It is imperative that young children hear both languages from an early age in order to become bilingual.'

Sabrina shrugged her acquiescence, even though she knew he would be wasting both his money and the tutor's time. 'As you wish, but don't say I didn't warn you.'

'I would also like you to update your wardrobe,' he continued. 'I will make sure you are well funded to do so.'

Pride stiffened Sabrina's spine. 'There is nothing wrong with my wardrobe as it is,' she said. 'I like my clothes.'

'In my opinion you would look better without them,' Mario teased.

Colour burned in her cheeks as she tried to stare him down. 'You haven't seen, and nor will you see, me without them,' she said. 'That is not part of the deal.'

His eyes roved over her, scorching her, making her feel as if she was standing in nothing but her goose-bumped skin. 'We could always make it part of the deal,' he said, locking his searing gaze on hers. 'How about it, Sabrina? How about another five-hundred-thousand euros to warm my bed?'

Sabrina felt her legs loosen and fought to stand firm. 'N-no,' she said, annoyed that her voice sounded so thready.

He undid the buttons on his shirt. 'If you change your mind, let me know.'

She tried not to stare as his masculine chest was revealed: dark, springy hair, tanned skin, sculptured pectoral muscles and a stomach that was flat and rock-hard. She felt her mouth go dry as she forced her eyes back to his smiling ones. 'What do you think you are doing?' she asked.

'I am getting undressed.'

'Here?' The word came out like a tiny squeak.

'Where else do you suggest I do so?' he asked. "This is *my* hotel room, is it not?'

Sabrina set her mouth into a prim line. 'Yes, but—'

He unhooked his belt. 'I could always do it in the corridor, but then the manager or other guests might have something to say about that, *sì*?'

'I am sure there are changing rooms on the pool deck,' she said, swallowing as he heeled himself out of his shoes.

'Yes, I suppose there are.'

She spun away when she heard the rasp of his zipper. 'Do you mind?' she choked.

'Sabrina, we are going to be officially married within days,' he said.

She hunched her shoulders, keeping her back turned. Did he have to keep reminding her? She was having enough trouble dealing with the reality of being tied to him, without him figuratively hitting her over the head with it at every opportunity. Was he doing it on purpose to show how he had all the power and control? 'So?' she said in a tone that asked 'what does that have to do with anything?'

'So you will have to get used to seeing me without clothes. I do not want my staff to think I have an unwilling wife in my bed.'

Sabrina felt her consternation increasing. 'You said it wasn't going to be a real marriage,' she said hollowly, still with her back turned towards him, every vertebrae feeling as if it was being unhinged as she listened to the rustle of his clothes being dispensed with.

'Nevertheless, we will have to share a bedroom from time to time.'

She spun back to face him, her heart pounding in her chest. *'What?'*

'I have dependable, trustworthy household staff at my villa in Rome, but when we stay abroad I must insist we share a bedroom like any other married couple,' he said, folding his trousers over the back of a chair. 'I do not wish the press to make a laughing stock out of me for not having a normal relationship with my wife.'

Sabrina stared at him in rising alarm, her heart rate soaring. 'But…but can't we have separate beds at such times?'

'No.'

Something about his intractable tone annoyed her beyond measure. 'You think I am going to sleep with you without a fight?' she asked, still trying not to look below his waist. He was still wearing his underwear, but with one involuntary glance she had seen enough to make her body crawl all over with traitorous desire.

'I expect you to know which side of your bread is buttered and how thickly, Sabrina,' he returned. 'I am paying you to act as my wife, and that is what you will do when I need you to do it.'

'I am not sharing a bed with you and that is final,' she said with a glittering glare.

'Then I will have to think of a way to convince you to do so,' he said. 'Leave it with me. I am sure I will come up with something.'

Sabrina was immeasurably annoyed that he was so confident she would cave in just like every other woman in his life had before. She was even more annoyed because she suspected he was going to succeed with her in spite of her paltry attempts to hold him off. 'How?' she asked with a curl of her lip. 'By using blackmail?'

His eyes held hers with steely purpose. 'If necessary.'

She drew in a wobbly breath. She was in no doubt of his ruthlessness. He had a hard edge to him that for some inexplicable reason was part of his lethal charm. He was aloof, untouchable, in control and powerful at all times and under all circumstances. 'I hardly think you could say anything about me that hasn't already been said,' she pointed out. 'My reputation is hardly pristine and worth protecting.'

'I was not thinking about using the threat of exposure to the press as my tool,' he said. 'As you say, what would be the point? Everybody already knows what sort of woman you are.'

Sabrina ground her teeth. Oh, how she wished she could prove him wrong. He would not look down at her in that imperious manner of his then. What would he say if she were to tell him the truth—that he wasn't marrying a sleep-around slut but a totally inexperienced virgin?

He would laugh at her, that was what he would do, she reminded herself. It was hardly something you could prove one way or the other, or at least not these days when women were physically active from a young age. It would be her word against her reputation, hardly a level playing-field, given what the press had said about her from day one of the Roebourne affair.

'Not going to deny it?' he asked in the throbbing silence.

'What would be the point?' she asked in return. 'You have already made up your mind about me.'

He held her gaze for endless seconds. 'You are rather a surprise package, Sabrina Halliday. Behind that demure façade you pack quite a sensual punch. I am almost tempted to refresh my memory of how passionate and tempting that soft mouth of yours can be.'

Sabrina stepped backwards, her heart giving a little skip and trip of alarm. 'Don't even think about it.'

He smiled an indolent smile that creased up the corners of his eyes. 'Oh, I am thinking about it, Sabrina,' he assured her. 'I think about it all the time.'

Panic beat a rapid tattoo in her chest as he stepped closer. 'S-stop it, Mario,' she said a little desperately. 'Stop flirting with me. That's what started it, you know—you flirted with me non-stop at the wedding. Don't do it. It…it annoys me.'

'Do you know what I have been thinking?' he asked as if she hadn't spoken, his dark eyes holding hers like head-lights aimed on a frightened fawn.

'No,' she said, running the tip of her tongue over her lips. 'No, I do not want to know what you've been think—'

'I have been thinking about how it would feel to have that soft mouth around me, your tongue licking me, until I—'

Sabrina pressed her fingers against his firm lips to stop him from going any further. 'No, don't say it,' she said hoarsely.

His eyes continued to burn their way into hers as he pushed his tongue against the pads of her fingers, the erotic action sending zigzags of electric heat right to her toes and back.

She pulled her hand away as if it had been burnt, her chest going up and down as she tried to control her erratic breathing.

'We could have fun together, Sabrina,' he said, still holding her gaze. 'Lots and lots of fun.'

She pursed her lips, trying her best to sound firm. 'I would rather watch paint fade…I mean dry.'

He laughed, the deep, rich sound having much the same effect on her as his tongue had against her fingertips. 'It will be interesting to see if that holds true once we are legally married,' he said, reaching for his bathrobe.

'You think putting a ring on my finger is going to suddenly make me find you irresistible?' Sabrina asked with a scowl.

'Diamonds have usually done the trick with all the women I have known,' he said with a mocking smile. 'Did you know I have recently acquired an investment in a large diamond company?'

She shook her head. 'No, but that's of no interest to—'

'I will have a ring made up with Marcolini diamonds, and then we will see just how irresistible I am, shall we?' he carried on in that arrogant manner of his.

Sabrina was steadily fuming. 'You really have an appalling opinion of women, don't you?'

'I am a realist,' he said, tying the ends of the bathrobe around his waist. 'I know the games women like you play. Money and prestige are paramount. You do not let feelings get in the way of position and power. That would ruin everything, would it not? You didn't love Howard Roebourne, for instance. He was just a meal ticket, a means to an end. What a pity it all went sour for you.'

Sabrina tightened her mouth even further. 'You don't know what you are talking about,' she said.

His dark eyes hardened with cynicism. 'He's told me what you were like, Sabrina. From your activities so far, I have no reason to doubt him.'

Colour flowed into Sabrina's cheeks. She had been so naïve in her handling of Howard Roebourne. She had not recognised the subtle moves he had been making on her until it was too late. 'He was lying,' she said through clenched teeth.

Mario picked up his room card from the table. 'After I have a swim I will have dinner brought up to the suite,' he said. 'That is, unless you think Molly is not too young to be taken out to a restaurant.'

Sabrina pressed her lips together. Dinner with others around would certainly be less threatening than sharing a meal in the room, commodious and luxurious as it was. But then Molly was only four months old, and the clatter of crockery and cutlery would hardly be conducive for a restful sleep. 'Um…I think today has been rather a big day for her,' she said at last.

His eyes held hers for a second longer than she felt comfortable with. 'As you wish,' he said.

Sabrina waited until he had left the suite before she let out her breath in a ragged stream. 'What were you thinking, Laura?' she whispered hollowly. 'For God's sake, what were you and Ric thinking?'

CHAPTER FOUR

SABRINA was sitting on one of the plush leather sofas, flicking through a magazine, when Mario returned from the pool. In spite of every attempt to ignore him, she felt her eyes drawn to his tall, imposing frame. He was wearing the hotel bathrobe but it was now hanging open to reveal the close-fitting black bathers that shaped his male form lovingly. The long, strong, tanned muscular length of his legs made her breath suddenly hitch in her throat. He was so intensely male she seriously wondered if any other man could hold a candle to him without it being snuffed out in shame. His slicked-back hair revealed the handsome contours of his face: his high, intelligent forehead, his patrician nose, his devil-may-care mouth and his dark eyes fringed with thick, black lashes still spiky with moisture from the pool.

'I'm going to have a shower,' he said with a glinting smile. 'Would you like to come in and scrub my back for me?'

Sabrina rolled her eyes and returned to her magazine. 'No thank you.'

'Afraid you might enjoy it?' he asked.

She closed the magazine and gave him a reprimanding

adult-to-recalcitrant-child look. 'Do you *ever* think about anything else besides having your physical desires met?'

His eyes locked with hers in a challenging duel. 'Yes, I do, as a matter of fact,' he answered. 'I think about how you slept with Roebourne under his wife's nose.'

Sabrina stood up and tossed the magazine down with a slap of glossy paper on marble. 'I did nothing with him,' she bit out.

One of his dark brows lifted in derision. 'I just can't quite believe you, Sabrina. I wonder, how much did he pay you to say that?' he asked.

'Have you ever considered I might actually be telling the truth?' she asked with a jut of her chin.

His eyes scanned her face for long seconds, as if making up his mind about her. Sabrina hated that she had a propensity to blush and fidget when under pressure. It made her look guilty and ill at ease, the opposite of what she wanted to convey. But then from the first moment she had been introduced to him Mario had made her feel like a naughty school-girl meeting the headmaster for some supposed misdemeanour.

'I have found in life there is not often smoke without some sort of heat behind it,' he said. 'The rumours that stick are usually the ones that have a grain of truth in them.'

'It seems to me it doesn't matter what I say, as you have already made up your mind about me,' Sabrina said. 'I would have thought someone who has spent most of his adult life subjected to the speculation of the press would have realised how unjust that is.'

'Ah, yes, but you have consistently refused to speak to the press,' he said. 'If you had nothing to hide, why not tell your own side of the story?'

Sabrina folded her arms against her chest as an image of Teddy and Amelia Roebourne came into her mind. Their young innocence was worth protecting even if it meant compromising herself. 'I don't have to explain anything to anyone,' she said. 'What I do or don't do in my private life is my own business and no one else's.'

'What you do once we are husband and wife will be very *much* my business,' he said, with a thread of steel underpinning his statement. 'I am sure I do not need to remind you, I am a high-profile businessman with many important clients across the globe. I do not want any personal scandals to disrupt my life, or indeed that of Molly's.'

Sabrina bristled at his autocratic stance. 'I suppose you want me to have no life at all while you carry on as normal? That's called a double standard, Mario, and in this country women don't take too kindly to it.'

'Then it is just as well you will not be in this country but in mine,' he returned. 'Of course, if you don't want to go through with the arrangement I can always find someone else to take up the position.'

Sabrina reined in her temper with an effort. She was dancing on thin ice with him, and he was ruthlessly reminding her of it. He didn't need her half as much as she needed him. The chances of her finding a husband at short notice were very slim indeed; the chances of finding a man who would love and protect Molly as if she was his own were even slimmer. She would have to see this arrangement through, no matter what the cost. There would be compensations, surely. She would have loads of time to be with Molly, to be the best substitute mother possible. And living in a foreign country would be an adventure of sorts. She had often toyed with the idea of working abroad and this was a perfect chance to do so.

'I am not going to desert Molly,' she said, with a determined set to her mouth.

His mouth was tilted in its usual mocking angle. 'Not to mention turn your back on a truckload of money. That would go against everything written in the gold-digger's guide to amassing a fortune, would it not?'

Sabrina glowered at him. 'I can see why your relationships only last a few weeks. No woman in her right mind would put up with your arrogance and rudeness any longer than that.'

'On the contrary, I make a point of always being the one to bring a liaison to an end,' he said.

'Have you ever been in love?' she asked.

'No.'

She couldn't quite stop her lip from curling. 'So your relationships are basically about sex.'

'More or less,' he said with another indolent smile.

Sabrina felt a faint shiver pass over her as his dark eyes held hers. There was something about him that deeply unnerved her when he looked at her like that. It was as if he knew what she was thinking, how her mind was conjuring up images of him pleasuring her, kissing her senseless, crushing her beneath him as he plunged into her moist softness.

She felt her womb contract as his gaze went to her mouth, each and every one of the pulsing seconds swollen with erotic promise. Her tongue darted out to moisten her lips, her heart thundering in her chest as he brushed the pad of his thumb where her tongue had just been, the caress so intimate, so sensually stirring, she felt her lips tingle all over with need.

She wanted to feel his mouth on hers, to taste his maleness, to feel the rasp of his unshaven jaw against her skin, to thread her fingers through his silky black hair, to feel his hard body pressed against hers in mutual longing. She tipped up her face, her eyes half-closed in silent appeal, a soft whimper of need sounding at the back of her throat as his head slowly came down towards hers.

Molly's cry from the bedroom was soft but it was enough to break the spell. Sabrina stepped backwards, one of her hands shakily brushing back her hair, her eyes slipping out of reach of his. 'I—I think she needs changing,' she mumbled as she slipped away.

As she saw to the baby's needs, Sabrina remonstrated with herself for being so foolish as to be tempted by Mario's touch. She had been so close to losing her head. She had been a whisker away from begging him to kiss her. Was she so pathetically weak? She had always been so sensible and in control, but for some reason Mario Marcolini made her feel out of control and reckless. He awakened in her a side of her personality she hadn't known existed. He made her aware of her body in a way no one else had ever done. He had only to look at her and she felt as if her skin had been set alight. Her body pulsed with longing, a persistent ache, that tortured her whenever he was around. It was like an itch she couldn't reach to scratch, a hunger she couldn't satisfy.

Sabrina could hear the shower running as she came back out to the lounge area with Molly in her arms. She tried not to think of Mario's naked body standing under the fine needles of spray, but her mind played traitor all the same. Even after she heard the water being turned off, she began to picture him drying himself with one of the big fluffy white towels.

'Oh, for God's sake,' she chastised herself after a few more minutes of mental torture. 'This must stop.'

'Everything all right?' Mario asked as he sauntered in with a towel slung low around his hips.

Sabrina swallowed tightly as her eyes ran over him. 'Er…yes. Fine…' she stammered.

He came over and tickled Molly under the chin. *'Come è la mia bambina?'* he asked.

Sabrina felt her nostrils flare to take in the clean, sharp tang of his aftershave. He was standing so close she felt his body heat; she could even see tiny droplets of water clinging to his slicked-back hair. He was smiling down at the baby, his eyes like melted chocolate, and his finger now stroking the tiny, dimpled cheek.

'She is so young and defenceless,' he said, meeting Sabrina's gaze.

'Um, yes. Yes, she is,' she said, scarcely able to breathe.

The baby grasped his finger with her tiny hands and gurled at him, her little legs kicking up and down in excitement.

'Is she hungry?' he asked. 'She seems to want to gnaw on my finger.'

'She might be teething,' Sabrina said. 'Some babies get them earlier than others.'

'Does it hurt?' he asked, looking at her again.

Sabrina felt herself drowning in the dark pools of his eyes. His forehead was creased slightly, his expression serious and concerned. 'Sometimes,' she said. 'Their gums can get a little red and sore just before the tooth breaks through.'

His gaze shifted back to the baby in her arms. 'Can I have my finger back, *mio piccolo*?' he asked.

Molly smiled and kicked her legs some more, still clutching his finger with her little dimpled hands.

Sabrina watched as his mouth curved upwards in another smile, the effect on her making her feel as if someone was slowly pulling a long silk ribbon out of her insides. She could see why Ric had insisted Mario be appointed as Molly's guardian. He might be an out and out playboy, but there was no question over his attachment to the child. She had seen biological fathers show less affection for their children than Mario did towards Molly.

Mario gently freed his finger and stroked the baby's wispy dark hair. 'Have you thought about what Molly should call us?' he asked.

Sabrina captured her bottom lip for a moment. 'I'm not sure,' she said. 'Mummy and Daddy seems—I don't know—not quite right under the circumstances.'

'Yes,' he said, frowning slightly. 'I have been thinking the same, but I suppose that is because it has been such a shock. We are not used to thinking of ourselves as her parents. I think in time I will get used to her calling me Papa. I don't want her to address me as "Uncle" or by my first name. I want her to look upon me as her father, even though I am not.'

Sabrina couldn't help noticing he didn't offer any suggestions over what she should allow Molly to call her. She could only suppose it was because he didn't envisage her being around in the long term. She looked down at the baby in her arms and felt her heart tighten at the thought of being shunted aside some time in the future. She couldn't let it happen, even if it meant fighting him tooth and ten bitten nails every step of the way.

Mario stepped back once Molly released his finger. 'Have you decided what you want from the room-service menu?' he asked Sabrina.

'I haven't had time to look,' she said, transferring Molly to her shoulder and gently patting her on the back to soothe her.

He picked up the hotel services guide and handed it to her. 'The chef will do anything to order if there is nothing on the menu that takes your fancy,' he said. 'Help yourself to a drink from the bar while I get dressed.'

Sabrina glanced at the bar once he had left the room, but in the end she decided against a unit or two of Dutch courage. The intimacy of sharing a suite was doing enough damage to her equilibrium. She was already having trouble keeping her mind focussed and in control. The last thing she needed was to have her inhibition blurred by alcohol, given what had happened the last time she had indulged.

Mario came out a few minutes later dressed in black trousers and a casual light blue shirt. His hair was still damp and finger-combed back, giving him a rakish look that was disturbingly attractive. 'Is Molly asleep?' he asked, looking at the baby snuggled peacefully against her neck.

'Yes; I was just waiting for you to come out so I could put her back down,' Sabrina said, moving past him towards the bedroom he had just vacated.

Once she had left, Mario poured himself a drink and wandered over to the bank of windows to look at the view. The city and harbour lights twinkled in the spring evening air, and he watched as a train crossed the Harbour Bridge like a long, golden centipede.

He felt a pang of loss deep in his gut at the thought of never seeing Ric Costelli again. How many times had they shared a drink and chatted about their lives and interests? When he'd received the news of the accident he had been rocked to the core. He had thought it was a mistake, a sick joke someone was playing on him. How could someone so vital and alive like Ric be lying now in a cold, dark grave?

Memories came flooding back: the childhood pranks he

and Ric had got up to when they'd been in elementary school; the day Ric had left with his family to come to Australia; the various trips they had taken when Mario had flown over to visit, most especially the skiing, when they had both stared mortality in the face and won.

Mario remembered Ric phoning him two years ago to tell him he had fallen in love with an Australian woman called Laura, and then just four months ago calling him in the middle of the night to tell him he was the father of a baby girl. Now Molly was an orphan; she would never know her mother or her father, never hear their voices, never look into their eyes and see the love they had had for her.

Mario was determined to do the right thing by Molly, even though it meant sacrificing his freedom for the time being at least. Although, the more he thought about it, it might not be such a hardship being temporarily tied to Sabrina Halliday. She had a certain allure about her—that defiant grey gaze, that stubborn chin, that quick-firing tongue and that slim but feminine-in-all-the-right-places body stirred him more than he had thought possible. She certainly wasn't his usual type. But he could not remember a time when he had wanted a woman more. Was it because she had held him at arm's length thus far? It wouldn't be for long, of that he was sure. She was as on-fire for him as he was for her; he could feel it every time their eyes met. It was like a vibration in the air, a high frequency of energy that passed between them. He saw the way her pupils flared, the way her tongue swept over her lips, making them moist and soft and so very tempting to taste.

God, he was getting hard just thinking about it. She would be dynamite in bed; he could tell from the way she had come on to him at the christening. Her soft, full mouth had barely touched his before it had flowered open beneath the responding pressure of his. Her tongue had tangled with his, her small, white teeth nipping at his bottom lip until he had been close to losing control. Her body had been so tightly clamped against his he had felt every delicious contour of hers, and he hadn't been able to wait to have her naked in his arms, to feel her creamy, satin skin against his. He had been tempted to take her up against the nearest wall, but the sound of someone coming had prevented him taking things that far. His body had throbbed and ached for hours afterwards, and he'd determined then that one day, somehow, he would have her.

He would make her forget all about Howard Roebourne and any of her other lovers. It would be *his* name she gasped when she came, it would be *his* bed she occupied, no one else's.

Mario turned and looked at her when she came back into the room. She met his gaze and he felt another surge of blood in his groin.

Yes, she would be *his*, he determined, and he had a feeling it would be sooner rather than later.

'Can I get you a drink, Sabrina?' he asked.

She shook her head. 'No, thank you.'

He twirled the contents of his glass as he held her gaze. 'I can order some champagne, if you would like it.'

A rosy hue came into her cheeks and she shifted her eyes away from his, although her voice was curt. 'No, thank you.'

'Have you decided what you would like to order?' he asked.

Her teeth worried her bottom lip as she flicked through the menu. 'I'll just have some soup and a roll,' she said, briefly meeting his gaze.

He raised one brow in a teasing arc. 'Surely you need more than that to satisfy you?' he said. 'You strike me as a woman of—shall we say—robust appetites.'

Sabrina felt her face grow hot at his *double entendre*. 'No, on the contrary, I am not one for over indulging,' she said, forcing herself to hold his satirical look.

He smiled a knowing smile. 'Only when you think you can get away with it, right?'

She set her mouth. 'Are we talking about food…or something else?' she asked.

'If Roebourne is to be believed, you are insatiable,' he said, still idly twirling the spirits in his glass. 'He said he had trouble keeping up with you.'

Sabrina silently ground her teeth. She could just imagine the light she had been painted in, one that made her look like a predatory trollop with no regard for anyone but herself. However, instead of defending herself, this time out of a perverse desire to annoy him she fed right into his assumptions with her response. 'I am surprised he admitted his failings in that regard. Don't all men like to portray themselves as full-blooded studs no matter what their age?'

A brittle look came into his eyes as they held hers. 'What did you see in him besides his money, I wonder?' he asked. 'He's at least thirty or forty kilograms over-weight and as ugly as a hatful, as the saying goes.'

'Unlike men, who place a high value on looks, women are much more accommodating when it comes to choosing a lover,' Sabrina clipped back. 'We choose a mate on other criteria.'

'Money being the primary one,' he inserted with a curl of his lip.

Sabrina gave her head a little toss. 'I am the first to

admit that money is not everything, but it does show a man who is going somewhere. No woman wants to be tied to someone who can't enhance her life in some way. What would be the point?'

'What about love?' he asked.

She raised her brow. 'Love, Mario?' Her tone was just shy of scoffing. 'I thought you didn't believe in love. I thought for men like you it was all about the physical, that you would never allow emotions to have a foothold.'

'Just because I have not felt love for a sexual partner does not mean I am incapable of ever feeling such an emotion,' he countered. 'The point is I have not met anyone who has that effect on me as yet.'

'What happens if you were to meet such a woman during the period of our marriage?' Sabrina asked, trying to ignore the strange, tight little ache she felt in her chest.

He put his glass down on the nearest surface before returning his eyes to hers. 'That would indeed be a difficult situation to be in,' he admitted. 'I have made a commitment to Molly, and yet I do not think Ric or Laura would have wanted me to sacrifice my own happiness indefinitely.'

'What if *I* meet someone?' she asked, deciding to play devil's advocate.

The hardness in his eyes turned to black marble. 'I would expect you to do the right thing by Molly,' he said. 'We both have to make some sacrifices until she is of an age where she can understand the circumstances of her life.'

'It's easier for you as a man,' Sabrina said. 'You can hold off having children of your own for years and years to come. I am twenty-five years old. I don't want to have children in my mid-to-late thirties. I would have liked to settle down in the next couple of years and have children while I am young and fit and healthy.'

'I understand that, and that is why this marriage between us is a temporary arrangement,' he said. 'By the time Molly is of school age, you will still be young enough to get on with your life.'

Sabrina frowned at him. 'But I've already told you, I can't just walk away from Molly like that. And what if the woman you eventually fall in love with resents having someone else's child to bring up? I know of several friends who have had to deal with stepmothers or stepfathers who made their lives absolutely miserable, especially when they have their own biological children. They always felt like the odd one out, like they didn't belong.'

'I will do my best to ensure Molly never feels like that,' he said. 'In any case, I do not envisage falling in love with a woman who does not also love Molly. As far as I am concerned, that child is a part of my life now and will be until the day I die.'

'It's very commendable of you, Mario, but life doesn't always work out the way you think it will,' she said. 'Love isn't something you can switch on and off. It happens, and it can happen between people who are totally unsuitable in other ways.'

'I am not planning on complicating my life in such a way,' he said. 'For the time being my life will continue as it has done. I work hard and I play even harder.'

'Will you be discreet with your playing hard, or am I to constantly be made a fool of?' Sabrina asked with an excoriating look.

'That, of course, is entirely up to you,' he said with an arcane smile.

She eyed him suspiciously. 'What do you mean?'

His dark gaze ran over her lazily, slowly undressing her as each second throbbed past. 'I would have no reason to make a fool of you by playing around if you were willing to entertain me at home.'

Sabrina felt her spine tingle at his indecent proposal, even though the rational part of her brain baulked at what he was suggesting. 'You think I would agree to be used by you?' she asked.

'For a price, I think you would do just about anything,' he responded cynically.

'I think you need to extend your social circle,' she said crisply. 'You have obviously been mixing with people who are not representative of how normal and decent people behave.'

'Come now, Sabrina,' he chided her. 'You can hardly describe yourself as normal and decent after what you have done. You have been accused of tearing apart a loving family for a roll in the sack with a man almost old enough to be your father.'

Sabrina mentally counted to ten. *Think of the children*, she told herself. It was not their fault they had a sleaze of a father and a cold and vindictive mother. 'In spite of what you might think, I am quite choosy in whom I sleep with,' she said. 'And you, I am afraid, do not qualify.'

Before she could move to counteract it, he suddenly pulled her up against him with such force the breath was knocked right out of her. She felt every hard ridge of him against her; his belt-buckle dug into her almost painfully, his fingers on her upper arms were like steel clamps and his eyes were like black diamonds as they clashed with hers. 'You are doing this deliberately, are you not?' he

ground out savagely. 'Teasing and taunting me with this
touch-me-not game. There is of course a rather coarse name
for a woman like you. Do I need to remind you of it?'

Sabrina pulled back against his grip but it was impossible to gain any leverage. She felt fear climb up her spine
on long, spidery legs, her heart picking up its pace and her
mouth going completely dry. 'Y-you're hurting me,' she
gasped, even though it wasn't quite true. Her traitorous
body wasn't feeling pain; it was feeling desire, hot and
strong. The blood was thundering through her veins,
making her breathless. Her breasts were swelling, her belly
turning to liquid, and her legs trembling as his strong ones
bracketed them either side. She felt the bulge of his erection
swelling against her, the erotic reminder of all that had
pulsed between them from the moment they had first met.

He wanted her.

She wanted him.

And in spite everything she felt about him Sabrina suspected it might not be too long until they both got what
they wanted.

'You would open your legs right here and now if the
price was right. But I am not going to pay you any more
than I have already agreed on.'

'I don't want your filthy money,' she spat at him, eyes
blazing with hatred.

'But you want me,' he said, his fingers tightening a frac-
tion. 'I can see it in your eyes and I can feel it in your body.
When we do it, Sabrina, you will not forget it in a hurry, I
can assure you. Your body will hum and throb for days afterwards—I guarantee it.'

Sabrina felt her head spin at his sensual promise. She
could feel his potency, the dangerous heat of him burning

its way through her paltry resistance. She was in no doubt making love with him would be totally unforgettable. One stolen kiss had shown her how vulnerable she was to him. She had practically melted in his arms, just like she was doing now. He had only to bring his mouth down to hers now and she would be his willing slave. It galled her to think she was so weak where he was concerned. What was wrong with her? Was she turning into the sensual witch he took her for?

'Admit it, damn you,' he continued in the same rough tone. 'You want me to beg like all the others have done. That is how you get off, is it not? You like to have power over the men in your life. That way, you can get what you want from them.'

Sabrina was way out of her depth, but doing her best to struggle to the surface. 'You are wrong, Mario,' she said somewhat shakily. 'I don't want any such thing.'

'So innocent,' he said with the customary cynical twist to his mouth. 'Even Ric fell for it, and he was usually so adept at identifying a fraud.'

'I am not a fraud,' she said. 'I am just like you—trying to do the best thing for Molly under incredibly difficult circumstances.'

He put her from him almost roughly. 'I have no idea why Ric and Laura nominated you as co-guardian,' he said. 'But I swear to God, if you put one foot wrong you will never see that child again. Do you understand?'

Sabrina held her ground but on legs that were trembling. 'You can't take her away from me,' she said in a voice that was nowhere near as strong and determined as she had intended.

His eyes burned like a laser beam into hers. 'You just watch me.'

CHAPTER FIVE

SABRINA made herself scarce until their room-service order arrived. Her stomach was in knots of tension and she wondered if she would be able to do the light meal justice with Mario sitting opposite her looking at her in that contemptuous way of his. The injustice of it all was stinging. She had nothing to be ashamed of, other than her blindness to the devious ways of men like her previous employer. If only she had suspected Howard Roebourne's motives from the start she could have done something to prevent the shame of being labelled as the seductress who had shattered the harmony of a supposedly loving family. Imogen Roebourne had latched on to Sabrina as the culprit, not for a moment listening to her denials of any wrongdoing. Imogen had been determined to switch the anger she should have been feeling towards her wandering husband on to the babysitter instead. Sabrina still cringed when she thought of how poorly she had been portrayed in the press. She was almost grateful now she had no living relatives to witness the shame that had been dumped on her. Her foster parents now lived interstate, and rarely kept in touch, but if they were to hear of the rumours Sabrina knew they would automatically assume she was the guilty party.

Sabrina's mother had been a young single-mother in the days when it had still been a stigma to have no man claiming paternity of the child. Sabrina had never known who her father was in spite of her longing to do so, especially since her mother's death. The sense of not belonging to anyone by blood made her longing for a family of her own all the more intense. From a very young age she had dreamed of building a relationship with a reliable and faithful man, bearing his children and raising them in a home that was happy, loving and secure.

Her hopes and dreams would have to be shelved now, for she could see no way how she could abandon Molly—and, attractive as he was, Mario was not the sort of man to settle down and agree to provide Molly with a stepbrother or sister or two. He was intent on doing the right thing by Molly, certainly, but only as far as it didn't interfere with his easygoing playboy lifestyle. That was where Sabrina came in. She would be the wife on paper, the substitute mother, until he found someone more suitable to occupy his bed. Whether or not his future bride if he chose to have one would also occupy his heart was not something Sabrina could decide. It was hard to imagine Mario Marcolini falling in love. He didn't seem the type to allow himself to be vulnerable to anyone. There was an element of the bad boy about him, a fast-living playboy who was untameable in every possible way. And the way he had orchestrated everything so far made her realise how seriously outclassed she was in dealing with him.

But, while Mario was wild and worldly, Sabrina on the other hand desperately wanted to find someone who would love her and protect her—someone who would be there for her no matter what, the sort of man who would look at her with love shining in his eyes, adoring her for who she was, not for how she looked. Not that her looks were anything to be ashamed of. She knew she was fortunate to have inherited her mother's slim figure and model-like cheekbones. Her grey eyes were thickly fringed with dark lashes that hardly needed the boost of mascara, and her skin was fine and clear apart from a light dusting of freckles on her nose.

But men like Mario Marcolini wanted perfection in their partners, and she was hardly that. She didn't possess anything glamourous in her wardrobe, which he had already alluded to; nor did she have expensive make-up in her cosmetic bag, nor did she wear handmade designer shoes. She was a chain-store girl out of necessity, not choice, although she knew how to highlight her best features when the situation called for it. No wonder Mario thought she was trash, she thought. Men born to privilege could be appalling snobs when it came to mingling with the other half, and she was very definitely the bottom end of the other half.

The room-service attendant arrived with a loaded trolley, the aroma of delicately prepared cuisine stimulating Sabrina's flagging appetite.

Mario tipped the attendant, and once the door closed after the young man's exit Sabrina felt the intimacy of the set-up all over again. She was alone in the luxury suite with him, a delicious meal set before them with no possibility of interruptions by other guests or staff like there would be in a restaurant. A bottle of wine was on ice, the scene set for seduction if he put his mind to it.

She chanced a glance at him, trying to read his expression. She felt that tiny quiver in her belly when her eyes met his, the rumble deep inside like a miniature earthquake, reminding her of how much he affected her. Those dark brown, almost black eyes of his contained both cynicism and something else that she suspected was a glint of determination. He wanted to conquer her, to show her to be the wanton woman he thought she was.

The trouble was Sabrina thought he might very well be right. She felt wanton and out of control when in his presence. It wasn't just his debonair looks and worldly charm; it was something else she couldn't quite put her finger on. She wanted to toss caution to one side and experience the passion he promised in every taut and muscular line of his body. As lovers went, she suspected he would be right up there on the scale of demanding, adventurous and earth-shatteringly satisfying. He would expect full participation and do everything possible to achieve it. Her intimate muscles contracted in delight at the thought of experiencing his sensual attentions. She suspected her body would shatter into a thousand pieces of pleasure under the expert touch of his mouth, hands and very male body.

She had seen enough of him so far to know he was not lacking in that department. He wore his sensual expertise like a second skin; she could feel it whenever he touched her. Just minutes ago when he'd had her rammed tightly against him she had felt the power and potency of him, the need building in him to subdue her, to claim her, to make her his in the most primitive and yet natural way possible. Her body recognised him as her nemesis. He was the one man she had no resistance to. She turned into putty when he touched her.

It frightened her to think she had no defences to hold him off. That one kiss four weeks ago still taunted her. She had thought of nothing else since. Her mouth even now was tingling with the need to feel the commandeering pressure of his, to feel his thrusting, searching tongue conquering hers. She had seen how powerfully he was made; she had felt him swollen and erect against her. His dynamic male body would totally consume her smaller one, stretching her, making her a woman in the real sense of the word, showing her a world of feeling that was way beyond what she had experimented with so far.

She had been kissed before, but not with the heated passion Mario's mouth offered. He made every kiss she had ever received seem like a chaste peck on the cheek in comparison. After that first move of hers, he had plundered her with a ruthlessness that had shocked and delighted her at the same time. He had triggered a response in her that she had not been able to damp down since. It was simmering there, keeping the network of nerves under her skin in semi-arousal mode, actively waiting for the next caress, the next touch, that would activate them into hot, throbbing life again.

Sabrina knew she had to be extra vigilant around him. He was too practised at this. He had women all over the globe falling over to experience his possession. She would lose valuable ground in joining them. She had never been one for jumping into the fire; unlike many other women her age, she could delay gratification. It was more or less her hallmark. For all of her adult life she had ignored the advances of men to keep her goals in sight. She wanted more for her life than a temporary liaison that had the potential for heartbreak, as her mother had experienced. And as far as Sabrina could tell Mario Marcolini had 'heartbreak' written all over him. God knew how many women he had already cast aside with their hearts in tatters. She certainly didn't want to be one of them.

'Take a seat,' Mario said as he lifted each of the silver dome-lids covering their meals on the trolley.

Sabrina sat on the edge of her chair, her tastebuds responding to the array of dishes set before her. The delicious-smelling cream-of-mushroom soup and the crusty bread-roll with its shell-like curl of fresh butter made her empty stomach rumble hollowly.

Mario had ordered a man-size meal: tender fillet wagyu-steak, steamed vegetables and a potato dish that was creamy and crispy at the same time.

He poured her a glass of chilled white wine and a glass of red for himself. 'Does Molly usually sleep through the night?' he asked as he picked up his glass of ruby-red wine.

Sabrina picked up her own glass, wondering if it was wise to indulge when she was already teetering on the edge of losing her self-control. 'The last couple of nights she hasn't woken, but usually by about three or four months most babies get into a routine of sleeping through the night,' she said.

Mario spread his napkin across his lap. 'How did you get into nannying?' he asked. 'Was it something you always aspired to?'

Sabrina put down her untouched glass of wine and picked up her water glass instead. 'I have always loved children. I was an only child, so I guess that might have had something to do with it. I worked in a childcare facility for a while, but I felt I wanted to bond with the children, and it was not always possible to do that when kids came and went so often. Becoming a nanny and spending extended periods of time with infants and small children in their own home was much more satisfying for me. I could really get to know them and their routines, as well as become part of the family unit. That in itself is very beneficial for very young children. Of course, no one else could ever replace their mother and father, but having another caregiver who is involved in every aspect of their lives is tremendously comforting to them—especially when both parents are busy professionals and very often time-poor.'

'So how did you come to work for the Roebournes?' he asked with an unreadable look.

Sabrina felt her colour start to rise. Looking back, she could see how stupid she had been in accepting the post. There was no way she could frame it without it sounding as if she had inveigled her way into the Roebourne household in order to conduct a clandestine affair with Imogen's husband.

She switched glasses and took a deep sip of her wine, hoping it would settle her nerves—but all it did was demonstrate how shaky her hand was, a sign of guilt if ever there was one, or so she thought by the way Mario's dark gaze zoned in on it like a hawk swooping down on unsuspecting prey.

She took an uneven breath and, bringing her gaze back to his, explained, 'I met Howard Roebourne at a charity event I was attending. He mentioned his wife was hoping to return to work after staying at home with their two children, who were four and six. He also mentioned how their attempts to find a suitable nanny had failed to find anyone remotely suitable.'

'You were unemployed at the time?' he asked, still watching her with that piercing gaze.

Sabrina tried not to fidget under his scrutiny. 'The family I had previously been working for had recently accepted a posting abroad. I would have gone with them if they had offered me the position, but the children were of school age by then, and the mother decided she wanted be a stay-at-home wife for a change. So, yes, I was at a bit of a loose end at the time.'

'Did you get on with Roebourne's wife?' Mario asked after another short pause.

Sabrina had never been all that good at lying and had to rely on every scrap of acting ability she possessed to answer his question. 'She was always very professional towards me.'

'But you were not friends…' It was neither a question nor a statement, but something in between.

'I was an employee,' she said, becoming increasingly annoyed by his attitude. 'Are you best friends with all the people who work for you?'

'Some I consider friends,' he answered. 'But obviously Mrs Roebourne did not take to you from the word go.'

'Mrs Roebourne was a disinterested and at times harsh mother, who in my opinion should never have had children in the first place,' she blurted unguardedly.

Mario's dark brows lifted. 'You clashed with her over the handling of the children?' he asked. 'Or perhaps it was because you had designs on her rich husband and wanted her out of the way?'

Sabrina wished she had kept her mouth closed. It seemed no matter what she said she painted herself in a bad light. 'I don't want to talk about it,' she said, picking up her glass again and taking another incautious mouthful.

Mario put his glass down with a dull thud on the table. 'How long did the affair go on?' he asked.

She glared at him resentfully, playing him at his own game. 'What is it to you? You are hardly one to call the pot

every shade of black, considering how many affairs you've
conducted over the years.'

His dark eyes speared hers. 'I am not denying my sexual
profligacy, but to date I have never stolen a married woman
from her husband.'

'Marriage is just a piece of paper,' Sabrina threw back. 'It
means nothing if the couple are not committed emotionally.'

'So I suppose Howard Roebourne told you his wife was
cold and did not understand him?' he said. 'That's the way
it usually goes, does it not?'

Sabrina gripped her glass so tightly her fingers went
white. 'She was cold and hostile towards her husband, and
even the children sometimes. I don't know why he stayed
with her, or her with him, to tell you the truth.'

Mario's top lip curled in disgust. 'So you eased his
marital suffering by offering your young and nubile body
at every available opportunity.'

'Look, Mario,' she said in rapidly rising frustration,
'The Roebournes' marriage was a mess well before I
entered the fray. Howard was having an affair—I suspect
not his first—with someone else long before I came into
their employ.'

Mario studied her for a long moment. Her colour was
heightened, her body tense, as if desperate to convince
him of her lies. But he wasn't going to fall for it. He'd
known Howard for years, and Howard had told him everything—how Sabrina had orchestrated her seduction of him
from that very first meeting. She'd had her designs on a potential sugar-daddy, and who better than a wealthy man
who was struggling to keep his home life together for the
sake of his children? It would take a saint to resist a woman
like Sabrina Halliday. She had a sensual allure about her

that was intoxicating. That intriguing combination of doe-eyed innocence and surly defiance made every drop of Mario's blood drain from his brain to his groin even now. The way she pouted at him made him want to crush his lips to hers. She could snip and snarl at him all she liked, but it did nothing to disguise the naked hunger he could see in her eyes. Howard Roebourne obviously hadn't been able to satisfy her, which left the field right open for him. And it would be very satisfying, very satisfying indeed, to have her writhing and gasping in his arms.

He could hardly wait.

He topped up her wine glass before attending to his own. 'You expect me to believe your word over his?' he asked.

'What possible reason would I have to lie to you?' she asked, frowning at him.

He leaned back in his chair and surveyed her for another lengthy moment. 'I have no reason to doubt Roebourne's account, having personally experienced your seductive wiles.'

'Oh, for pity's sake!' Sabrina threw back in outrage. 'If anyone is to blame for that kiss, it's you. You took advantage of me.'

His eyes raked her mercilessly. 'Careful, Sabrina,' he warned. 'Those are very serious charges you are laying at my door. Are you sure your recollection of the day in question is accurate?'

Sabrina wasn't sure who she hated more: him for reminding her of her one moment of weakness, or herself for responding to him so feverishly at the time. 'I was not in control of myself,' she said, knowing it sounded rather feeble. 'I don't usually drink more than one glass of alcohol, especially on an empty stomach. If I gave you the wrong impression back then, I am sorry. I can assure you it will not happen again.'

He smiled at her indolently. 'I am counting on it happening again—tomorrow, in fact, when we get married. The groom always gets to kiss the bride, correct?'

Sabrina felt her eyes widen to the size of the soup bowl in front of her. *'Tomorrow?'* she choked.

'I have applied for a special licence,' he said evenly. 'The magistrate has made special dispensation in order for us to travel to Italy as Molly's legal guardians. I have already activated the adoption formalities, but they will take some time.'

Sabrina felt as if her life was spinning out of control. She had comforted herself with the hope that she would at least have a few days to get used to the idea of marrying Mario and moving abroad. Now it seemed she would barely have enough time to pack a bag before she was legally his wife. Her heart began to hammer in panic. It was too soon. She needed more time. But then would *any* amount of time be enough?

'Of course it will by necessity have to be a registry-office affair,' Mario continued.

'Too bad if I wanted a white wedding with all the trimmings,' Sabrina put in, unable to refrain from sounding churlish.

His eyes glinted with derision. 'A white wedding?' he asked. 'Would that not be rather hypocritical, given your sexual history?'

She brought up her chin. 'Most women regardless of their sexual experience dream of being a proper bride,' she said. 'It's the one day in a girl's life she can feel like a princess.'

He sat looking at her for so long without speaking, Sabrina began to wish she hadn't spoken. She sat, trying not to squirm in her chair, her cheeks growing hotter by the second, her stomach in tight knots and her girlhood dreams in tatters. Just like her mother, all she had ever wanted was to be married—to wear a beautiful dress and veil, to wear something old, something new, something borrowed and something blue. But just like her mother she was going to be cheated out of it. She chided herself for being so senti-mental. It wasn't as if it was going to be a real marriage in any case. And it was certainly not going to last any length of time if Mario had his way. But still…

'I fail to see why you should desire a huge fuss for a marriage that for all intents and purposes will not be a normal one,' Mario said, voicing her thoughts out loud.

'That's not the point,' she said. 'People with the sort of wealth and public profile you possess will expect you to have a proper wedding, not some hole-in-the-corner affair.'

Mario began to drum his fingers on the table, his eyes still tethering hers. 'What is this about, Sabrina?' he asked.

She caught her bottom lip between her teeth. 'Nothing,' she said. 'Forget I said anything. You're right—a registry office makes perfect sense under the circumstances.'

Mario wondered what she was playing at. Did she hope to make him think twice about ending the marriage by making him commit to the formality of a full-blown, church-sanctified ceremony? He was Italian, after all; the church was a deeply entrenched part of his culture, and she could hardly be ignorant of it. She was a devious little madam, perhaps far more devious than he had first allowed. Did she want the world to know she had landed herself a wealthy business tycoon? Perhaps, to whitewash her reputation over her involvement with Howard Roebourne. But there was no way Mario was going to dance to her particular tune. He would marry her—but on his terms and his terms only.

'I have chartered a private jet for our trip to Rome,' he said, changing the subject. 'I thought it would make it more comfortable for Molly. Long-haul flights are not the most pleasant experience in a commercial plane, even in business class, and particularly so for an infant, I would imagine.'

'You seemed to have thought of everything,' she said, still looking at him with a sulky expression.

'I am doing my best to cover all bases,' he answered. 'However, I have not yet purchased a wedding or engagement ring for you to wear. I thought I would wait until we are in Rome. I have a jeweller friend who acts as an agent for the Marcolini diamonds.'

She gave a 'couldn't care less' shrug. 'You can get one from a fairground slot machine for all I care. I am quite sure that's what you would really prefer to do.'

Mario felt his jaw lock with tension. 'Do not push me too far, Sabrina,' he said. 'It is not too late for me to find someone else to step up to the plate and be a mother to Molly.'

Her grey eyes were stormy as they warred with his. 'I am not going away without a fight,' she said. 'I am going to hate every minute of being married to you, but I love Molly enough to endure whatever torture you dish out.'

Mario tossed his napkin aside, his mouth set in an intractable line. 'You can hate me all you like, but one thing I absolutely insist on is that you keep your ill feelings out of the sight and hearing of Molly. She might be too young to speak as yet, but she has eyes and ears. I do not want her poisoned against me by you.'

Sabrina wished her nails were long enough to score down his arrogant face. Anger raged inside her, red spots of it almost blinding her as she returned his heated glare. How she hated him! He was everything she most despised in a man. She was unused to feeling such powerful, over-whelming emotions. She was normally such an even-tempered person, slow to anger, patient to a fault—and yet in Mario Marcolini's presence something inside her burned like a hot flame, threatening to totally consume her. But she knew if she gave in to her fury he would use it against her. He had the power to do whatever he wanted. She would never see Molly again, and he would not have a twinge of conscience about it.

In less than twenty-four hours they would be married. That would at least give her some sort of security and a rightful place in Molly's life, for the time being at least. All she could hope for was that he would see in time how much Molly needed her and allow her a permanent place in the little girl's life, even if it meant she had to suffer regular contact with him as joint custodian.

Taking a deep breath to calm herself down, she picked up her wine glass and took another sip, all the time watching the way Mario's dark eyes surveyed her with brooding intensity. 'You know something, Mario?' she said after a moment. 'I think that works both ways, don't you? If Molly hears you calling me names and other such opprobrious names, what sort of husband and father figure will she think you are?'

He reached for his glass, his eyes still on hers. 'I dare say we will both have to watch our tongues when interacting with each other,' he conceded. 'But I am sure all parents have to at times shelve their differences for the sake of their children.'

'Children are highly perceptive,' Sabrina pointed out. 'They can nearly always sense when their parents are at loggerheads, even when the parents think they are hiding it. It can cause great emotional distress for youngsters when they feel undercurrents of tension all the time.'

'Then we will have to make sure we settle our differences well before Molly is of an age to be affected by them,' he returned.

'How do you suggest we do that?' Sabrina asked, frowning in wariness.

'We shall have to call a truce,' he said, raising his glass in preparation for a toast. 'How about we make a toast?'

She cautiously touched her glass against his. 'What exactly are we drinking to?' she asked.

He gave her an enigmatic smile. 'To making love, not war,' he said and, lifting his glass to his lips, he drained the contents.

CHAPTER SIX

SABRINA put her glass down on the table with a hand that trembled slightly. 'I…I need to check on Molly,' she said, and pushed back her chair.

Mario got to his feet. 'I have a few calls to make and some emails to send, but I will do it downstairs in the business centre so I don't disturb Molly,' he said. 'Feel free to get into bed whenever you are ready.'

Sabrina felt her body tense. 'Um…I think I would be more comfortable sleeping on the sofa,' she said.

His eyes smouldered as they held hers. 'You do not fancy sharing my bed, Sabrina?' he asked. 'What—is it too soon after leaving Roebourne's?'

She tightened her mouth, refusing to respond to his taunt, beyond caring if it confirmed his opinion of her as a tart. Let him think what he liked. He was hardly one to throw the first stone, given his easy-come easy-go approach to the women in his life.

Mario came to stand in front of her, blocking her exit. 'I can make you forget all about him,' he said.

Sabrina sucked in a breath when he stroked his finger-tip down her cheek to just within reach of her mouth. Every sensitive nerve in her face bloomed in response. Her lips began to tingle; the anticipation of feeling the brush of his mouth against hers became almost unbearable. Her eyes were trapped by the mesmerising heat of his, the silent communication of attraction and hot-blooded desire making her heart begin to pound and her legs feel as if they were turning to water.

She watched as his mouth slowly descended towards hers, millimetre by millimetre, the light, warm breeze of his breath caressing her expectant lips, thrilling them, ramping up her excitement until she was tilting towards him, her eyes fluttering closed as his mouth finally, bliss-fully met hers.

It was a potently explosive kiss. But then Sabrina wondered if any of Mario's kisses were anything else. Everything about him communicated his sexual power, most particularly his utterly sensual mouth. She felt the hot, hard heat of him as his mouth commandeered hers, his lips firm and demanding, and yet strangely gentle and persuasive. She opened her mouth on a shuddering sigh, her whole body shaking in reaction when his tongue drove through the small opening in a thrust-like movement, an erotic imitation of what his lower body would do if she let her resolve slip.

She felt him explore every corner of her mouth in erotic detail, his teeth taking her bottom lip in a nip-like tug that sent a zigzag of lightning down her spine. His tongue tangled with hers again, playing with it, teasing it, stroking it and then subduing it, reminding her just exactly who was in control. It certainly wasn't her, Sabrina thought ruefully. She was giving a pretty fair imitation of a lustful libertine, and yet there seemed to be nothing she could do to stop it.

As soon as his lips met hers, she felt as if he had turned

a switch on in her body. It was programmed to respond to him and only him. It wasn't that she hadn't been kissed before, but never so thoroughly, and never to the point where her body melted like honey under a blow torch. She could feel the slick moisture of desire between her thighs, her intimate cleft swelling with need, the on-off pulse deep inside her aching for the delicious friction of his thick, hard possession. She could feel him against her, the outline of his maleness inciting her to kiss him back with heated fervour. Her tongue was stroking his boldly, her teeth tugging at his lips, both top and bottom, in little kittenish bites that brought a primitive groan of approval from deep within him.

'*Lei è una tentatrice,*' he growled, and deepened the kiss even further, pushing her back against the wall, his hands going to the proud mounds of her breasts.

Sabrina felt her spine almost collapse when he cupped her, for even through the layers of her clothing she felt the exhilarating electricity of his touch. But, impatient to feel her skin on skin, he tugged her top out of her skirt, and with a deftness that spoke of his monumental experience he unclipped her bra, freeing her aching, swollen breasts to the ministrations of his warm, caressing hands.

It was mind-blowing to feel her nipples embed themselves in his warm palms, the intimacy of his touch taking her by surprise, and yet delighting her at the same time. The weight and shape of her breasts seemed to be a perfect match for the cup of his hands. Never had she felt so feminine, so in tune with her body. Every pore of her skin seemed to be throbbing with feeling, her senses shuddering with the need for fulfilment. She squirmed against him, rubbing against his touch, wanting more, so much more.

She wanted to feel his hot mouth sucking on her, to feel those white, hard teeth of his pulling on her erect nipples, to feel the rasp of his tongue on her sensitive flesh, to feel him delight in her femaleness as she was delighting in everything that made him a man: the evening shadow peppering his jaw, the insistent pressure of his mouth, the driving heat of his tongue, and the thundering pulse of his blood that left her in no doubt of his erection and the pressure for release building within him. She could feel his hardness against her, so tantalisingly close to where her body ached and pulsed with need.

Her mind began to picture him, imagining how long and thick he was. She was shocked at where her thoughts were leading her, but with his magical mouth setting hers alight and his hands shaping her so possessively she was lost to the traitorous workings of her brain.

His mouth moved from its sensual assault of hers to suckle her right breast, the moistness, the heat and fire of him making her gasp out loud. The caress of his hands on the creamy, smooth skin of her breasts had sent her pulses soaring, but the feel of his tongue rolling over her tightly budded nipple was beyond anything she had felt before. Her nerves exploded with feeling as the rasp of his tongue circled her before he drew on her with his hot, moist mouth.

Desire flooded her being, sending sparks up and down her spine, buckling her legs, loosening every ligament, until she felt as if she was going to melt into a pool at his feet. She dug her fingers into the thick thatch of his hair, holding on to anchor herself as he subjected her to even more of his earth-shattering caresses. Every nerve-ending fizzed with sensation. She was on fire for him, every atom of her being screaming for the fulfilment he was holding, tantalisingly just out of her reach.

Just when she thought she could take no more, his mouth came back to hers, swallowing her whimper of pleasure as his tongue found hers and swept it up in a dance that shook her to the core of her being. She clung to him, her body pressed so tightly against him she felt every hard ridge of him, each point of contact thrilling her beyond description. Her mind took her on another erotic journey, conjuring up images of his body naked against hers, their limbs entwined, their bodies rocking in the quest for satiation.

Almost without realising she was doing it, Sabrina slid her hands down his back, exploring the well-formed, tightly bunched muscles that even his shirt could not disguise. She went lower, underneath his jacket, to feel the tautness of his buttocks, her stomach giving a little hollow gulp when she felt him surge against her in response to her touch.

The need to feel him in her hands, to shape the hot, hard potency of his aroused body, was a temptation she suddenly could not resist. With tentative shyness her hands skimmed over his slim hips before she brushed against the front of his trousers where the fabric was stretched with the heated trajectory of his arousal. She stroked his outline, her fingertips quivering at the latent power of him. She felt him flinch, as if her touch had burned him, and a rough, primal-sounding groan sounded from deep within his throat as his mouth ground against hers with increasing fervour.

Suddenly the kiss was over.

Mario stepped back, capturing both of her shameless hands in one of his, a blade of disdain sharpening his dark-as-pitch gaze. 'You know, that is quite some sensual repertoire you have perfected, Sabrina,' he said. 'I was within moments of letting you have your wicked way with me.'

Sabrina had to give herself a mental shake to reorient herself. Her senses were skyrocketing all over the place, her heart-rate galloping, her lips still throbbing and her colour at an all-time high. She lowered her gaze and, wrenching out of his hold quickly, covered herself, hating him for making her lose control in such an abandoned way. No doubt he had done it deliberately, showing how he could pick her up and put her down like a toy that amused him one minute and bored him the next.

When she finally met his gaze once more, she made sure her features were blank, even though her body was still screaming out in frustration. 'It was just a kiss, Mario,' she said in an offhand tone. 'It was never going to be anything more than that.'

'Perhaps. But if you change your mind about occupying that sofa, let me know,' he said with a glinting smile. 'You never know where the next kiss might lead, now, do you?'

It annoyed Sabrina that he was so clearly unaffected by what had happened just moments earlier. He showed no signs of a man pushed to the limits of physical control. Instead he looked cool and calm as if they had done nothing more than exchange a quick, platonic peck on the cheek.

She on the other hand felt completely undone; her emotions were all over the place, not one of them making any sense to her. She wasn't in love with him, far from it, but neither was she as immune to him as she so dearly wanted to be. What was it about him that made her feel so out of sorts?

Well, maybe that wasn't so hard to answer after all. He had 'casual sex' written all over him. She had known it the moment Laura had introduced her to him the day of her wedding. The memory was as clear as if it had been yesterday.

'Just wait until you meet Ric's best man, Mario Marcolini,' Laura had said with a twinkling smile as she'd made a last-minute adjustment to her veil. 'I am sure you two will get on like a house on fire.'

Sabrina had rolled her eyes as she'd handed Laura another bobby pin. 'I hope you are not trying to match make, Laura,' she cautioned. 'You know how I feel about that sort of thing.'

Laura had given her a guileless look as she'd slid the pin in place. 'I wouldn't dream of doing any such thing. It's just that Mario is quite a catch. He's disgustingly rich, and now that he's past thirty he's surely going to be thinking about hanging up his playboy hat for something a little more substantial in terms of a relationship. You are perfect for him. It's that "opposites attract" thing. He's a man of the world; you are a young woman who hasn't even been around the corner, let alone the block several times. He's so cynical; you're so fresh and trusting. I tell you, it's a match made in heaven.'

Sabrina had grimaced in embarrassment. 'Oh, please, you don't have to keep reminding me how unsophisticated and inexperienced I am.'

Laura had given her a fond smile. 'Don't be so hard on yourself. Not every man these days wants an experienced temptress in the bedroom. Ric loved the fact he was my first lover. I am so glad I waited. I know it's considered terribly old-fashioned, but I never felt I was ready before I met him. He told me it was the greatest gift I could have given him.'

Sabrina blinked herself back to the present. Mario was

looking at her in that cynical way of his, probably thinking of how he could cajole her into his bed with the crook of one finger. 'If you want a wife in the real sense of the word, you are going to have to pay for it,' she said, goaded beyond reasonable caution.

He gave her a mocking look as he reached inside his jacket for his wallet. He unfolded it, took out a thick wad of notes and fanned them out on the coffee table next to her like a hand of cards. 'I hope that covers the entertainment so far,' he said. 'It was quite a floor show. I am looking forward to an encore.'

Sabrina glowered at him, her anger towards him like a swirling hot tide of lava inside her. 'You think you can get whatever you want by opening your wallet, don't you?'

His hard gaze raked her mercilessly. 'I know I can, Sabrina,' he drawled. 'You, my little gold-digger, just proved it.'

Sabrina thought of several stinging retorts to hurl his way, but before she could utter even one of them he had turned on his heel and left.

The sofa in the end made quite a comfortable bed, and even though Sabrina hadn't expected to be able to relax enough to sleep she found herself drifting off regardless. Molly was asleep in her pram nearby, and apart from the occasional snuffle she slept soundly until about four in the morning, when she began to whimper on and off.

When it was clear Molly wasn't going to settle back down again, Sabrina turned on a lamp and changed the baby's nappy before heating her bottle. Once Molly was fed, Sabrina sat on the sofa and gently rocked the pram with her foot to settle the baby back to sleep.

The front door opened and Mario came in, still dressed in the clothes he had been wearing earlier, although he'd pulled his shirt free from the waistband of his trousers. His hair looked as if he had run his fingers through it several times, and his jaw was heavily shadowed with stubble. Although his eyes had shadows beneath, they still contained a devilish light when they collided with hers.

'Waiting up for me, sweet Sabrina?' he asked.

She gave her eyes a quick roll of disdain. 'I can see why you have booked the largest suite in the hotel—no doubt it is to make room for your ego.'

Mario laughed as he undid a couple of buttons on his shirt. 'And I can see how it might be rather fun being married to you. The challenge of taming that quick tongue of yours could prove to be very entertaining.'

Sabrina threw him a filthy look. 'I can't stand men who think they can control the women in their lives.'

'Ah, but you are not really the woman in my life, are you, Sabrina?' he said. 'But perhaps you would like to be, *sì*? That would be the icing on the cake, would it not? A rich man for a husband, a child thrown into the bargain and a lifestyle other people only dream about.'

She gave him a withering look. 'I can think of nothing worse than being tied to you.'

A light of challenge came into his eyes. 'I think you are playing a very clever game,' he said. 'No doubt you have played it many times before. But with me, young lady, you have taken on much more than you realise. I am not going to be manipulated by you. I know what you want and how far you will go to get it. The next thing, you will be telling me you are in love with me and want our marriage to continue indefinitely.'

She rolled her eyes. 'As if.'

Mario smiled. He liked nothing better than a woman who was quick with a come back; it showed a level of intelligence that was a match to his. Sabrina's feisty nature was becoming increasingly attractive to him. He was so used to women simpering around him, bowing to his demands without a whimper of protest.

Sabrina on the other hand fought him tooth and nail, snarling at him like a cat cornered by a snapping terrier. It made him all the more determined to tame her, to have her purring in submission in his arms, welcoming him like a lioness who recognised the alpha male of the pride, giving herself to him because she realised there was no other male who could satisfy her the way he could.

And he *could* satisfy her. He knew it as surely as he knew where his next breath was coming from. He had not felt anything like the heat he felt in her kiss; he had not felt anything like the fire in her touch as her hands had skimmed over him, barely touching, but setting fires on his flesh all the same. His skin was still smouldering, the ashes of banked down desire still glowing, threatening to erupt into consuming flames if she so much as pressed her soft mouth to his.

'I am going to catch a couple of hours' sleep,' Mario said. 'Are you sure you will not join me in my bed?'

The disparaging look she gave him made his skin tighten all over with excitement.

Later today she would be his wife.

Legally.

Officially.

And from what he had seen and tasted of her so far he did not think it would be too long before she agreed to be his wife in every sense of the word.

CHAPTER SEVEN

THE registry-office ceremony was just as disappointing as Sabrina had imagined it would be. A disinterested official conducted the short, impersonal exchange of vows and the paperwork was signed and sealed in less time than it would have taken a real bride to walk down the aisle of a church. The only thing that stood out for Sabrina was the part where the marriage celebrant gave Mario permission to kiss the bride.

Sabrina had been preparing herself for that moment for hours, but even so when his mouth came down on hers she felt every bone in her body melt. Her lips clung to his, her body sinking into the leanly muscled strength of his tall frame. The kiss was brief but intense—but because Mario was the first to bring an end to it Sabrina felt cheated, wondering if he knew she was secretly longing for more. It was so hard to read his expression; he gave no indication of the event of their marriage affecting him whatsoever, which in a perverse sort of way upset her even more.

The press were in their droves on the street outside, but Mario had already organised a security team to keep them at bay. It was impossible to prevent them from taking a few snapshots, however, and Sabrina was glad she had gone to the trouble of wearing her best outfit, a pale-pink suit and a string of pearls and earrings that had belonged to her mother. She had piled her hair in a casual but still elegant knot on her head, and taken extra care with her make-up, recognising she was now playing a role that required all the poise and sophistication she could muster. She didn't want any of Mario's previous and future lovers to look at her and think he had married trailer trash. She was determined to show everyone, including Mario himself, that she was a young woman who knew how to carry herself in the public eye.

There was no reception following the service, no crystal flutes of the best champagne to toast the future, no throwing of the bouquet—there wasn't even a single flower for her to toss. Instead there was a flurry of activity as Mario's driver ushered them into the waiting limousine to take them to the airport for her departure to Rome.

Molly thankfully had slept through the proceedings and didn't wake until Sabrina had to lift her out of her baby carrier in order to go through the security check-point.

In no time at all they were led to the waiting jet, and once the safety demonstration was over, the sleek plane taxied along the runway before it finally took off like a giant metallic bird.

Sabrina was glad she had Molly's needs and comfort to see to as it kept her attention away from the silent figure seated beside her. She was intensely aware of him, however. He only had to turn over the page of the thick folder of documents he was reading for her to shiver in reaction at the occasional brush of his arm against hers.

Eventually the stress and emotional turmoil of the day got the better of her, and, with Molly asleep in the bassinet against the bulkhead, Sabrina closed her eyes, promising herself she would have a little power-nap to refresh herself before Molly next woke.

Mario breathed in the sweet light fragrance of Sabrina's light brown hair as she leant against his shoulder. She smelt of fresh spring flowers, sweet peas and jasmine, a subtle but alluring combination that made his concentration drift away from the article on fund management he was supposed to be reading.

He looked at her small, slim hands lying on his right thigh, their ringless state reminding him of his need to organise an engagement and wedding ring to add credence to their sudden marriage.

He had phoned his brother and briefly explained the situation, and Antonio had encouraged him to concentrate on what was best for Molly. Building a long-term relationship with Sabrina was not something Mario had ever considered, but he was starting to see how the baby responded to Sabrina as if she was indeed her biological mother. He didn't want to think too far into the future, but he comforted himself that lots of children survived the divorce of their parents or guardians. Being stuck in a loveless marriage was not an option for him; his parents had enjoyed a mostly happy and fulfilling relationship up until his father had suffered a fatal heart attack. His mother's decline over the last five years and recent death had made Mario even more convinced marriage was not for him. He didn't like the thought of being dependent on someone for anything, including emotional support. He had seen what had happened to Antonio and his wife, how the tragedy of their stillborn first child had torn them apart for five long years.

Did he want that sort of emotion in his life? It was hard enough being responsible for Molly, whom he loved as if she was indeed his own. He didn't like the uncertainty, the sense of vulnerability, that giving all of yourself to another person created. He had never been in love, and often wondered if it was an overrated emotion to cover more base desires, which in the end usually burned out all by themselves. He knew too many married couples who could barely stand the sight of each other, grudgingly staying together for the sake of children or combined assets.

Even if he had been thinking along the lines of marriage Sabrina was not the sort of woman Mario had ever envisaged as wife material. She might have a knack with infants and children, but what man wanted a wife who was likely to stray at the first opportunity? For the duration of their marriage he would have to keep a very close eye on her. He didn't want her making a fool of him behind his back. He was the first to admit he had more than his share of pride, and he had no doubt from what he had seen so far that Sabrina was just the type who would find it entertaining to grind it into the dust.

Although, looking at her now totally relaxed in sleep, it was hard to imagine her with the bed-hopping reputation she had been tarred with. He supposed that was why she was so successful at luring unsuspecting men into her orbit. She had a little-girl-lost look at times that had the potential to confound the hardest of hearts. He knew he had to watch himself around her. He was so used to playing the game with women who had the same motives as himself: sex without ties, fun on the run, nothing permanent and certainly no emotional investment. Sabrina challenged all that with one look with those smoky-grey eyes, not to mention her all-female body with its promise of passion in every delicious curve.

Mario moved his arm to encircle her as she nestled closer. A soft sigh escaped her lips, her hands moving farther up his thigh to where his blood was already pumping like a piston. She was so practised at her game she could seduce a man in her sleep, he thought wryly.

She murmured something and lifted her head, blinking at him groggily. 'What time is it?' she asked, brushing at her disordered hair, the action releasing another whiff of its fragrance into the air.

'Rome time or Sydney time?' he asked, trying to resist the urge to tuck a loose tendril of her hair behind her ear.

She straightened in her seat, her eyes going straight to the sleeping baby. 'Has she woken?'

'No, she slept like a…' He suddenly smiled. 'Like a baby.'

Sabrina turned and looked at him, her heart giving a little jerky movement in her chest at his smile. The smile had travelled all the way up to his eyes, making him look so utterly gorgeous that her breath stalled. She swallowed and tore her gaze away, concentrating with fierce intent on the sleeping baby. 'Yes, well, whoever made up that adage obviously hadn't had a baby,' she said to fill the silence.

'Perhaps you are right,' he said, stretching out his legs.

'How soon before we land?' she asked as she looked out of the window to distract herself from the proximity of his long legs so close to hers.

'The pilot has already started his descent,' he said. 'It won't be long before the cabin crew will want us to prepare for landing. It seems a shame to wake Molly, but she is safer strapped in one of our laps than in the cot.'

The announcement came through as Mario had predicted, and Sabrina cuddled Molly close as he helped fix the infant seatbelt-attachment to hers. She barely breathed as his long-fingered hands dealt with the clip and straps, her stomach sucked in tightly in case he inadvertently or indeed deliberately touched her. She could feel her heart doing crazy back-flips at his proximity, the masculine scent of him dancing around her face.

Before he sat back in his seat his gaze found hers, holding it for a pulsing beat or two of silence. Sabrina was the first to pull her gaze away, her desperate attempt to act cool and composed spoilt somewhat by the blush she could feel spreading over her cheeks. She drew Molly close and, taking a shallow breath, settled back in her seat as the plane began to make its way down.

Within a few minutes they were safely on the ground and soon after they'd made their way through customs, and finally to the chauffeur-driven vehicle waiting outside. The press took a couple of photographs, and Sabrina noticed Mario seemed to be particularly annoyed by the intrusion as he swore at one of the paparazzi as he shouldered his way past, keeping Molly close against his chest.

Sabrina absorbed the view as they drove towards the city. The ancient ruins of the Colosseum went past, and a flicker of excitement travelled through her belly in spite of the circumstances of their paper marriage. Her only overseas trip prior to this had been to New Zealand, and, although stunningly beautiful and with its own ancient Maori history, it was nothing like the eternal city of Rome. There was so much to see, so much history and so much beauty, it was almost too much for her to take in.

Mario pointed out the various points of interest along the way, including the Celian Hill and then the Vatican in the distance. 'I will be busy at work but I will organise someone to accompany you on a guided tour of all the sights,' he offered as they drew close to his *palazzo*.

Sabrina was surprised at the tiny jab of disappointment she felt. It wasn't as if she even liked his company; why then should she want him to be the one to show her around? 'I am sure I will be perfectly able to find my way around by myself,' she said as the car purred to a stop outside an imposing-looking *palazzo*.

'I am sure you are more than capable, but I must insist on Molly's welfare being attended to at all times,' he said as he helped her out of the car. 'Rome is a beautiful city, but like a lot of cities its size it has it dangers—congested traffic being one of them. You are not used to cars being on the other side of the road, for instance. You would only have to push Molly's pram out on the road ahead of you for tragedy to strike if you were not concentrating.'

Sabrina could see his point, but she couldn't help noticing it was Molly's safety he was primarily concerned about, not hers. If anything it could prove to be rather convenient for him if something was to happen to her. He hadn't wanted a wife, and certainly not one with the sort of reputation she had.

She pushed her pique aside as Mario led the way inside the *palazzo*. The housekeeper came bustling towards them, barely gracing Sabrina with a glance before turning in delight at the baby, who was soundly asleep in the baby carrier.

Mario made a few cursory introductions, but it was clear to Sabrina he had been brutally honest with his staff about the woman he had married. A hard nut of anger lodged in her throat and she clenched her teeth behind her coolly polite smile each time another staff member was introduced to her. She was determined to have it out with Mario in private, however. Surely it had been unnecessary to swing the jury before she had even stepped over the threshold?

It didn't help that everyone spoke Italian in a rapid-fire manner that made it impossible for her to pick up some of the very few words she had managed to learn from Laura. It made her feel all the more shut out, as if they were determined not to make any allowances for her.

'Giovanna will show you to your room,' Mario informed her. 'I have to call in at my office to catch up on some paperwork which needs my immediate attention. I will no doubt see you later this evening.'

Sabrina wondered if the paperwork he was going to catch up on was slim and blonde with breasts you could serve a meal off. She pushed her resentment down with an effort, turned and followed the housekeeper up the huge flight of stairs, trying not to show how overawed she was by the opulent furnishings on the way. Priceless works of art hung upon the walls, marble statues and busts were displayed along the lower and upper landings, and even the runner of carpet that followed the curve of the staircase felt as it if had been woven from air.

The housekeeper opened a door about halfway down the second-floor landing. 'This your room,' she said. 'The *bambino* next door. Signore Marcolini next door to that.'

Sabrina thanked her, and without another word Giovanna left with a disapproving rustle of her starched, black uniform.

Molly made a noise from the carrier, and Sabrina sighed and bent down to take her out. She held her close, silently promising she would see this through for the baby's sake, no matter how difficult it turned out to be.

* * *

Sabrina resisted falling asleep too early in case she couldn't sleep that night. She felt jet-lagged, but with Molly to bathe and feed it gave her a focus to keep going. But once Molly was settled in the nursery next to her room there was little else for her to do but wait until it was a reasonable time to go to bed.

The housekeeper had informed her earlier that evening that dinner would be served at eight-thirty, but when Sabrina went downstairs she ended up eating alone as Mario hadn't yet returned. There was no message from him that she could find, and although she longed to ask Giovanna if Mario had told her when he would be back she resisted doing so.

The large dining-room with its solitary place-setting on the highly polished, seemingly endless table made her feel all the more isolated. The food was delicious, however, and although her appetite was affected by the change of time zone she still managed to do the meal justice. She even drank a glass of wine, figuring it would help her to relax when it came time to go to bed.

She thought about waiting until Mario got home to speak to him about the housekeeper's coldness towards her, especially in view of Molly—who although still so young would before too long become aware of undercurrents of tension—but she decided against speaking with him until she was more rested. He was hard enough to resist with all her faculties working; God only knew what would happen if she locked horns with him in the edgy state she was currently in. She felt jittery and agitated, restless and frustrated. Trapped might be a better word, Sabrina thought as she finished the last of her wine. She was trapped by her own traitorous thoughts of Mario pleasuring her, introducing her to the sensual world of sexual pleasure. She felt a little shudder rumble through her as she remembered the passion in his kiss, the teasing of his tongue and the way her body had responded.

Was this energy always going to be simmering between them? she wondered. Or was he dealing with his desire by taking the edge off it with his mistress? Jealousy tightened Sabrina's insides to coils of barbed wire. She hated thinking about him with another woman—*any* other woman. For all the weeks since that kiss she had tortured herself with thoughts of his mouth passionately exploring other women's mouths. It was stupid of her to act like a put-upon wife, but she couldn't help it. She had taken his name and she was damned if she was going to be made of fool of, even if it was just in front of his household staff.

Sabrina made her way upstairs and, once she was confident Molly was still sleeping peacefully, she found herself eyeing the other door leading off the nursery. What would it hurt to have a quick peek into Mario's domain? He wasn't home, and even if he did return she would surely hear him come along the landing, as she had heard Giovanna earlier. She wavered for a moment. *Will I or won't I?* The temptation was dangling there, just waiting for her to give in to it.

There was so much she didn't know about her new husband. Surely it was her right to inspect his private quarters? How else could she find out who he was, what he liked, what he didn't like, what things he chose to have around his private space? She had read somewhere that the three keys to knowing someone was to meet their family, go for a drive with them behind the wheel, and look into their bedroom. Well, Sabrina hadn't yet met Mario's older brother, but she had been for a drive with Mario behind the wheel, so this was the next step. Maybe she was rationalising her intrusion into his privacy, but he had railroaded her into marriage, so surely she had a right to get her own back?

Sabrina watched as her hand slowly reached out to the door knob. It was still not too late to pull back, but instead of doing so she turned it clockwise and the door opened. And then, taking an uneven breath, she stepped over the threshold.

It was a very masculine room.

A large, king-size bed was made up with linen that looked every bit as luxurious as that on her own bed two doors away, but instead of the pink-and-white ensemble on her bed his was starkly black and white. The bedside tables followed the theme; they were black marble, and the lamp-stands polished white marble, the shades a muted grey.

Sabrina could smell him in the air she breathed, the hint of his aftershave, the musk of his male body, and something else she felt drawn to in a way she could neither explain nor understand.

She wandered over to the huge bed, stroking her hand over the spread, her fingertips tingling with sensation as she thought about his long, strong body stretched out in sleep or in the process of hot, passionate sex. How many women had he entertained in here? How many women had he pleasured with his leanly toned body—not to mention that sensual mouth of his?

Sabrina stumbled backwards from her wayward thoughts, only to come up against a wall of warm, hard, male muscle. She spun round, her eyes going wide when she came face to face with Mario. 'I…I was just…just…' Her voice trailed off, her colour rising, her heart stuttering behind her ribcage like a two-stroke engine.

Mario's cynical gaze stripped her naked. 'Come to play, Sabrina?' he asked.

Sabrina brushed at her loose hair with a hand that wasn't quite steady. 'I was just, um, looking around.' It sounded so pathetic, so contrived. It sounded like a woman who was on the prowl, and she could see from the dark glint in his eyes that was exactly the way he had read it.

'Looking around for what?' he said, snaking an arm out to block her exit, his eyes like steel darts pinning hers.

She felt the searing brand of his hand on her forearm, his long fingers overlapping each other around her slim wrist. The air pulsed with tension, a tension she could feel passing from his body to hers. It was as if by merely touching their blood was heating, the temperature rising by the second, until she felt sure she was going to boil unless he let her go. 'N-nothing,' she said in a cracked whisper.

He pulled her up close to his body, chest to chest, thigh to thigh, temptation to temptation. 'We both know what you are looking for, don't we, Sabrina?'

Sabrina could see her own desire reflected in the black pits of his eyes. His pupils were dilated, so much so she had trouble distinguishing the irises from them. Could he see what she was feeling? she wondered. Could he see how she longed for his mouth to capture hers and titillate her senses into overload?

The tip of her tongue came out over her lips, and her stomach folded as his eyes dipped to follow its movement. His eyes came back to hers, the message in them plucking at the strings of her desire, playing a melody she had no hope of resisting. She felt each and every one of the vibrations throughout her body, her breasts aching as they pushed against the lacy restraint of her bra. Her legs felt unsteady, her heart rate equally so. Her body was suddenly outside of her control; it was acting of its own accord, doing things she had not thought possible just a few moments ago. It was moving against his, seeking his hot, hard heat, her hips melting into the thrust and grind of his like the wanton woman he took her to be.

'God damn you,' he growled and, bringing his head down, crushed her mouth beneath his.

It was just like his last two kisses, explosive and out of control within seconds. Sabrina relished every sweep and thrust of his brandy-scented tongue; she revelled in every guttural groan he tried to suppress as she moved against him instinctively. It felt so good to be in his embrace; it felt so right for some strange reason. Her body fitted so neatly against his, her feminine softness against his hardness in a way that made her feel as if this was meant to be, that this moment was inevitable, and had been from the moment they had first met. That first spark of interest in his dark eyes had awakened her femininity, made her become aware of her body and its needs, and how only he could meet them. No one else had affected her the way he did. She didn't think anyone else could, not now she had been singed by the sensual heat of his touch.

She could have stopped him, she *should* have stopped him, but still she returned his kiss—inciting him to caress her breasts, to shape them with his hands, to tug her clothes out of the way so he could feel her skin on skin, so he could open his mouth over one erect nipple, sucking, licking and drawing on her until she was whimpering in pleasure. He moved to her other breast, subjecting it to the same passionate assault before he pressed her backwards towards the bed.

Sabrina considered telling him of her inexperience. She

even opened her mouth in that brief moment when his left hers, but all she could manage to say was his name: 'Mario…'

His dark eyes swept over her hungrily, making her blood race through her veins at a terrifying pace. 'I told myself I would not do this,' he said, breathing hard. 'But the truth is I have wanted to do this since the first day we met.'

'I wanted it too,' she breathed against his lips as they sealed hers again with a kiss that left her in no doubt of where they were heading from here.

Sabrina felt the mattress at the back of her knees, but even then she didn't stop him. It was like someone else was in charge of her senses; it wasn't the sensible Sabrina Halliday who rarely dated, let alone kissed a man she barely knew. It was someone else, a sensual addict who pulsed and throbbed with lust for a man she all but hated.

She fell back on the bed with his weight coming over her, his muscled thighs entrapping hers, his hands dealing with her clothes in much the same manner as she was dealing with his—frantically. Buttons popped, fabric ripped, and still it didn't register that she should call a halt. She wanted this. She wanted to feel his passion, she wanted to feel him lose control because of her, because of the electric heat that had been passing between them like lightning bolts from the moment they had met.

She lay beneath him, naked except for her knickers, her body writhing beneath the one last barrier that separated them. He had somehow dispensed with everything but his briefs, his aroused length pushing against that final, fragile shield like a tightly clenched fist pushing its way against a pair of closed velvet curtains.

She sucked in a breath as he drew the lace from her body, the slow but steady slide of fabric down her thighs making her arch her spine in readiness for him. She quickly moistened her mouth. 'Mario…' she began. 'I'm not—' She stopped, pulled up short by the fear of him not going on if she told him the truth. She wanted this so much; she needed him to make her feel complete. Stopping now would leave them both stranded and unsatisfied.

His eyes questioned hers. 'Sabrina?'

She ran her hands over his broad shoulders, relishing in the feel of the strength in his bunched muscles. Somehow she wasn't so sure about hating him as much now. She wasn't quite sure if it was possible to hate someone who had such an amazing ability to make her feel the way she was feeling.

'Nothing,' she said, letting out a breath that prickled like a tiny free-floating thorn in her chest.

After a moment he reached across her to open the bedside-table drawer to retrieve a condom. 'Don't worry,' he said. 'I have protection. We don't want any accidents.'

It was a timely reminder of how many times he had done this in the past, but somehow Sabrina managed to ignore that in order to follow the instincts of her body. She watched as he sheathed himself, his length sending another wave of feverish excitement through her.

He positioned her beneath him, locking his mouth on hers as he drove into her warm, moist heat in one deep, slick thrust that brought a gasp of sharp pain from Sabrina's mouth into his.

She felt his whole body freeze above hers.

She blinked back the tears that had sprung to her eyes, feeling exposed in a way that was deeply unsettling as his frowning gaze sought hers.

'What's the matter?' he asked in a gravel-rough tone.

Sabrina chewed at her lip, her eyes falling away from his. 'I...I should have told you.'

He anchored her chin to bring her gaze back to his. 'Should have told me what?' His eyes, those dark, melted-chocolate eyes, contained a flicker of uncertainty, something she had never seen in them before.

She ran the point of her tongue across her lips, the taste of him still lingering there. His body was still encased in hers, hot, hard and stinging her slightly, although she did her best to conceal it. She felt foolish, gauche and foolish, like an immature child pretending to be an adult. She also felt a failure, a miserable failure at pleasuring a man. This was her first sexual experience and it was forever going to linger in her memory as a fiasco of monumental proportions. Shame coursed through her. She felt it in her cheeks, a burning fire that his dark intense gaze was stoking as each throbbing second passed.

'Sabrina?' he prompted.

She fought against the wobble in her voice. 'I—I'm not very experienced.'

Mario slowly eased himself away from her. He had not for a moment considered she was a virgin. How could he have? He thought back over each and every conversation they had had and couldn't remember a single clue to suggest she was anything but the slut the press had made her out to be. If anything she had on one or two occasions actively encouraged him to believe the stories about her were true.

Guilt drove a dagger into his gut, ripping him wide open with remorse. He had hurt her; he had stolen from her the preciousness of her innocence, slaking his lust with no thought for anything but doing it, and doing it roughly and quickly.

For all the years he had been dating and sleeping with

partners, he had not once encountered a virgin. All the women he slept with had been as experienced as him, and, in his early-adult years, some even more so.

He was deeply ashamed. He was not used to feeling so out of his depth. He was used to being in control, used to having things his way. He had always trusted his judgement. He had rarely got it wrong in the past.

And yet he had got it horribly wrong about Sabrina.

Horribly, horribly wrong.

He looked at her grey eyes shining with moisture, and another blade of blame sliced through him. He cleared his tight throat, swallowing against the golf ball of guilt that had lodged there.

'Sabrina…' He sat upright, pulling the covers to shield her nakedness, wincing again when he saw her blood on the stark white of the sheet between her slender legs.

'It's all right,' she said, blushing like a rose. 'It was my fault for not telling you. I was going to, but I felt so embarrassed. I let you believe—'

Mario cut the air with a sharp, coarse oath. 'I will not have you take the blame for what just happened,' he insisted. He clawed his fingers through his hair as he got off the bed, turning his back to dispose of the condom, before he reached for a robe.

Once he was covered, he turned back to face her. 'Damn it, Sabrina, I hurt you. I was so rough with you I could have damaged you.' He swallowed again, but his guilt would not move, either up or down; it remained to choke him until he could barely speak. How could she ever be the same after what he had done? He rubbed at the back of his neck, his guilt crawling beneath every pore of his skin. He had acted like an animal. He had hunted her down and mated with her, not taking the time to get to know her as she deserved to be known.

He dragged his gaze back to her slim body lying in his bed. She hardly took up any room, her light weight barely making an impression on the mattress. He was six-feet-four and, although lean, he was close to twice her weight. He couldn't bear to think of how tiny she was. He was disgusted with himself. He could barely stand to be in the same room as her for the shame he felt.

He strode, agitated, to the *en suite*, came back with a warm, damp face cloth and handed it to her. 'Is there anything I can get you?' he asked, deeply ashamed of how inadequate it sounded.

She shook her head, her small fingers clutching at the face cloth, her cheeks going a deeper shade of pink. 'No, thank you. I just need to have a shower and…and get some sleep. I think it was the jet lag, you know? Why I allowed things to get so out of control…'

Mario swore again. 'Do not let me off the hook so lightly, Sabrina. I deserve to be horse-whipped for what I have done.'

Her small, white teeth sank into her bottom lip again, her eyes moving out of reach of his. 'I was with you all the way,' she said so softly he almost didn't hear it.

'Not quite all the way,' he said, and with a ragged sigh left her to dress in privacy.

CHAPTER EIGHT

SABRINA crawled out of Mario's bed and, using the sheet as a wrap, bent down to pick up her scattered clothes. She winced as her inner muscles protested and another wave of embarrassment washed over her.

Stupid. Stupid. Stupid.

What had she been thinking?

She could blame it on the jet lag or the glass of wine she'd had with dinner, but deep down she wondered if that was just a cop out. She knew exactly why she had allowed him to make love to her: she wanted him. It was as simple as that.

Was that wrong?

No, of course not. What young woman of her age worried about having sex with someone they were deeply attracted to? She was old-fashioned, out of date and naïve to think sex was only for those who were in love. She wasn't in love with Mario. She didn't even like him. And yet there was something about him that drew her inexorably towards him. She felt like a small fluttering moth attracted to a dangerously hot flame. She had just got burnt and had only herself to blame.

Sabrina checked on Molly before she went to the *en suite* off her room. After a shower she curled up on her bed, hugging a pillow to her chest, torturing herself with wondering if Mario had left the *palazzo* to have his needs met elsewhere. Her mind began to picture him with his blonde mistress, the catwalk model she had seen him with in the newspapers several times. No doubt *she* would not have flinched at his touch, nor would she have blushed like a schoolgirl at seeing his naked body in full arousal. Sabrina groaned and put the pillow over her face, trying to block the taunting images.

When there was a soft knock at her door, she blinked in surprise. 'Y-yes?' she said.

'Sabrina, it's me,' Mario said. 'May I come in?'

'Um, yes.' She sat upright as he came into the room.

He too had showered. He was dressed in jeans and a T-shirt, not nightwear as she was, but then she assumed he didn't own any. She couldn't imagine that long, leanly muscled body encased in boring old-fashioned flannelette or cotton pyjamas.

His gaze ran over her for a moment. 'How are you feeling?' he asked.

Sabrina felt her face heating under his scrutiny. 'I'm fine.'

He came over to the bed and sat on the edge of the mattress, his brow heavily furrowed. 'Why did you not defend yourself about the Roebourne affair?' he asked.

She hugged her knees to her chest, her flesh tingling with awareness with him so close. She couldn't stop looking at his mouth, thinking of how it had burned so fiercely against hers.

Mario tipped up her chin so her gaze met his. 'Sabrina?'

She pressed her lips together, trying to keep herself from pitching forward into his arms to finish what they had started. Her body was still aching for him. Every nerve was on high alert for his touch, even her chin felt like fire where his fingers were holding her.

'I didn't want to upset the children,' she finally said.

His brow furrowed. 'The Roebourne children?'

'Yes. They are very young, but not too young to hear what would have been said about their father in the papers if I had told the truth about what had happened.'

Mario released her chin and picked up one of her hands instead, stroking the back of it with his thumb as he held her gaze. 'What did happen?' he asked.

She looked down at her hand in his before bringing her eyes back to his. 'I was very naïve about him,' she said. 'I didn't realise he was grooming me to be his scapegoat. By the time I did realise what was going on it was too late to do anything. The children had enough to deal with, without learning about their father's attempts to seduce me. Besides it was his word against mine. I couldn't see how anyone would believe me.'

Mario's hand tightened around hers. 'Did he threaten you in any way?' he asked.

Her grey eyes became shadowed for a brief moment. 'A couple of times, yes.'

Mario felt his insides burn with bile. He was not a violent man, but right now he wanted to drive his fist into Howard Roebourne's face for how he had maligned Sabrina's reputation. But he was just as angry at himself for treating her the way he had. If he had been thinking with his head instead of other parts of his anatomy he would have realised she couldn't possibly be as bad as she had been portrayed. In spite of her friendship with Laura, Ric would never have agreed to have Sabrina nominated as guardian of Molly if he had not had complete trust in her.

Mario brushed the pad of his thumb across her bottom lip, surprised yet again at how soft her mouth was. A tight little silence pulsed for a beat or two.

'Are you still sore?' he asked hollowly.

She shook her head. 'Please, Mario, don't make a fuss about it. It was my fault for not telling you.'

Mario got to his feet, raking his hand through his hair as he paced the floor. 'Maybe—but if you had told me do you think I would have believed you?' he said in self-disgust. 'I would probably have laughed at you, Sabrina, and carried on regardless.'

'I don't believe that,' she said in a soft voice. 'I don't believe you would have forced me to do anything I didn't want to do.'

He turned to face her, his expression grim. 'I forced you to marry me.'

She gave a little shrug of her slim shoulders. 'For Molly's sake—yes.'

He blew out a breath. 'The thing is, Sabrina, I can't undo what has been done, not yet, at least. You deserve much better than this.'

Sabrina hugged her knees again. 'I'm not sure what you are saying.'

His eyes were very dark as they meshed with hers. 'Why did you let me make love to you earlier this evening?' he asked.

'I'm not sure.' Her teeth sank into her lip again.

'It can not happen again,' he said. 'You do understand that, don't you?'

Sabrina didn't want to examine why her chest suddenly felt so tight. The thorn was back in her throat, making it hard for her to speak past it. 'If that's what you want.'

He muttered a coarse swear-word as he began to pace the floor again. 'What I want is immaterial. Molly needs us both, and we will have to stay married for the time being to keep her out of the clutches of the Knowles, who will no doubt push for custody if we suddenly announce our separation.'

Sabrina could see the sense in what he was saying even though a part of her—the feminine, romantic part of her—was already starting to play with the fanciful scenario of him falling in love with her and asking her to be his wife for real.

Love?

She mentally flinched. Was she in love with him? She had never been in love before but she imagined it would feel exactly like this. Her stomach felt hollow, her heart felt like it was being squeezed between two book-ends and her body was burning for more of his touch.

She chided herself for being so foolish. It was clear he was no longer attracted to her now he knew she was so inexperienced. Some men were like that. They didn't want to spend time tutoring a novice; they would much rather have an experienced lover in their bed. If not his current mistress, no doubt he would find someone else to entertain him during the course of their marriage, maybe even several women. As much as it pained her all she could hope for was that he would be discreet—although that seemed unlikely, given the press's fascination with anything Mario did and who he did it with.

'You are very quiet,' he said. 'Do you not agree we should remain married?'

Sabrina pasted a bland expression on her face. 'I just want to do what is best for Molly.'

'Good,' he said, blowing out a breath. 'That is settled, then.'

Another silence began to suck at the air in the room.

Sabrina held her breath as he came back to where she was sitting on the bed. Her stomach did a crazy little somersault when he brushed the back of his knuckles down the curve of her cheek, his eyes holding hers like the powerful beam of a searchlight. She hoped he couldn't see what she was so desperately trying to hide. If she blurted her feelings to him, now how would he interpret it? He had said at the start he would not take seriously any avowals of love. How she had scoffed at the thought; was it only a day or so ago? What a bitter irony to find herself so deeply in love with him. How had it happened, and so quickly? Was it his deep, dark eyes that had unlocked her heart? Or was it his mouth, the way it kissed her with such potent passion? Or was it the way his touch set fire to her skin, making every pore pucker in excitement?

'I am sorry for hurting you,' he said in a low, deep voice that sounded as if it had been dragged across coarse gravel. 'I will do my best to make it up to you.'

Sabrina could barely get her voice to work. 'You don't have to do anything, Mario.' *Just love me, because I think I'm falling in love with you,* she added silently.

He bent forward and pressed a soft, chaste kiss to the middle of her forehead, making her feel about three years old. '*Buonanotte*, Sabrina,' he said softly.

Sabrina waited until the door had closed behind him before she let out her tightly held breath.

Stupid. Stupid. Stupid.

Over the next few days Sabrina began to see a softening in the housekeeper's attitude towards her. She could only assume Mario had somehow reversed Giovanna's opinion of her as a gold-digger, for the housekeeper had gradually dropped her surliness and had even offered to help Sabrina learn Italian, with limited success.

Sabrina saw very little of Mario, however, just briefly in the mornings when she first got up to tend to Molly and last thing at night when he came home from his office well past dinner. He was polite but distant, asking her about her day and what Molly was up to, but he mentioned nothing personal. It was as if he was building a wall around himself, keeping her on the other side of it. It made her wonder if he had already hooked back up with his model mistress. All the clues were there: the late nights, the slightly ruffled look of his clothes and appearance when he did finally come home, and his stiff formality when speaking to her.

Sabrina constantly berated herself for falling for him. It showed just how naïve she was to have let that one foray into sensuality turn over her heart. He had probably put the whole episode out of his mind by now. He would not be torturing himself over what could have been if things were different between them.

On Friday afternoon while Molly was having a nap Giovanna informed Sabrina there was a delivery of goods for her. 'It is from Signore Marcolini,' she said. 'I think you will be very happy with what he has bought for you.'

Sabrina stood to one side as the courier brought in bag after bag of designer clothes. There were evening dresses, shoes, handbags and evening bags, a range of separates and even some gossamer-fine lingerie. She fingered each item once the courier had left, marvelling at the exquisite fabrics, wondering who Mario had asked for help in selecting such a fabulous wardrobe. While she was grateful for his generosity, she couldn't quite shake off the feeling that he wanted to remodel her into the sort of glamourous wife people would expect a man of his standing to have by his side. Clearly her chain-store clothes and decade-old shoes were not going to cut it. It made her feel tawdry and mousy, like a common sparrow being dressed up as a rare and exotic colourful bird.

'Signore Marcolini will be home early this evening,' Giovanna said when Sabrina came into the salon carrying Molly in her arms later that evening. 'He just called to say he would be here for dinner.'

Sabrina felt another twinge of pique that he hadn't asked to speak to her personally, but pushed it aside to smile at the housekeeper. 'That is nice,' she said. 'Would you like some help with preparing the meal?'

Giovanna looked shocked. '*No, no, no!* I am the house-keeper—you are his wife, *sì*?'

Sabrina put Molly down on the rug so she could kick her little legs. 'You know very well I am not really his wife,' she said with a despondent sigh. 'Not apart from on paper. We don't even share a bedroom.'

Giovanna knelt down beside her to tickle Molly under the chin. 'You are his wife, Signora Marcolini,' she said, still looking at the baby. 'He just does not realise it yet.'

Sabrina turned her head to look at her. 'I think he has a lover,' she said, trying not to choke up.

Giovanna got to her feet in a matter-of-fact manner. 'Rich Italian men often have mistresses,' she said. 'It means nothing.'

'It means something to *me*,' Sabrina returned. 'I don't want to share him with someone else.'

'Perhaps you would not be sharing him with someone

else if you were seeing to his needs yourself,' Giovanna pointed out.

Sabrina felt her cheeks ripen with colour. She turned to look at Molly, and resumed idling playing with her tiny feet. 'We don't have that sort of relationship. It's not what he wants.'

'Has he told you that?'

'Pretty much.'

Giovanna folded her arms across her ample chest. 'I see the way he looks at you, Signora Marcolini. Maybe you need to make the first move, *sì*?'

Sabrina felt herself quake at the thought. What if he rejected her? How would she bear it? She would feel an even bigger fool to have him spurn her clumsy, awkward advances.

'Ah, that is him now,' Giovanna said as the sound of the front door closing echoed through the *palazzo*.

The housekeeper bustled out and within a few moments Mario came in. He reached up to loosen his tie, shrugging himself out of his suit jacket, his smile as he saw Molly kicking and giggling on the floor totally transforming his face. *'Come è il mio piccolo prezioso ragazza?'* he asked, flinging his jacket aside. 'How is my precious little girl?'

Molly cooed at him in delight, kicking her legs all the harder, her tiny starfish hands waving in the air. Mario scooped her up from the floor and kissed her on both cheeks, before turning to face Sabrina. 'Did you get the clothes I sent you?'

Sabrina raised her chin. 'There are lovely. Thank you. You must have spent a fortune.'

He held her gaze for a pulsing moment. 'If you do not like anything in the collection it can always be returned,' he said. 'It will not offend me, I can assure you.'

Pride stiffened her spine a little more. 'I am not used to having someone select my clothes for me.'

He continued to hold her look. 'You are angry, *cara*.'

Sabrina blinked at the endearment, her heart giving a jerky kick of surprise inside her chest. 'No—no, I'm not. It's just I… Some of the things you bought are very personal, and I…'

'Did I get the size right?' he asked before she could finish.

'Yes.' She tucked a strand of hair behind her ear, her face still burning at the thought of those lovely lacy bras and barely there knickers he had chosen for her.

'I have something else for you,' he said. 'It is in my jacket pocket.'

She glanced at his jacket where it was hanging lopsidedly over the back of one of the sofas. 'W-what is it?'

'Go and see.'

Sabrina stepped past him to pick up his jacket. She could feel his body warmth still clinging to it, and his particular male smell. She felt tempted to hold the fabric up to her face to breathe in the essence of him, but stopped herself just in time. Instead she reached inside one of the pockets and found a velvet-covered ring box. She brought it out, her heart thumping wildly as she met his gaze.

'Open it,' he said.

She opened it with careful fingers, her eyes going wide when she saw the two-ring ensemble inside. Diamonds and white gold sparkled back at her brilliantly. She had never seen anything quite so beautiful before. It made her chain-store costume-jewellery collection look like fairground trinkets in comparison.

'Like the clothes, I had to take a guess on your ring size,' he said into the silence. 'If they don't fit the jeweller will adjust them for you.'

Sabrina took the rings out with meticulous care, sliding each one easily over the knuckles of her ring finger.

'They are too loose,' he observed.

'Not by much,' she said, looking up at him shyly.

His eyes held hers for an infinitesimal moment, his expression difficult to read, although his voice when he spoke sounded gruff. 'You are far smaller than I realised. I should have known after the other night.'

She lowered her gaze as she examined the rings on her finger. 'They are truly beautiful.' She looked up at him again. 'I have never had anything quite so beautiful before.'

'I had it specially designed using diamonds from the Marcolini collection.'

Sabrina looked back at the exquisite rings on her finger, thinking wryly of how willingly she had dived into his bed without the lure of priceless diamonds. Was he thinking the same? she wondered as she glanced back at him.

He transferred Molly to his other arm, holding her with casual ease as if he had been taking care of infants all of his life. 'I have made some enquiries about a nanny for Molly,' he said.

Sabrina felt her scalp prickle in apprehension. She feared once a nanny was firmly established in Molly's life there would be no need for her any more. Had the clothes and rings he had given her been part of a consolation prize to make her go away without a fuss?

'Do we need a nanny?' she asked. 'It's not as if I have anything I would rather do with my time.'

Mario cradled Molly's head against his chest with one of his large hands. 'Some of my business associates are keen to meet you.'

'They could meet me here,' she offered. 'We don't have

to go out to entertain. I could help Giovanna with the meal. I've done some gourmet cooking courses, and—'

'What is the problem, Sabrina?' he asked, looking at her intently.

Sabrina lowered her gaze again. 'I am not sure I can be all that convincing as a pretend wife. I have the clothes and the rings, but I'm not sure that's really going to be enough to convince anyone.'

'It will have to be enough,' he said, drawing in a breath. 'The press have already announced our union. We will be expected to be out and about like any other recently married couple. I have an important business dinner scheduled for tomorrow evening. People will start to ask questions if you are not there with me.'

She began to twist her hands together. 'But who is going to look after Molly?' she asked. 'We can't leave her with a total stranger.'

'Giovanna will stay overnight,' Mario said. 'She has several grandchildren of her own, so she is used to babies. I am sure she will have no trouble for three or four hours while we are out.'

Sabrina looked at Molly, who had fallen asleep against his broad chest. No wonder the little baby felt so safe and secure in his arms. He was such a big man, tall and strong, and yet surprisingly gentle when the need for it arose. How she longed to feel him touch her again, to tantalise her with his mouth, to captivate her senses until she could think of nothing but how he made her feel. Her body craved him; even now she could feel the pining of her flesh, the nerves so sensitive to his nearness they were making her skin feel too tight for her frame. Her breasts ached for his touch, the graze of his teeth and the sweep of his tongue. Her inner core had stopped hurting days ago, but she missed that tender, intimate reminder of how he had so briefly possessed her. He had been so kind and considerate afterwards, so apologetic it had made it impossible for her not to fall in love with him.

'I think this little girl is ready for bed,' Mario said, carefully handing her back to Sabrina.

She took the sleeping baby from him, her heart racing like a Formula One engine as one of his hands inadvertently brushed against her breast. Her eyes met his for a beat or two before she lowered them to the child in her arms. 'You are very good with her, Mario,' she said. She lifted her gaze back to his. 'She is lucky to have such a wonderful guardian.'

A shadow passed through his dark eyes, like strong sunlight blocked by the passing of thick clouds. 'She would have been much better off with her real parents,' he said. 'There is no substitute for the real thing, is there?'

'No, I guess you are right,' Sabrina said on the back of a sigh. She had often wondered what it would have been like to have a father, especially after her mother had been taken from her when she'd been so young. She had often dreamt of what he would look like, how he would sound and the things he might say to her if they ever met. Why he had not stayed to support her mother she would never know. She had been too young to ask, and now it was too late. When she had seen the words "father unknown" on her birth certificate it had felt like an arrow piercing her heart. It was so hard to accept she didn't belong to anyone. She wondered now if she ever would belong to anyone. Mario had made it pretty clear he was only interested in a temporary arrangement, but how she longed for things to be different.

* * *

When she came back downstairs after putting Molly to bed, Mario was mixing himself a drink at the bar in the salon. He turned as she came into the room. 'Would you like an aperitif?'

'Just tonic water, no gin. Thank you,' she said as she sat on the edge of one of the sofas.

He gave her an ironic look as he handed her the glass of tonic water. 'Keeping a clear head, *cara*?' he asked.

Sabrina took the glass with fingers that felt as if the nerves had been severed. 'Why do you keep calling me that when there is no one around to hear you?'

'Does it bother you?'

She pressed her lips together and looked at the cubes of ice rattling in her glass. 'Not really. It just seems a little unnecessary.'

'I do not find it unnecessary,' he said. 'It is all part of the act, no?'

Sabrina met his satirical gaze. 'How are people ever going to believe you chose someone like me to be your wife?' she asked.

He took a leisurely sip of his drink before he answered. 'You underestimate your charms, Sabrina. You are a very beautiful young woman. I have always thought so, right from the first moment we met.'

She couldn't hold back a churlish retort. 'You thought I was a gold-digger.'

His mouth momentarily tightened. 'And I was wrong. I have apologised, Sabrina. I can do no more.'

She crossed her legs, cradling her drink in both hands in case she spilt it. 'If you thought I was so beautiful, why did you feel the need to revamp my wardrobe?'

His eyes warred with hers for a tense moment. 'I can

see that has become somewhat of an issue with you,' he said. 'Believe it or not, I was trying to help you. I would imagine it is not easy shopping with a small infant in tow. But, since you don't appreciate the gesture, I will have everything taken back. I will arrange for you to have your own credit card with maximum credit.'

Sabrina felt sudden tears thicken her throat as he turned away from her to refresh his drink. The tension in his back and shoulders made her regret her childish response to his act of thoughtfulness. 'I'm sorry,' she said softly. 'It was wrong of me to be so ungrateful. I realise you were only trying to be helpful.'

Mario turned to face her. 'You are not used to people being kind to you, are you, *tesore mio*?'

Sabrina brushed at her prickling eyes with the back of her hand. 'I'm sorry for being so…so emotional right now.'

He put down his drink and came over to where she was sitting, hunkering down in front of her like he would a small child. His eyes were soft as they held hers, his fingers as he stroked her tear-stained cheek even softer. 'You are not the one who should be apologising for anything, Sabrina,' he said. 'We have both been through a dreadful time. It is to be expected that we will have shifts of mood in these early days and months of grief.'

'I know.' She gave a deep, shuddering sigh. 'I know…'

Mario traced a fingertip over her trembling bottom lip. Again he was amazed at how soft and pillowy her mouth was. He ached to feel it under his, but he knew where it would lead if he kissed her again. She had affected him much more than he had realised; that bittersweet taste of her had left him wanting in a way he had never wanted before. His body throbbed to feel her moist warmth again, but she was shy and hesitant around him, and he could hardly blame her for it. He had treated her appallingly. He loathed recalling some of the things he had said to her; doing so made his guilt all the harder to bear. He had done his best to make it up to her, but she seemed to be offended no matter what he did. Most women would have been mollified with gifts of jewellery and designer clothes, but she had turned her freckled, *retroussé* nose up at them.

He had lain awake the last few nights thinking of how he had hurt her. She was so petite, it tortured him to think of what damage he might have done. He had brutalised her in his savage desire for satiation, arrogantly assuming she was with him all the way when she had probably not even been aware of what she had been doing, nor what she had been communicating. Her instincts had taken over and he had exploited them.

'You have such a soft mouth,' he said. 'Do you realise I have never seen you smile at me?'

She gave him a tentative half-smile. 'Really?'

He smiled back. 'Really.'

She shifted her gaze from his, her mouth turning down at the corners. 'I guess I haven't had all that much to smile about just lately.'

Mario got to his feet and, taking one of her hands, pulled her up to stand in front of him. He slid his hands down the length of her arms, relishing the silky feel of her smooth skin, his groin tightening in response. He held himself away from her, not wanting to reveal how turned on he was in case she was frightened. She looked up at him with her clear grey eyes, and he felt something move inside his chest, like a lever being shifted to a position it had never been in before.

The silence swelled and swelled, making the air thick, heavy and drugging.

Mario's gaze went to her mouth, his heart rate picking up its pace as he saw her moisten her lips with the tip of her tongue. He felt the blood surge in his veins, the primal urge to feel her against his hardness too much for him to withstand. He muttered a short, sharp imprecation and then lowered his mouth to hers.

CHAPTER NINE

SABRINA melted against him as his kiss deepened, the movement of his tongue against hers unlocking every vertebra of her spine. Her legs felt woolly, and her belly did crazy zigzags, like a Buick on black ice, as his hands found the small of her back and pressed her up close to his erection. Her body burned at the intimate contact; it felt like flames were leaping beneath her skin, scorching her in every secret place. The feminine heart of her began to ache with an on-off pulse, a deep, throbbing ache that she knew instinctively no one could ever satisfy but him.

His kiss became more and more urgent as she laced her arms around his neck, his tongue calling hers into a fast-paced tango. Electric sensations danced along her skin, her chest wall reverberating with the pounding of her racing heart.

He tasted so fresh and so arrantly male, his unshaven skin scraping her tender face as he angled his head to change position. The kiss this time was slower, tantalisingly so. Sabrina could feel herself being swept away on a sensual tide of longing so intense she felt as if her body had completely taken over her mind. There was no room for rational thought, her body had already decided what it

wanted and was doing everything in its power to commu-
nicate it to him. She nipped at his bottom lip with her teeth,
gently, playfully, teasingly, until he growled deep in his
throat and did the same to her. Shivers cascaded down her
spine as his strong white teeth captured her kiss-swollen
lip, his tongue sweeping over it before his teeth made her
his slave again.

Sabrina felt his hands move from her lower back to
skate up her sides, resting just beneath the gentle swell of
her breasts. Her nipples tingled in excitement, the puckered
flesh pressing against the lace of her bra, desperate for the
hot, sweet suck of his mouth and the lick and glide of his
raspy male tongue.

She gave a little whimper when his thumbs brushed
over her, his mouth still commandeering hers. Her heart
thundered in her chest, the drum beat of her pulse roaring
in her ears like the tumultuous waves of a wild ocean.

Mario lifted his mouth from hers and looked down at
her with eyes blazing with desire. 'This might be a good
time to stop,' he said. 'Before things get out of hand.'

Sabrina's body felt cold and unstable without the solid
prop of his. His hands were now holding her by the upper
arms, but she longed for the hot press of his body against
hers. She swallowed the ropey lump of disappointment in
her throat, her spirits wilting at the realisation of how easy
it was for him to release her. His desire for her was a tran-
sient, controllable thing, unlike hers, which had reduced her
almost to the point of begging.

'I suppose your mistress might not be too happy about
you sleeping with your wife as well as her.' She spoke her
thoughts out loud.

His eyes studied hers. It seemed a decade before he spoke.

'You know, for a moment there I thought you sounded jealous.'

Sabrina felt her colour rise but raised her chin regardless. 'I don't want to be laughed at by everyone.'

'No one is laughing at you, *cara mia*.'

Tears burned like acid at the back of her eyes. 'Stop calling me that,' she said, desperately trying to control the wobble of her chin. 'Please don't make fun of me. I can't bear it.'

Mario's hands moved from her upper arms to encircle her wrists, his fingers overlapping each other. 'What is this about, Sabrina? What is it *really* about?'

Her throat moved up and down as if she was shuffling through the words before she spoke them. 'I'm not sure…'

'Look at me.'

She slowly raised her eyes to his, her bottom lip quivering ever so slightly.

'I do not have a mistress right now,' he said.

Her pupils went wide, like black saucers. 'Y-you don't?'

He gave her a rueful smile. 'No, *tesore mio*. But perhaps it would be a good idea if I did, for then I would not be so tempted to sleep with you.'

She licked her blood-red lips with a quick dart-like movement of her tongue. 'You're…' She swallowed again. 'You're…tempted? Really?'

He stroked the undersides of her small wrists with the pads of his thumbs, watching as her whole body reacted. He felt her faint shiver, saw the way the grey pools of her eyes darkened, and the way her pulse leapt and fluttered beneath his touch. 'I am sorely tempted, but I swore I would not touch you again,' he said. 'A promise is a promise, even if it was only to myself.'

There was a pregnant pause.

'What if…?' She moistened her mouth again before continuing, 'What if I wanted you to sleep with me?'

Mario drew in a long breath, holding it for a few beats before releasing it, along with her wrists. He put some distance between them, dragging a hand through his hair, searching for patience, strength, resolve. 'Sabrina…you don't know what you are asking.'

'I think I do,' she said quietly.

He looked at her again, his heart feeling as if a clamp was pressing the sides together. It seemed strange to him how young she seemed now, when only weeks ago he had thought her so streetwise and worldly. How could he have been so blind? She was so innocent; she didn't know what the hell she was getting in to by asking him to be her lover. She was vulnerable and sweet, and he would be a cad to have a short-term 'affair' with her. She wasn't the affair type. 'Sabrina…' He finger-combed his hair again. '*Cara*, listen to me.'

Her limpid eyes began to glisten. 'It's all right,' she said stiffly, turning her back to him as she moved to the other side of the room. 'I understand, really I do. I'm not your type. You've made it clear right from the start.'

Mario swore in both English and Italian, a perverse part of him pleased at how she flinched as the words cut the air. 'For God's sake, Sabrina, you are still in my mind a virgin.'

'I wasn't aware it was something to be ashamed of.'

'Of course it's nothing to be ashamed of,' he said. 'You should be proud of it, especially in this day and age.'

She turned to look at him. 'If you don't mind, I think I will give dinner a miss. I'm not hungry.'

Mario swore again, this time under his breath. 'Sulking is for small children, Sabrina.'

She put her chin up at him. 'You think I'm in a sulk?'

'I think you are young and vulnerable and in way over your head, *tesore mio*,' he said, with a crooked smile to soften the words.

She set her mouth so tightly he could see brackets of strain around the soft lips he had kissed only minutes ago. 'I guess I'll see you in the morning,' she said, her shoulders slumping as she made to move past.

Mario placed one of his hands on the cup of her shoulder, holding her in place. 'Don't run away, Sabrina,' he said gently. 'Stay with me. Talk to me.'

Her bottom lip trembled slightly and her white, even teeth sank down to steady it. Her eyes skittered away from his, her cheeks flushed with colour.

Mario cupped the nape of her neck with his palm, his fingers tangling in her silky hair, tying her to him. 'Look at me, Sabrina,' he commanded again, softly this time.

She raised her eyes to his, her tone short and self-deprecating. 'I'm sorry for embarrassing you. But I guess you must be pretty used to women falling all over themselves to sleep with you.'

He brushed his thumb over the pouting protrusion of her bottom lip. 'Firstly, I am not at all embarrassed, and secondly, I do not have as many women in my life as you might think. If I did everything the press said I did, I would not have any time for my work.'

Her eyes moved away from his again. 'You say you don't have a current mistress, but I'm guessing it won't be long before you do.'

Mario studied her features for a long moment. She had lilac thumbprint-like shadows beneath her eyes, and her brow was networked with fine lines of uncertainty. He had become so used to a certain arrogant confidence in all his previous partners, he had not thought anything of it until now. Now all he wanted was the shy innocence of Sabrina. He ached for it—for her hesitant touch, for her sweet-but-feverish kisses and the feminine pulse of her body against his. He wanted to claim her as his, to tutor her in the wild, secret world of her sensuality, to fill her with his hardness, to spill himself as she convulsed around him. His body leapt at the thought, his blood rocketing through his veins, surging to his loins until he was throbbing with need.

He clenched his teeth, fighting the temptation, but it was impossible to ignore the magnetic pull of her body so close to his.

'Is…is everything all right?' she asked in a voice so soft he had to strain to hear it.

'No,' he said gruffly as he took her by the hips and pulled her up against him.

Her eyes flared as she felt him. 'I—I thought you said—?'

'Forget what I said,' he growled as he bent his head to hers. 'Forget the hell what I said.'

Sabrina stifled a gasp as his mouth seared hers, the hot urgency of it sweeping her up into a maelstrom of heady sensation. Desire licked along her veins like a river of fire, lightning-fast, lightning-hot and equally electrifying. His fingers dug into her hips, holding her tighter against his hot, hard need. Her body quivered at the intimate contact, the outline of his erection making her legs weaken.

His mouth continued its sensual assault, his tongue stroking and stabbing at hers simultaneously, drawing her into a whirlpool of wanting that was uncontrollable. Her tongue danced with his, darting and diving to evade, and then licking and stroking to cajole. He responded by kissing her harder and deeper, his lower body grinding against hers as the pressure built.

His hands moved from her hips to slide up her ribcage and possess her breasts, the warm cup of his palms making the pores of her flesh stand up in goose bumps of excitement. Her spine felt as if it had been injected with warm, smooth honey, her limbs equally malleable, as his mouth moved from hers to the scaffold of her collarbone. She shivered as his lips whispered over her sensitive skin, every nerve arching its back to feel more of his touch.

'I told myself I wasn't going to do this,' he said. 'I *promised* myself.'

Sabrina felt another shiver dance over her skin as his lips moved against her neck when he spoke. 'It's all right,' she said on a breathless gasp. 'I'm a big girl now.'

He brushed her mouth with a hard, possessive kiss, his dark eyes hooded and brooding. 'I'm afraid I'll hurt you again.'

Sabrina felt his erection thick and swollen against her, making her insides melt like candle wax. 'You won't hurt me,' she whispered against his mouth. 'I am sure you won't.'

He kissed her again, deeply and lingeringly, exploring every contour of her mouth before he moved his lips to the breast he had deftly uncovered. His mouth closed over one puckered nipple, sucking on her hungrily, before he circled her with his tongue. Pleasure ricocheted through her like gunfire, piercing the sound barrier. Waves of feeling washed over her, tossing her about until she was clinging to him like a raft.

'We need to go upstairs,' he said, and lifted her off her feet.

'Put me down,' Sabrina protested. 'I'm too heavy.'

'You weigh next to nothing,' he said, and carried her out of the room and up the sweeping staircase.

Sabrina linked her arms around his neck, her belly feeling as if a hundred tiny fists were trying to punch their way out. She breathed in his scent; the exotic spices of his aftershave mixed with the essence of his maleness made her nostrils flare in excitement. Nervousness and anticipation were jostling for position inside her, making her feel dizzy and light-headed at the thought of finally being possessed by him. Her body was preparing itself, the moist dew of desire already secretly anointing her, the deep throb of her inner core like a low, deep drum-beat.

Mario shouldered open his bedroom-suite door, kicking it shut with his foot once they were inside. He let her slide down his body as he set her down, his eyes searing hers with passionate promise. 'Are you sure this is what you want?' he asked. 'It's not too late to change your mind.'

Sabrina snatched in a scratchy breath. 'I want you, Mario. I want you to make love to me.'

His gaze darkened to a black, bottomless pool of desire. 'I wanted you the moment I met you,' he said as he walked her backwards to the bed, slowly, inexorably.

'I—I know,' she said shakily, her thighs bumping against his.

He ran his hands down her arms, entrapping her wrists as her knees came up against the mattress. There was a primitive element to his hold, a heated charge of energy she could feel passing from his body to hers. His body simmered with it; hers felt like it was boiling.

He slowly undressed her, kissing her flesh as it was revealed to him until she was standing in just her bra and knickers, her skin tingling wherever his lips had burned and branded her as his. 'Now you get to undress me,' he said with a smouldering look that lifted every hair on her scalp.

Sabrina's fingers fumbled with the buttons on his shirt, but somehow she got them undone. She tugged it out of his trousers and slid it off his broad shoulders, pausing to kiss his bronzed flesh, tasting the saltiness of him, relishing in the feel of his sculptured muscles under the soft press of her fingertips. Her lips brushed against his hard, flat nipples, her tongue sweeping and curling over him, her belly turning over in excitement when he groaned in pleasure.

Her fingers came to the waistband of his trousers. She glanced up at him shyly, wondering if she had the courage to follow through. His eyes glittered darkly with expecta-tion, and she took a shallow breath and unhooked his belt from its buckle, slowly pulling it through until it dropped to the floor with a serpent-like slither.

'You are in control, Sabrina,' Mario said, although it sounded rough and uneven. 'Any time you want to stop, you stop.'

Sabrina traced the pathway of masculine hair from his belly button to his waistband with her fingers, delighting in the taut flatness of his abdomen, the ridged muscles contracting even more at her touch. 'I don't want to stop,' she said lightly, skating her fingertips over the tenting of his trousers.

She heard him suck in a harsh breath, his body whipcord-tight as she continued stroking him, exploring the length and breadth of him through the barrier of his clothes.

One of his hands came over hers, holding her against him as he fought for control. 'Give me a moment,' he bit out.

Sabrina looked up at him in alarm. 'Am I doing some-thing wrong?'

'No, *cara*,' he said, shuddering as her fingers moved against him. 'I am getting a little ahead of myself, that is all.'

Her hand stilled but she could still feel him throbbing against her palm. He was so magnificently male, so magnificently aroused. She moved her fingers experimentally, feeling him, shaping him, and then, with a swiftly indrawn breath for courage, she unzipped him.

He stepped out of his trousers, his black underwear the only remaining barrier. Sabrina's fingers danced over him, and then with increasing boldness she peeled back the stretchy black fabric and exposed the proud length of him.

She saw the muscles of his abdomen clench in preparation for her first skin-on-skin touch, the pearl-like bead of moisture at his blunt tip making her stomach free-fall.

She ran her fingertip down him from shaft to tip, amazed at how silky his taut skin felt. He was satin-covered steel, sexual energy still leashed but visibly straining. She felt the latent power of him against her curling fingers; she felt too the deep all-over shudder he gave as her hand finally enclosed him.

'My turn, I think,' he said, and captured her hand.

The look in his eyes made her stomach drop another fifty floors. He turned her hand over and kissed the middle of her palm, his tongue circling it, teasing the sensitive nerves, until they were screaming for mercy beneath her skin.

His other hand moved to the small of her back, sliding upwards until he came to the clasp of her bra. She pulled in an uneven breath as it fell to the floor with a lacy silence.

His eyes consumed her greedily, taking in her small-but-neat, creamy-white form, the rosy-red nipples already pert and aching for his lips and tongue. He bent his head and suckled on her, taking his time over each breast, torturing her with his caresses until she was clutching at his shoulders, panting breathlessly.

'You are so dainty and yet so perfect,' he said against the satin smoothness of her right breast, his lips making the tender flesh shiver in reaction.

Sabrina couldn't speak when his mouth closed over her nipple again. She felt the rough glide of his tongue over her, the moist heat of his mouth making her whimper in pleasure.

His hands settled on her hips, holding her against his arousal with just the fragile cobweb of her lacy knickers between his body and hers. He nudged against her experimentally, his eyes smoky as they held hers. 'It is still not too late to stop,' he said. 'You are still in control, Sabrina. Always remember that—you are the one in control.'

Sabrina felt her heart give an almighty squeeze that was almost painful. He was being so tender and considerate; how could she not love him? She wanted to tell him, but held back just in time. He had not given any indication of feeling anything but lust for her. Why spoil the moment with confessions of a love that had no future? She was only in his life because of his guardianship of Molly. His physical desire for her was a bonus, a temporary diversion, until he moved on to his next mistress.

His reputation said it all. Yes, the papers whipped it up a bit, but even so it was obvious he was a no-strings-sex guy. He liked to play and to play hard. Sabrina was a novelty to him, a naïve innocent who made a stark change from the worldly, streetwise women he normally bedded. But it wouldn't matter how experienced she became; Sabrina knew Mario was the only man who could make her feel the way she was currently feeling. No one else had kissed her until she was senseless. No one else had made her ache with a need so strong she felt as if her breathing was going to stop altogether unless he assuaged it.

'Touch me, Mario,' she whispered as she leant into his hardness.

He moved his hand down to cup her through the lace, her intimate dampness making his pupils dilate. 'You are beautiful,' he said, low and deep.

With him touching her like that, Sabrina *felt* beautiful. She felt powerful, too, full of feminine power to attract a mate. She moved against his hand, her body thrilling at the contact, her feminine flesh quivering. His fingers moved aside the lace of her knickers to trace her moist cleft, gently separating her before he slowly inserted one finger. She gasped at the sensation of feeling him move inside her, exploring her tenderly, preparing her for the ultimate possession of his body.

After a moment he guided her down onto the bed. 'Relax, *cara*,' he said as he came down beside her, his long legs entwining with hers. 'Don't tense up on me.'

Sabrina tried to loosen up, but every nerve in her body seemed to be switched to hyper-vigilance mode. She wanted him so badly she felt twitchy and restless, feverish with excitement and escalating need. She arched her spine as he peeled away her underwear, her breathing coming in ever-shortening intervals as his hand came back to cup her.

'You are so very tempting.'

Sabrina shivered as his fingers explored her again, stretching her to accommodate him. Her muscles fought him at first, but he kissed her to distract her, and after a moment he went deeper.

It wasn't enough. It wasn't what she wanted. She wanted *him*, deep and hot and hard, inside her.

She pulled his hand away and nestled closer, touching him, squeezing her fingers around his length. He bit back a groan and lay back, propped up on his elbows while she caressed him, his laboured breathing making his chest rise and fall like a pair of bellows. 'I am going to come if you don't stop that,' he said through tightly clenched teeth.

'I would like to see you,' Sabrina said, surprising herself at her boldness.

'Not this time,' he said, and flipped her on to her back. 'We'll save that for another time. This time it is all about you.'

Sabrina watched as he opened the bedside-table drawer to retrieve a condom. Again she had to push aside the thought of how many other women had lain on this bed with him; this was not the time to reflect on his past. This was her time with him, a time to enjoy the pleasure of her body under the tutelage of his. And her body was enjoying it. It was pulsing with longing, quaking all over with it, as she watched him roll the condom over his erection.

He moved over her to kiss her mouth lingeringly, teasing her with his tongue, the stab and thrusting action mimicking the intimate union that was to come.

Sabrina made room for him between her legs, her heart giving a little jump of exhilaration as he brushed her moist entrance.

'Not so fast, *cara*,' he chided her gently as he pulled back. 'There are things I have to do first.'

A small frown tugged at her brow. 'What things?'

He gave her a smouldering look. 'These things,' he said, and kissed his way from her breasts over her quivering belly until he got to the dark, neatly trimmed curls that shielded the secret heart of her.

Sabrina stopped breathing when his mouth separated

her, his tongue sending electric pulses of sensations to her curling toes and back. Her back lifted off the bed as he intensified the movement of his caressing tongue, all the delicious feelings seeming to gather at one tight point, hovering there, waiting for the final moment to explode.

'Go with it, *cara*,' he coaxed her gently. 'Don't fight it. Let go.'

She couldn't believe her body could contain so much feeling as the first waves rolled over her, lifting her up higher and higher, until she was spinning in a vortex of sensation. Spasm after spasm rocketed through her, making her aware of nothing but her body and how Mario had made it feel. Her limbs felt deliciously loose, the lassitude of physical release flowing through her like a warm tide.

He slowly moved back up her body, stroking her, caressing her, until she felt the need building again. She moved against him, aching for the primal connection of their bodies.

'Please,' she said, beyond caring that she was almost begging. *'Please...'*

'Don't be impatient, *mio piccolo*,' he growled playfully as he positioned himself, a leg over one of hers, an intimate tangle of limbs. 'I am trying to be careful with you, but you are making it almost impossible for me to slow down.'

Sabrina felt him at her entrance, the heat of him just hovering there making her breath hitch in her throat. 'I don't want you to slow down,' she said, clutching at his shoulders. 'I want to feel you...all of you.'

He kissed her on the mouth, lingering there before he pushed in slowly, just the tip, waiting until she accepted him before going further. 'Tell me if I am hurting you,' he said against her lips.

'You're not hurting me,' she breathed back, her lips

tingling from the movement of his own against their sensitive surface.

He thrust a little deeper, gauging her response, waiting until she stretched before he moved again. 'You feel so good,' he said in a deep, throaty tone. 'So unbelievably good.'

Sabrina felt the stirring of her senses as he moved more deeply within her, the pleasure he was feeling evident by the contorted expression on his face as he fought for control. She ran her hands over his back and shoulders, delighting in the feel of him teetering on the edge of release. So much power, so much strength, and yet he was so tender with her. The love she felt for him swelled in her chest, taking up so much room she could barely breathe without feeling like she was snagging on something deep inside.

Mario slowly built his pace, the tantalising friction sending Sabrina's senses into another wheel-spin. Instinct told her he was getting closer and closer to the point of no return. She could feel the tension in his body, the way his breathing became more hectic, and the way his hold on her subtly tightened.

She wriggled beneath him, arching her back like a sinuous cat, wanting that final trigger to make her pleasure complete.

He delved between their rocking bodies, stroking her swollen dampness until she plunged headfirst into the abyss of paradise, her body shaking, convulsing and twitching as he emptied himself in a series of hard pumps that left her breathless and gasping.

Sabrina listened to the sound of his breathing for a long time without moving. Her body felt boneless, her senses so satiated she could barely tie two thoughts together in her head.

'Am I too heavy for you?' Mario asked after what seemed an extraordinarily long time.

'No. You feel…nice.'

'Nice is not a word usually used to describe me,' he said wryly as he rolled away.

Sabrina felt the cooler air rush at her like an icy slap on the face. He was distancing himself. There had been no loving aftermath, no lingering over a final kiss or two. There had been a long silence, and then…nothing. Was he regretting sleeping with her? Or had she not pleased him the way he normally expected a woman to please him?

He had done this a thousand times, she reminded herself. It was nothing special. This was not an experience that would live in his memory as it would hers. She was a fill-in, an amusing diversion while they were shackled together for the sake of a small child.

'I need to check on Molly,' she said, and clutching at the sheet, used it like a wrap to cover her nakedness as she got off the bed.

'Is the baby monitor not working?' he asked.

Sabrina pressed her lips together as she glanced at the device he had installed in every room. 'Yes, but it doesn't hurt to look in on her,' she said. 'Sometimes she wriggles out from beneath the covers.'

There was still nothing in his expression to indicate the intimacy they had just shared, or even if he had been affected by it. 'I will check on her while you get dressed for dinner,' he said, tying the ends of his bathrobe firmly around his waist. 'Giovanna has gone to a lot of trouble. I would hate to disappoint her.'

Sabrina flinched as the door clicked shut on his exit; all things considered, it seemed a rather fitting punctuation-mark on her hopes.

CHAPTER TEN

MARIO was on his second drink when Sabrina came into the dining room half an hour later. She brought the fresh fragrance of summer flowers with her, a light, carefree scent that teased his nostrils. She had pulled her still-damp hair up into a pony-tail-cum-knot that looked both casual and elegant, and her face was lightly made up, her lips shining with lip gloss. Her eyes, however, were not quite making the distance to his.

He wasn't sure what else he had been expecting. He wasn't even sure if he had a right to expect anything. He suspected she had wanted to sleep with him more out of a sense of adventure than anything else. Now it was over with, she was regretting it. He didn't regret making love with her, not for a moment, it was more that by doing so he felt he had crossed a boundary and now he couldn't uncross it. He had travelled into unchartered territory; the feelings he was experiencing were foreign to him. He hardly knew what to make of them.

He had slept with lots of women in the past, and not one of them had left a lasting impression on his senses. And yet his body was still humming from making love with Sabrina earlier. His skin had lifted in a frisson of excitement as soon as she'd walked into the room. He felt the tension building in him as each second ticked past, the roar of his blood, the tightening of his flesh and the ache in his loins.

He put the gossip magazine he had been flicking through aside, wondering if Sabrina had seen the photographs of him carrying Molly at the airport on the day of their arrival in Rome. The caption had read: *high-flying playboy now a tamed family man*. It had shocked him a little to see himself portrayed in such a domestic way. It made him think longingly of his freedom, of the come-and-go lifestyle he had always taken for granted. There would be compensations, he knew. Molly was an engaging infant, and would no doubt grow into a beautiful child. He owed it to Ric to concentrate on giving Molly the most secure and happy childhood he could. The other compensation of course was Sabrina—but he wasn't so sure he wanted to linger too long on what to make of his ambiguous feelings where she was concerned.

'Would you care for a drink?' Mario asked, to break the silence.

Her lips moved in the semblance of a smile, but it was fleeting; it disappeared as soon as her eyes met his. 'Thank you. White wine, if you have it.'

Mario poured her a glass of chilled white wine and handed it to her wryly, noting how her hand shook slightly as she took it from him. 'There is no need to be nervous, Sabrina.'

Her eyes skittered away from his. 'I'm not nervous.'

He picked up his glass and twirled the contents, the sound of the ice cubes bumping against the sides loud in the silence.

'I would like to talk to you about our future,' he said.

Her finely arched brows lifted, making her grey eyes larger than a startled fawn's. 'I see…'

'Actually, I don't think you do,' Mario said, putting his glass down.

Her chin rose a little, although she sneaked in a quick lick of her lips which totally belied her cool composure. 'I understand this arrangement between us is temporary,' she said. 'I also understand that a marriage of convenience is only workable if it is convenient to both parties.'

'In our case it is convenient for three parties,' Mario pointed out. 'Molly needs both of us.'

'Yes, but you said—'

'I have changed my mind.'

She stepped backwards as if he had slapped her. 'W-what?'

'I have changed my mind about how long our marriage should continue.' He paused for a beat or two before adding, 'I would like it to continue indefinitely.'

He watched as her throat moved up and down, the motion like a small mouse wriggling under a blanket. Her tongue came out again, a quick flash of movement across her lips, her eyes flickering with alarm. 'But you don't… I mean, we don't love each other,' she said.

Mario leaned back against the bar, crossing one ankle over the other as he held her gaze.

'Any marriage is a bit of a gamble,' he said, uncrossing his ankles and straightening to his full height. 'But, when two people are prepared to make it work, it can be very satisfying in the long term.'

'What about love?' she whispered

'Sabrina, we have a chance to make this work for Molly's sake,' he said. 'I believe it is the best thing for her to have two parents who live together in companionship if nothing else.'

Sabrina felt her stomach clench in despair. 'But what

about what I want?' she asked. 'I want children of my own. How can I have the family I've always wanted if I am tied indefinitely to you?'

He held her questioning look for a pulsing moment before he shifted his gaze. He sent his hand through his hair and moved to the other side of the room. 'I do not want to have children,' he said. 'I am sorry, but that is not something I have ever seen for myself. The responsibility of Molly is more than enough for me.'

She stared at him in bewilderment. 'You're expecting me to give up that lifelong dream for you?'

His eyes came back to hers, hot, hard and determined. 'Not for me—for Molly,' he said. 'If it is too much to ask you to sacrifice having children, then after a suitable time I will release you from our marriage.'

Sabrina felt her stomach fold over in panic. 'Define "a suitable time".'

His eyes moved away from hers again. 'I can't put an exact time on it. It will depend on many things.'

She lifted her chin. 'Like my turning a blind eye to what you do on the side?' she asked.

His expression tightened. 'If you are not happy with the conditions, you know what you can do. You will be more than adequately compensated.'

She put her wine glass down and brushed back her hair with an unsteady hand. 'I'm not sure what has motivated this,' she said. 'But if it has anything to do with what happened earlier, I—'

'It has everything to do with what happened earlier.'

Sabrina rolled her lips together, her eyes hunting his for a sign of what he was feeling, but his expression was as neutral as if they had been discussing the weather.

'Wow, I must have really impressed you in bed!' She affected an airy tone.

A smile flashed through his dark eyes. 'You did.'

'The novelty factor, right?'

'Wrong.'

She stopped breathing as he closed the distance between them. Her heart began to hammer as his hands settled about her waist, his long fingers warm and strong as he brought her that little bit closer. She felt the stirring of his body against her, the slow and steady burn of his gaze making her toes curl up inside her shoes. Her eyes flicked to his mouth, his sexy half-smile sending another hot rush of liquid longing between her thighs.

He brought one hand up to her face, cupping her cheek as he brushed the pad of his thumb over her lips in a caress that was as gentle as it was potent. She felt every sensitive nerve snap to attention, each one buzzing with expectation.

When he touched her like this it was all too easy to put aside her hopes and dreams to have another moment of magic in his arms. But Sabrina wondered how long it would be before she began to resent him, to hate him for holding her back, for not allowing her to access his heart. He was not willing to give up his freedom. That hurt, so too did the fact that he would never commit to her emotionally. Why else would he refuse to blend his blood with hers and have a child together? That was the biggest slap in the face of all—he didn't want any permanent reminders of their liaison. Molly was enough responsibility for him; dear, little motherless Molly, who would very likely be the one to get hurt in the long run when her guardians were eventually torn apart with bitterness and recrimination.

Sabrina pulled out of his hold, rubbing at her arms as if

her skin was itchy from a rash. 'Don't do this, Mario,' she said. 'This is not how normal people behave.'

'What is normal about our situation?' he asked. 'We have been thrown together by circumstances beyond our control. I think it is up to us to make the best of the hand we have been dealt.'

'I don't know about how you live your life, but mine is not and never has been a game,' Sabrina shot back with a glare.

He let out a breath as he raked his fingers through his hair. 'I am not suggesting we treat this lightly. I am sorry if I have given you that impression. Having a child is a big step. It is too big a step for me. I watched my brother and his wife go through a painful separation after the loss of their first baby. I am the first to admit there are no guarantees, but I want this to work, Sabrina. I want it to work for Molly, but also for Ric and Laura. They chose us for a reason. Think about it for a moment—they must have been confident we could make a go of it as a couple, otherwise they would never have nominated us.'

She threw her hands in the air. 'I've thought about it, Mario, and I still can't believe they did what they did. We are polar opposites. If we had met under any other circumstances, you wouldn't have given me a second glance.'

'You underestimate yourself, *cara*,' he said. 'You are one of the most beautiful women I have ever met. But unlike a lot of other women I know you don't choose to display it at every opportunity.'

She rolled her eyes and swung away again. 'You only want me because of my inexperience. It's a primal thing; it has nothing to do with emotion, but everything to do with evolution.'

'I admit that I find your innocence refreshing,' he said.

'But it is not just about that. There are many things I like about you.'

Sabrina pursed her lips as she waited for him to continue.

'I like the fact that you let the public think what they wanted over the Roebourne affair in order to protect the children,' he said. 'I also like the fact that you agreed to marry me even though you disliked me intensely. Once again, you put your feelings aside for the sake of a small child. Those are very admirable qualities, *cara*.'

She let out a small sigh. 'I don't really dislike you intensely—at least, not now.'

His expression contained a hint of wryness. 'I kind of figured that.'

Sabrina wondered what else he had figured out. Did he know how much she loved him? Was he laughing at her naivety for falling for a man who had no intention of returning that love? Although he said he wanted their marriage to continue indefinitely, he had spoken of *liking* her—not loving her. There was a very big difference, and it mattered to her. It mattered a great deal. How could she settle for second best when all her life she had dreamed of having it all—a man who adored her, a child or two to cement that love? Bringing up their little family as a solid unit, the sort of unit she had been denied during her childhood.

The loneliness of her upbringing had always tormented her. That was why she had married Mario; to protect Molly from experiencing the same—or at least it had been one of the reasons. He could have looked like the proverbial bell-ringer at Notre Dame and she still would have married him to protect her little god-daughter—although it was rather a bonus that he didn't, she thought as her eyes went to his again. He was the most amazingly good-looking man; her heart fluttered every time she looked at him. Would she still feel this way in two, ten or even twenty years? Or would she end up hating him for locking her into a loveless marriage that existed only for the sake of Molly?

She shifted her weight, forcing her eyes to make the full distance to his penetrating gaze. 'Just because we…had sex doesn't mean I am in love with you.'

'It would be hypocritical of me to expect you to be,' he returned. 'I have had sex with many women without once falling in love.'

Sabrina tried to ignore the spike of jealousy that jabbed at her at his statement. 'Women you will continue to sleep with?' she asked.

His eyes never once moved away from hers. 'I told you before, I expect our marriage to be an exclusive arrangement.'

She cocked a finely arched brow at him. 'You mean you won't keep a mistress on the side?'

'Why would I want a mistress when I have you to warm my bed?' he asked with a look that smouldered like hot coals.

Sabrina felt her breath catch inside her chest. 'So…so you want our marriage to be a normal one, but without actually falling in love with each other?'

He studied her for a pregnant pause, not speaking, barely even moving.

Sabrina supposed that was his answer: no answer. He was not prepared to commit himself emotionally. He had never been in love with any of his lovers, why should she be any different? Why torture herself with foolish hopes that would only break her heart in the end?

'Signore and Signora Marcolini?' Giovanna's voice sounded from the doorway. '*La cena è pronta.*'

'*Grazie*, Giovanna,' Mario answered. 'Dinner is ready,' he translated for Sabrina.

She followed him to the elegantly laid-out table, sitting down on the chair he pulled out for her. 'Thank you.'

'My brother and sister-in-law are keen to meet you,' he said once he had taken the seat opposite. 'Remember the business dinner I mentioned?'

'The one tomorrow evening?'

'Yes,' he said, spreading his napkin across his lap. 'As joint heirs to our father's estate, Antonio tries to attend most of the bigger functions, although he leaves most of the business end of things to me due to his surgical commitments. He and Claire will be there tomorrow. They have just returned from abroad. He called me while you were having a shower.'

Sabrina toyed with the rings on her finger before meeting his gaze. 'What sort of business is it that you do?'

'Corporate lending and fund management,' he answered. 'I also have a commercial-property portfolio that I run on the side. Lots of eggs in lots of baskets.'

'It sounds very demanding.'

'It is, but then I have always liked a challenge.'

Sabrina shifted her gaze from his glinting eyes, her fingers moving from her ring to fiddle with her soup spoon instead. 'I suppose you treat everything in life, including women like me, as a challenge to be conquered.'

He reached across the table to capture her hand, bringing it up to his mouth, his eyes holding hers as he pressed a ghost of a kiss to her bent knuckles. 'You, *tesore mio*, have been a delightful challenge,' he said. 'I have enjoyed every minute of it.'

Sabrina pulled her hand out of his and tucked it away from temptation in her lap. 'I need some time to think about the no-children issue.' She took an uneven breath and continued, 'It's a big step to take, and I don't want to do anything I will later regret.'

Mario poured some wine into both of their glasses. 'Take all the time you need,' he said. 'I will have Giovanna move your things into my room after dinner.'

Her eyes flared. 'You want me to move into your room *straight away*?'

'That is what husbands and wives do, is it not?' he asked. 'Sharing a room and a bed are pretty standard, I would have thought.'

She swallowed and reached for one of the bread rolls Giovanna had left earlier, systematically crumbling it in her fingers without actually eating any of it.

'Would you like some butter or olive oil with your crumbs?' he asked drily.

She looked down at her plate and grimaced. 'Sorry…'

He smiled as he picked up his wine glass. 'I am not sure why I make you so nervous, *cara*—especially now that we have consummated our relationship. Believe me, it will only get better from now on.'

Sabrina knew she was blushing again but there was little she could do about it. He made her feel hot all over just by looking at her. The thought of experiencing more of his sensual expertise made her stomach dip and dive in excitement. When she squeezed her legs together she could feel where he had been earlier.

Giovanna came in with their entrée, and Mario instructed her to transfer Sabrina's things into his room before she left for the evening. The housekeeper gave Sabrina a twinkling look as she moved past to leave, making Sabrina's cheeks flame all over again.

'Now that is one very happy housekeeper,' Mario commented.

'Yes, well, one room is easier for her to clean than two,' Sabrina said.

'She has taken rather a shine to you, has she not?'

'No thanks to you,' she said with a sour set to her mouth. 'She was absolutely awful to me when I first arrived.'

A frown appeared between his eyes. 'You think I deliberately set her against you?'

She gave him an arch look. 'Didn't you?'

'Of course not,' he said, still frowning. 'Perhaps she read something in the press. I will have a word with her about it.'

'There's no need to do that,' Sabrina inserted quickly. 'Whatever she heard or read, she has obviously disregarded. She is lovely towards me now, and she adores Molly.'

'Giovanna has been in the service of my family for a long time,' he said. 'I know for a fact she is delighted I have finally settled down.'

'You don't strike me as the tameable, settling-down type,' Sabrina said as she picked up her spoon.

The smile fell away from his face as he reached for his glass. 'Perhaps I will change,' he said, swirling the red wine for a moment. He met her eyes once more and added, 'But don't hold your breath.'

She gave him an 'I wouldn't be so foolish' look. 'Believe me, I wasn't going to.'

Once the meal was over, Mario led her into the salon for a liqueur. He turned on the sound system; the strains of a mellow-sounding ballad made Sabrina's nervous tension gradually fade away. She laid her head back on the cushioned sofa, closing her eyes as the sweet cadences floated over her.

She felt the depression on the seat next to her as Mario joined her. The strong band of his arm lay on the back of the sofa, his fingers idly playing with her hair at the nape of her neck. She suppressed a tiny shiver of delight as he loosened the clip holding her hair up, the tresses falling down over his hand.

'You have beautiful hair,' he said in a throaty tone. 'Promise me you won't cut it.'

Sabrina turned her head to look at him. She felt ready to promise him just about anything when he looked at her like that. His eyes were dark and intense, his mouth so close she could see every pinpoint of stubble around its sensual curve. Almost without realising she was doing it, she raised her hand and gently traced over the sculptured contours of his lips, her belly giving a little, punching-fist-like movement as his tongue came out and brushed over her fingertip.

'Kiss me, Sabrina.'

She leaned towards him, her eyelids going down as she felt the gentle breeze of his breath caress her lips. She pressed her mouth to his, softly, hesitantly, tasting him, feeling the simmer of sexual heat spring fervently to boiling life.

He took over the kiss with a sweep of his tongue across the seam of her mouth, taking possession of her moist warmth, calling her tongue into a Latino salsa that was smoulderingly sexy. Sparks of reaction raced up and down her spine as his hands brought her nearer, one hand splayed at the back of her head, the other cupping the swell of her breast. She pressed herself closer as his thumb found her nipple, teasing it until it ached for the intimate caress of his mouth.

Her body throbbed with an insistent pulse, an on-off rhythm that resounded deep in her womb. Moisture pooled between her thighs, the humidity of need that would not be denied now it had been awakened. She felt the raw ache consume her as she strained to get closer to him; she ached to feel the power of him under her touch.

She groped blindly for his shirt buttons as his mouth continued its passionate command of hers, undoing each one until her hands found his warm, hard flesh. She moved lower, undoing his belt and unhooking his waistband, rolling down his zip until she took him in her hand.

He broke the kiss to watch her caress him, his breathing becoming deep and uneven. 'Harder, *cara*—don't be frightened to use more pressure. I like it that way.'

Sabrina made a circle with her fingers and massaged him, taking her cue from his reaction. He sucked in a breath, his jaw clenched as he fought to keep his head, pleasure written all over his features. He beaded with moisture, and she bent her head and tasted him, delighting in the way he quivered against her mouth. She licked him again, using her tongue to tantalise him, to string out the pleasure. She could feel the tension building in him with every smooth stroke of her tongue.

'Enough,' he groaned as he pulled away. He took a couple of deep breaths and then began to work on her clothes. 'Let's even the score, shall we?'

Sabrina tried to control her frantic breathing as he slowly undressed her. Each item of clothing was taken from her body with a series of burning kisses that branded her flesh, sending an electric current of need to her inner core. She lay back on the sofa as he came over her, his mouth sucking on her breast as his fingers explored the moist heart of her. The stroking motion stirred her senses into a frenzy; she arched her back, striving for the ultimate moment, hovering precariously on the edge, not quite there, but so close she could feel every nerve tensing and twitching.

His mouth left her breast to kiss its way down her body, lingering over the tiny bowl of her belly button before going lower. Sabrina snatched in a sharp breath as his lips nibbled at the sensitive curve of each of her hips, a tiny, teasing nip that made every nerve beneath the skin leap in awareness.

'You have such silky, creamy skin,' he said as he began to trace her inner thighs with his fingers in a lazy 'I've got all the time in the world' motion that made her nearly scream out loud in frustration. 'It is like satin; so smooth and warm. I want to taste every inch of you.'

Her heart rate soared as his fingers moved closer, millimetre by millimetre, the tight coil of tension in her body threatening to snap. She gasped when he separated her, the gentle caress making her quiver all over in pleasure.

'You are so slick and warm, so ready for me,' he said as he continued stroking her.

'I want you inside…' she said in a breathy whisper.

'It's probably too soon after the last time,' he said. 'You are new to this, *cara*. Your body will be tender. Let me pleasure you this way.'

Sabrina grasped his hand, her eyes pleading. 'No, please, Mario. I want you to make love to me. I want to feel you again.'

He held her gaze for a moment before he lowered his mouth to hers, kissing her until she was writhing with longing.

He reached for where he had thrown his trousers, and, taking out his wallet, retrieved a tiny square that contained a condom. He quickly applied it before coming down over her, positioning himself so she wasn't taking all of his weight.

His first thrust was gentle, making Sabrina's skin leap

in excitement, a rush of feeling so intense it took her breath away.

'Am I hurting you?' Mario asked, tensing.

She let out a sigh of bliss. 'No, it's perfect. You are perfect.'

Mario gradually increased his pace, becoming lost in the sensations flooding his system. She was such a generous lover, so willing to give as well as receive. He was blown away by the power her body had over him. Making love with her was so different from his other experiences. She somehow lifted him to another sphere, a place where mind, body and soul were inextricably linked, where feelings he had not thought possible began to unfurl inside him like a tight bud blossoming under the first rays of warm spring sun.

He loved the way her body fit his as if it had been made especially for him. Her slim limbs wrapped around him so naturally; her soft mouth received his with such warmth, and her feminine heart gripped him as if she never wanted to let him go.

Mario felt her shudder as he drove a little harder, her body starting to convulse around his as she came. He felt a powerful surge of emotion as she gasped and whimpered his name, her slender arms holding him tightly as the tumult of her orgasm ricocheted through her. His own release was just as powerful; it bulleted through him like a pump-action rifle, sending him tumbling in a vortex of sensation that was totally earth-shattering.

Mario lay with her encircled in his arms as their heart rates gradually returned to normal, his fingers idly playing a rhythmic tune on the silky skin of her arm as if on a keyboard. It wasn't a song he recognised—it had no words—but he knew he didn't want it to end.

Not yet.

CHAPTER ELEVEN

THE baby monitor sounded and Sabrina moved out of Mario's arms, retrieving her clothes from the flaoor, trying not to feel embarrassed at her nakedness. 'I'd better go and see if she needs changing or something,' she said as she dressed with as much dignity as she could.

Mario seemed less concerned about his lack of covering. He sat upright and brushed his hair back with his hand. 'I'll come with you,' he said, and reached for his trousers.

Sabrina's eyes fell away from his. She was annoyed with herself for feeling ashamed of the intimacy they had shared. It made her seem so unsophisticated and homely. 'Don't worry,' she said. 'It might wake her up too much to have both of us fussing over her.'

'As you wish.'

Sabrina didn't let out her breath until she was in the nursery tending to the baby's needs. Molly was soon re-settled, and Sabrina tiptoed out, leaving the door ajar.

She was on her way back from a visit to the bathroom when she heard Mario talking to someone. At first she thought it must be Giovanna, but then she realised he was speaking on the phone in the master bedroom, as she could only hear his side of the conversation. She had always loathed people who eavesdropped, but something about the tone of his voice stopped her in her tracks just outside the door. Although he was speaking in Italian, she heard her name mentioned a couple of times, the urgency in his voice making her wonder who exactly he was talking to. When she considered the possibility of him discussing her with another woman, after the intimacy they had so recently shared, her heart began to pound like a pendulum that had been knocked out of kilter, each strike against her chest-wall making her feel as if her fragile hopes were being bludgeoned one by one.

Sabrina was not aware of making a sound, but suddenly Mario pulled the bedroom door fully open, the mobile in his hand now flipped closed. His mouth was pulled tight, his jaw even tighter. 'I am sorry about this, Sabrina, but I have to go out for a while,' he said, his eyes moving out of range of hers. 'I might not be back until late.'

She frowned as he snatched his car keys off the bedside table, his hand going through his hair once more. 'Mario?'

His eyes cut to hers. 'Leave it, Sabrina,' he said, his tone edgy. 'We will talk in the morning. I have to get going. Someone is waiting for me.'

She opened her mouth, but closed it again as he brushed past. Her shoulders went down, her spirits plummeting in despair.

Someone was waiting for him.

The words taunted her as each minute of each hour dragged past, as she lay listening in vain for Mario's return.

It was the longest and loneliest night of her life.

When Sabrina came downstairs the next morning, bleary-eyed and with a pounding headache, she saw Giovanna start as she entered the kitchen, the newspaper she had been reading hastily snatched out of sight.

'*La prima colazione*, Signora Marcolini?' she asked, wiping her hands on her apron.

Sabrina lifted her hands in a gesture of helplessness. 'I'm sorry, Giovanna. Can you say it in English, please?'

'Breakfast,' the housekeeper said, not quite meeting Sabrina's gaze. 'I have some fresh rolls and preserves, or if you like I have cured ham and cheese, and—'

'It's all right, Giovanna,' she said with a sigh. 'I am not feeling like food just now.'

'Did the *bambino* keep you awake last night?' Giovanna asked as she surreptitiously put the newspaper in the bin under the sink.

'She only woke once, and only briefly,' Sabrina said, peering past the housekeeper's shoulder to the bin. 'Is that today's paper?'

Giovanna pursed her lips for a moment. 'You not able to read it, *signora*. It is in Italian.'

It suddenly became absolutely imperative for Sabrina to see it. She moved past Giovanna and pulled the scrunched-up paper out of the bin, smoothing it out to see the front page. Looking at the photograph of Mario and a blonde woman draped all over him made her chest feel as if someone had kicked her whilst wearing a concrete boot. She swallowed tightly, trying to control her emotions. 'What does it say, Giovanna?' she asked, lowering the paper to look at the housekeeper.

Giovanna lifted her apron to wipe the beads of perspiration off her face. 'It say…' she gave Sabrina a wincing look '…it say Mario Marcolini resumes affair with Glenda Rickman.'

Sabrina swallowed again, her throat feeling razor-blade raw. 'Glenda Rickman the model?'

Giovanna nodded grimly. 'She was his mistress before he married you.'

Sabrina drew in a breath that burned all the way down into her lungs. 'I see…'

'I told you before, lots of rich Italian men have mistresses,' Giovanna said. 'You are his wife. That is all that matters.'

Sabrina closed the paper and handed it back to the house-keeper. 'When—or should I say *if*—Signore Marcolini comes home some time today, I would like you to inform him I am taking Molly with me for a few days to think over his offer.'

Giovanna frowned uncertainly. '*Sì?*'

Sabrina straightened her spine in resolve. 'I want some time to consider my options,' she said. 'I am not sure I am cut out for the life he expects me to live here with him.'

Giovanna began to wring her hands. 'You must not go where he cannot find you, Signora Marcolini,' she insisted. 'He will be very angry.'

Sabrina remained implacable and calm, although inside she felt cut to ribbons. 'Let him be angry,' she said. 'I am angry too. We can't go on like this without some give on his part.'

'He give you diamonds!' Giovanna threw her hands in the air. 'He give you a *palazzo* and expensive clothes. He treat you like a *principessa*—how you say in English?—a princess. You are his wife, *signora*. You share his bed.'

Sabrina felt her bottom lip quiver as tears came to her eyes. 'I don't want his priceless diamonds and his stupid designer-clothes.'

Giovanna looked confused. 'What do you want from him?'

I want his heart, Sabrina said, but not out loud. 'Tell him

I will call him in three days,' she said. 'My mobile will be switched off until then.'

Mario slammed his fist on the kitchen counter as he grilled the housekeeper for the umpteenth time. 'What do you mean, she has taken Molly away?' he roared. 'Where the hell is she? She *must* have told you where she was going.'

Giovanna flinched, blinking back tears. 'I tell her not to go, but she not listen to me. She not tell me anything about where she was going. She called a cab and was gone before I could contact you.'

Mario swore viciously as he left the room, pacing up and down, trying to think where Sabrina could possibly have gone. She had money and she had Molly. She could be on a plane to anywhere by now.

His chest tightened at the thought of something happening to either of them. He wasn't used to feeling so utterly powerless. How had he not foreseen this? He had trusted Sabrina too much. He had thought she had been softening towards him; each day he had felt her move closer to him, letting her guard down. God damn it, she had given herself to him, fooling him into believing she might be developing feelings for him, when all the time she was planning an escape route. He suddenly recalled how he had overheard her telling Molly she was going to think of a way out of the situation on the day of the funeral.

All this time—he clenched his teeth until they almost cracked—*all this time* she had been planning a revenge so complete it would destroy him. If the press heard of it he would look a complete fool. He could handle that, but he could not handle Sabrina deserting him just when he had begun to realise how much he needed her. It wasn't just about Molly; perhaps it had never been about Molly. From the first moment he had met Sabrina he had felt strangely unsatisfied, felt an irksome feeling that something was missing from his life, but until now he hadn't been able to identify exactly what it was.

The *palazzo* was so achingly empty. Had it always been that way? Why hadn't he noticed it before? His footsteps echoed ominously throughout the corridors as he searched every room again and again, looking for some clue as to where Sabrina had gone.

The nursery smelt of baby powder, and Mario felt his insides clench as he picked up a tiny pink all-in-one baby suit. His fingers tightened around it, thinking of the pain his brother must have gone through when his tiny daughter had been stillborn.

He loosened his grip on the little suit, its softness slipping through his fingers as he laid it gently back down on the dresser. He swallowed a thick lump of emotion as he thought about Antonio being brave enough to take on the prospect of another child with the woman he had loved enough to put his life on pause for for five long, lonely years.

Mario felt ashamed of how shallow and selfish he had become. Antonio had been rather blunt about it last night before they'd been rudely interrupted by both the press and Mario's playboy past. Mario could see now it was no wonder Sabrina had baulked at his plan for a loveless, childless marriage. Children were everything to her. She lived to look after and nurture others. He had seen her grey eyes light up whenever she looked at Molly. But he had denied her the dream of having her own child, blackmailing her into a relationship that gave her money and jewels and prestige, but not the thing she most desired.

'Signore Marcolini?' Giovanna spoke tentatively from the door.

He turned and faced her, stripping his face of emotion. '*Sì?*'

'The dinner tonight…' she said, pausing as if waiting for the fall out. 'I have pressed your suit for you.'

Mario swore as he glanced at his watch. 'Call my brother and tell him I can't make it,' he instructed Giovanna as he strode out of the nursery towards his study to check his computer. 'He'll understand. Tell him I have decided I have other things to see to that are far more important.'

Sabrina sat on the sunny terrace with Molly asleep in her pram just inside the doors, where she could hear her if she stirred. The villa she had rented at Positano was small but perfectly placed so she could have the peace and quiet she needed to face the biggest decision of her life.

She had read of the village in an Internet tour-guide and had felt immediately drawn to it. It was a haven-like place, or so the guide had said. It was protected from the winds by the Lattari Mountains, the dry, mild climate attracting tourists all year round. The guide had also pointed out that the author John Steinbeck had once written in an essay published in the 1950's:

> Positano bites deep. It is a dream place that isn't quite real when you are there, and becomes beckoningly real after you are gone.

Those words seemed hauntingly relevant to Sabrina's relationship with Mario. Her love for him had bitten deep; she felt the teeth marks of it in her soul.

Their marriage wasn't real—more hauntingly familiar words—but now she was gone it seemed very real indeed. Could she walk away from Molly and leave Mario to his life of luxury and freedom? Or could she stay and shelve her hopes for a family of her own to make that ultimate sacrifice for him?

In the end it was not such a hard decision to make. She had been away from him just one day and she knew if he was standing here right now what she would say.

Sabrina looked up in surprise when she heard the sound of footsteps on the terrace. Her heart knocked against her ribcage when she saw Mario standing there, looking down at her.

'Next time you want to cover your tracks, *cara*,' he said in an unreadable tone, 'It might be an idea to delete all the sites you have been surfing on the Internet.'

She got up from the sun lounger on unsteady legs. 'Mario, I…I have something to say to you.'

He thrust his hands deep into his trouser pockets as if he was worried he might use them inappropriately. He looked haggard, drawn and hollow under the eyes, as if he had not slept. She took a step towards him, but he set his mouth and turned his back to look at the ocean below.

His voice when he spoke sounded empty; it echoed with regret. 'I don't blame you, Sabrina.'

Sabrina flicked her tongue across her lips, waiting for him to go on.

He stood there a moment or two before he turned back to face her, his expression rueful but composed.

'I don't blame you for leaving me,' he said. 'It is what I deserve for how I have treated you from the start.'

She stood very still, barely moving her chest up and down to breathe.

'I have been a fool,' he continued. 'It was only after you left that I realised how much of a fool I have been.'

Sabrina suddenly realised what it would be like. Year after year it would be exactly like this—him coming to apologise for yet another indiscretion, a little fling that the press had got wind of and run in the next day's paper to spread her shame at not being able to keep him happy at home. He would apologise, she would forgive him and the hurt would eat away at her until there was nothing left.

Anger bubbled up inside her—anger at how she had fallen for him when she had always known it would end like this, with her shattered while he was barely affected. She clenched her hands into tight balls of resentment, her voice coming out higher and shriller than she had expected as her emotions got the better of her. 'Why did you have to sleep with me?' she choked over the words. 'Why did you have to turn me into yet another one of your cheap bedmates? *Why?*'

Mario took her tightly clenched hands in his, holding them securely as he looked down at her flushed face. 'Sabrina, you are not listening to me. Stop shouting at me for a moment and let me tell you what I came here to say.'

'Did you do it deliberately?' She flashed grey lightning at him with her eyes. 'Did you make me fall in love with you for a laugh? Were you laughing about me to *her*?'

'*Cara...*' Mario swallowed to clear the emotion that had surged up from deep inside him at her words. *She loved him.* It hardly seemed possible given what he had done.

'Why?' she asked again, her eyes now glistening with tears as she struggled to get out of his hold. 'Why did you sleep with me? Did you have to take it that far?'

Mario tightened his hold. 'I slept with you, *mio piccolo*, because I could not resist you. I slept with you because I wanted you to be mine.' He took a deep breath and added, 'I slept with you because I've fallen in love with you.'

Sabrina went slack in his grip. 'But…but you can't love me. The paper said you've gone back to your mistress. That was who you went to see the night before last, wasn't it?'

His expression darkened. 'I met with my brother. We met in one of our favourite bars, but we were interrupted by the arrival of Glenda and, of course, the press. She is insanely jealous I married you so soon after I ended things with her. She has never been rejected before, and decided to orchestrate a little payback.'

Sabrina bit her lip until it hurt. 'But the photo?'

'I know it looks incriminating, but the press always play on that sort of shot,' he said. 'I had just told her to stay away from me and my loved ones—in particular you—and she threw herself at me. What the press failed to report is that a few minutes later Security hauled her out of the building with the threat of an assault charge ringing in her ears.'

Sabrina looked into his dark eyes, her heart shifting in her chest as she saw how meltingly soft they were. 'You're not just saying it, are you? I mean, about the being in love part…?'

He wrapped his arms around her, bringing her close. 'I only realised it last night as I was talking to my brother,' he said. 'I was asking his advice on what to do about our situation. But while we were talking it made me think back over the last year or two since we first met at Ric and Laura's wedding, and then again at the christening. I started to see it then—how I had always been drawn to you. I couldn't get you out of my mind. I guess I was always a little bit in love with you. I think Ric and Laura sensed it too.'

She gave him a sheepish look from beneath her lashes as she confessed, 'I think I was always a little bit in love with you too.'

His hands came up to tenderly cup her face, his eyes centred on hers. 'Just a little bit in love?' he asked with a twinkling smile.

She beamed back at him radiantly. 'A big bit in love,' she said. 'Totally, irrevocably and immeasurably in love.'

'So will you marry me, Sabrina?' he asked.

She frowned at him in puzzlement. 'But, darling, we *are* already married.' She held up her hand to show him her wedding and engagement ring. 'See?'

'I mean a real wedding, *tesore mio*,' he said, looking even more serious now. 'I want to see you walk down the aisle towards me. I want to see you dressed in a beautiful white dress and long, trailing veil. I want to give you the best honeymoon you can dream of.' He paused for a second and added in a deeper, gruffer tone, 'And I want to give you a baby, maybe two.'

Her eyes opened wide. 'You're serious? Are you sure?'

He nodded and gripped her hands tightly in his. 'It took a few lonely hours without you and Molly to make me realise what I was throwing away. I want it all, Sabrina. I want you and Molly and a family of our own.'

She nestled closer, and linking her arms around his neck, pressed a soft kiss to his mouth. 'I love you,' she said. 'I love you so much, I was planning on telling you when I got back that I would stay with you, children or no children.'

Mario held her from him, looking into her grey eyes, feeling a sense of completeness he had never dreamed possible. 'You are the most giving and loving person I have ever met. What did I do to deserve you?'

She sighed and hugged him tight, her head pressed against his heart. 'I can't believe this is happening I was so miserable when I thought you were seeing someone else.'

Mario eased her away from him to look down at her again, his expression sombre. '*Cara*, it is always going to be like it was the other night—the press, I mean. They make money out of people like Antonio and I, making up scandals, speculating on our movements all the time. I need you to trust me otherwise it will destroy us as it very nearly destroyed him and Claire.'

Sabrina held his sincere gaze with love shining in her eyes. 'I do trust you, Mario. Ric and Laura trusted you. Molly trusts you. I think you are the most trustworthy and loyal man I've ever met.'

He kissed her softly. 'Thank you for saying that. It means the world to me. I never thought I would find someone like you. In fact, I didn't think people like you existed anymore. I thought my brother had found the last one.'

'About that honeymoon you spoke of,' Sabrina said smiling as she rubbed up against him like a sinuous cat against a pole. 'Do we have to wait until we get married for real?'

He scooped her up in his arms, his dark eyes glinting back at her sparkling ones. 'Who said anything about waiting? We're married, right?'

Sabrina smiled a blissful smile, hugging her arms tightly around his neck. 'Right,' she said.

* * * * *

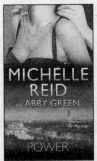
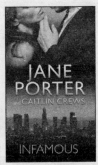
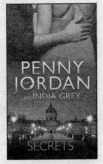
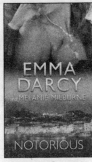
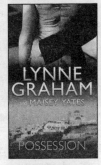

Happy ever after is only the beginning!

Callie Grey has got a great job, a great man and, fingers crossed, a whopping great diamond—then her boss/boyfriend gives her dream and her sparkly ring to someone else…

She's spent her life reaching for the moon. Now Callie's let go and, falling among the stars, who will be there to catch her?

www.millsandboon.co.uk

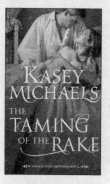
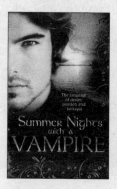
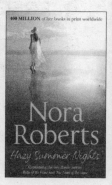

The World of Mills & Boon®

There's a Mills & Boon® series that's perfect for you. We publish ten series and with new titles every month, you never have to wait long for your favourite to come along.

Blaze®   Scorching hot,
                  sexy reads

By Request   Relive the romance with
                  the best of the best

Cherish™   Romance to melt the
                  heart every time

Desire™   Passionate and dramatic
                  love stories

Have Your Say

You've just finished your book. So what did you think?

We'd love to hear your thoughts on our 'Have your say' online panel
www.millsandboon.co.uk/haveyoursay

- Easy to use
- Short questionnaire
- Chance to win Mills & Boon® goodies